DIANE DUANE IS T
AND *TO VISIT*
THE BOOK OF NIGHT WITH MOON
ARE PURE CATNIP!

"Fans of Duane's *The Book of Night with Moon* will be equally pleased with TO VISIT THE QUEEN. Duane has taken traditional fantasy themes and breathed new life into them. I'm looking forward to more stories of the feline wizards."

—*SF Site*

✦

"An entertaining tale . . . magical high adventure and humor. . . . Even readers with no fondness for felines may be surprised to find themselves enjoying this one."

—*Millennium SF & Fantasy*

✦

"Intriguing, with a well-worked backdrop. . . . Fantasy-loving ailurophiles will curl up and purr."

—*Kirkus Reviews*

✦

"Cat lovers who enjoy fantasy will delight in this well-constructed tale. . . . Highly recommended."

—*Kliatt* magazine

✦

"Did I love it? I could not put it down."

—Jane Yolen

more . . .

"A fast-paced, fun read. Anybody who likes fantasy will enjoy this novel."

—*Explorations* (Barnes & Noble newsletter)

"A fun fantasy adventure. [Duane's] deft touch keeps the action moving. Her eye for human—and feline—nature makes all the character development here vivid and sensical. Her knowledge of and comfort with the genre allow her to play games with her story that keep a seasoned fantasy reader hopping. And her genuine relish for her storytelling makes the reader enjoy the book as much as Duane obviously enjoyed writing it."

—*Talebones* magazine

"Diane Duane is a skilled master of the genre."

—*Philadelphia Inquirer*

TO VISIT THE QUEEN

Other Books By Diane Duane

The Book of Night with Moon
available from Warner Aspect

The "Middle Kingdoms" Quartet:
The Door into Fire
The Door into Shadow
The Door into Sunset
*The Door into Starlight**

The "Young Wizards" Series:
So You Want to Be a Wizard
Deep Wizardry
High Wizardry
A Wizard Abroad

Novels Set in the *Star Trek*™ Universe:
The Wounded Sky
My Enemy, My Ally
The Romulan Way†
Spock's World
Doctor's Orders
Dark Mirror
Intellivore

Novels Set in the Marvel Comics™ Universe:
Spider-Man: The Venom Factor
Spider-Man: The Lizard Sanction
Spider-Man: The Octopus Agenda
*X-Men: Empire's End**

*Forthcoming
†With Peter Morwood

TO VISIT THE QUEEN

DIANE DUANE

A Time Warner Company

For Mike Hodel

WARNER BOOKS EDITION

Cover design by Don Puckey
Cover illustration by Robert Goldstrom

Warner Books, Inc.
1271 Avenue of the Americas
New York, NY 10020

Visit our Web site at
www.twbookmark.com

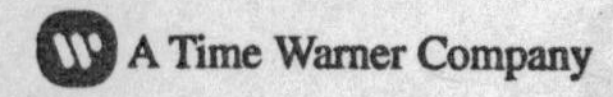

Printed in the United States of America

Originally published in Trade Paperback by Warner Books
First Mass Market Paperback Printing: May 2000

10 9 8 7 6 5 4 3 2 1

Acknowledgments

Many thanks to:

Chris Pond, in the Public Information Office at the Palace of Westminster; the Public Information Office, Number Ten Downing Street; the Yeoman Ravenmaster, Her Majesty's Tower of London.

A Note on Feline Linguistics

Ailurin is not a spoken language, or not *simply* spoken. Like all the human languages, it has a physical component, the cat version of "body language," and a surprising amount of information is passed through the physical component before a need for vocalized words arises.

Even people who haven't studied cats closely will recognize certain "words" in Ailurin: the rub against a friendly leg, the arched back and fluffed fur of a frightened cat, the crouch and stare of the hunter. All of these have strictly physical antecedents and uses, but they are also used by cats for straightforward communication of mood or intent. Many subtler signs can be seen by even a human student: the sideways flirt of the tail that says "I don't care" or "I wonder if I can get away with this . . ." the elaborate yawn in another cat's face, the stiff-legged, arch-backed bounce, which is the cat equivalent of making a face and jumping out at someone, shouting "Boo!" But where gestures run out, words are used—more involved than the growl of threat or purr of contentment, which are all most humans hear of intercat communication.

"Meowing" is not counted here, since cats rarely seem to

meow at each other. That type of vocalization is usually a "pidgin" language used for getting humans' attention: the cat equivalent of "Just talk to them clearly and loudly and they'll get what you mean sooner or later." Between each other, cats subvocalize using the same mechanism that operates what some authorities call "the purr box," a physiological mechanism that is not well understood but seems to have something to do with the combined vibration of air in the feline larynx and blood in the veins and arteries of the throat. To someone with a powerful microphone, a cat speaking Ailurin seems to be making very soft meowing and purring sounds ranging up and down several octaves, all at a volume normally inaudible to humans.

This vocalized part of Ailurin is a "pitched" language, like Mandarin Chinese, more sung than spoken. It is mostly vowel-based—no surprise in a species that cannot pronounce most human-style consonants. Very few noncats have ever mastered it: not only does any human trying to speak it sound to a cat as if he were shouting every word, but the delicate intonations are filled with traps for the unwary or unpracticed. *Auo hwaai hhioehhu uaeiiiaou,* for example, may look straightforward: "I would like a drink of milk" is the Cat-Human Phrasebook definition. But the people writing the phrasebook for the human ear are laboring under a terrible handicap, trying to transliterate from a thirty-seven-vowel system to an alphabet with only five. A human misplacing or mispronouncing only one of the vowels in this phrase will find cats smiling gently at him and asking him why he wants to feed the litter-box to the taxicab? . . . this being only one of numerous nonsenses that can be made of the above example.

So communication from our side of things tends to fall back on body language (stroking, or throwing things, both of which cats understand perfectly well) and a certain amount of monologue—which human-partnered cats, with some resignation, accept as part of the deal. For their communications with most human beings, the cats, like so many of us, tend to fall back on shouting. For this book's purposes, though, all cat-to-human speech, whether physical or vocal, is rendered as normal dialogue: that's the way it seems to the cats, after all.*

One other note: two human-language terms, "queen" and "tom," are routinely used to translate the Ailurin words *sh'heih* and *sth'heih.* "Female" and "male" don't properly translate these words, being much too sexually neutral—which cats, in their dealings with one another, emphatically are not. The Ailurin word *ffeih* is used for both neutered males and spayed females. —DD

*Cat thoughts and silent communications are rendered in italics.

Pussy-cat, pussy-cat, where have you been?
I've been to London to visit the Queen.
Pussy-cat, pussy-cat, what did you there?
I frightened a little mouse under her chair.

CHILDREN'S RHYME

In Life's name, and for Life's sake, I assert that I will employ the Art which is Its gift in Life's service alone. I will guard growth and ease pain. I will fight to preserve what grows and lives well in its own way: nor will I change any creature unless its growth and life, or that of the system of which it is part, are threatened. To these ends, in the practice of my Art, I will ever put aside fear for courage, and death for life, when it is fitting to do so—looking always toward the Heart of Time, where all our sundered times are one, and all our myriad worlds lie whole, in That from Which they proceeded. . . .

THE WIZARD'S OATH,
SPECIES-NONSPECIFIC RECENSION

Prologue

Patel went slowly up the gray concrete stairs to the elevated Docklands Light Railway station at Island Gardens; he took them one at a time, rather than two or three at once as he usually did. Nothing was wrong with him: it was morning, he felt energetic enough—a good breakfast inside him, everything okay at home, the weather steady enough, cool and gray but not raining. However, the package he was carrying was heavy enough to pull a prizefighter's arms out of their sockets.

He had made the mistake of putting the book in a plastic shopping bag. Now the thing's sharp corners were punching through the bag, and the bag's handles, such as they were, were stretching thinner and thinner under the book's weight, cutting into his hands like cheesewire and leaving red marks. He had to stop and transfer the bag from right hand to left, left hand to right, as he went up the stairs, hauling himself along by the chipped blue-painted handrail. When he finally reached the platform, Patel set the bag down gratefully on the concrete, with a grunt, and rubbed his hands, looking up at the red LEDs of the train status sign to see when the next one would be along. 1, the sign read, BANK, 2 MINUTES.

He leaned against the wall of the glass-sided station-platform shelter, out of reach of the light, chill east wind, and thought about the morning's class schedule. This was his second year of a putative three years at London Guildhall University, up in the City. He was well on his way toward a degree in mathematics with business applications, though what good that was really going to do him, at the end of the day, he wasn't certain. There would be time to start worrying about job hunting, though, next year. Right now Patel was doing well enough, his student grant was safe, and whatever attention he wasn't spending on his studies was mostly directed toward making sure he had enough money to get by. Though he didn't have to worry about rent as yet, courtesy of his folks, there were other serious matters at hand: clothes, textbooks, partying.

From down the track came a demure hum and a thrum of rails as the little three-car red-and-blue Docklands train slid toward the station. Patel picked up the book in his arms—he had had enough of the bag's bloody handles—satisfied that at least this would be the last time he would have to carry the huge god-awful thing anywhere. One of the jewelry students, of all people, had seen the for-sale ad on Patel's Web page and had decided that the metallurgical information in the book would make it more than worth the twenty quid Patel was asking for it. For his own part, Patel was glad enough to let it go. He had bought the book originally for its mathematical and statistical content, and found to his annoyance within about a month of starting his second semester that it was more technical than he needed for the courses he was taking, which by and large did not involve metallurgy or engineering. He had put the book aside, and after that, most of the use it had seen involved Patel's mother using it to press flowers.

The train pulled up in front of him, stopped, and chimed: the doors opened, and people emptied out in a rush of brief-cases and schoolbags going by, and here and there a few white uniforms showing from under jackets and coats—people heading to the hospital in town. Patel got on the last car, which would be the first one out, and sat in what would have been the driver's seat, if there had been a driver; there was none. These trains were handled by a trio of straightforwardly programmed PCs based somewhere in the Canary Wharf complex. The innovation left the first seats in the front car open, and gave the lucky passenger a beautiful view of the ride in to town.

Patel, though, had seen it all a hundred times, and paid little attention until the train swung round the big curve near South Quay and headed across the water. Even though he knew a little about the place's history, Patel found it hard to imagine this landscape not full of construction gear and scaffolding, but jostling with the hulls of close-berthed ships, the air black with smoke from a thousand smoke-stacks, cranes loading and unloading goods: the shipping of an empire filling these man-made harbors and lagoons that had been dredged out of oxbows of the Thames. It had all vanished a long time ago, when Britain stopped being an empire and the mistress of the seas. This whole area had undergone a terrible decline after the war, during which it had been bombed nearly flat, and whatever was left had fallen into decrepitude or ruin. Now it was growing again, office space abruptly mushrooming on the waterside sites where the ships had docked to disgorge their cargoes. Only the street names, and the names of the Docklands stations, preserved the nautical memories. Some of the old loading cranes still stood, but the warehouses behind them had been converted to expensive loft apartments. Slim black cormorants fished off Heron Quays, though the quays themselves were gone, slowly being replaced by more apartments and office space, and shining hotels and still more office buildings looked down on waters that were no longer so polluted they would catch fire if you dropped a match in them.

Patel got out at Shadwell to change for the little spur line to Tower Gateway, and stood there waiting for a few minutes. All around were four- or five-story brick buildings, their brick all leached and streaked with many years' weather, tired looking. Scattered among them was much council housing, ten-story blocks of flats done in pebble-dash and painted concrete, looking just as weary. These were not slums anymore, not quite, though his father never tired of telling Patel and his mother how lucky they were to be able to afford someplace better. It was true enough, though it meant Patel had a three-quarter-hour commute to school every morning instead of a fifteen-minute walk.

No matter. Today he was grateful enough not to have to walk more than a few minutes carrying the Book from Hell. The train for Tower Gateway came rumbling along, stopped, and opened its doors. It was crowded, and Patel slipped in through the door and put the book down on the floor, bracing it between his shins lest it fall on someone's foot and get him involved in what would probably be a completely justified lawsuit for grievous bodily harm.

The train swung south the few blocks to Tower Gateway. There Patel got out with his burden, walked along the platform, and took the escalator up through the tubelike corridor that led to the overpass that avoided the main-line BR tracks: then down the other side again, and out across the open concrete plaza from which jutted several large slabs of ancient wall, not much more than fieldstones mortared together—a remnant of the old days when the City of London was all the London there was and that tiny square mileage had a proper defensive wall of its own. Nothing to do, of course, with the other walled edifice just this side of the river . . .

As he went down the stairs to the underpass-tunnel that dove under the traffic stream of Minories Street, Patel glanced up and caught a glimpse of crenellated tower against the clouds: one of the metal windvane-banners mounted on a pinnacle of the Tower's outer wall stood frozen in midswing against the wind, then spun suddenly to point west in a gust off the Thames. *Sky's getting nasty,* Patel thought. *Might rain. Hope it stops by the time I'm aboveground again.*

He headed through the underpass, breathing a little harder now from the weight he was carrying—*Am I getting out of shape? I can't wait to get rid of this thing*—and up the stairs on the far side; past some more "islands" of old preserved City wall, and then down again into the Tower Hill Underground station.

He pushed his train ticket into the turnstile before him, waited for the machine to spit it out again. Here he would catch the last leg of his trip, the tube train to Monument, and meet Sasha at the coffee shop at Eastcheap and Gracechurch Street, and she would take this thing off his hands. *And arms, and shoulders, but particularly the hands,* Patel thought, and headed down the stairs, stepping a little to one side so as not to be trampled by the people behind him. A direction sign just ahead of him read PLATFORMS 2 AND 3, DISTRICT AND CIRCLE LINES, WEST.

He headed for the sign, changing the bag again from left hand to right hand with a slight grimace as he went, and turned the corner left toward the tube platform—

Dark. Why was it dark all of a sudden? *Power failure,*

Patel thought. *Though where's the light behind me?* He turned—

The smell was what hit him first. *My God, what* is *that? Did the sewer break through in here or something?* But there was no way to tell. He couldn't see. Patel turned again, took a few hesitant steps forward. There was something wrong with the ground. It felt mushy—

—and then suddenly light broke through again, the watery gray light of the morning he had just left. A few spits and spatters of rain reached him even here in the tunnel, blown in on that chilly wind. Some part of Patel's mind had now begun to go around and around with thoughts like *How the heck is there daylight down here—I must be fifty feet underground* and *The smell, what is that smell?* but that part of him felt strangely far away, like a mind belonging to someone else, in the face of what he saw before him. A street, and the gray day above it, those made sense: buildings pressing close on either side, yes, and the enameled metal sign set high in the brick wall of the building opposite him, reading COOPER'S ROW—that was fine too: the math/business building of the university was up past the end of the Row, on Jewry Street, and he would have been heading there after meeting Sasha. But there was no pavement to be seen. There was hardly any road visible either: It was covered ankle-deep in thick brown mud, the source of the god-awful smell. *Must have been a sewer break,* said some hopeful part of his mind, steadfastly ignoring the basic issue of how he was suddenly standing at ground level.

Patel walked forward slowly, trying not to sink into the mud, and failing—it came up over the tops of his shoes. *Boy,* these *trainers are going to be a loss after this, and they were only three weeks old. How am I going to explain this to Mum?* Squelch, squelch, he walked forward, and came to the corner of Cooper's Row and Tower Hill, looked down to his right in the direction of the Monument tube station.

It was not there. The road was lined with old buildings, three- or four-story brick edifices all crowded together where multistory office buildings should have been. The traffic was gone too. Or rather, it was all replaced by carriages, carriages pulled by *horses,* their hooves making a strangled wet clopping noise as they pounded through the mud, up and down Byward Street and Tower Hill. Patel staggered, changed the bag mechanically from the right hand to the left, and took a few more steps forward, looking away from the traffic—*Don't want to see that; doesn't make sense*—and across to the Tower.

It, at least, was still there: The great square outer walls defining the contours of Tower Hill stood up unchanged, the lesser corner towers reached upward as always, the windvanes on them wheeling and whirling in the gusts of wind off the river—the wind that bore the stink forcefully into Patel's nostrils and the rain, now falling a little harder, into his face, cold and insistent. That wind got into his hair and tried to find its way under his jacket collar; and around him, the few trees sprouting from the unseen pavement rocked in the wind, their bare branches rubbing and ratcheting together. Bare. That was wrong. It was September. And other things were moving, rocking, too—

Momentarily distracted by the motion, he looked past the Tower, down toward Lower Thames Street and the great bend of the river that began there. *A forest,* he thought at first, and then rejected the thought as idiotic. No trees would be so straight and bare, with no branches but one or two sets each, wide crosspieces set well up the trunk; nor would trees be crowded so close together, or rock together so unnervingly, practically from the root. The "trees" were masts—masts of ships, fifty or seventy or a hundred of them all anchored there together, the wind and the water pushing at the ships from which the masts grew; and the bare shapes silhouetted against the morning gray were all rocking, rocking slightly out of phase, making faint, uneasy groaning noises that he could hear even at this distance, for they were perhaps a quarter of a mile down the river from where he stood. From that direction too came a mutter of human voices, people shouting, going about their business, the sound muted by the wind that rose around him and rocked the groaning masts together.

That groan got down inside Patel, went up in pitch and began to shake him until he rocked like the masts, staggering, failing, the world receding from him. The bag fell from Patel's hand, unnoticed.

A man came around the corner right in front of Patel and looked at him, then opened his mouth to say something.

Patel jumped, meaning to run away, but his raw nerves misfired and sent him blundering straight into the man. As Patel came at him, the strangely dressed man staggered hurriedly backward, panic-stricken, tripped, and fell—then scrambled himself up out of the mud with an unintelligible shout and ran crazily away. Patel, too, turned to flee, this time getting it right and going back the way he had come. He ran splashing through the stinking mud and, for all the screaming in his head, ran mute: ran pell-mell back toward sanity, toward the light, and (without knowing how he did it) finally out into the bare-bulb brilliance of the white-tiled Underground station, where he collapsed, still silent, but with the screaming ringing unending in his mind, insistently expressing what the shocked and gasping lungs could not.

Later those screams would burst out at odd times: in the middle of the night, or in the gray hour before dawn when dreams are true, startling his mother and father awake and leaving Patel sitting frozen, bolt upright in bed, sweating and shaking, mute again. After several years, some cursory psychotherapy, which did nothing to reveal the promptly and thoroughly buried memory causing the distress, and a course of a somewhat overprescribed mood elevator, the screaming stopped. But when he and his wife and new family moved up to the country, later in his life, Patel was never easy about being in any wooded place in the wintertime, at dusk. The naked limbs of the trees, all held out stiff against the falling night and moving, moving slightly, would speak to some buried memory that would leave him silent and shaking for hours. Nor was he ever able to explain, to Sasha, or to his parents, or anyone else, exactly what had happened to his copy of *Van Nostrand's Scientific Encyclopedia.* Mostly his family and friends thought he had been robbed and assaulted, perhaps indecently; they left the matter alone. They were right, though as regarded the nature of the indecency, they could not have been more wrong.

Patel fled too soon ever to see the men who came down along Cooper's Row after a little while, talking among themselves: men who paused curiously at the sight of the dropped book, then stooped to pick it up. One of them produced a kerchief and wiped the worst of the mud away from the strange material that covered the contents. Another reached out and slowly, carefully, peeled the slick, thin white stuff away, revealing the big heavy book. A third took the book from the second man and turned the pages, marveling at the paper, the quality of the printing, the embossing on the cover. They moved a little down the street to where it met Great Tower Street, where the light was better. As they paused there, a ray of sun suddenly pierced down through the bleak sky above them, that atypical winter's sky here at the thin end of summer. One of the men looked up at this in surprise, for sun had been a rare sight of late. In that brief light the other two men leaned over the pages, read the words there, and became increasingly excited.

Shortly the three of them hurried away with the book, unsure whether they held in their hands an elaborate fraud or some kind of miracle. Behind and above them, the clouds shut again, and a gloom like premature night once more fell over the Thames estuary, a darkness in which those who had ears to hear could detect, at the very fringes of comprehension, the sound of a slowly stirring laughter.

One

At just before 5 P.M. on a weekday, the upper-track level of Grand Central Terminal looks much as it does at any other time of day: a striped gray landscape of long concrete islands stretching away from you into a dry, iron-smelling night, under the relentless fluorescent glow of the long lines of overhead lighting. Much of the view across the landscape will be occluded by the thirteen Metro-North trains whose business it is to be there at that time, and by the rush and flow of commuters through the many doors leading from the echoing main concourse to the twelve accessible platforms' near ends. The commuters' thousands of voices on the platforms and out in the concourse mingle into a restless, undecipherable roar, above which the amplified voice of the station announcer desperately attempts to rise, reciting the cyclic poetry of the hour: "Now boarding, the five-oh-*two* departure of Metro-North train number nine-five-*three,* stopping at One Hundred and Twenty-*fifth* Street, *Scars*dale, *Harts*dale, *White* Plains, *North* White Plains, Val*hal*la, *Haw*thorne, *Pleas*antville, *Chap*paqua . . ." And over it all, effortlessly drowning everything out, comes the massive basso B-flat *bong* of the Accurist clock, echoing out there under the blue-painted backward heaven, two hundred feet above the terrazzo floor.

Down on the tracks, even that huge note falls somewhat muted, having as it does to fight with the more immediate roar and thunder of the electric diesel locomotives clearing their throats and getting ready to go. By now Rhiow knew them all better than any train spotter, knew every engine by name and voice and (in a few specialized cases) by temperament, for she saw them every day in the line of work. Right now they were all behaving themselves, which was just as well: she had other work in hand. It was no work that any of the other users of the Terminal would have noticed—not that the rushing commuters would in any case have paid much attention to a small black cat, a patchy black-and-white one, and a big gray tabby sitting down in the relative dimness at the near end of Adams Platform—even if the cats *hadn't* been invisible.

Bong, said the clock again. Rhiow sighed and looked up at the elliptical multicolored shimmer of the worldgate matrix hanging in the air before them, the colors that presently ran through its warp and woof indicating a waiting state, no patency, no pending transits. Normally this particular gate resided between Tracks 23 and 24 at the end of Platform K; but for today's session they had untied the hyperstrings holding it in that spot, and relocated the gate temporarily on Adams Platform. This lay between the Waldorf Yard and the Back Yard, away off to the right of Tower C, the engine inspection pit, and the power substation. It was the easternmost platform on the upper level, and well away from the routine trains and the commuters, though not from their noise. Rhiow glanced over at big, gray-tabby Urruah, her colleague of several years now, who was flicking his ears in irritation every few seconds at the racket. Rhiow felt like doing the same: this was her least favorite time to be here.

Nevertheless, work sometimes made it necessary. *Bong,* said the clock: and clearly audible through it, through the voices and the diesel thunder and the sound of the slightly desperate-sounding train announcer, a small, clear voice spoke. "These endless dumb drills," it said, "lick butt."

WHAM!—and Arhu fell over on the platform, while above him Urruah leaned down, one paw still raised, wearing an expression that was surprisingly mild—for the moment. "Language," he said.

"Whaddaya mean? There's no one here but you and Rhiow, and you use worse stuff than *that* all the—"

WHAM! Arhu fell over again. "Courtesy," Urruah said, "is an important commodity among wizards, especially wizards working together as a team. Not to mention more ordinary People working as teams or in-pride, as you'll find if you survive that long. Which seems unlikely at the moment. *My* language isn't at question here, and even if it were, I don't use it on my fellow team members, or to them, even by implication."

"But I only said—" Arhu suddenly fell silent again at the sight of that upraised paw.

Dumb drills, Rhiow thought, and breathed out, resigned. *This is* not *a drill,* life *is not a drill, when will he get the message? Lives* . . . She sighed again. *Sometimes I think the One made a mistake telling our people that we're going to get nine of them. Some of us get complacent. . . .*

"Let's be clear about this," Urruah said. "Our job is to keep the worldgates down here functioning. Human wizards can't do this kind of work, or not nearly as well as we can, anyway, since we can see hyperstrings, and *ehhif** can't without really working at it. That being the case, the Powers That Be asked us very politely if we would do this job, and

*A glossary of words used by the People appears at the back of this book.

we said yes. You said yes, too, when They offered you wizardry and you took it, and you said yes again when we took you in-pride and you agreed to stay with us. That means you're stuck with the job. So you may as well learn how to do it right, and part of that involves working smoothly with your teammates. Another part of it is practicing managing these gates until you can do it quickly, in crisis situations, without having to stop to think and worry and 'figure out' what you're doing. And this is what we are teaching you to do, and will continue teaching you to do, until you can exhibit at least a modicum of effectiveness, which may be several lives on, not that it matters to me. You got that?"

"Uh-huh."

"Uh-huh what?"

"Uh-huh, I got it."

"Right. So let's start in again from the top."

Rhiow sighed and licked her nose as the small black-and-white cat sat up on his haunches again and thrust his forepaws into the faintly glowing warp and woof of the worldgate's control matrix, and muttered under his breath, very softly, "It still licks butt."

WHAM!

Rhiow closed her eyes and wondered where she and Urruah would ever find enough patience for this job. Inside her, some annoyed part of her mind was mocking the Meditation: *I will meet the terminally clueless today,* it said piously: *idiots, and those with hairballs for brains, and those whose ears need a good shredding before you can even get their attention. I do not have to be like them, even though I would dearly love to hit them hard enough to make the empty places in their heads echo. . . .*

She turned away from that line of thought in mild annoyance as Arhu picked himself up off the platform one more time. This late on in this life, Rhiow had not anticipated being thrust into the role of nursing-dam for a youngster barely finished losing his milk teeth, and certainly not into the role of trainer of a new-made wizard. She had gained her own wizardry in a different paradigm—acquiring it solo, and not becoming part of a team until she had proven herself expert enough to survive past the first flush of power. Arhu, though, had broken the rules, coming to them halfway through his Ordeal and dragging them all through it with him. He was still breaking every rule he could find, having apparently decided that since the tactic had worked once, it would probably keep on working.

Urruah, however, was slowly breaking him of this idea, though getting anything through that resilient young skull was plainly going to take a while. Urruah, too, was playing out of role. Here he was, the very emblem of hardy individuality and independence, a big, muscular, broad-striped tom, all balls and swagger, wearing the cachet of his few well-placed scars with an insouciant, good-natured air—but now he leaned over the kitten-becoming-cat the Powers had wished upon them, and acted very much the hard-pawed pride-father. It was a job to which Urruah had taken with entirely too much relish, Rhiow thought privately, and she was at pains never to mention to him how much he seemed to be enjoying the responsibility. *Does he see himself in this youngster,* Rhiow thought, *does he see the wizard he might have been if he'd had this kind of supervision? But then, who among us* wouldn't *see ourselves in him? The way one feels one's way along among the uncertainties—and the way you try to push your paw just a little farther through the hole, trying to get at what's squeaking on the other side. Even if it bites you . . .*

Arhu had picked himself up one more time, with no further mutters, and was putting his paws into the glowing weave again. *You have to give him that,* Rhiow thought: *he always gets back up.* "I've given the gate some parameters to work with already, though I'm not going to tell you what they are," Urruah said. "I want you to find locations that match the parameters, and open the gate for visual patency, not physical."

"Why not? If I can—"

"Visual-only is harder," Rhiow said. "Physical patency is easy, when you're using a preestablished gate: anyway, in a lot of them, the physical opening mechanism has become automated over time. Restricting the patency, refining control . . . *that's* what we're after here."

Arhu started hooking the control strings with his claws, slowly, pulling each one out with care—which was as well: the gates were nearly alive, in some ways, and if misused or maltreated, they could bite. "I wish Saash was here," Arhu muttered. "She was better at explaining this. . . ."

"Than we are? Almost certainly," Rhiow said. "And I wish she was here too, but she's not." Their friend and fellow team-member Saash had passed through and beyond her ninth life within the past couple of months, under unusual circumstances. *Though* none *of our circumstances have actually been terribly usual lately,* Rhiow thought with some resignation. They all missed Saash in her role as gating technician, where her expertise at handling the matrices had come shining through her various mild neuroses with unusual brilliance. But Rhiow found herself just as lonely for her old partner's rather acerbic tongue, and even for her endless scratching, the often-misread symptom of a soul long grown too large for the body that held it.

"Saash," Urruah said to Arhu, "knowing her, is probably explaining to Queen Iau that she thinks the entire structure of physical reality needs a serious reweave: so you'd better get on with this before she talks the One into it and the Universe dissolves out from under us. Quit your complaining and pick up where you left off."

"I can't figure out where that is! It's not the way I left it, now."

"That's because it's returned to its default configuration," Urruah said, "while you were recovering from sassing me."

"Start from the beginning," Rhiow said. "And just thank the Queen that gate structures are as robust as they are, and as forgiving, because those qualities are likely to save your pelt more than once, in this business."

Arhu sat there, narrow-eyed, with his ears back. "Two choices," Urruah said, after a moment. "You can sulk and I can hit you, or you can get on with your work with your ears unshredded. Look at you, sitting here wasting all this perfectly good gating time."

Arhu glanced back down the station at the other platforms, which were boiling with *ehhif* commuters rushing up and down and in some cases nearly pushing one another onto the tracks. "Doesn't look perfect to me. I know we're sidled, but what if one of them sees what we're *doing?*"

"There won't be much *for* them to see at the rate you're going," Urruah said.

"*Ehhif* don't see wizardry half the time, even when it's hanging right in front of their weak little noses," Rhiow said. "The odds against having anyone notice anything, down here in the dark and the noise, are well in your favor—if you ever get *on* with it. If you're really all that concerned, rotate the gate matrix a hundred and eighty degrees and specify one-side-only visual patency. But I don't think you need to bother. These are New Yorkers, and no trains of interest to *them* are due on these side tracks, so for all that it matters, we and the gate and this whole side of the station might as well be on the Moon."

"Not a bad idea," Arhu muttered, putting his whiskers

forward in the slightest smile, and reached more deeply into the weft of the gate matrix.

He fell over backward as Urruah clouted him upside the head. "*No* gatings into vacuum," he said. "Or under water, or below ground level, or into any other environment that would be bad if mixed freely with this one."

Arhu got to his feet, shook himself, and glared at Urruah. "Aw, I was just thinking . . ."

"Yes, and I heard you. No offplanet work for you until you're better with handling the structural spells for these gates."

"But other wizards can just get the spell from their manuals, or the Whispering, or whatever way they access wizardry, and go—"

"*You're* not 'other wizards,' " Rhiow said, pacing over to sit down beside Urruah as a more obvious gesture of support. "You are part of a gating team. You *have* to understand the theory and nature of these structures from the bottom up. And as regards the established gates like this one, you've got to be able to *fix* them when they break—take them apart and put them back together again—not just use them for rapid transit like 'other wizards.' Yes, it's specialized work, and the details are a nuisance to learn. And yes, the structure is incredibly complex: Aaurh Herself made the gates, Iau only knows how long ago—what do you expect? But you've got to know this information from the inside, without having to consult the Whisperer every thirty seconds for advice. What if She's busy?"

"How busy can gods get?" Arhu muttered, turning his attention back to the gate.

"You'd be surprised," Urruah said. "Queen Iau's daughters have their own lives to lead. You think the Silent One has all day to sit around waiting to see if *you* need help? Get off those little *thaith* of yours and do something."

"They're *not* little," Arhu said, and then fell silent for a moment. "All right, should I just collapse this and start over?"

"Sure, go ahead," Rhiow said.

Arhu reached out a paw and hooked one claw into one of the glowing control strings of the gate. The visible gate-locus vanished, leaving nothing behind it but the intricate, faint traces of hyperstring structure in the air.

And he's right about them not being little, Rhiow said privately, from her mind to Urruah's.

When even you *notice that, o spayed one,* Urruah said, *it suggests that we may shortly have a problem on our hands.*

Rhiow stifled a laugh, keeping her eye on Arhu as he studied the gate matrix, then sat up again and started slowly hooking strings out of the air to "reweave" the visible matrix. *It surprises me that* you *would describe the concept of approaching sexual maturity as a problem.*

Oh, it's not, not as his affects me *anyway,* Urruah said. *We're in-pride now: he's safe with me—it helps that the relationship between you and me isn't physical. Though I do feel sorry for* you, Urruah said, magnanimous.

Rhiow simply put her whiskers forward and accepted the implied compliment without comment. *But for him,* Urruah said, *there's likely to be trouble coming. Hormonal surges don't sort well with the normal flow of wizardly practice.*

I'm not sure there's going to be anything normal about his *practice for a while,* Rhiow said, dryly, as they watched the structure of the gate reassert itself in the air, rippling and flowing, wrinkling as if someone were pulling it out of shape from the edges. Arhu had not actually started his task on the gate yet, but he was thinking about it, and the gates were susceptible to the thoughts of the technicians who worked with them.

"Uh," Arhu said.

"Don't just pull it in all directions like a dead rat, for Iau's sake," Rhiow said, trying not to sound as impatient as she felt. "Take time to get your visualization sorted out first."

"Remember what I told you about visualizing the entire interweave of the gate's string structure as organized into five-stranded structures and groups of five," Urruah said. "Simplest that way: there are five major groupings of forces involved in worldgates, and besides, we have five claws on each paw, and these things are never accidental—"

"Wait a minute," Arhu said, sitting back again, but with a slightly suspicious look this time. "Are you trying to tell me that the whole species of People was built the way we are just so that we could be gate technicians?"

"Maybe not *just* for that purpose, no. But don't you find it a little strange that we're perfectly set up to handle strings physically, and that we can see them naturally, when no other species can?"

"The saurians can."

"That's a recent development," Rhiow said wearily. It was one of many "recent developments," which they were all slowly digesting. "Never mind that for now. No other species *could*. Meantime, do something before the thing defaults again."

"All right," Arhu said. "Group one is for phase relationships." He plucked that control string out as he named it, held it hooked behind one claw, and a series of strings in the matrix ran bright golden as he activated them. "Two is for . . ." He continued reciting the basics of string activation as Urruah listened, alert to any errors.

Arhu leaned in to bite the strings that he was having trouble managing with his paws. "Just be glad this is all you have to worry about at the moment," Urruah said. "Once we get up into second-order stuff, your head will hurt a *lot* worse than if I'd hit you for your rude mouth, which may come later. And don't think I can't hear you thinking, with your teeth and claws full of hyperstrings: you think the laws of science are broken, or I'm deaf? Thought runs down those things like water: that's partly what they're built for. All you have to worry about now is the path this piece of Earth is describing through space at the moment, and the path that the piece you're trying to gate to is describing. You keep them in sync while the gate's open, and that'll be more than a lot of wizards can do. It's a complex helical locus in motion, but no more complex than a trained Person can handle. Let's see how you do."

Rhiow sat and wondered how Urruah could sound so casual about the management of forces that, if Arhu let them slip, could peel the whole mass of Grand Central Terminal off its track-tunneled lower layers and toss it up into the stratosphere the way you would toss a new-killed rat. That was Urruah's teaching style, though, and it seemed to work with Arhu. *Tom stuff,* Rhiow thought, and kept her whiskers still; unwise to let the amusement show. *For toms, it all comes down to blows and ragged ears in the end. Never mind: whatever works for them . . .*

The weave of the gate before them suddenly shimmered and misted away to invisibility. They got a glimpse of light streaming golden through rustling green leaves, a bustle and rush of *ehhif* along a checkered black-and-white pavement before them: and suddenly, with a huge clangor of bells, a huge, boxy blue-and-white shape turned a corner in front of them and came rushing directly at the gate.

Arhu's eyes went wide: he yowled and threw himself backward, dropping the mouthful and double pawful of strings. The view through the gate vanished, leaving nothing but the snapped-back rainbow weave of the hyperstrings, buzzing slightly like strummed guitar strings in the dark air as they resonated off the energy that had built up in them while the gate was open.

Arhu lay on the cinders and panted. "What did I—I didn't—"

Rhiow yawned. "It was a tram."

"What?"

"A kind of bus," Rhiow said. "It runs on electricity; some *ehhif* cities use them. Don't ask me where that was, though."

"Blue-and-white tram," Urruah said. "Combined with that smell? That was Zürich."

"Urruah . . ."

"No, seriously. There's a butcher just down the road from there, on the Bahnhofstrasse, and they have this sausage that—"

"Urruah."

"What? What's the matter?"

Rhiow sighed. Urruah had four ruling passions: wizardry, food, sex, and *o'hra.* They jostled one another for precedence, but you could guarantee in any discussion with Urruah that at least one of them would come up, usually repeatedly. "We don't need to hear about the sausage," Rhiow said. "Was that the location you had set into the gate?"

"I didn't set a specific location. Just told it to hunt for population centers in the three-hundred-to-five-hundred-thousand range with gating affinities."

"Then you did good," Rhiow said to Arhu, "even if you did panic. You had 'here' and 'there' perfectly synchronized."

"Until I panicked." Arhu was washing now, with the quick, sullen movements of someone both embarrassed and angry.

"It didn't do any harm. You should always brace yourself, though, when opening a gate into a new location, even on visual-only. It's another good reason to make sure the gate defaults to invisible/intangible until you've got your coordinates solidified."

"Take a break," Urruah said. But Arhu turned back to the gate-weave and began hooking his claws into it again, in careful sequence.

Stubborn, Rhiow said silently to Urruah.

This isn't a bad thing, Urruah said. *Stubborn can keep you alive, in our line of work, at times when smart may not be enough.*

Rhiow switched her tail in agreement. They watched Arhu reconstruct the active matrix and pull out the strings again, two pawfuls of them: then he leaned in and carefully began taking hold of the next groups with his teeth, pulling them down one by one to join the ones already in his claws. The gate shimmered.

Traffic flowed by in both directions right before them, cars and buses in a steady stream, but there was something odd about the sight, regardless. In the background, beyond some lower buildings, two great square towers with pointed pyramidal tops stuck up: a roadway ran between them, and some kind of catwalk, high up.

"The cars are on the wrong side," Arhu said suddenly.

"Not wrong," Rhiow said, "just different. There are places on the planet where they don't drive the way *ehhif* here do."

"*No* one on the planet drives the way *ehhif* here do," Urruah muttered.

Rhiow put her whiskers forward in a smile. "No argument."

People were walking back and forth before what would be the aperture of the gate, were it to open physically. "Look at them all," Arhu said, somewhat bemused. "It keeps coming up cities."

"It would whether Urruah had set the parameters that way or not," Rhiow said to Arhu. "Worldgates inhere to population centers."

Make it a little drier for him, why don't you? Urruah said good-humoredly into her mind as he looked out at the *ehhif* hurrying by. "See, Arhu, if you pack enough people of whatever species into a tight enough space, the fabric of physicality starts fraying from the pressure of all their minds intent on getting what they want. Pack even more of them in, up to the threshold number, and odd things start to happen routinely in that area as the spacetime continuum rubs thinner—places get a reputation for anything being available there, or at least possible. Go over the threshold number and gates start forming spontaneously."

"Much smaller populations can produce gates if they're there for long enough," Rhiow said. "The piled-up-population effect can be cumulative over time: there are settlements of *ehhif* that have been established for many thousands of years, and therefore have gates even though only a small population lives there at any one time."

"Catal Huyuk," Urruah said, "and Chur, places like that. Those old gates can be tricky, though: idiosyncratic . . . and over thousands of years, they pick up a lot of strange memories, not all of them good. The newer high-population-locus gates can be a lot safer to work with."

"What's the threshold number you were talking about?" Arhu asked, studying the gate.

"A variable, not a constant," Rhiow said. "It varies by species. For *ehhif,* it's around ten million. For People, eight hundred thousand, give or take a tail."

Arhu flirted his own tail, a gesture of disbelief. "Where would you get that many People?"

"Right here in this city, for one place," Rhiow said. "All those 'pets,' all those 'strays' "—the words she used were *rhao'ehhih'h* and *aihlhih,* "human-denned" and "non-aligned." "There might be as many as a million of us just in this island. Either way, there's more than enough of us to sustain a gating complex without *ehhif* being involved . . . and they're here too. With such big joint populations, it's no surprise that this complex is the most senior one in the planet."

"And besides, there's the 'master' gating connection to the Downside," Urruah said. "Every worldgate on the planet has 'affectional' connections to it: for all we know, its presence made it possible for all the other gates to spawn."

Arhu shook his head. "What's this city, then?"

"London," Urruah said.

"Don't tell me . . . you can smell the local butcher."

Urruah took a swipe at Rhiow, which she ducked with her whiskers forward, amused to have successfully put a claw into his near-impervious ego. "As it happens," Urruah said, "I recognize the landscape. That's Tower Bridge back there."

Rhiow looked at the bridge between the two towers: it was starting to rise in two pieces, to let a ship past. "Isn't that the one the *ehhif* have a rhyme about? It fell down. . . ."

"Wrong bridge. This is a younger one; the location it serves started developing gates around the beginning of the last millennium, when the last bunch of *ehhif* with a big empire came through."

"The 'Hrromh'ans.' "

"That's right."

"Not a very old complex, then," Rhiow said.

"Nope. A little finicky, this one. The population pressure built up around it in fits and starts rather than steadily, and it kept losing population abruptly—the city kept getting sacked, having plagues and fires, things like that. The matrices formed under touchy circumstances. But the Tower

Bridge complex is good for long-range transits: better than ours, even. No one's sure why. Convergence of ley lines, gravitic anomalies under that hill close to the bridge, who knows?" Urruah waved his tail. "Leave it to the theorists."

"Like you, now."

He put his whiskers forward, but the expression in his eyes was ironic. "Well, we're all diversifying a little at the moment, aren't we? Not that we have much choice."

"You miss her too," Rhiow said softly.

Urruah watched Arhu for a little, and then said, "She used to go on and on about these little details. Now I wonder whether she had a hint of what was going to happen. . . ."

"The interesting thing," Rhiow said, "is that you *remembered* all this."

He looked at her sidewise. "Shouldn't surprise you. 'He lives in a Dumpster, he's got a brain like a Dumpster,' isn't that what you always say?"

"I never say that," Rhiow said, scandalized, having often thought that very thing.

"Huh," Urruah said, and his whiskers went farther forward. "Anyway, this complex handles a lot of offplanet work—emergency interventions, and the routine training and cultural exchange transits involving wizards here and elsewhere in the Local Group of galaxies. Bigger scheduled transits than that tend to go to Chur or Alexandria or Beijing, to keep Tower Bridge from getting overloaded, Saash told me. It overloads easily—something to do with the forces tangled around that hill with the old castle on it."

"Should I try somewhere else?" Arhu said, now bored with looking at the traffic.

"Sure, go ahead," Rhiow said, waving her tail in casual assent, and Arhu sat up on his haunches again and hooked his claws into the control matrix, while Rhiow looked thoughtfully for a moment more at that old tower. There were a lot of physical places associated with *ehhif* that acquired personality artifact over many years, probably as a result of the *ehhif* tendency to stay in one place for generations. People didn't do that, as a rule, and found the prospect slightly pathological: but there was no use judging one species by another's standards—the One doubtless had Her reasons for designing them differently. *Ten lives on, maybe we'll all be told.*

"It's stuck," Arhu said suddenly.

"What? Stuck how?"

"I don't know. It's just stuck."

Urruah got up and stalked over to look the gate-web up and down. To a Person's eyes, its underweave, the warp and woof of interwoven hyperstrings that produced the gating effect, was still plainly visible through the image of sunshine on that other landscape, the tangle of buildings and traffic beyond. Arhu was sitting up with the brilliant strings of the "control weave" now stretched again between his paws, pulled taut and in the correct configuration for viewing. "Look," Arhu said, and twisted his paws so that the weave changed configuration, went much more "open," a maneuver that should have shut down the gate to the bare matrix again.

The gate just hung there, untroubled and unmoved, and showed the bridge and the traffic, and the *ehhif* hurrying by.

Rhiow came up beside Urruah. "Do it again."

"I can't, not from this configuration, anyway."

"I mean take that last move back, then reexecute."

Arhu did.

Nothing changed. The morning was bright, and shone on the bridge and the river.

"Let me try," Urruah said.

"Why?" Rhiow said. "He did it right."

Urruah looked at her in astonishment. "Well, he . . ."

"He did it right. Let's not rush to judgment: let's have a look at this."

They all did. The strings looked all right, but something else was the matter: nothing that they could see. As she peered at the view, and the gate, Rhiow started to get the feeling that someone was looking over her shoulder . . .

. . . and then realized that Someone was. She did not have to look to see: she knew Who it was.

There's a problem, the voice whispered in her ear.

Urruah's ears flicked: nothing to do with the ambient noise. Arhu's eyes went wide. He was still adjusting to hearing the Whisperer. It took some getting used to, for the voice in your mind sounded like your own thought, except that it was not. It plainly came from somewhere else, and at first the feeling could be as bizarre as feeling someone else switch your tail.

Rhiow's was switching now, without help. *Well, madam,* she thought, *do You know what this problem is?*

The gate with which yours is presently in affinity is malfunctioning, said the silent voice inside their heads. *The London gating team requires your assistance; they will be expecting you. You should leave as soon as you can make arrangements for covering your own territory during your absence.*

And that was it: the voice was silent, the presence gone, as suddenly as it had come.

Arhu blinked, though this time he didn't drop the strings. "What did She mean?" he said. "And where *is* London exactly?"

"About a tenth of the way around the planet," Rhiow said, glancing at the bridge again. "Look in that fourth group of strings and you'll see the coordinates."

"You mean we have to go *away?*"

"That's what She said," said Urruah, dismayed. "To London, yet."

"I would have thought you'd be happy, 'Ruah," Rhiow said, slightly amused despite her own surprise and concern. "The butchers and all."

"When you're visiting, that's one thing," Urruah said, sitting down and licking his nose. "Working, that's something else. It wasn't so much fun the last time."

"We have to go work on someone *else's* gates?" Arhu said, letting the strings go, carefully, one at a time. "And you did this before?"

"We had to go help a team in Tokyo," said Rhiow, "halfway around the planet: it was about a sunround and a half ago. We were there for nearly three weeks. It was something of a logistical nightmare, but we got the job done."

" 'Something' of a nightmare!" Urruah muttered, and lay down on the platform, looking across at the commuters as they came and went. "You have a talent for understatement."

"There's no telling how long we'll be gone on one of these consultational trips," Rhiow said, "but they're not normally brief. Usually we're only called in for consultation when the local team has exhausted all its other options and still hasn't solved the problem."

"Why us, though?" Arhu said.

"We're the senior gating team on the planet," Urruah said, "because we work with Grand Central. It's not that we're all that much better at the job than anyone else"—and Rhiow blinked at this sudden access of humility from Urruah—"but the main gating matrices in the Old Downside are the oldest functioning worldgate complex on the planet. All the other gating complexes that have since come into being have 'affinity' links through Grand Central to the Downside matrices."

"Think of all those other gating complexes as branches of

a tree," Rhiow said, "and Grand Central as the last of the really big complexes that branched out closest to the trunk. There have been others that were bigger or older, but for one reason or another they're gone now . . . so Grand Central is the last of the 'firstborn' gating complexes, the ones that Aaurh the Maker set in place Herself when the world was young. Since we routinely work with Grand Central, and less routinely with the Downside matrices, we're expected to be competent to troubleshoot gates farther up the 'tree' as well."

"Wow!" Arhu said.

" 'Wow,' " said Urruah, rather sourly.

Rhiow was inclined to agree with him. *Who needs this now?* she thought. Life had just begun to be getting a little settled again, after the craziness of the late summer, after the desperate intervention in the Old Downside, in which Arhu gained his wizardry and Saash lost hers, or rather took it up in a more profound version after her ninth death—though either way she was lost to the team now. Arhu had filled her spot, though not precisely. Saash had been a gate technician of great skill, and Arhu was primarily a visionary, gifted at seeing beyond present realities into those past or yet to come. That talent was still steadying down, as it might take some years yet to do; and it would take a lot of training yet before Arhu was anything like the gating technician Saash had been. Since they got back, Rhiow and Urruah had been spending almost all their free time coaching him and wondering when life would get back to anything like "normal." *So much for* that! Rhiow thought.

"What are we going to do about our regular maintenance rounds?" Urruah said.

Rhiow flirted her tail. "The Penn Station team will have to handle them."

"Oh, they're going to just love *that.*"

"We can't help it, and they'll know that perfectly well. All of us wind up subbing for People on other teams every now and then. Sometimes it's fun."

"*They* won't think so," Urruah said. "How long is this going to go on?"

Rhiow sighed. The human school year was just starting, and *ehhif* businesses were swinging back into full operation after the last of their people came back from vacation. The city was sliding back into fully operative mode, which meant increased pressure on the normal rapid transit. That in turn meant more stress on the gates, for the increased numbers of *ehhif* moving in and out of the city meant more stress on the fabric of reality, especially in the areas where large numbers of humans flowed in and out in the vicinity of the gate matrices themselves. String structure got finicky, matrices got warped, and gates went down without warning at such times: hardly a day went by without a malfunction. The Pennsylvania Station gating team had their paws full just with their normal work. Having the Grand Central gates added to their workload, at their busiest time . . .

" 'Ruah, it can't be helped," Rhiow said. "They can take it up with the Powers themselves, if they like, but the Whisperer will send them off with fleas in their ears and nothing more. These things happen."

"Yeah, well, what about you?"

"Me?"

"You know. Your *ehhif.*"

Rhiow sighed at that. Urruah was "nonaligned"—without a permanent den and not part of a pride-by-blood, but most specifically uncompanioned by *ehhif,* and therefore what they would call a "stray": mostly at the moment he lived in a Dumpster outside a construction site in the East Sixties. Arhu had inherited Saash's position as mouser-in-chief at the underground parking garage where she had lived, and had nothing to do to keep in good odor with his "employers" except, at regular intervals, to drop something impressively dead in front of the garage office, and to appear fairly regularly at mealtimes. Rhiow, however, was denned with an *ehhif* in a twentieth-story apartment between First and Second in the Seventies. Her comings and goings during his workday were nothing that bothered Iaehh, since he didn't see them; but in the evenings, if he didn't know where she was, he got concerned. Rhiow had no taste for upsetting him—between the two of them, since the sudden loss of her "own" *ehhif,* Hhuha, there had been more than enough upset to go around.

"I'll have to work around him the best I can," she said. "He's been doing a lot of overtime lately: that'll probably help me." Though as she said it, once again Rhiow found herself wondering about all that overtime. Was it happening because the loss of the household's second income had been making the apartment harder to afford, or because the less time Iaehh spent there, being reminded of Hhuha in the too-quiet evenings, the happier he was? "And besides," she said, ready enough to change the subject, "it can't be any better for you. . . ."

Urruah made a *hmf* sound. "Well, it's annoying," he said. "They're starting *H'la Houhème* at the end of the week."

"I don't mean that. I had in mind your ongoing business with the 'Somali' lady you've been seeing over at the Met. The diva-*ehhif*'s 'pet.' "

Urruah shook his head hard enough that his ears rattled slightly. It was a gesture Rhiow had been seeing more often than usual from him, lately, and he had picked up a couple more scars about the head. "Yes, well," he said.

Rhiow looked away and began innocently to wash. Urruah's interest in the art form known to *ehhif* as "opera" continued to strike her as a little kinky, despite Rhiow's recognition that this was simply a slightly idiosyncratic personal manifestation of all toms' fascination with song in its many forms. However, lately Urruah had been discoursing mostly in the abstract mode as regarded *oh'ra* proper, and a lot more about one of the Met's star dressing rooms and the goings-on therein. Urruah's interest in Hwith, the Somali, was apparently less than abstract, and appeared mutual, though most of what Rhiow heard of Hwith's discourse had to do with the juicier gossip about the steadily intensifying encounters between her "mistress" and the *oh'ra*'s present guest conductor.

"Well, what the *houff,*" Urruah said after a moment. "This is what we became wizards for, anyway, isn't it? Travel. Adventure. Going to strange and wonderful places . . ."

And getting in trouble in them, Rhiow thought. "Absolutely," she said. "Come on, let's start getting the logistics sorted out."

She turned and walked back up the platform, jumped down onto the tracks, and started to make her way over the iron-stained gravel to the platform for Track 24. Urruah followed at his own pace: Arhu leaped and ran to catch up with her. "Why're you so down about it?" he said. "This is gonna be great!"

"It will if you don't act up," Rhiow said, and almost immediately regretted it.

"Whaddaya mean, act up? I'm very well behaved."

Rhiow gave Urruah a sidewise look as he came up from behind them. "Compared to the Old Tom on a rampage," she said, "or the Devastatrix in heat, doubtless you are. As *People* go, though, we have some work to do on you yet."

"Listen to me, Arhu," Urruah said as they jumped up onto Track 24 and started weaving their way down it toward the entrance to the main concourse. "We're going into other

People's territory. That's always ticklish business. Not only that: we're going there because something's going on that *they* couldn't handle by themselves. They have to have feelings about that . . . and that we're now going to come strolling in there with our tails up to fix things, supposedly, can't make them overjoyed either. It makes them look bad to themselves. You get it?"

"Well, if they *are* bad—"

Arhu broke off and ducked out of the way of the swipe Rhiow aimed at his head. "Arhu," Rhiow said, "that's not your judgment to make. Certainly not of another wizard: not of regular People, either. Queen Iau has built us all with different abilities, and just because they don't always work perfectly right now doesn't mean they won't later. As for their effectiveness, sometimes a wizard comes up against a job he can't handle. When that happens, and we're called to assist, we do just that . . . knowing that someday we may be in the same position."

They came out of the gateway to 24, squeezing hard to the left to avoid being trampled by the *ehhif* who were streaming in toward the waiting train, and came out into the concourse. "We're a kinship, not a group of competitors," Urruah said as they began making their way toward the Graybar Building entrance, hugging the wall. "We don't go out of our way to make our brothers and sisters feel that they're failing at their jobs. We fail at enough of our own."

"So," Rhiow said. "We've got a day or so to sort out our own business. Urruah, fortunately, doesn't have an abode shared with *ehhif,* so his arrangements will be simplest—"

"Hey, listen," Urruah said, "if I go away and they take my Dumpster somewhere, you think that isn't going to be a problem? I'll have to drop back here every couple of days to make sure things stay the way I left them."

Rhiow restrained herself mightily from asking what Urruah could possibly keep in a Dumpster that was of such importance. "Arhu, at the garage, have any of them been paying particular attention to you?"

"Yeah, the tall one," he said, "Ah'hah, they call him. He was Saash's *ehhif;* he seems to think he's mine now." Arhu looked a little abashed. "He's nice to me."

"Okay. You're going to have to come back from London every couple of days to make sure that he sees you and knows you're all right."

"By myself?" Arhu said, very suddenly.

"Yes," Rhiow said. "And Arhu—if I find that, in the process, you've gated offplanet, your ears and my claws are going to meet! Remember what Urruah told you."

"I never get to have any *fun* with wizardry!" Arhu said, the complaint acquiring a little yowl around the edges, and he fluffed up slightly at Rhiow. "It's all work and dull stuff!"

"Oh really?" Urruah said. "What about that cute little marmalade tabby I saw you with the other night?"

"Uh . . . *Oh,*" Arhu said, and abruptly sat down right by the wall and became very quiet.

"Yes indeed," Urruah said. "Naughty business, that, stealing groceries out of an *ehhif*'s trunk. That's why you fell down the manhole afterwards. The Universe notices when wizards misbehave. And sometimes . . . other wizards do too."

Arhu sat staring at Urruah wide-eyed, and didn't say anything. This by itself was so bizarre an event that Rhiow nearly broke up laughing. "Boy's got taste, if nothing else," Urruah said to her, and sat down himself for a moment. "He was up on Broadway and raided some *ehhif*'s shopping bags after they'd been to Zabar's. Caviar, it was, and smoked salmon and sour cream: supposed to be someone's brunch the next day, I guess. He did a particulate bypass spell on a section of the trunk lid and pulled the stuff out piece by piece . . . then gave every bit of it to this little marmalade creature with the big green eyes."

Arhu was now half turned away from them while hurriedly washing his back. It was *he'ihh*, composure-washing: and it wasn't working—the fur bristled again as fast as he washed it down. "Never even set the car alarm off," Urruah said, wrapping his tail demurely around his toes. "Did it in full sight. None of the *ehhif* passing by believed what they were seeing, as usual."

"I *had* to do it in full sight," Arhu said, starting to wash farther down his back. "You can't sidle when you're—"

"Stealing things, no," Rhiow said, as she sat down too. She sighed. The child had come to them with a lot of bad habits. Yet much of Arhu's value as a Person and a wizard had to do with his unquenchable, sometimes unbearable spirit and verve, which even a truly awful kittenhood had not been able to crush. Had his tendencies as a visionary not already revealed themselves, Rhiow would have thought that Arhu was destined to be like Urruah, a "power source," the battery or engine of a spell that others might construct and work, but he would fuel and drive. Either way, the visionary talent, too, used that verve to fuel it. It was Arhu's inescapable curiosity, notable even for a cat, that kept his wizardry fretting and fraying at the fabric of linear time until it "wore through" and some image from future or past leaked out.

"If nothing else," Rhiow said finally, "you've got a quick grasp of the fundamentals . . . as they apply to implementation, anyway. I can see the ethics end of things is going to take longer." Arhu turned, opened his mouth to say something. "Don't start with me," Rhiow said. "Talk to the Whisperer about it if you don't believe us; but stealing is only going to be trouble for you eventually. Meanwhile, where shall we meet in the morning?"

Urruah looked around him as Arhu got up again, looking a little recovered. "I guess here is as good a place as any. Five thirty?"

That was opening time for the station and would be fairly calm, if any time of the day in a place as big and busy as Grand Central could accurately be described as calm. "Good enough," Rhiow said.

They started to walk out down the Graybar passage again, to the Lexington Avenue doors. "Arhu?" Rhiow said to him as they came out and slid sideways to hug the wall, heading for the corner of Forty-third. "An hour before first twilight, two hours before the Old Tom's Eye sets."

"I know when five thirty is," Arhu said, sounding slightly affronted. "They do shift change at the garage a moonwidth after that."

"All right," Urruah said. "Anything else you need to take care of, like telling the little marmalade number—"

"Her name's Hffeu," Arhu said.

"Hffeu it is," Rhiow said. "She excited to be going out with a wizard?"

Arhu gave Rhiow a look of pure pleasure: if his whiskers had gone any farther forward, they would have fallen off in the street.

She had to smile back: there were moods in which this kit was, unfortunately, irresistible. "Go on, then—tell her good-bye for a few days: you're going to be busy. And Arhu—"

"I know, 'Be careful.' " He was laughing at her. " 'Luck, Rhiow."

" 'Luck," she said as he bounded off across the traffic running down Forty-third, narrowly being missed by a taxi taking the corner.

She breathed out. Next to her, Urruah laughed softly as they slipped into the door of the post office to sidle, then waited for the light to change. "You worry too much about that kit. He'll be all right."

"Oh, his survival is between him and the Powers now," she said, "I know. But still . . ."

"You still feel responsible for him," Urruah said as the light turned and they trotted out to cross the street, "because for a while he *was* our responsibility. Well, he's passed his Ordeal, and we're off *that* hook. But now we have to teach him teamwork."

"It's going to make the last month look like ten dead birds and no one to share them with," Rhiow said. She peered up Lexington, trying to see past the hurrying *ehhif*. Humans could not see into that neighboring universe where cats went when sidled and in which string structure was obvious, but she could just make out Arhu's little black-and-white shape, trailing radiance from passing resonated hyperstrings as he ran.

"At least he's willing," Urruah said. "More than he was before."

"Well, we owe a lot of that to you . . . your good example."

Urruah put his whiskers forward, pleased, as they came to the next corner and went across the side street at a trot. "Feels a little odd sometimes," he said.

"What?" Rhiow said, putting hers forward too. "That the original breaker of every available rule should now be the big, stern, tough—"

"I didn't break *that* many rules."

"Oh? What about that dog, last month?"

"Come on, that was just a little fun."

"Not for the dog. And the sausage guy on Thirty-third . . ."

"That was an intervention. Those sausages were *terrible.*"

"As you found after tricking him into dropping one. And last year, the lady with the—"

"All right, all right!" Urruah was laughing as they came to Forty-fifth. "So I like the occasional practical joke. Rhi, I don't break any of the real rules. I do my job."

She sighed, and then bumped her head against his as they stood by the corner of the building at Forty-fifth and Lex, waiting for the light to change. "You do," she said. "You are a wizard's wizard, for all your jokes. Now get out of here and do whatever you have to do with your Dumpster."

"I thought you weren't going to mention that," Urruah said, and grinned. " 'Luck, Rhi."

He galloped off across the street and down Forty-fifth as the light changed, leaving her looking after him in mild bemusement.

He heard me thinking.

Well, wizards *did* occasionally overhear one another's private thoughts when they had worked closely together for long enough. She and Saash had sometimes "underheard" each other this way: usually without warning, but not always at times of stress. It had been happening a little more frequently since Arhu came. *Something to do with the change in the makeup of the team?* she thought. There was no way to tell.

And no time to spend worrying about it now. But even as Rhiow set off for her own lair, trotting on up Lex toward the Upper East Side, she had to smile ironically at that. It was precisely *because* she was so good at worrying that she was the leader of this particular team. Losing the habit could mean losing the team . . . or worse.

For the time being, she would stick to worrying.

✦

The way home was straightforward, this time of day: up Lex to Seventieth, then eastward to the block between First and Second. The street was fairly quiet for a change. Mostly it was old converted brownstones, though the corner apartment buildings were newer ones, and a few small cafés and stores were scattered along the block. She paused at the corner of Seventieth and Second to greet the big stocky duffle-coated doorman there, who always stooped to pet her. He was opening the door for one of the tenants: now he turned, bent down to her. "Hey there, Midnight, how ya doing?"

"No problems today, Ffran'hk," Rhiow said, rearing up to rub against him: he might not hear or understand her spoken language any more than any other *ehhif,* but body language he understood just fine. Ffran'hk was a nice man, not above slipping Rhiow the occasional piece of bologna from a sandwich, and also not above slipping some of the harder-up homeless people in the area a five- or ten-dollar bill on the sly. Carers were hard enough to come by in this world, wizardly or not, and Rhiow could hardly fail to appreciate one who was also in the neighborhood.

Having said hello in passing, she went on her way down the block, not bothering to sidle even this close to home. Iaehh rarely came down the block this way anyhow, preferring for some reason to approach from the First Avenue side, possibly because of the deli down on that corner.

She strolled down the sidewalk, glancing around her idly at the brownstones, the garbage, the trees, and the weeds growing up around them; more or less effortlessly she avoided the *ehhif* who came walking past her with shopping bags or briefcases or baby strollers. Halfway down was a browner brownstone than usual, with the usual stairway up to the front door and a side stairway to the basement apartment. On one of the squared-off tops of the stone balusters flanking the stairway sat a rather grungy-looking white-furred shape, washing. He was always washing, Rhiow thought, not that it mattered much to how he looked. She stopped at the bottom of the stairs.

"Hunt's luck, Yafh!"

He looked down at her and blinked for a moment. Green eyes in a face as round as a saucer full of cream, and almost as big; big shoulders, huge paws, and an overall scarred and beat-up look, as if he had had an abortive argument with a meat grinder: that was Yafh. However, you got the impression that the meat grinder had lost the argument. " 'Luck, Rhi," he said cheerfully. "I've had mine for today. Care for a rat?"

"That's very kind of you," she said, "but I'm on my way to dinner, and if I spoil my appetite, my *ehhif* will notice. Bite its head off on my behalf, if you would. . . ."

"My pleasure." Yafh bent down and suited the action to the word.

She trotted up the steps and sat down beside Yafh for a moment, looking down the street while he crunched. Yafh was one of those People who, while ostensibly denned with *ehhif,* was neglected totally by them. He subsisted on scraps scavenged from the neighborhood garbage bags, and on rats and mice and bugs—not difficult in this particular building, its landlord apparently not having had the exterminators in since early in the century.

"You off for the day?" Yafh said when he finished crunching.

"The day, yes," she said, "but tomorrow early we have to go to Hlon'hohn."

"That's right across the East River, isn't it?"

"Uh, yes, all the way across." Rhiow put her whiskers forward in a smile. So did Yafh.

"They're making you work again, 'Rioh," Yafh said. The name was a pun on her name and an Ailurin word for "beast of burden," though you could also use it for a wheelbarrow or a grocery cart or anything else that *ehhif* pushed around. "It's all a plot. People shouldn't *work.* People should lie on cushions and be fed cream, and filleted fish, and ragout of free-range crunchy mouse in a rich gravy."

"Oh," Rhiow said. "The way *you* are."

Yafh laughed that rough, buttery laugh of his: he leaned back and hit the headless body of the rat a couple of times in a pleased and absent way. "Exactly. But at least I'm my own boss. Are you?"

"This isn't slavery, if that's what you're asking," Rhiow said, bristling very slightly. "It's service. There *is* a difference."

"Oh, I know," Yafh said. "What wizards do is important, regardless of what some People think." He picked up the rat one more time, dangled it from a razory claw, flipped it in the air and caught it expertly. "And at least from what you tell me you have it better than the poor *ehhif* wizards do: your own kind at least know about you. But Rhi, it's just that you never seem to have much time to yourself. When do you lie around and just be *People?"*

"I get some time off, every now and then. . . ."

"Uh huh," Yafh said, and smiled slightly: that scarred, beat-up, amiable look that had fooled various of the other cats (and some dogs) in the neighborhood into thinking he was no particular threat. "Not enough, I think. And things have been tough for you lately."

"Yes," Rhiow said, and sighed. "Well, we all have bad times occasionally: not even wizardry can stop that."

"It stops other people's bad times, maybe," Yafh said, "but not your own. . . . It just seems hard, that's all."

"It is," Rhiow said after a moment, gazing up toward her *ehhif*'s apartment building near the corner. Sometimes lately she had dreaded going home to the familiar den that suddenly had gone unfamiliar without Hhuha in it. But Iaehh was still there, and he expected her to be there on a regular basis. As far as he knew, she was only able to get out onto the apartment's terrace and from there to the roof of the building next door, from which Iaehh supposed there was no way down . . . and if she didn't come in every day or so, he worried.

"You sure you don't want the rest of this rat?" Yafh said quietly.

Rhiow turned toward him, apologetic. "Oh, Yafh, I appreciate it, but food won't help. Work will . . . though I hate to admit it. You go ahead and have that, now. Look at the size of it! It's a meal by itself."

"They're getting bigger all the time," Yafh said, lifting the headless rat delicately on one claw again and examining it with a more clinical look. "Saw one the other night that was half your size."

Rhiow's jaw chattered in relish and disgust at the thought of dancing in the moonlight with such a partner. The dance would be brief: Rhiow prided herself on her skill in the hunt. At the same time, it was disturbing, for the rats did keep getting bigger. "The rate they're going," she said as she got up, "we're going to start needing bigger People."

Yafh gave her an amused look. "I've done my part," he said, and Rhiow put her whiskers forward, knowing he had sired at least fifty kittens in this area alone before he was untommed.

"You've done more than that," she said. "Hunt's luck, Yafh. . . . I'll see you in a few days. Can I bring you something from Hlon'hohn?"

"How are the rats?" he said.

"Oh please," Rhiow said, laughing, and trotted down the steps toward home.

✦

For the last part of the run, she sidled, since the building next to her *ehhif*'s apartment house had windows that were not blind. Down by the locked steel door that separated the alley beside the building from the street, Rhiow looked up and down to make sure no one was looking directly at her, and then stepped sideways without moving. Whiskers and ear-tips and Rhiow's tail-tip sizzled slightly as she sidled, making the shift into the alternate universe where the hyperstrings that stitched empty space and solid matter together were clearly visible, even in the afternoon light. They surrounded her now, a jangle and jumble of hair-thin harp strings of multicolored light, running up toward vanishing points up in space and down to other vanishing points in the Earth's core or beyond it. Rhiow threaded her way among them, and slipped under the gate and into the alleyway.

The garbage was piling up again. She paused to listen for any telltale rustling among the black plastic bags: nothing. *No rats today. But then for all I know, Yafh's been here already.* Rhiow stalked past the bags, looked up toward the roof of the building whose left-paw wall partly defined the alleyway, and said several words under her breath in the Speech.

Everything living understands the Speech in which wizards work, as well as many things that are not living now, or once were, or that someday might be. Air was malleable stuff, and could be reminded that it had once been trapped in oxides and nitrates in the ancient stone. It had been in and out of so many lungs since its release that there was controversy among wizards whether air should any longer simply be considered an element, but also something once alive. Either way, it was easy to work with. A few words more and the hyperstrings in the empty air of the alley knotted themselves together into the outline of an invisible stairway: the air, obliging, went solid within the outlines.

Invisible herself, Rhiow trotted up eight stories to the roof of the building on the left, and leaped up over the parapet to the gray gravel on top. Wincing a little as always at the way it hurt her feet, she glanced over her shoulder and said the word of release: the strings unknotted, and the air went back to being no more solid than the smog made it. Rhiow made her way along to the back left-paw corner where the next building along, her *ehhif* 's building, abutted this one's roof.

When the *ehhif* who built her building had done its brickwork, they had left a repeating diamond pattern down its side of bricks that jutted out an inch or so. The bottom of one of these diamonds made a neat stairstep way straight up to where her *ehhif*'s apartment's terrace jutted out.

Rhiow jumped up onto the parapet of the building she had just ascended, and then stepped carefully onto the first of the bricks. Slowly she made her way up, sure of the way but in no rush: a fall would be embarrassing. Just before coming up to the last few bricks, she unsidled herself and then jumped to the terrace: slipped under the table and chairs there, nosed through the clear plastic cat door, and went in.

"Hey, there you are."

He was sitting halfway across the room, in the leather chair under the reading lamp. The apartment was a nice enough one, as far as Rhiow understood the denning requirements of *ehhif:* a "one-bedroom" apartment with a living room full of leather furniture and bookshelves, a big, soft comfortable rug on the polished wood floor of the main room. It was clean and airy, but still had places where a Person could curl up and sleep undisturbed by too much sun or noise: a place not too crowded, not too empty.

Well, Rhiow thought, *until recently not too empty.* She went over to Iaehh and jumped up into his lap before he had time to get up. It was always hard to get him to sit still, more so now than it had been even a month ago.

"Well, hello," Iaehh said, scratching her behind the ears, "aren't we friendly today?" He sighed: he sounded tired. Rhiow looked up into his face, wondering whether the crinkles around the eyes were a sign of age or of strain. He was good-looking, she supposed, as *ehhif* went: regular features, short dark hair, slim for his height and in good shape—Iaehh ran every morning. His eyes sometimes had the kind of glint of humor she caught in Urruah's, a suppression of what would have been uproarious laughter at some wildly inappropriate thing he was about to do. All such looks, though, had been muted in Iaehh's eyes for the last month.

"I'm always friendly with you," Rhiow said, stepping up onto the arm of the chair to bump her head against his upper arm. "You know that. Except when you hold me upside down and play Swing the Cat."

"Oooh," Iaehh said, "big purr . . ." He scratched her under the chin.

"Yes, well, you look like you can use it—you've got that busy-day look. I hope yours wasn't anything like mine." It was folly to talk to *ehhif* in normal Ailurin, Rhiow knew: Iaehh couldn't hear the near-subsonics People used for most of the verbal part of their speech. But like many People who denned with *ehhif,* Rhiow refused to treat him like some kind of dumb animal. At least her work meant she could clearly understand what he said to her—an advantage over most People, who had to guess from tone of voice and body language what was going on with their *ehhif.*

"You hungry? You didn't eat much of what I left you this morning."

"You forgot to wash the bowl again," Rhiow said, starting to step down into his lap, then pausing while Iaehh re-settled himself. "With all the dried stuff from yesterday and the day before yesterday stuck to it, it wasn't exactly conducive to gourmet dining. I'll get some of the dry food in a while."

She settled down in his lap and made herself comfortable while he stroked her. "You're a nice kitty," Iaehh said. "Aren't you?"

"Under the throat," Rhiow said, "yes, right there, that's the spot. . . ." She stretched out her neck and purred, and for a while they just sat there together while bright squares of the late afternoon sun worked their way slowly across the apartment.

"Now why can't the people at work be as laid back as you," Iaehh said after a while. "You just take everything as it comes. . . . You never get stressed out."

She stretched out her forepaws and closed her eyes. "If you only knew," Rhiow said.

"You don't have any worries. You have a nice bed to sleep on, nice food whenever you want it. . . ."

"As regards the food, 'nice' is relative," Rhiow said with some amusement, kneading with her paws on Iaehh's knee. "That 'choice parts' thing you gave me the day before yesterday was parts, all right, but as for 'choice'? Please. I'd be tempted to go out and kill my own cows, except that getting them in the cat door would be a nuisance."

"Ow, ow, don't do that! You go in and out whenever you like, you don't have a job, you don't have to worry about anyone depending on you. . . ."

Rhiow's tail twitched ironically. "Wouldn't it be nice if it were so," she said softly, and sighed. Any wizard had daily concerns over whether or not she was doing her job well: you pushed past those doubts and fears as best you could, secure in the knowledge that the Powers That Be would not long allow you to go on uncorrected if you were messing up. Yet that routine, negative sort of approval sometimes fell short of one's emotional needs; it left you wondering, *Am I giving enough? The Powers that made the Universe have poured Their virtue into me for the purpose of saving that Universe, piece by piece, day by day. Am I giving enough of it back? And—more to the point—is it working?*

"What a life," Iaehh said.

"You're not kidding," Rhiow said.

"But I still wonder . . . is it good enough. . . ."

She opened an eye and looked up at him.

"I don't know sometimes," Iaehh said, stroking her steadily, "if it's fair for me to keep you. Just because . . . you're all that's left of her. I don't know, is that a fair reason to keep a pet?"

Rhiow sighed again. His tone was reflective, his face was still, but the intensity of Iaehh's grief for Hhuha was no less obvious for lacking tears. For one thing, Rhiow could hear the echoes of his emotions: even nonwizardly People could manage that much with the *ehhif* with whom they spent most of their time. For another thing, Rhiow was an experienced wizard, fluent in the Speech. Understanding it, you could thereby understand anything that spoke. You could also speak to anything that spoke, and make yourself understood: but this was strictly forbidden to wizards except when engaged in errantry, on wizardly business that required it. Rhiow had sometimes been tempted to break her silence, but she had never done it—not even when Iaehh had clutched her and wept into her fur, moaning the name that Rhiow herself also would have moaned aloud in shared grief, if only it had been allowed: *Susan, Susan . . .*

Iaehh stroked her, and Rhiow could hear and feel his pain, a little blunted from that first terrible night, but no less easy to bear. She knew the way it came to him in sudden stabs, without warning, at the sound of a telephone ringing or a *ra'hio* commercial that had always made Hhuha laugh. "I worry that you're lonely," Iaehh said slowly. "I worry that I don't take care of you right. I worry . . ."

"Don't worry," she said, snuggling a little closer to him.

"And this place is expensive," he said. "Too big for one, really. I think I ought to move, but finding another building that allows pets is going to be such a hassle. I wonder if I shouldn't find you somewhere else to live."

Rhiow's heart leaped in instant reaction: fear. *He's going to try to rehome me,* she thought. Someone would adopt her whom she hated, and she wouldn't be able to get out and go about her business. Or there were *ehhif* who, meaning nothing but the best, would not give away a pet if they could no longer keep it. They would take their cat to the vet and have it—

Ridiculous, another part of her mind snapped. *You're a wizard. If he seriously starts thinking about giving you away, then one day you can just vanish.*

Yes, said another part of her mind, *and to where? To live with whom?* Wizard Rhiow might be, but she was also a Person, and the one thing People hate above all is to have their routine disrupted. To lose the comfortable den, the sympathetic tone of mind of Iaehh, the food at regular intervals, and find herself . . . where? Living in a Dumpster, like Urruah? Rhiow shuddered. "Iaehh," she said, "this is a *bad* idea, I'd really rather you didn't follow this line of thought any farther."

But what about him? said still another part of her mind, and Rhiow much disliked its tone, for it was like the voice that often spoke of wizardry and its responsibilities. *What about* his *needs? How much pain do you cause him by being here, reminding him of Hhuha every time he sees you?*

And what about my *needs?* Rhiow retorted, fluffing up

slightly. *Don't you think* I *miss her? Damn it, what about* my *pain? Haven't I done enough in service to the Queen and the worlds to be allowed a little comfort, to think of myself first, just this once?*

No reply came. Rhiow disliked the silence as much as she had the voice when it spoke. It sounded entirely too much like the Whisperer, like Hrau'f the Silent, that daughter of Iau's who imparted knowledge of wizardry and the worlds to feline wizards, and who often seemed to have left a kind of goddaughter to herself inside you, stern as a goddess, inflexible as one, asking the questions you would rather not answer.

What then? Rhiow said silently. *Do I have to let him do this? Do I have to let him get rid of me?*

Silence: and Iaehh's stroking, all wound up with his pain and the way he missed Hhuha. Rhiow licked her nose in fear. She could practically feel his anguish through her fur.

The Oath was clear enough on the matter, the Oath that every wizard of whatever species took in one form or another. *I will guard growth and ease pain.* . . . And you kept the Oath, or soon enough you began to slip away from the practice of your wizardry into something that did not bear consideration: into the service of the Lone Power, Who had invented death and pain. Entropy was running, the energy bleeding slowly away out of the universe: the Lone One would widen the wound, hurry the bleeding in any way It could. Tricking or manipulating wizards so that they used their power to Its ends was one of the Lone One's preferred techniques.

I will not be Its claw, to rip the wound wider, Rhiow thought. Brave words, the right words for a wizard. But it was inside her that she felt the claw, already beginning to set in deep. She looked away from Iaehh.

If this situation doesn't improve . . .

. . . then leaving may be something I have to consider.

"No," Iaehh said, "of course not, stupid idea, it's a stupid idea. . . ." He stroked her. "If I have to move, it'll be to somewhere with pets, of course it will. Sue would be furious if I ever let anything happen to you."

He put her aside suddenly, got up. Rhiow, climbing up to stand on the arm of the chair where he had set her down, looked after Iaehh, not at all reassured.

If he keeps hurting this way—then you may have to let him think that something has "happened" to you. Regardless of how well you like this warm, snug place.

"Look at that, it's half an hour past your dinnertime," Iaehh said, fumbling at the kitchen cabinet where the cat food was, as if he were having trouble seeing it: and he sounded stuffed up. "Come on, let's get you fed. Oh, jeez, look at this bowl, I keep forgetting to wash it—no wonder you didn't want to eat out of it."

Rhiow jumped down from the chair and went to him.

If this doesn't get better . . .

Sweet Queen about us, what will become of me?

Two

She was out early the next morning, as (to her relief) Iaehh was: on mornings when the weather was fair, he did his jogging around dawn, to take advantage of the city's quietest time. Rhiow had already been awake for a couple of hours and was doing her morning's washing in the reading chair when he bent over her and scratched her head. "See you later, plumptious—"

She gave him a rub and a purr, then went back to her washing as he went out, shut the door behind him, and locked all the locks. Iaehh was pleased with those locks—their apartment had never been broken into, even though others in the building had. Rhiow smiled to herself as she finished scrubbing behind her ears, for she had heard attempts being made on all those locks at one time or another during the day when she happened to be home. Some of those attempts might have succeeded, had there not been a wizard on the other side of the door, keeping an eye on the low-maintenance spell that made access to the apartment impossible. Should anyone try to get in, the wizardry simply convinced the wall and the door that they were one unit for the duration: and various frustrated thieves had occasionally left strangely ineffectual sledgehammer marks on the outside—the whole door structure having possessed, for the duration of the attack, a nongravitic density similar to that of lead. Rhiow was pleased with that particular piece of spelling: it required only a recharge once a week, and kept her *ehhif*'s routine, and hers, from being upset.

Rhiow finished washing, stretched fore and aft, and headed out the cat door to the *hiouh*-box on the terrace. There she went briefly unfocused in the cool darkness as she did her business, thinking about other things. She had reviewed the basic structures and relationships of the London gates in the Knowledge, the body of wizardly information the Whisperer held ready for routine reference: she had looked at the specs for the gates' operation under normal circumstances. Being rooted in the Old Downside's gates, the London "bundle" had similarities to them, but being sited a continent away and subject to much different spatial stresses, there were also significant differences. She would assess those more accurately when she was right down in the gating complex with their hosts.

Rhiow finished with the box, shook herself, and stepped out onto the terrace and then down onto the brick "stairway," making her way down to the roof of the next building. There she made her way across the gravel again, this time to leap up on the Seventieth Street side of the roof's parapet and balance there for a moment, breathing the predawn air. For once it was very quiet, no car alarms going off, even the traffic over on First muted, as yet. The low, soft *hhhhhhhhh* of the city all around her was there: the breathing of all the air-conditioning systems, the omnidirectional soft sound of traffic that almost never went away. Only during a significant snowstorm did that low, breathing hiss fade reluctantly to silence—and even then you imagined you heard it, though softer, as the breathing in and out of ten million pairs of lungs. It was the sound of life: it was what Rhiow worked for.

She looked eastward toward the river. Her view was partially blocked by the buildings of New York Hospital and Cornell Medical Center, but she could smell the water, and faintly she could even hear it flowing, a different soft rushing noise than that of the traffic. Past the East River and the hazy sodium lights of Queens on the far side, she could smell the dawn, though she couldn't yet see it. *Another job,* Rhiow thought, *another day.*

She closed her eyes most of the way, in order to more clearly see, and be seen by, the less physical side of things. *I will meet the cruel and the cowardly today,* Rhiow thought, *liars and the envious, the uncaring and unknowing: They will be all around. But their numbers and their carelessness do not mean I have to be like them. For my own part, I know my job; my commission comes from Those Who* Are. *My paw raised is Their paw on the neck of the Serpent, now and always. I shall walk through Their worlds as do the Powers That Be, seeing and knowing with Them and for Them, tending Their worlds as if they were mine, for so indeed they are. Silently shall I strive to go my way, as They do, doing my work unseen; the light needs no reminding by me of good deeds done by night. And in this long progress through all that is, though I will know doubt and fear in the strange places where I must walk, I will put these both aside, as the Oath requires, and hold myself to my work . . . for if They and I together cannot mend what is marred, who can? And having done my work aright, though I may know weariness at day's end, come awakening I shall rise up and say again, with Them, as if surprised, "Behold, the world is made new!"*

There was more to the Meditation, of course: it was more a set of guidelines than a ritual in any case, a reminder of priorities, a "mission statement." It was perhaps also, just slightly, what *ehhif* might term a call to arms: there was always a feeling after you finished it that Someone was listening, alert to your problems, ready to make helpful suggestions.

Rhiow got up, shook herself, and headed over to the side of the building to make her stairway down. *The joke is,* she thought, getting sidled and heading down the briefly hardened air, *that knowing the Powers are there and listening doesn't really solve that many problems.* It seemed to her that *ehhif* had the same difficulty, though differing in degree. They were either absolutely sure their gods existed or not very sure at all: and those who were most certain seemed no more at peace with the fact than those who doubted. The city was full of numerous grand buildings, some of them admittedly gloriously made, in which *ehhif* gathered at regular intervals, apparently to remind their versions of the Powers That Be that They existed (which struck Rhiow as rather unnecessary) and to tell Them how wonderful they thought They were (which struck her as hilarious—as if the Powers Who created this and all other universes, under the One, would be either terribly concerned about being acknowledged or praised, or particularly susceptible to flattery).

She thanked the air and released it as she came down to the alley level and made for the gate onto the sidewalk, thinking of how Urruah had accidentally confirmed her analysis some months back. He had some interest in the vocal music made in the bigger versions of these buildings, some of it being of more ancient provenance than most *ehhif* works he heard live in concert in town. He'd gone to one service in the great "cathedral" in Midtown to do some translation of the music's verbal content, and had come back bemused. Half the verses addressed by the *ehhif* there to the Powers That Be had involved the kind of self-abasement and abject flattery that even a queen in heat would have found embarrassing from her suitors, but this material had alternated with some expressing a surprisingly bleak worldview, one filled with a terror of the loss of the Powers' countenance—even, amazingly, the One's—and a tale of the approaching end of the Worlds in which any beings who did not come up to standard would be discarded like so much waste, or tortured for an eternity out of time. Rhiow wondered how the Lone Power had managed to give them such ideas about the One without being stopped somehow. Such ideas would explain a lot of the things some *ehhif* did.

Rhiow stood at the corner of Seventieth and Second, by the corner of the dry cleaner's there, waiting for the traffic to finish passing so that she could cross. *They're scared,* she thought: *they feel they need protection from the Universe. Nor does it help that though they may know the Powers exist,* ehhif *aren't sure what* their *role is. They're not even sure what happens to them when they die.* There was an unsettling sense of permanence about *ehhif* death, in which Rhiow was no expert despite her recent brush with it. The *ehhif* themselves seemed to have been told a great many mutually exclusive stories about what happened After. Her own *ehhif* was somewhere benevolent, Rhiow knew. But where? And would Hhuha ever come back, the way you might expect a Person to, during the first nine lives at least? Not that, certainties aside, it wasn't always a slight shock when you looked into the eyes of some new acquaintance and suddenly saw an old one there, and saw the glint of recognition as they knew you, too. Rhiow's fur had stood up all over her the first time it had happened, a couple of lives back. You got used to it, though. Some People tended to seek out friends they had known, finishing unfinished business or starting over again when everyone had moved on a life or so, in new and uncontaminated circumstances.

She came to Second and turned south, trotting down the avenue at a good rate, while above her, against the brightening sky, the last yellow streetlights stuttered out. Rhiow crossed Second diagonally at Sixty-seventh and kept heading south and west, using the sidewalk openly for as long as the pedestrian traffic stayed light. It was unwise to attract too much attention, even this early: There were always *ehhif* out walking their *houiff* before they went to work. *But you can't really feel things as clearly when you're sidled,* Rhiow thought, *and anyway, there's no* houff *I couldn't handle.* If the sidewalk got too crowded, Rhiow knew five or six easy ways to do her commute out of sight. But she liked taking the "surface streets": more of the variety of the life of the city showed there. There were doubtless People who would feel that Rhiow should be paying more attention to her own kind, but by taking care of the *ehhif,* she took care of People, too.

Southward and westward: Park Avenue and Fifty-seventh. Here there was considerable pedestrian traffic even at this time of morning, people heading home from night shifts or going to breakfast before work, and the two greenery-separated lanes of Park were becoming a steady stream of cabs and trucks and cars. Though she was fifteen blocks north of Grand Central proper, Rhiow was now right on top of the terminal's track array: at least the part of it where it spread from the four "ingress" tracks into the main two-level array, forty-two tracks above and twenty-three below. As she stood on the southwest corner of Fifty-seventh and Park, beside one of the handsome old apartment buildings of the area, Tower U was some fifteen or twenty feet directly below her. From below came the expected echoing rumble, the tremor in the sidewalk easily felt through her paw-pads—one of the first trains of the morning being moved into position.

Five twenty-three, Rhiow thought, knowing the train in

question. She looked up one last time at the paling sky, then headed for the grate in the sidewalk just west of the corner by the curb.

She slipped in between the bars, stepped down the slope of the grainy, eroded concrete under the grating, and paused for a moment to let her eyes adjust. Ahead of her the slope dropped away suddenly.

It was a moderately long drop, ten feet: she took a breath, jumped, came down on top of a tall cement-block wiring box, and jumped from there another eight feet or so to the gravel in the access tunnel. Rhiow trotted down the cast-cement tunnel, all streaked with old iron stains, to where it joined the main train tunnel underneath Park. There in front of her was the little concrete bunker of Tower U, its lights dark at the moment. To her left were the four tracks, which almost immediately flowered into ten—seven active tracks, three sidings—by the time they reached Fifty-fifth.

Rhiow looked both ways, listened, then bounded over to the left-paw side of the tracks and began following them southward, along the line of the eastward sidings. Ahead, the fluorescents were still on nighttime configuration, one-quarter of them on and three-quarters off, striping the platforms in horizontal bands of light against the rusty dimness. She trotted toward them, seeing something small move down by the bottom of Track 24: and she caught a glimpse of something that didn't belong down here, a glitter of white or hazy blue light concentrated in one spot.

Bong, said the ghost-voice of the clock in the main concourse, as Rhiow cut across a few intervening tracks and jumped up onto the platform for 24. There was Urruah, sitting and looking at the dimly seen warp and weft of the worldgate, the oval of its access matrix a little larger than usual.

" 'Luck, 'Ruah," Rhiow said, and stood by him a moment

with her tail laid over his back in greeting. "Where's the wonder child?"

"Upstairs begging for pastrami from the deli guy."

Rhiow sighed. "There's one habit of his I wish you wouldn't encourage."

"Oh, indeed? I seem to remember where he got it. *Some*-one took him upstairs and—"

"Oh, all right." Rhiow grinned. "We all slip sometimes. Did you open this?"

"No, he did, while he was waiting for us."

"For us? You weren't here?"

"He was early. Got impatient, apparently."

Rhiow put one ear back. "Not sure I like him doing this by himself, as yet . . ."

"How were you planning to stop him? Come on, Rhi, look at it. The synchronization's exact. He would have stayed here to keep an eye on it," Urruah added, forestalling her as she opened her mouth, "but I told him to go on upstairs and get himself a snack. The guy likes him: he won't get in trouble."

Rhiow put her ear forward again, though she had a definite feeling of being "ganged up on by the toms." *It may be something I'm going to have to get used to.* "All right," she said, studying the gate. It was open on London, set for nonpatency and a nonvisible matrix on the far side: this side would have been invisible to her too, except that she could see where Arhu had carefully laid in the "graphic" Speech-form of her name, and Urruah's and his own, in the portion of the spell matrix that controlled selective visibility and patency configurations. Beyond the matrix, light glittered off the river that ran by the big old stone building on which the view was centered: a huge square building of massive stone walls, with what appeared to be more buildings inside it, like a little walled city.

"The Tower of London," Urruah said.

"Doesn't look like a tower . . ."

"There's one inside it," Urruah said, "the original. The gating complex proper is a little to the north: this is a quieter place for a meeting, the Whisperer suggested. Local time's four hours or so after sunrise."

"Ten thirty," Rhiow said. "Is this a good time for the gating team there?"

"Don't know how *good* it is," Urruah said, "but it's what She specified. She may have spoken to them already. Ah hah—here he comes."

The small black-and-white form came trotting insouciantly down the platform, not even sidled. "Arhu," Rhiow said as he came up to them, "come on. You know how they are about cats in here—"

"Not about cats they can't find," Arhu said, licking his chops, and sidled. Rhiow sighed, leaned over, and breathed breaths with him: and she blinked. "Sweet Iau in a basket, what's *that?*"

"Chili pickle."

Rhiow turned to Urruah. "You have created a *monster,*" she said.

Urruah laughed out loud. "Your fault. You showed him how to do the food-catching trick for the deli guy first."

"Yes, but *you* encourage him all the time, and—"

"Hey, come on, Rhi, it's good," Arhu said. "The guy in there likes hot stuff. He gave me some on a piece of roast beef last week as a joke." Arhu grinned. "Now the joke's on him: I like it. But he's good about it. I ate a whole one of those green Hungarian chilies for him the other day. He thinks it's cool: he makes other people come and see me eat it."

"Not the transit police, I hope," Rhiow said.

"Naah. I wouldn't go if I knew they were up there. I always know when they're down on the tracks," Arhu said.

Rhiow flicked one ear resignedly: there were plainly advantages to being a fledgling visionary. "All right. Are you ready?"

"I was ready an hour before you got here."

"So I hear. Well, the parameters are all set: You did a good job. Turn the gate patent, and let's go."

Arhu sat up in front of the great oval matrix, reached in, and pulled out a pawful of strings. The clarity of the image in the matrix suddenly increased greatly, a side effect of the patency.

"Go ahead," Arhu said. Urruah, already sidled, leaped through into the day on the far side of the gate: Rhiow sidled and followed him.

The darkness stripped away behind her as she leaped through the gate matrix. She came down on cobblestones, found her footing, and looked around her in the morning of a bright day, blinding after the darkness of the Grand Central tunnels. Off to her right, just southward, was the wide river, which she had earlier seen glinting in the distance: in the other direction, up the cobbled slope, was a small street running into a much larger, busier one. Traffic driving on the left charged past on it. She turned, looking behind her at where the smaller street curved away, running parallel to the river. Black taxicabs of a tall, blocky style were stopping in the curve of the street, and *ehhif* were getting out of them and making their way in one of two directions: either toward where she and Urruah stood, looking toward an arched gate that led into the Tower, or toward a lesser gate giving on another expanse of cobblestones, which sloped down toward the river.

As Rhiow looked around, Arhu stepped through the worldgate, with one particular hyperstring still held in his teeth. He pulled it through after him and grounded it on the cobbles. Gate matrix and string vanished together, or seemed to; but Rhiow could see a little parasitic light from the anchor string still dancing around one particular cobble.

"That's our tripwire," Arhu said. "Pull it and it activates the gate to open again."

"And what about the other wizards who might need the gate while we're gone?" Rhiow said.

Arhu put his whiskers forward, pleased with himself. "It won't interfere—the gate proper's back in neutral again. I only coded these timespace coordinates into one string."

"Very good," Rhiow said: and it was. He was already inventing his own management techniques, a good sign that he was beginning genuinely to understand the basics of gating.

They looked around them for a few moments more in the sun. It was a breezy morning: clouds raced by, their shadows patterning the silver river with gray and adding new shades to the gray-brown-silver dazzle-painting of the battleship that was moored on the other side of the river. Arhu had no eyes for that, though, or for the traffic, or for the *ehhif* passing them by. He was looking at the stone walls of the Tower, and his ears were back.

"It's *old* here," Arhu said. His ears went forward, and then back again, and kept doing that, as if he were trying to listen to a lot of things at once . . . things that made him nervous.

"It's old in New York, too," Urruah said.

"Yeah, but not like this. . . ."

"It's the *ehhif,*" Rhiow said. "They've been here so long—first thousands, then hundreds of thousands of them, then millions, all denning on the two sides of this river. A thousand years now, and more."

"There's more to it than that," Arhu said. He was staring at the Tower. "I smell blood. . . ."

"Yes," said a big deep voice behind them. "So do we."

They turned in some surprise, for he had come up behind them very quietly, even for a Person. Rhiow, taking him in at first glance, decided that she should revise her ideas about bigger cats being needed in the world: They were already here. This was without any question one of the biggest cats she had ever seen, not to mention the fluffiest. His fur, mostly black on his back, shaded to a blended silver-brown and then to white on his underparts, with four white feet and a white bib making the dark colors more striking. He had a broad, slightly tabby-striped face with surprisingly delicate-looking slanted green eyes in it, and a nose with a smudge: the splendid plume of gray-black tail held up confidently behind him looked a third the thickness of his body, which was considerable. If this Person was lacking for anything, it wasn't food.

"We are on errantry," Rhiow said, "and we greet you."

"Well met on the errand," said the Person. "I'm Huff: I lead the London gating team. And you would be Rhiow?"

"So I would. Hunt's luck to you, cousin." They bumped noses in meeting-courtesy. "And here is Urruah, my older teammate: and Arhu, who's just joined us."

Noses were bumped all around: Arhu was a little hesitant about it at first. "I won't bite," Huff said, and indeed it seemed unlikely. Rhiow got an almost immediate impression from him that this was one of those jovial and easygoing souls who regret biting even mice.

"I'm sorry to meet you without the rest of the team," Huff said, "but we had another emergency this morning, and they're in the middle of handling it. I'll bring you down to them, if you'll come with me. Anyway, I thought you might like to see something of the 'outside' of the gating complex before we got down into the heart of the trouble."

"It's good of you," Urruah said, falling into step on one

side of him, Rhiow pacing along on the other: Arhu brought up the rear, still looking thoughtfully at the Tower. "Did I see right from the history in the Whispering that the gates actually used to be aboveground here, and were relocated?"

"That's right," Huff said as he plodded along. He led Rhiow and her team through an iron gate in a nearby hedge, and down onto a sunken, paved walk, which made its way behind that hedge around the busy-street side of the Tower and into an underpass leading away under that street. "See this grassy area over to the right, the other side of the railings? That was the moat . . . but much earlier, before the Imperial people were here, it was a swamp with a cave nearby that led into the old hillside. That was where the first gate formed, when this was just a village of a few mud-and-wattle huts."

"How come a gate spawned here, then," Arhu said, "if there were so few *ehhif* around?"

"Because they were around for two thousand years before the Imperials turned up," Huff said, "or maybe three. There's some argument about the dates. It's not certain what kept them here at first; some people think the fishing was good." Huff put his whiskers forward, and Rhiow got, with some amusement, the immediate sense that Huff approved of fish. "Whatever the reason, they stayed, and a gate came, as they tended to do near permanent settlements when the Earth was younger." He flicked his ears thoughtfully as they all stepped to one side to avoid a crowd of *ehhif* making their way up to the admission counters near the gateway they'd come in.

"It's had a rocky history, though," Rhiow said, "this gating complex. So Urruah tells me."

"That's right," Huff said as they turned the corner and now walked parallel to the main street with all the traffic. "This has always been the heart of London, this hill . . . not that there's that much left of the hill anymore. And the heart has had its share of seizures and arrests, I fear, and nearly stopped once or twice. Nonetheless, everything is still functioning."

"What exactly is the problem with the gates at the moment?" Rhiow said.

Huff got a pained look. "One of them is intermittently converting itself into an unstable timeslide," he said. "The other end seems to be anchoring somewhere nearby in the past—it has to, after all; you can't have a slide without an anchor—but the times at which it's anchoring seem to be changing without any cause that we can understand."

"How long has it been doing this?" Urruah said. His eyes had gone rather wide at the mention of the timeslide.

"We're not absolutely sure," Huff said. "Possibly for a long time, though only for microperiods too small to allow anyone to pass through. In any case, none of the normal monitoring spells caught the gate at it. We only found out last week when Auhlae—that's my mate—was working on one of the neighboring gates . . . and something came out."

"*Something?*" Arhu said, looking scared.

"Some*one,* actually," Huff said, glancing over at the Tower as a shriek of children's laughter came from somewhere inside it. "It was an *ehhif*—and not a wizardly one. Very frightened . . . very confused. He ran through the gate and up and out into the tube station—that's where our number-four gate is anchored, in the Tower Hill Underground station—and out into the night. Right over the turnstiles he went," Huff added, "and the Queen only knows what the poor *ehhif* who work there made of it all."

"Have you made any more headway in understanding why this is happening?" Rhiow said. She very much hoped so: this all sounded completely bizarre.

But Huff flirted his tail no, a slightly annoyed gesture.

"Nothing would please me better than to tell you that was the case," he said.

Rhiow licked her nose. "Huff," she said, "believe me when I tell you that we're sorry for your trouble, and we wish we didn't need to be here in the first place."

"That's very kindly said," Huff said, turning those green eyes on her: they were somber. "My team are—well, they're annoyed, as you might imagine. I appreciate your concern a great deal, indeed I do."

Huff and Rhiow's team turned leftward into the underpass, which was full of *ehhif* heading in various directions, and one *ehhif* who was tending a small mobile installation festooned with colored scarves and T-shirts. Numerous prints of the Tower and other pictures of what Rhiow assumed were tourist attractions were taped to the walls, and some of what Rhiow assumed were tourists were studying them. "Huff," Urruah said, "what did the gate's logs look like after this ingress?"

"Muddled," Huff said as they walked through the underpass, up the ramp on its far side, and turned toward a set of stairs leading downward into what Rhiow saw was the ticketing area of the Underground station: above the stairway was the circle-and-bar Underground logo, emblazoned with the words TOWER HILL. "We found evidence of multiple ingresses of this kind, from different times into ours . . . and egresses from ours back to those times. The worst part of it is that only one of those egresses was a 'return': all the others were 'singles.' The *ehhif* went through, in one direction or another, but they never made it back to their home times."

Urruah's eyes went wide. "This way," Huff said, and led them under one of the turnstiles and off to the right.

Rhiow followed him closely, but Urruah's shocked look was on her mind. "What?" she said to him as Huff leaped up onto the stainless-steel divider between two banks of stairways.

"Single trips," Urruah said, following her up. "You know what that means. . . ."

Rhiow flirted her tail in acquiescence. It was an uncomfortable image, the poor *ehhif* trapped in a time not their own, confused, possibly driven mad by the awful turn of events, and certainly thought mad by anyone who ran into them. But then she started having other things to think about as she followed Huff steeply down. The steel was slippery; the only way you could control your descent was by jumping from one to another of the upthrust steel wedges fastened at intervals to the middle of the divider, almost certainly to keep *ehhif* in a hurry from using the thing as a slide. Rhiow started to get into the rhythm of this, then almost lost it again as Arhu came down past her, yelling in delight. Various *ehhif* walking up on one side and down on the other looked curiously for the source of the happy yowling in the middle of the air.

"Arhu, look out," Rhiow said, "oh, look out, for the Queen's sake *look*—" It was too late: Arhu had jumped right over the surprised Huff, but had built up so much speed that he couldn't stop himself at the next wedge: he hit it, shot into the air, fell, and rolled for several yards, then shot off the end of the divider to fall to the floor at the bottom of the escalator. Rhiow sighed. *He was so good there,* she thought, *for about ten minutes.*

She caught up with Huff as he jumped down. "Huff, I'm sorry," Rhiow said, watching Arhu do an impromptu dance as he tried to avoid crowds of *ehhif* stepping on him. It was something of a challenge: they were coming at him and making for the stairs from three directions at once. "He's a little new to all this, and as for being part of a team . . ."

"Oh, it's all right," Huff said, unconcerned. "Our team

has one his age: younger, even. She's left us all wondering whether we aren't too old for this kind of work. With any luck, they'll run each other down and give us some peace. Come on, over this way."

Huff led them from one hallway into another, where several stainless-steel doors were let into the tiled wall. "In here," said Huff, and vanished through the door: "through it" in the literal sense, passing straight into the metal with a casual whisk of his tail.

It was a spell that any feline wizard knew, and even some nonwizardly People could do the trick under extreme stress. Rhiow drew the spell-circle in her mind, knotted it closed. Then inside it she sketched out the graphic form of her name, and the temporary set of parameters that reminded her body that it was mostly empty space, and so was the door, and requested them to avoid one another. Then she walked through after Huff. It was an odd sensation, like feeling the wind ruffling your fur the wrong way: except the fur seemed to be on the *inside*—

—and she was through, into what looked like a much older area, a brick-lined hallway on the far side of the door, lit by bare bulbs hanging from the ceiling, all very much different from the clean, shining fluorescent-lit station platform outside. Rhiow looked over her shoulder, and Urruah came through after her. From the far side of the door there were a couple of soft bumping noises.

Urruah put his whiskers forward and looked ahead of them at Huff, who had paused to see where they were. "He has a little trouble with this one sometimes," Urruah said. *Bump*, and Arhu abruptly came blooming through the metal, spitting and growling softly to himself. "*Vhai*'d stuff, why doesn't it get out of the way when I tell it—"

"Language," Rhiow said, rather hopelessly, but for the moment, Urruah just laughed. "*Telling* it won't help," he said. "You've got to ask nicely. Most things in the Universe react positively to that. Sass them, and they get stubborn."

Arhu threw Urruah an unconvinced look as he padded by him in Huff's wake. Old wooden doors opened into side rooms off this hallway: storerooms, Rhiow thought—a smell of electrical equipment and tools hung about the place. "There are workshops down here," Huff said, "and there's an access to the tunnel junction where the Tower Hill station's tracks run near the access stairs to the Fenchurch Street railway station. That's where the number-four gate is."

He led them down one more stairway, a spiral one this time. It let out onto a small, dimly lit platform that ran for maybe ten yards along a double line of track, the track stretching away into darkness on both sides. Above the platform hung the faintly glimmering oval of an active gate matrix. In front of it sat three People, one of them up on his haunches and working with the gate's control strings: a youngish tabby tom who, except that his tabbying was marmalade rather than silver and gray, reminded Rhiow somewhat of Urruah.

One of the other two turned her head to look at the new arrivals. She was a slender gray shorthair queen, about Rhiow's own size but slimmer, with the most beautiful eyes Rhiow thought she had ever seen: they were a blue as deep as the skies on one of those perfect autumn days you sometimes got in the city, and the set of them was both indolent and kind. As she looked at Huff, the expression got kinder, and Rhiow knew immediately that the two of them were mates. The fourth Person, apparently concentrating on what the young tabby was doing, didn't move.

"Has it failed again?" Huff said as they walked toward the others.

"It *vhai* ing well has *not*," said the tabby, sounding very annoyed. "But that's what you'd expect, isn't it, since People are coming to look at it?"

Well, so much for any concerns about Arhu's *language,* Rhiow thought with resignation.

The handsome queen chuckled. "Huff, you weren't really expecting this gate to oblige you, were you? The cranky thing."

"No, I suppose not. Rhiow," Huff said over his shoulder. "Come meet Auhlae, my mate."

"You're very welcome," Auhlae said, touching noses delicately with Rhiow, "and well met on the errand. And this is . . ."

"My older partner Urruah," Rhiow said, "and my younger partner Arhu."

Noses were bumped all around: Rhiow was privately amused to note how shyly Arhu did it. He was apparently not immune to physical beauty in a queen. "And this is Fhrio," Auhlae said.

"Rrrrh," Fhrio said, a sound of general disgust, and dropped back down to all fours again, turning to the others. "Yeah, hunt's luck to you, hello there, well met." He bumped noses peremptorily, then sat down and started in on a serious bout of composure-washing, the action of a Person so annoyed that he didn't trust his reactions with others for the moment.

"And Siffha'h," said Auhlae.

The smallest of the London team got up, turned away from her single-minded concentration on the gate, and looked at Rhiow and the others. This little queen was maybe a couple of months younger than Arhu, Rhiow thought, and, like him, was a *hu-rhiw,* though a paler one; her coat had much more white than black, and two black "eyebrow" marks over her eyes gave her a humorous look. Her eyes were large, golden, and thoughtful, and the look she gave

Rhiow was surprisingly mature and measuring for someone who still had most of her milk teeth.

"I greet you," Rhiow said, "and hunt's luck to you."

"You too," said Siffha'h, and stepped over to touch noses, first with Rhiow, then with Urruah. Arhu, coming back from nosing Fhrio, met her last: they bumped noses cordially enough, and then, slightly to Rhiow's surprise, Siffha'h repeated the touch. She looked up at Arhu and said, "What's *that?*"

"Uh, chili pickle," Arhu said.

"Hhehhh," Siffha'h said scornfully, nose wrinkled and lips pulled back—the feline equivalent of an *ehhif* of tender years saying "Ewwww." She turned away, leaving Arhu looking rather stricken.

"I had wondered," Huff said genially to Arhu. "Remind me to take you along some night when I do Indian."

"Huff has been telling us about your problem," Rhiow said to Auhlae. "I take it there's been no improvement."

Fhrio looked up from his *he'ihh.* "I've been trying to get it to fail all morning," he said, "and I might as well have saved my time. The logs don't give us enough data about what the strictly physical conditions were doing when the last failures occurred. I'm going to have to sit down with the Whisperer and get Her to make me a list."

"That won't stop the problem, though," Siffha'h said. "You're going to have to shut the gate."

"I would rather not do that," Fhrio said, and began washing furiously again.

Auhlae looked over at Rhiow and Urruah with a sympathetic expression. "Fhrio is our gating specialist," she said softly. "He tends to take these things rather personally."

"I know the feeling," Urruah said. "Well, do you have any specific recommendations for us? Or should we just start running some diagnostics and see if there's any data we can add to what you've got already?"

"The only recommendation we have on which we're all in agreement," said Huff, "is that the gate has to stop functioning as a timeslide, and probably the simplest way to make it do that is to shut it down. But since we don't know how the gate's failing in the first place, we can't guarantee that this will work. It might make our problem worse, by forcing the malfunction to 'migrate' to another gate in the cluster—you know how they get 'sympathetic' malfunctions, like organs in a body. That would be pretty serious, if it happened. We're having enough trouble with just one of these gates presently out of use for transit: a lot of the northern European wizards depend on transfers through our cluster for access to the big long-range facilities in Rome and Tokyo. If the difficulty should spread by contagion to one of the others . . ."

Rhiow nodded. "I see your problem. Well, probably diagnostics are the way to go at the moment. Any help you might want to give us would be welcome: or if you prefer to leave us to get on with it—"

Fhrio looked up from his washing. "No one messes with my gates unless I'm here," he said, and there was a touch of growl in his voice.

"I would hope you'd stay and clue us in on the fine points," Urruah said. "Gates have a lot more personality than a lot of wizards would give them credit for . . . and no one knows a gate like its own technician."

"You sound just like Fhrio," Siffha'h said, sounding amused. "Are *you* the best in the business too?"

Urruah was purring, and trying not to do it too loudly. Rhiow and Auhlae exchanged a look of amusement of their own.

"This is the point at which Urruah makes noises of shy

agreement," Rhiow said, "and the safest thing to do under the circumstances is to make him get to work. Huff, we're entirely at your disposal. Tell us where you want us to start."

"The diagnostics sound like a good idea," Huff said, and then yawned, a prodigious yawn that showed every one of his teeth and made Rhiow reassess her idea that Urruah had the biggest ones she'd ever seen. "I'm sorry . . . it's late for me. Fhrio, if you want to stay with them and keep them from duplicating routines you've already run . . ."

Fhrio straightened up from his washing again. "Absolutely. Maybe the gate'll surprise us by failing in the middle of something. At this point, I wouldn't care if it did it in midtransit."

"Oh yes you would," Siffha'h said. "You should try it and see. You want me to stay and put the claw in it for you?"

"Sure. She's our power source," Fhrio said to Rhiow and the others. " 'The best in the business.' "

"This I want to see," Urruah said mildly. Rhiow shot him a sidewise glance, trying to keep it from being too obviously a warning look. True, queens rarely worked as power sources in team spelling, but there was nothing sex-linked about it—it seemed to be a preference grounded in the basic nature of the work, which (Urruah had occasionally admitted to Rhiow) was boring compared with building the spells themselves. There was a general tendency among People for the females to show more initiative than the males, and to go out of their way to get their paws on the most interesting work.

"You'll excuse me for a moment, then," Huff said, and headed up the stairs.

Urruah padded over and started examining the gate matrix in detail, with Fhrio looking over his shoulder and making mostly monosyllabic comments. Rhiow watched them, and watched Arhu watching them: being, for the moment, excessively well behaved. It was hard to believe the same youngster had been busy falling down the stairs not twenty minutes ago.

Auhlae came over to sit down beside Rhiow. "When it comes to diagnostics," Auhlae said, sounding weary, "there's no point in me watching what's happening. I spent all yesterday morning at them, with my teeth clenched so full of strings that they buzzed for the rest of the day." She shook her head.

Rhiow waved her tail in agreement. "I feel a bit like the sixth claw myself, at the moment," she said, and strolled over to the edge of the platform, looking down the tracks into the darkness. From here she could still keep a general eye on what was going on, as Huff headed up the stairs again and Fhrio turned his attentions back to the gate—Urruah and Arhu looking over his shoulder, and Siffha'h slipping one foreleg shoulder-deep into the gate matrix to hook her claws into the strings and the spell, supplying the power it would need. "Are most of you denned near here?" Rhiow asked, noticing the interested looks that Arhu was throwing in Siffha'h's direction, which Siffha'h was ignoring.

"Not all of us," Auhlae said, following Rhiow's glance. She put her whiskers forward in a smile. "But when you're a gating team, there are certain perquisites—the Whisperer is hardly going to cavil if we need to use the gates to get to work. Anyway, it keeps us alert to their condition: it's hard to miss something wrong with them when you use them every day."

Rhiow did not say out loud that someone seemed to have missed something about the number-four gate, repeatedly, no matter how often it was used. *But then, if the failure was happening a fraction of a second here, another fraction there, and nothing was actually passing* through *the gate, how was anyone going to notice?* It would have taken an obsessively thorough review of the logs to find the occurrences—

Which there should have been. That was something else Rhiow was not going to say out loud. Saash had routinely reviewed the complete logs for each of the Grand Central gates once every week, and Rhiow had gotten used to that kind of thoroughness from her teammates. *Still,* she thought, *different teams, different management techniques . . .* And Huff seemed to run his team more casually than Rhiow did hers. She was in no position to complain: if the Powers That Be didn't care for the way his team was working, Huff would have been relieved long ago.

"I see your point," Rhiow said after a moment, and lifted one paw to lick at it reflectively. "Do you have a long way to come?"

"Not I, thank the Dam," Auhlae said. "Fhrio commutes in from Ealing, some miles away—he's with a family pride there, one that lives on gardening-land that some *ehhif* keep, what's called an allotment. Siffha'h, on the other hand, is local, very local in fact—she was born just across the river, in an outdoor den not far from HMS *Belfast,* that big ship anchored there. She's nonaligned, and undenned so far. Huff and I aren't so close, but we're nowhere near as far away as Fhrio is. Huff has a den with an *ehhif* who owns a pub in the City and lives in a flat above it: I'm denned just around the corner with a futures trader who works at the securities exchange. Huff's *ehhif* is used to him coming and going as he pleases, and that kind of thing isn't a problem for me either, fortunately. My Rrhalf keeps such weird hours that he hardly notices that I'm there."

Then why on Earth do you stay with him? Rhiow was tempted to ask, and didn't. She couldn't imagine a Person who was also a wizard going through the inconvenience of denning with an *ehhif* if it wasn't because you liked him or her. "Did you two meet locally, then?" Rhiow said.

"Oh, yes, the usual thing. A friend of his is one of the big *hauissh* players in the area: we ran into each other during a tournament, got friendly. Then I went into heat, and . . ." She waved her tail, a graceful and amused gesture.

"Kittens?"

"Oh, plenty. My *ehhif* is very good about finding them good places to live: otherwise I wouldn't let the heat happen."

That brought Rhiow's ears forward. "I used to wonder how a wizard managed when she was in heat," she said. "I never had the chance, myself: my *ehhif* took me and had me unqueened before I started."

"Oh, how terrible for you!" Auhlae said.

"Oh, no, it wasn't that bad. Afterwards I tended to see it as an advantage. No interruptions . . . no toms fighting over me. It looked like a release."

Auhlae was silent for a moment, and started to wash one ear. "Well," she said, "I suppose I can see your point of view. But truly, I haven't found it to be all that much of a problem. You can always use wizardry to adjust your own hormones a little, and delay the onset. But of course it's not too good to do much of that kind of thing. Fortunately, it doesn't seem to be necessary very often. Only very rarely have I had to be on call while I was in heat, and never while I was kittening. The Whisperer seems to keep track of such things." Auhlae put her whiskers forward, a demure smile with a slightly wicked edge to it. "I suppose we should be grateful that it's the Queen running the Universe and not the Tom: who knows if we'd ever get any rest?"

Rhiow chuckled. "I think you're right there . . . in all possible senses of the word."

"But anyway," Auhlae said, "Huff and I usually come

down in the early evenings and troubleshoot the gates. There's always trouble," she said, sounding very resigned. "You know how even inanimate objects can start betraying evidence of personalities, over time—"

"*Oh,* yes," Rhiow said.

"Well, the gates have been here a lot longer than we have, and believe me, they have personalities. Mostly annoyed and suspicious ones. I think it may have had to do with their 'upbringing,' their history. Populations would rise here and then be swept away without warning . . . and to a certain extent, the gate 'learns' to adapt to the pressure of the population around it. Take that population away suddenly, and it must be like suddenly being thrown off something that you've always slept on safely before. The shock makes you stop trusting . . . you don't know whether things will be the same from one day to the next. So the gates act fairly 'calmly' for a period of time—a week, a month—and then—*pff!*" Auhlae made a soft spitting hiss of the kind that an annoyed Person would use to warn another away. "It can take endless time to calm them down. Do you have the same problem?"

Rhiow flicked her tail no. "Oh, they're alive enough, all right," she said. "Aaurh Herself made them, after all: I'm not sure anything with that level of wizardry incorporated into it could avoid being alive, to some degree. But, fortunately, New York grew very steadily, and our gates behave themselves . . . except when they don't," she added, wryly. "Often enough . . ."

Auhlae purred in amusement. "You must run into the personality problem with other things, though. You sounded pretty definite."

"Well, it crops up from time to time." And glancing over at Arhu again (who was still gazing thoughtfully at Siffha'h, apparently without effect) and at Urruah and Fhrio (now leaning right into the gate's matrix structure again, with their heads bent close together and almost invisible among the tangle of strings), Rhiow began to tell Auhlae about the diesel locomotives that ran the trains in and out of Grand Central. Theoretically, they should have been just great complex hunks of metal and wiring. But they were not, as the *ehhif* who drove them and took care of them loudly attested. The engines had noticeable personalities, which manifested in the ways they worked (or didn't): some good-natured and easygoing, some spiteful and annoying, some lazy, some overtly hostile. Rhiow had wondered whether she and the engineers and mechanics were all projecting the traits of life onto dead things for which, admittedly, they all felt affection. But finally she had realized that that wasn't it. She started wondering whether this acquisition of personality might be caused by something specific about the way the locomotives' complicated shapes and structures affected the local shape of spacetime—the way the atomic and molecular structure of water, for example, manifested itself as wetness. The Whisperer had no answers for her, or none that made sense: and when Rhiow had taken the problem casually to the *ehhif* advisory wizards for New York, Tom and Carl, they had shaken their heads and confessed an ignorance on which even their wizard's manuals could not shed light. Finally Rhiow had simply given up and started talking to the locomotives in the course of her rounds, despite being unable to tell whether it was making any difference. *But certainly something with a personality, no matter how undeveloped, deserves to be talked to as if it exists.*

Auhlae looked bemused at that, for a moment. "Now there's something I hadn't given much thought to," she said. "The Underground trains . . . you get a faint sense of personality off them, but nothing like *that.* Or is it just because I haven't been looking?"

"Hard to say," Rhiow said. "But beware. Do you really need another area of interest? The one we share is trouble enough."

Auhlae laughed softly. "Tell me about it," she said as Huff came back down the stairs again and padded toward them.

"Problems, *hrr't?"* Auhlae said.

"Oh, I wanted a look at number three," Huff said, "since this one's being worked on." He sat down beside Auhlae and leaned against her slightly. "You know how they tend to interfere with each other—their catenary links are close together." He paused a moment, then said, "Is it true that you were there? Down deep, right where the catenaries meet, at the roots of things?"

"We were there," Rhiow said, "but it's not a memory I'd call up willingly just now. For one thing, we lost a partner of my age there: if we had her here now, I'd bet we'd have solved your problem already. As it is, we're all learning new jobs, and everything is so confused."

"I'm sorry for your trouble," said Huff, and Auhlae blinked somber agreement, stirring her tail slowly.

"Oh, it wasn't all sad," Rhiow said, "not at all. A great many things changed for the better; and the Downside has new guardians."

"The great cats live there," Auhlae said, "don't they? Our ancestors, our ancient selves. The Old People . . ."

"Yes," Rhiow said, "and nothing will remove them from where they have been since the Beginning. But there are two peoples there now." Maybe this was not the time to start that particular story, but the facts still made Rhiow wake up in the middle of the night, wondering. For all the years there had been dry-land creatures in this world, cat and serpent had expressed in a specific symbolism the two sides of an ancient enmity: creatures of the Sun and light against creatures of Earth and the dark beneath the Earth, warm blood against cold blood, the Powers That Be against the Lone Power that went rogue, both sides battling for the world. But suddenly Rhiow found herself running across new concepts, in which at least some of the great saurians were warm-blooded, and images in which serpent was born of cat (despite the older mythologies, which suggested that cat had been born of serpent)—all too predictable a development, since Arhu had become "father" to the new serpent-kind, the great saurians who had become the new guardians of the Old Downside.

Of course the Universe was full of these jokes and ironies, mostly born of the misapprehension, native to beings living serially in time, that time itself was serial. Naturally, it was not. Time was at least Riemannian, and tended to run both in circles and cycles: outward-reaching spirals that repeated previous tendencies and archetypes reminiscent of earlier ones, but the repetitions came in "bigger" forms, and with unexpected ramifications. Now time bit its own tail one more time, and in the process of that biting pulled off the old skin, revealing the new shiny skin and the bigger body underneath: more beautifully scaled and intricately patterned, more muscular, and, as usual, harder to understand. Rhiow had seen these hints before the last months' troubles began, but hadn't been able to make much of them at the time. Now, with the events and the history behind her, the myth was easier to understand. But it still made her blink, sometimes, and wonder what happened to the good old days, when things were simpler: when cats were cats, and snakes were snakes, and never the twain would meet.

Of course, for most cats and serpents, they never would. But as a wizard, Rhiow came of a bigger worldview, one that held that cats were equal, under the One, to any other sentient species—say, whales, or humans, or some dogs or birds of prey, or various other creatures intelligent enough to have emotional lives and to understand the existence of a world outside their own selves. Most People would have trouble with the idea that *ehhif* were equal to them. And dogs? Birds? They would hiss with indignation at the very idea. Rhiow knew better, but was glad she did not often have to indulge in explanations to her less tolerant kindred.

"It's been a very strange time," Rhiow said at last, "and I look forward to telling you about it in detail: for, truly, there are parts of it I don't understand myself. 'Ruah . . . any news?"

Urruah had strolled over to where they sat, and now threw a look over his shoulder at the gate. "I really hate to admit it," he said, "but at first glance, I'm stumped. Rhi, Huff, I'll want to examine the logs in detail, of course." He looked over his shoulder at Fhrio for approval: Fhrio waved his tail in a "don't-care" way. "Good. I'll do that later this evening. I need a break."

Urruah did sound tired, but that was no surprise: even though the gates had their diagnostic procedures built in, there were other, more sophisticated ones that Rhiow's team routinely used to make sure that a given gate's own diagnostics were "honest." It had always seemed a wise precaution to Rhiow, since a deranged gate might conceivably lose the ability to diagnose itself correctly.

"You'll want to sort your schedule out with Fhrio, perhaps," Huff said.

"Yes," said Urruah, "I'll do that." He headed back over to the gate, where Fhrio and Siffha'h were withdrawing themselves from the gate matrix and letting the strings snap back into place.

Huff sighed. "We'll leave it shut down for another day," he said, "and come and tackle it afresh tomorrow. Rhiow, I think we've made a good start."

"I hope so too," she said. "I have a feeling that this won't be one of those quickly solved problems, but we won't be out of your fur until it's handled."

"Then we'll see Urruah later this evening," said Auhlae, "and you tomorrow?"

"Tomorrow let it be," Rhiow said, and bumped noses with their hosts, though she threw a look over her shoulder first. Urruah and Fhrio had their heads together again: but Arhu was looking in one direction, and Siffha'h in another, as if they were on opposite sides of the same planet.

Rhiow smiled slightly *"Dai stihó,"* she said, the non-species-specific greeting and parting words of one wizard to another: *Go well.* "Come on, Arhu, 'Ruah," she said, getting up, "let's call it a day."

✦

"Very nice People," Urruah said as they came out on the Grand Central side of their own gate. "Competent."

That assessment surprised Rhiow slightly. "You're satisfied with their inspection routines?" she asked.

"They're much like what I'd be doing if *I* were stuck with their gate complex," Urruah said. "I mean, Rhi, look at their transit figures. Three or maybe four times the number of wizards and unaffiliated outworlders use their gates every day as use ours, or the ones at Penn. London is a major on-planet transit center for western Europe, and if you tried to read all the gate logs there once a week, the way Saash did for ours, you'd never have time to do anything else, such as fix the gates when they broke. I'm going to take some time to read those logs in more detail, as I said. But I don't know what I'm looking for as yet, and I'm hoping the tracers we've left in place will pick something up to give me a hint. Without a specific event track to follow, a signature attached to the kind of access we're looking for, we're walking in the dark without whiskers."

Rhiow waved her tail slowly in agreement. "All right," she said.

"But one thing, Rhi—and this may be more important, even, than the problem with the gate itself. Remember when Huff was telling us about the 'single' egresses?"

"Uh, yes." She paused. "He was telling us that people were going one way, not 'round trip.' "

"That's right. Rhi, do you realize how big a problem that is? Times can get imbalanced, just as spaces can: the 'pressure' of times against one another has to be kept equal, and lives displaced from their proper times can seriously skew that balance. Those people from other times have to be recovered and put back where they belong, or the gates will become more unstable than they are already. Not just Huff's gates: *all* the gates."

"Ours too," Rhiow said under her breath.

"Ours would take longest to imbalance," Urruah said. "They're 'senior,' and their connection to the Old Downside and the power sources there is direct: that lends them some immunity. But, inevitably, the imbalance will spread. Gating around the planet will start failing without warning and without reason. The rapid-transit system that wizards use so as not to have to waste their powers on minor business like travel spells will go down. The Universe will start dying faster. I just thought I'd mention."

"Thank you," Rhiow said, and her stomach turned over inside her. "What's your estimate of the time when these imbalances will begin to affect other gates?"

"If there have been only a few imbalanced egresses," Urruah said, "it would take some weeks. If there have been, say, as many as ten or more, I would expect them within ten to fourteen days. Twenty or so—well, we would already be seeing random failures. So it's not that bad. But we have to help the London team track down the *ehhif* from backtime and restore them to their proper periods."

"And how much diagnosis is *that* going to take?"

"A fair amount, the longer the *ehhif* have been loose in a nonnative time. There's a temporal signature you can search for, like a target scent, in someone out of their proper time, but first you need to know exactly which time they're native to, and the longer they're in a nonnative period, the less detectable it is. A fresh ingress through the malfunctioning gate would be the best thing we could hope for. All ingresses through a given gate would have a similar 'signature,' like DNA from different members of the same family, and others could be tracked using it."

Oh gods, Rhiow thought, *and I thought things were going fairly well.* "All right," she said, "we'll take it up with Huff tomorrow. Arhu? You?"

"Huh?" He was walking along in an unusual state of self-absorption. "Me what?"

"What do you think of the London team," Rhiow said, "and their gates?" It wasn't as if he was likely to have a terribly sophisticated assessment at this point, but Rhiow was always careful to make sure everyone had their say after coming back from an "outcall" job.

"Huff and Auhlae are nice," Arhu said, still looking somewhat distracted. "Fhrio's a snot: he thinks he knows everything." And there Arhu fell silent.

Aha, Urruah said privately to Rhiow.

She was inclined to agree. "And Siffha'h?" Rhiow said.

There was a long pause. "I think maybe she doesn't like me," Arhu said, "and I don't know why."

"Well," Rhiow said, "it's early to tell that, yet. You can't have exchanged more than ten words the whole time we were there."

"I know," Arhu said, dejected. "That's the trouble."

"Give it time," Urruah said. "It'll come right in the end. You can't rush the queens, Arhu, especially the young ones: they have their whole lives ahead of them, maybe as many as nine of them, and they don't impress easily. Take your time, talk to them. . . ."

"That's just the problem. She *won't* talk to me."

"So let actions say what words won't. She probably hears all kinds of bragging these days, if she's just coming into her day . . . isn't she?"

Arhu looked up at Urruah with a kind of heartsick hope that made Rhiow's heart turn over at the sight of it. "I think so," Arhu said. "That's how it smells."

Rhiow turned her attention away from the conversation and let the toms gain some walking-space in front of her. It was at times like this that she missed Saash most, her slightly sardonic turn of phrase that could make anything, even something as serious as non-round-trip time travel, seem less crucial until you were actually able to get around to handling it. But Saash was out on the One's errantry now: Rhiow would just have to manage without her, and hold her own against the boys as well as she could. *Fortunately,* she said to the Whisperer with a pride-queen's arrogance, *it isn't hard.*

From the depths of reality came the feeling of divine whiskers being put forward, and the sound of tolerant laughter.

✦

The whole team made the commute to London the next morning to check the diagnostics and the logs, and found nothing: and they did so the next morning, and the morning after that, with no sign of any unusual ingresses or egresses at all. On the fourth day of this, Rhiow began to wonder whether the Powers had sent her team on one of those useful but temper-fraying jobs that her old mentor and teacher Ffairh would have described as "trying to herd mice at a crossroads": a lot of trouble to very little effect for a long, long time, until you lost patience and started eating the mice, which might be what the Powers had in mind in the first place. Urruah was beginning to feel the strain, and was getting short with everybody, especially Arhu. Arhu, for his own part, was getting bored.

"He won't let me *do* anything," he said to Rhiow one morning as they went in to work together.

"That's possibly because he's not sure of your level of mastery as such," Rhiow said, "and possibly because it's other People's gates we're working with, not our own. No, Arhu, listen. Don't look that way. If you want to get a job done—that being the whole reason we have to keep going to London—sometimes you have to do it a little more slowly, a little more cautiously, than you otherwise would. At home, with our own gates, it's usually no big deal. If one of us makes a mistake, she gets her head smacked, we clean up the mess, and the matter stays in the family. But when you're dealing with other People's territory, things slow down. And this *is* their territory, be sure of that."

"I thought you told me 'We are guardians and nothing more,' " Arhu said with some annoyance.

"That's as true of the London team as it is of us. But it's Her business to tell them that, not ours."

They paused in front of the number-three gate, which was anchored over by the Waldorf Yard again because of track maintenance going on near its usual location. "Territory," Rhiow said, "it's a problem."

"Yeah. Oh, Urruah said he might be late this morning. Something about the Dumpster."

"I wish he'd tell me these things," Rhiow said, and sat down in front of the gate. "How late did he think?"

"He didn't say."

She waved her tail, resigned. *Toms* . . . "You'd better take care of the gating, then," she said. "They're going to be wondering where we are."

"Probably not," Arhu said, sitting up and slipping his forepaws into the control weave. "I don't think Fhrio cares one way or the other."

"Oh, I wouldn't be so sure," Rhiow said. "He's likely enough to care, but not to show it."

Arhu was busy with the weave, pulling strings out and hooking them under and through one another with his claws. He was getting quick at this work, whatever Urruah might think: after a few days' practice with the London configuration, the pattern had become second nature to him. Or else the gate itself was beginning to answer his requirements, falling into "heart-configuration" with Arhu—a development very much to be hoped for. It was the kind of sympathy, not quite a symbiosis, that Saash had had with the Grand Central gates: a sort of mutual understanding of what needed to be done, based to be sure on a sound theoretical knowledge, but on something much more in execution. It was as if the gates had liked Saash, and wanted to cooperate with her because she liked them. If Arhu was acquiring that kind of almost-affection, Rhiow thought, there would be little limit to what he could do as a gate technician later in life, or in other lives to come, if the wizardry followed him.

And we could use someone with that kind of basic affinity, she thought. *For all my theoretical work, I don't have it: and for all Urruah's, he's more an engineer than a technician. Probably it comes of being a power source—of seeing the gate as something to be done* to *rather than someone to be done* with.

Arhu stopped. "Does that look right?" he said suddenly, sounding rather confused.

Rhiow looked over the gate-weft. The colors were running correctly, the hyperstrings all seemed to be making the correct "itch" in the air, the resonances of sound and texture were all in place. "It looks fine."

"It doesn't *feel* fine. It feels like something's come unsnagged."

Arhu was blinking, looking a little vague. Rhiow had learned to recognize that particular danger sign. "Now," Rhiow said, "or later?"

"I think . . ." Arhu's eyes narrowed, a look of abrupt and uncomfortable concentration. This was always the most difficult part of the work for a visionary, the matter of learning to "ride" the vision rather than simply being ridden by it: though the question of which was finally master, the seer or the seen, was always one that caused most seers a certain amount of unease over their careers. "I think later. But not much later. Short term . . ."

Oh wonderful, Rhiow thought. "Today? Tomorrow?"

"What am I, some *ehhif* weather forecaster?" Arhu said, still squinting, with his paws all tangled up with hyperstrings. "Do you want percentages of probability, too?"

"Whatever you can come up with," Rhiow said. "And whatever idiom works for you. I'm not picky."

"I can See the Sun," Arhu said after a moment, "but I'm not sure which one it is, which day. Just a sense of things . . . unraveling. Something unsnags, and then everything sorts itself out. Though it *smells* really bad at first."

He blinked again, shook his ears until they rattled, and looked at Rhiow. "Gone. I *hate* it when it does that!"

"Calm down, Arhu. Take it easy, don't let the strings go—"

"I wasn't going to—do you think I want the whole place

to jump off into space?" But his ears were flat back, and he hissed softly. "Rhiow," Arhu said, sitting up still with that unkittenish perfect balance of his, "I can hear Her. I can See what She Sees . . . just for a second. Everything together: images, thoughts in minds, lots of minds all together, a hundred paws' worth of places all at once. But all broken, like light in water when the wind blows. My brains won't hold a whisker's worth of it . . . and then it's *gone*. What's the use, this becoming one of the Powers, but not enough of one to be any good to anybody, or for long enough to figure it out, long enough to make a difference!"

Rhiow sighed and paced over to him, balanced on her hindquarters just long enough to bump her head against his. "You know it's going to be hard at first," she said, settling down again. "It's going to take so much practice, and it's going to be hard for a long time yet. The Seer's talent is one of the worst ones in its way, tough to manage. But if you can stay with it . . ."

"Do I have a choice?" Arhu said, and the edge of bitterness and sadness was impossible to miss. "If I don't learn it, I'll lose it."

He sat back on his haunches then and said, "Never mind. At least I can still gate."

He glanced sidewise at Rhiow, and gave the strings a quick pull.

The other side of the gate flickered abruptly into black night over a white land—pale silver and white dust and stone with every stone's shadow laid out long and black and razorlike behind it. Over everything hung a shape that burned at first so blue that the eye refused it: then you saw the white swirls, and the shades of green and haze-brown, but the main color was blue, shining down pale on that white desolation, and Rhiow's abrupt first thought was of the shade of Auhlae's eyes.

She gave Arhu a look. "Very cute," she said. "If you're demonstrating that you've learned to keep a gate patent when there's a vacuum on the other side, I take your point. Otherwise, you know what I told you."

"And what Urruah keeps telling me," Arhu said. "Yeah, I know."

Rhiow opened her mouth, then shut it again, remembering what Urruah had said about Arhu's early morning gate work the other day. And slowly she put her whiskers forward. *If he was going to go,* she thought, *how would we stop him?* And: *Not so long ago, this was the kitling we were worried wasn't doing* enough *wizardry. He's finding his way. Let him be.*

"We've no business there today," Rhiow said, working to sound lazy about it. "Maybe later this week we'll go. I'll see you off, in fact, if you'd rather do it on your own. Meanwhile, let's get going: They'll be waiting for us. Urruah will catch up."

The look Arhu threw her was a little odd, but very featly he flipped his paws and changed the configuration of the strings again, and the view through the gate shifted to that of darkness again, but this time it was the unstarred darkness of the Underground tunnels near London Bridge.

"I'll let it snap back into its default settings afterwards," Arhu said. "Urruah'll be able to pull this setting out of memory and alter it for changed time with no problem."

"Right," Rhiow said, and stepped through; Arhu followed her.

They made their way over to the platform where the malfunctioning London gate hung, shimmering dully in a nonpatent configuration. Only Fhrio was with it at the moment, sitting by it and yawning.

" 'Luck, Fhrio," Rhiow said. "Have you been waiting long?"

"Half the night, but don't let that bother you," the orange tabby said, and tucked himself down into what Rhiow's *ehhif* called the "meat loaf" shape.

Rhiow threw an amused glance at Arhu, who was looking off into the darkness to avoid having Fhrio see him rolling his eyes. She felt a little sorry for him on his first outcall, having half the team they were working with turn out to be such difficult cases: but this kind of thing happened occasionally. She still thought often of one of the Brasília team who, though a wizard of tremendous talent, was also so scarred by some old trauma that he would jump up in the air hissing anytime you spoke to him before he could see you, and would come down with claws out and fur standing on end, ready to murder anyone who was standing too close. Working with him had driven her nearly insane, and as for Urruah, it had been all Rhiow could do to keep him from walking off that job every day, at the occurrence of the first jump-and-hiss. At least Fhrio wasn't quite so unnerving to work with, but Rhiow was increasingly wondering what his problem was, or, if there was no problem, why he was this way all the time.

"No incursions, I take it," Rhiow said, sitting down in front of the gate and eyeing it thoughtfully.

"Nothing," Fhrio said. "I almost wish for one: at least it would make sitting here a little less boring."

She twitched her tail in agreement. "Have Auhlae or Huff been along yet today?"

"Auhlae's home with her *ehhif,*" Fhrio said. "He's sick or something. Huff was here earlier and then went off." Fhrio yawned. "I think probably to take a nap; he was up watching the gate all night."

Arhu was standing behind Rhiow now, looking over her shoulder at the shimmer of light in the gate-web. She wasn't sure how much he was able to make out of its function as yet just from the configuration of the light patterns and the juxtaposition of the various braids and bundles of hyperstrings. Reading a gate that way took time to learn.

"It's changed since yesterday," Arhu said.

"Of course it's changed," Fhrio said, and yawned again. "The Earth's not where it was yesterday, is it? Basic changes in spacetime coordinates show in the web as a matter of course—"

"I don't mean that. I mean the sideslip and tesseral string bundles in the control weft have changed position slightly. And one of the sideslip subarrays has a string loose."

"What?" Fhrio sat up, looked at the part of the gate-web that Arhu was staring at. "Where are you—oh. No, that's all right, this gate does that sometimes. It's a locational thing—I think it has to do with the gravitational anomaly in the substrate under the hill. The loose ends always weave themselves back in after a few minutes: this isn't a static construct, after all, it 'breathes' a little."

"I know—our gates do that too. But look at the way the sideslip bundle is interweaving with the hyperextensor braid. . . ."

Fhrio was beginning to look confused. "Yes, as I say, it does that. I don't see what the—"

"Well, look," Arhu said, padding forward, and Rhiow gave him a Now-you-be-careful look, which he ignored. "See the way this is hanging out—shouldn't it be tucked in? I mean, it has no anchor. If you just—"

"No, don't pull that!"

It was too late. Arhu had already snagged a claw around the string in question, and pulled.

The gate shimmered: a brief storm of many-colored light ran down it—

—and someone stumbled out of it. An *ehhif.*

The two teams sprang back in horror as the man crashed

to the concrete almost on top of them. He lay there moaning, then grew quiet.

"Well," Arhu said, his eyes big with surprise and his voice full of badly hidden satisfaction. "You wanted it to fail the same way? There you go."

Fhrio gave Arhu a look suggesting that he would be seeing him later, outside the line of business.

"He's got a point, Fhrio," Rhiow said hurriedly. "You said you wished for an incursion, and a wizard has to watch what he wishes for. The Universe is listening."

Fhrio gave her an annoyed look, but then almost visibly let the mood go, aware that they had more important issues to deal with. They all bent down together over the sprawled *ehhif:* Fhrio patted him gently on the face with one paw. There was no response. "Unconscious . . ."

"Not for long, I think."

"But, great Queen of us all, where did he *spring* from?" Fhrio said.

"From his clothes, I'd say not our time, that much is certain," Rhiow said. "And no time close to it. I'm no expert on *ehhif* styles, but this looks more like what tom-*ehhif* wear for formal wear in our time. It used to be everyday clothing once, though, so Urruah told me."

The *ehhif* was mostly in black: long narrow trousers, a white shirt with a peculiar cloth wrapped around the neck and tucked into the shirt's collar: then a sort of short close coat that came down only to the waist, and over that a bigger coat, dark again. The *ehhif* himself was tall, and fair-furred, and had a lot more fur around the face than was popular these days: he might have been in middle age.

"He's stopped breathing," Fhrio said suddenly.

Rhiow looked at him more closely. "It might just be a sigh," she said. "But just in case, we'd better spell-fence him. He's going to need support spelling anyway when he wakes up."

She started walking the beginning of a wizard's circle around the *ehhif* and the gate together. Arhu had dropped the string he had pulled and was looking off down the old train tunnel. "Now what in the Dam's name," said a voice from a little distance down the tunnel, and a second later Auhlae jumped up onto the platform, with Siffha'h in tow. Arhu looked at her, then turned and sat down hurriedly and began to wash.

"Auhlae," Fhrio said, "where's Huff?"

"He'll be along shortly," she said, walking along to the *ehhif* and peering at him. "Iau's name," Auhlae said, "it's another one."

"Yes," Fhrio said, and said nothing more for the moment, but Rhiow could hear trouble in his voice. She ignored it for the moment. "Has he started breathing again?"

Auhlae looked closely at him, and put her face down close to the *ehhif*'s, feeling for breath. "None at the moment. Siffha'h," she said, "when Rhiow finishes, put some power into her circle. This poor *ehhif*'s going to need it. I think he's in shock."

"Doesn't surprise me," Siffha'h said, coming over to look at the circle Rhiow was building as she paced and assembled the spell in her mind. "Pretty standard," she said. "Which part do you want me to fuel first?"

"The main strand and the life-support part," Rhiow said. "I want to feel if there's anything actually wrong with his body before we start interfering." She completed the circle, tying the "wizard's knot" in the air with a flirt of her tail: pale fire followed it briefly and died away. Normally she would have preferred to see her guidelines in visible light, but the appearance of strange fires from nowhere was not likely to do this poor *ehhif* any good when he became conscious.

"Now then," she said. The basic spell-circle lay traced in ghost lines on the concrete around the *ehhif*. Rhiow now made one more turn around it, her paws pressing into the circle the graphic forms of those words of the Speech that Rhiow was assembling in her mind, the words that would control the function of the spell. One by one they appeared in graceful ghost curves and arabesques interwoven around the main curve of the circle, like vines twining around a support, until the last few words rooted themselves into the wizard's knot and became one with it.

"Ready," she said. Siffha'h looked the circle over, found the power-supply access point, and stood on it: the circle flared for just a second with power, then damped down again.

Rhiow, still standing on the control point of the circle at the wizard's knot, nearly jumped off it at the abrupt access of power into the spell, and, secondarily, into her. It was partly the suddenness of its inrush, and partly the sheer volume of it, and the unusual taste of it when it came—mostly the taste of Siffha'h's mind: young and fierce and bold, surprisingly so for such a young queen, with a great sense of potential unused and potential still developing, and behind everything, driving it all, some huge and dimly perceived desire. Rhiow shied away from any attempt to look more closely at that—it was none of her business—but she was impressed by it all the same. This young queen was going to be quite something as she grew into more certainty about her work and her life.

"That enough to work with for the moment?" Siffha'h asked.

"For several hours, if you ask me," Rhiow said, impressed. "Thanks, cousin!" She turned her attention to the spell. She had no proper name for the *ehhif,* and so had used one of the species-generic terms and an indicator for his gender: now her mind ran down through that connection to his, and felt about gingerly in the *ehhif* 's mind. The part of his brain that ran breathing and blood pressure and other functions was undamaged, but the emotional shock had thrown his blood chemistry badly out of kilter, and left him in a "sigh" that was much more prolonged than the usual fifteen seconds. That chemistry was getting worse as she watched, but fortunately the problem was a simple one, already partially rectified. Rhiow cured it by increasing the acidity of his blood ever so slightly, a process already under way, and the automatic response to such an increase took over, so that the *ehhif* gasped, and then started to breathe normally again.

"Nothing too serious, then," Auhlae said, putting her ears forward in relief.

"No, just the kind of thing that causes hiccups, but a little more severe," Rhiow said, relieved herself, and shook herself a little to get rid of the peculiar cramped, narrow feeling of an *ehhif* 's mind. "It's his emotional state that I'm more worried about, when he becomes conscious again. He may need quieting. Let's see how he does."

The *ehhif* was stirring a little already. "Hey, sorry I'm late," said another voice from down the tunnel, and Urruah leaped up onto the platform. "There were some things I had to take care—" He broke off, going wide-eyed as he took in the whole scene in a second. "Hey," he said then. "So wishing works after all."

"Whether it does or not, we'd better shut this gate down," Fhrio said. "The last thing we need at the moment is another access, especially one into a spell-circle when whoever might come through isn't named in the spell."

Urruah stared at him. "Are you kidding? Lock it open!"

"What?"

"If we don't lock it open I won't be able to get a reading on where the other end is anchored," Urruah said, "and that's information we badly need. Are you set up to do it? Then let me."

Fhrio bristled at that, but Auhlae bumped him from one side, distracting him. "He's right," she said. "Rhiow, you'll want to put his personal information into the spell so that he can step through. Just make sure you lock it in nonpatent configuration, Urruah. Come on, Fhrio, we have other things to attend to. Poor *ehhif,* look at him, he's in a state."

The *ehhif* 's eyes were open now. He lay there staring around him at the darkness, and tried to sit up once: failed, and slumped back again.

"Where . . ." he said, and then trailed off at the sound of his own voice in the close darkness of the tunnel.

The wizards exchanged glances. "If this isn't errantry," Auhlae said, "what is?"

She padded over to the edge of the circle and sat down where the *ehhif* could see her. Once again he tried to sit up, and did a little better this time, managing at least to hitch himself up on one elbow and look around. The light here was not good, even by feline standards; it was questionable how much he could see.

"Don't be afraid," Auhlae said to him in the Speech. "You've had a fall. Are you hurt?"

"No, I—I mean, I think not, but where—where is this?" He tried to sit up again. "Where are you?"

"Here in front of you," Auhlae said, with a look at Rhiow.

She was ready. The *ehhif* looked around him and saw Auhlae, then looked past her. "Where?"

"Right here, in front of you," she said, and even in the rather dire circumstances, Rhiow could hear the sound of slight amusement in Auhlae's voice. "The cat," she added, and this time the amusement was genuine.

The *ehhif* looked at Auhlae, and then actually laughed out loud, though the laughter was shaky. "Oh surely not," he said. "Some kind of ventriloquism. I've seen illusionists' shows: I know what kind of tricks may be played on an unsuspecting audience."

Auhlae sighed a little. "In front of an audience, a skilled stage magician can produce all kinds of illusions, I know," she said, "but this isn't that kind of thing. Rhiow, maybe you'd better let the light of the circle come up a little."

She waved her tail in agreement, meanwhile watching the *ehhif* closely for any signs that he was about to go shocky again.

"Mr . . . Illingworth," said Auhlae after a moment, as the light of the circle grew and the *ehhif* looked around him, "please don't believe this a trick. It *is* something out of your experience, though. Perhaps you would prefer to think of it as a dream. Do you mind if we ask you some questions?"

The *ehhif* looked around at a circle, and the cat inside it with him, its paws thrust into the glowing webwork, which the circle surrounded, and the four other cats outside, and he blinked. "I suppose not, but where are you? And how do you know my name?"

"Please don't bother looking for any other humans, because you'll see none here," Auhlae said. "Just pretend, if you will, that the cats are speaking to you."

"But how do you know my name?" the *ehhif* demanded, more urgently now. "Is it—is this some kind of plot?"

Through the spell, Rhiow could feel the *ehhif*'s blood pressure beginning to spike. She watched it carefully, and felt down the spell for indications of any sudden physical movement: there were too many ways he could damage himself, physically and nonphysically, if he tried to break out of the circle before it was correctly disassembled.

"It's no plot," Auhlae said, "though I wouldn't mind hearing why you would think it was one."

The *ehhif* looked around him, still trying to find the source of the voice that spoke to him, and now he started to look suspicious. "There are plots everywhere these days," he said, and his voice sounded unusually troubled. "Everything used to seem so safe once, but now nothing is what it seems."

His blood pressure spiked again with his anxiety, and Rhiow could feel his muscles getting ready for a jump. *Better not,* she thought, and spoke briefly to his adrenal glands through the spell. They obligingly stopped the chemical process that was already producing adrenaline, and instead produced a quick jolt of endorphins that left Mr. Illingworth blinking in slightly buzzed bemusement, and much less prepared to get up and run anywhere. Rhiow was ready to lock his muscles immobile if she had to, but she preferred less invasive and energy-intensive measures to start with.

"How do you mean?" Auhlae said.

"The war," said Mr. Illingworth, and now his voice started to sound mournful. "What use is being the mightiest nation on the globe when we must be bombed for the privilege? There was a time when no one dared lift a hand to us. But now our enemies have gathered together and grown bold, and London itself is a prey."

At that Auhlae looked sharply at Fhrio. Fhrio's eyes were wide. *Bombed?* he said silently, to her and the others. *London hasn't been bombed for fifty years.*

"When did this start?" Auhlae said, and for all her attempts to keep her voice soothing, her alarm came through.

"A year or so ago," said Mr. Illingworth wearily. "There were troubles before then, but nothing like the crisis we face now." And much to Rhiow's surprise, the *ehhif* put his face down in his hands. "Not since the Queen died . . ."

The Queen? Urruah said then, pausing in his work with the gate. What's he talking about?

"The Queen? Which queen?" Auhlae said.

The *ehhif* looked up again, and looked around him with a much less fuzzy air: Rhiow felt his blood pressure start spiking again. "How can you not know about the great tragedy," Mr. Illingworth said, "for which a whole nation mourns, and at which the whole world looked on amazed? Only spies would pretend not to know how the Queen-Empress was assassinated, treacherously killed by—" He started to struggle to his feet.

Rhiow clamped the spell down on him, shorting out the neurotransmitter chemistry servicing his voluntary musculature but being careful to avoid his lungs. Still the *ehhif* gasped, though he couldn't struggle, and his fear began to grow. "Let me go!" he said loudly, and then started to shout, "Spies! Traitors! Let me go! *Police!*"

The sound of that cry could be kept from being heard, of course, but Rhiow had other concerns. *Auhlae,* she said silently, *there's no point in this. It takes doing for an* ehhif *to frighten itself to death, but this one's pretty emotionally labile: he might be able to do it. And he's been under a lot of stress.*

You're right, Auhlae said. *Better put him to sleep.*

Rhiow reached into the spell and spoke to the *ehhif*'s brain chemistry. A moment later his eyes closed, and his head sagged slightly, though he did not move otherwise; she kept the hold on his muscles, just for safety's sake.

"Bombed?" Urruah said then.

"One moment," Rhiow said. "Urruah, how's the gate?"

"Locked open but nonpatent, like Auhlae said."

"Have you got a time fix on the opening?"

"Not yet. The congruency with our present timeframe is *not* one-to-one, Rhi. The spatiotemporal coordinate readings I'm getting at the moment are not meshing in direct line with our own." Rhiow twitched at the sound of that, for she thought she knew what he meant—and she didn't like it. "Additionally, I think something's been fretting at the gate from the other side while it's been doing these 'rogue' openings . . . unraveling it. The unraveling's been starting to manifest itself on this side now." He put his whiskers back. "And I'm almost afraid to fix it. That might warn whoever's doing the unraveling, send them under cover."

I'd wait and talk to Huff about it, Rhiow said silently to him. *This is getting to be a jurisdictional matter, and I don't want to . . .* She glanced in Fhrio's direction.

Understood, Urruah said. *But if something sudden happens, we're going to have to intervene in the situation's best interest, no matter what local opinion might be.*

Rhiow waved her tail in agreement, though the prospect made her nervous: Urruah went back to "reading" the gate, letting the information in the string configuration sing down through his claws and into his nerves and brain. "Auhlae," Rhiow said aloud, "you managed enough rapport with him to get a name: Could you get in there and find out more?"

Auhlae shook herself. "Names are easy," she said, somewhat distressed. "They're so near the surface in any sentient being. But abstract information is a lot harder to get at, out of species. You know how *ehhif* minds look and feel inside: the imagery's all wrong, the language is bizarre and the mindset is stranger still. I'm no expert in *ehhif* psychologies—I'll get lost in there as readily as anyone else. And anyway, I can't do anything useful while our Mr. Illingworth's unconscious. If he *was* conscious, I could go in, all right, but I couldn't be sure I was getting the information absolutely correct. And if we're hearing from this *ehhif* what I *think* we're hearing—"

"If you think you're hearing evidence of an alternate timeline," Urruah said, "then I think you're right. Leaving aside all the other things he mentioned, most of which I don't understand, I do know that London hasn't been bombed recently—and it certainly was never bombed when *ehhif* wore clothes like that."

Rhiow suddenly became aware of Arhu looking over her shoulder, most intently, at Illingworth. "He's the unraveling," Arhu said softly. "Or a symptom of it: concrete rather than abstract. It's not a process that's finished yet. But if something's not done soon . . ."

"Hold that thought," Rhiow said. "Don't lose it, whatever you do."

"Oh, certainly," Fhrio said suddenly, sounding very annoyed. "Encourage him. He's been enough trouble already."

"Look," Arhu said, turning. "I tried to tell you—"

"No, *you* look." Fhrio leaned close to Arhu and stared at him straight on: leaned over him stiff-necked and tall, the classic posture of the threatening tom. "You may think that you've done us a favor by causing this incursion, but who knows if it's anything to do with the problems we've been having? All *I* see is that you've made a sweet mess of things. Don't you *ever* touch my gate again unless I specifically tell you to. You hear me? You come in here thinking you're so *vhai*'d smart, and you tamper with things that you don't—"

Arhu was staring right back at Fhrio, and his ears were back: he hadn't given an inch, and his lips were beginning to wrinkle away from his teeth. Urruah was looking on dispassionately. *Oh, dear Dam around us,* Rhiow thought, *please don't let Arhu—*

"Now what in the worlds," said another voice down the tunnel. Heads turned. A moment later Huff jumped up onto the platform, and looked at the bizarre tableau before him: the half-sitting, frozen *ehhif,* Urruah once again up to his armpits in the hyperstrings of the gate, Siffha'h sitting on the power junction and washing nonchalantly, Auhlae and Rhiow looking on in bemusement and distress, and Fhrio and Arhu.

Fhrio turned and glared at Huff, his ears still back. "Well, about time you got back here! While you've been off having one of your little catnaps, your precious imported *vhai*'d 'senior gating team' has—"

"Fhrio," said Huff. Fhrio subsided and sat down, though his ears stayed flat.

Huff sat down too. "For one thing, I was not having a catnap, much as I would have liked to be. I was off having a talk about this gate with Hni'hho." Rhiow immediately recognized this as the name of the present Senior Wizard for Western Europe, an *ehhif* living just across the water in one of the low countries near the sea. "And for another, I think you may owe Rhiow and her team an apology. They were brought here to produce the results. They are apparently producing them"—and he flicked a glance over at the wretched unconscious *ehhif*—"whether you like them or not. We were specifically instructed to expect 'somewhat unorthodox technique.' Or weren't you listening to Her?"

"Oh, I heard Her, it's just—"

"It isn't 'just.' If you're feeling obstructive, take it up with Herself, but you've got to resolve whatever conflicts you have about this work before you do anything further."

Fhrio turned away and began to wash. So did Arhu, with great intensity and speed.

Rhiow breathed out in relief. *"Somewhat unorthodox technique,"* she thought then, slightly amused. *Well, Arhu's off the sharp end of the claw for the moment. But what if "unorthodox" means me and Urruah too?*

Huff got up and walked to the edge of the circle, looking at the sleeping *ehhif* half sitting there. "*He's* a long way from home," he said.

"I'd say he's from the middle of the century before last, as *ehhif* count time," said Urruah. "The location is nearly congruent with this one, at least, but the exact time is proving elusive. It's somewhere within the spread of the previous micro-openings, though. No guarantee of whether it coincides with any of them."

"He spoke of bombings," Auhlae said, going over to stand by her mate.

"He was talking about the Queen, too," Arhu said, looking up from his own composure-washing and sounding a little bemused. "I wouldn't have thought *ehhif* knew about Iau."

"With him wearing those clothes, I would say he probably meant the *ehhif*-queen who was ruling then," Huff said. "A different usage of the same word we use for Her, and for shes. Hffich'horia, this queen's name was. A lot of the *ehhif* on this island count themselves as of the same pride, though they're not blood-related except distantly: and they have a kind of *hwio-rrhi'theh*, a 'pride of prides,' who're supposed to care for all the other *ehhif*, help them find food and do justice among them and so forth, though as usual for *ehhif*, it's never quite that simple. This *ehhif*-queen was a daughter of that chief-pride, which the *ehhif* then apparently found a little unusual: for a long time toms had run that chief-pride, not queens."

"Peculiar," Rhiow said. "Even among *ehhif*, queens still run things a lot of the time, no matter that the toms say otherwise."

Huff grinned at that. "I've never understood that myself. You'd think they'd be glad to have someone relieve them of the responsibility." He threw an affectionate look at Auhlae:

she half-closed her eyes in amusement. "Anyway, this *ehhif*-queen is still famous for the things done by her pride and the great ones of the prides under her: today's *ehhif* call that whole time period after her."

"He said she was assassinated, though," Urruah said.

Huff twitched his tail back and forth. "Certainly other *ehhif* tried to kill her several times," he said, "but none of them ever succeeded. She died of age and illness . . . in our world. But in his . . ." Huff looked at the *ehhif*.

"We really need to know when he comes from," Siffha'h said, "if this is going to make any sense."

"Yes, but if you've already had to tranquilize him, I don't think he's going to be much more help," Huff said. "If we try to get more information out of him, we might damage him, which contravenes the Oath, no matter how much we think may ride on what he knows."

"I'd have to agree," Rhiow said. "He was getting very distressed indeed."

"Well, at least we have other ways to get this information, since now we have a positive lock on where this particular *ehhif* came from. We can put him back where he belongs, and we can compare the gate's present configuration to the older gate logs, then see if we can find out how or why they've been malfunctioning and giving us less than useful records of these transits. Any other thoughts on this? 'Hlae?"

Auhlae waved her tail in negation. "Let's do it."

"Fhrio? Siffha'h?"

Fhrio said, "I don't like this gate being locked open, and even less do I like it when the other end may be anchored in an alternate reality. One gate stuck in the open position can begin to affect all the others in odd ways, and our sheaf of gates is sensitive enough in that regard."

"I understand your concern," Huff said, "and you're

right. But in this particular case, we're going to have to take the chance. As soon as we can put someone through to confirm the temporal coordinates at the other end and get them home again, we can close it down again. Sif?"

"Sounds like a good idea to me," Siffha'h said.

Huff turned to Rhiow. "Do you concur?"

"Absolutely," she said.

"All right," Huff said. "Let's send this pastling home, then. Do you think you need to alter his memories, Rhiow?"

"It wouldn't be easy," she said, "for the same reason Auhlae wasn't willing to go after abstract information. I might mess something up, and leave him worse off than he would have been if I hadn't meddled. But from the way he was answering us, I think it's likely enough that he *will* dismiss all this as a dream."

"All right. Siffha'h, you like the big showy physical spells."

"This isn't showy," Siffha'h said, and without twitching so much as a whisker or making any alteration to the "physical" spell-circle she sat on, Mr. Illingworth levitated gently into the air and toward the gate.

"Would you make it patent, and give me visual?" Siffha'h said. "I don't want to drop the guy."

Urruah, looking over his shoulder at her, grinned a little and slipped one claw behind into the patency bundle, pulling gently. A moment later they were looking into a dark vista that might have been a street: walls were visible not too far away, and a faint, yellow, wobbling light came off from one side.

"Gaslight," Auhlae said softly, waving her tail in fascination. The *ehhif* drifted slowly through the gate, into the darkness on the other side of the gate; Urruah edged sideways a little to let him pass unhindered. "How far down is the ground?" Siffha'h said.

"About your body's length."

The *ehhif* dropped down below the boundary of the gate, out of Rhiow's sight: Urruah craned his neck to see. "All right," he said, "he's down. I'm going to turn this nonpatent again and leave it locked." He started pulling strings again. "If we can."

The gate shimmered and rippled—and all the length of it heaved, a bizarre sight like some huge beast's skin shivering convulsively to get rid of a biting fly. Even the boundaries of the gate, which should have remained unaffected, twisted and warped. Urruah threw himself backward, twisted, and came down on his feet—just. Behind him, color drained from the warp and weft of the gate and it steadied: after a moment it hung in the air in its default configuration again, nonpatent, in "standby," though its colors looked very muted, almost drained.

"What in the Queen's name was *that?*" Huff said, staring.

No one had any answers. Fhrio padded up to the gate, looked at it, then looked angrily over at Urruah. *"What did you do to it?"*

"Nothing that you didn't see," Urruah said, getting up and shaking himself. "I've seen catastrophic closures before, but they didn't look anything like *that.* I wonder, though, if that was some kind of reaction to Mr. Illingworth being put back where he belonged all of a sudden?"

"You mean you don't think these gatings are accidental," Siffha'h said. "So it was like whatever engineered the opening, from way back then, didn't *want* him back."

"Meaning that he was meant to increase whatever imbalance in our universe is already present," said Auhlae, "from the pastlings who've come through and not yet been found again."

"There's another nasty possibility," Rhiow said. "That

transit might have been balanced for him alone, and when someone else either tried to accompany him through it or follow him to the source using the same 'settings,' they could have been damaged. Or possibly even killed."

"You're suggesting that it was a trap?" Huff said.

"There would be no way to be sure of that with the data we have. But I *am* suggesting that Siffha'h's right. This was not a malfunction . . . or not a very likely one. There was someone at the other end managing it, or someone who programmed it and walked away."

"But how do you open a gate *forward* in time?" Siffha'h asked, her eyes big.

Huff looked at her somberly. "Unless you've mastered contemporal existence," Huff said, "you don't. But the only ones who have done so, who simultaneously live in all times and none, are the Powers That Be."

"Including that one other Power," said Auhlae, "who gives us so much trouble."

Glances were exchanged all around.

"Well, the circle's served its purpose," Rhiow said. She flirted her tail at the "wizard's knot": it unraveled, and the rest of the circle vanished with it. "Thanks, Siffha'h. That was nicely done."

She looked smug. "Anytime."

Fhrio went over to the gate and put one paw into the control weave, hooking out first one string, then another. He hissed softly. "There's no telling what happened now," he said. "Those 'settings' wiped themselves from the logs when the gate collapsed, that doubtless being the 'operator's' intention. We're no farther along than we were before."

Urruah, who had stepped away to sit down and have a brief wash while Fhrio was looking the gate over, now glanced up. "Well," he said, "it's not that bad. I wove them into the gate's hard memory, stacked underneath your standard default routines, while I was locking the gate open. Just a precaution: I was afraid I might drop something vital when things got busy. But at least that way we could be sure of finding the settings again if something went wrong."

Fhrio blinked. "*How* did you get into my hard routines that fast?"

Urruah smiled one of those smug-tom smiles, and Rhiow said hurriedly, "Huff, I wouldn't mind taking a break for a little while, if it suits you."

"Certainly. Let's go up and get some fresh air, see if we can find some lunch. After that"—and Huff looked grim—"we must plan. If the Lone Power is behind what we just saw—and I can't think what else could be—then we've a nasty job ahead of us. Food first: but then the council of war."

✦

The food took less time than Rhiow had thought, most of it provided by *ehhif* whom she found astonishingly willing. Huff had simply led them around to the Mint, the pub where he lived with his *ehhif*, the pub's manager. Rhiow was not sure what to expect from a pub, except for thinking that perhaps, like many other things she had glimpsed so far in London, it might be fairly old: but this one was as much like a New York uptown bar as anything else, all plate glass and polished brass and hanging plants. Huff made his way through the pub's "lounge" area, graciously accepting bits of sausage and burger and sandwich and other treats from the patrons and bringing this food back to the others, who stayed discreetly sidled in one out-of-the-way corner of the pub otherwise populated only by a group of mindlessly dinging and hooting small-stakes gambling machines.

"You're very popular here," Urruah said after Huff came back with a rather large piece of fried fish.

"Oh yes," Huff said, watching with amusement as Arhu fell on the piece of fish and devoured it almost without stopping to breathe. "They're a nice enough bunch, by and large: and my *ehhif* doesn't mind. He describes it as 'goodwill' . . . says it helps business. It's my pleasure, I'm sure." Huff looked around the place with a satisfied air. "Always nice to be part of a successful undertaking. I just have to watch myself sometimes; it would be too easy to get fat."

Rhiow, busy washing her face after finishing a greasy but delectable half of a sausage, was glad of the excuse not to be looking at Huff when he said that. He had already achieved at least "portly" status, but he was not genuinely overweight—yet. *And who am I to stare at* him *in this regard? If I had unlimited access to food like this, who knows what I'd look like in a few months.* All the same, she wished she had the opportunity to find out.

Everyone was washing now but Fhrio: he had finished first and was hunkered down with his eyes half closed, perhaps consulting with the Whisperer about the status of his gates. *Or perhaps,* Rhiow thought, *wondering how much face he's lost, and how to get it back.* She sighed, and scrubbed her face harder.

Urruah was in comfort: after a chunk of burger, two fish sticks from someone's finicky child, and a big piece of gravy-soaked crust from someone's steak and kidney pie, he was lying on one side and putting his stomach fur in order. "So, Huff," he said, pausing and looking up, "let's consider options."

"I don't know that we have many," Huff said. He was taking his time about putting his broad snow-white bib in order: it had somehow gotten some ketchup on it after that last piece of hamburger, and Rhiow suspected that he would be pinkish there for a day or two. "We've got to try to trace back along the same path that Mr. Illingworth came by. But the modality is going to be difficult, considering how our problem gate is behaving." He sounded meditative.

"I think we're going to have to construct a timeslide," Urruah said. "To access what the *ehhif* wizards call a piece of time."

"You started to tell me about that once," Arhu said suddenly to Urruah. "And then you yelled at him," he said, turning to Rhiow. "And me."

"With reason," Rhiow said. "It wasn't germane to the problem at hand: and messing around with time without a specific goal, and approval from the Powers, is like playing in traffic. Worse, actually. But temporal claudication theory's been a hobby of Urruah's for a long time."

Urruah shook himself, then sat up and licked a paw as meditatively as Huff, started rubbing behind one ear, even though he had already washed there. "I started getting interested in it when I was still freelance," he said to Arhu. "Sometimes the Whisperer will talk about it, for whatever reasons. Can't be boredom, I wouldn't think: maybe it's her way of encouraging research, or just curiosity. She's sneaky that way."

"Temporal claudication," Arhu said. "I thought it was supposed to be 'temporospatial.' "

"It is," Urruah said. "Oh, there's no way you can ever completely lose the spatial coordinate-set on any temporospatial transit spell, no matter how still you try to hold it: not a planet-based one, anyway. But a timeslide's emphasis is always mainly on temporal change. You can either mount it 'freestanding,' by bending space locally and temporarily with spells and equipment tailored to that specific spot, or you can start a timeslide in 'parasitic' relationship to an existing worldgate, using the gate's power source to run the slide. There are more involved 'half and half' implementations for use when you want some of the gate's own functions to augment those of the timeslide, but that kind of implementation is kind of fiddly."

"A claudication is a squeezing, a constriction," Huff said to Arhu. "Squeeze space, and you enable things to pop from one side of the 'squeezed' area to another: that's worldgating at its simplest. Squeeze time as well—or squeeze the temporal component of the time/space pair harder than the spatial one—and you pop from one time to another. Present to past, and back again. That's a timeslide."

"You still have to control the spatial component very exactly," Urruah said, "or else you pop out at the right *time,* all right, but somewhere very different in the planet's orbit, not forgetting that the planet's primary has moved too, and taken its whole solar system with it, since the time you're aiming for. Hanging out there in the cold, dark vacuum and feeling very silly . . . assuming you remembered to bring some air with you." Urruah put his whiskers forward, amused by the image. Arhu licked his nose, twice, very fast. "You must choose a spot at one end of the timeslide," Urruah said, "ideally your 'present' end, as de facto anchor, and the other as the spot to which the anchor chain is fastened, and not lose control of either of them, despite their individual movements through space, which continue through the duration of the slide. There has to be enough flex in the connection to cope with unpredictable movements of the body . . . or bodies, since the temporal element means you have to treat this as a two-body problem. Then when you're done, you have to unhook both ends of the timeslide without causing temporal backlash at either insertion point. It's delicate work, my kit: you'll break a few claws on this one, if it's what we go for."

Arhu gave Urruah a look that suggested the usage of claws might be more imminent. "I can handle it," he said.

"We'll see," said Rhiow. "You're good with static

worldgates, for a beginner. Whether you'll do as well with a timeslide is another question."

"In any case," Urruah said, "I think options one and three are closed to us."

Fhrio looked up from his ruminations at that. "Why?"

"Well," said Urruah, flicking his tail, "for one thing, how often are we going to have to *do* this? Does anyone want to give me odds that we'll find out what's causing the trouble—from solving the original gate malfunction, to finding out what in Iau's name Mr. Illingworth was talking about—and fix it all, with just one trip?"

They all looked at each other. No one looked willing to suggest that they were witless enough to believe that this might happen.

"Right," Urruah said. "So there's no sense in running around trying to acquire three or four or five sets of the specialized equipment we'd need to execute a freestanding timeslide repeatedly from the same spot. We'd only waste huge amounts of energy, which the Powers hate, and drive ourselves crazy, which *we* would hate. Type three, the half-and-half timeslide implementations, are a nuisance to maintain; they get out of kilter at the drop of a whisker, and they fail without warning, which we do not need in these circumstances. This leaves us with type two, which has certain advantages in our case."

"A parasitic linkage has *advantages?*" Auhlae said, sounding dubious. "With a malfunctioning gate?"

"It does if you're trying to fix the malfunction," Urruah said. "It'll function as a diagnostic, for the power source, anyway. A clumsy one, but rugged. Nor will it be liable to the same kinds of failures that the malfunctioning gate is having."

"No, just different ones," Fhrio said.

Urruah shrugged his tail. "Who wants all mice to taste

the same? Variety keeps you young. We parasitize the gate's power source and use it to power the slide. *That* at least we'll be able to control precisely. It's a simple structure to build and troubleshoot: anything goes wrong with it, we'll know about it in seconds, and be able to fix it in minutes. You try doing that with one of *these* gates. They're complex."

"Tell me about it," Huff said wearily. "The others have been failing sporadically because of the extra strain due to this troublesome one being taken offline. They're just not built for larger access numbers than they're carrying at the moment."

"We can get you some help for that," Rhiow said. "We have authorizations to get assistance from the other congener gates in this bundle. The teams at Chur and its daughter-complex at Samnaun in the Alps will take some of the strain until we've resolved this: we can install a couple of direct access portals in the near neighborhood of the functioning gates."

"They may have to stay there awhile," Huff said. "We have all these incursions to resolve as well."

"The Whisperer says we'll have as much support time from the other gates as we need," Rhiow said. "It'll be all right."

"And meanwhile, at least we have one illicit gate transit that we caught live and can use for its coordinates," Urruah said. "More than that: Mr. Illingworth, wherever he is, will still be carrying some hint of wizardly 'transit residue' about him that we can isolate and track—and possibly get a better sense of who or what pushed him through that gate. Maybe even why, if we're lucky."

"The oldest lostlings' residue will have already worn off, though," Auhlae said. "Even after all the other problems are solved, we're still going to have to find *them* somehow. And when we do . . . are they native to the same universe Mr. Illingworth is?"

It was a problem that had been nagging at Rhiow. Theoretically, the number of potential alternate universes was almost infinite. Even postulating a completely cooperative *ehhif*, once found—and that itself was none too likely—the two teams would then have to identify correctly which universe was that *ehhif*'s home. If they accidentally sent the *ehhif* back to the wrong world, their own home universe's problem would be solved, but the same problem of growing instability would be created for some other world.

"It's something we're going to have to sort out," Rhiow said, "but at the far end of this process, not the near end. I'd say what we must now do is construct Urruah's parasitic timeslide, plug into it the coordinates he saved from Mr. Illingworth's transit, and see where it takes us: then find out what we can about that universe, especially about this Queen of theirs, and what happened to her. You said there had been other attempts on her life," she said to Huff.

"At least three or four," Huff said. "We've got to discover whether this assassination is one of the attempts that, in our world, failed: or if it's a new one, never recorded."

"Perhaps never recorded," Urruah said, "because in the past someone else has already stopped it. . . . Us, perhaps?"

"That would be reassuring," Auhlae said. "But somehow I don't think we can count on it."

There was quiet for a moment. Huff sat gazing thoughtfully at the floor, a weary reddish carpet that over much time had become an amalgam of stomped-in chewing gum, spilled beer, and other substances that Rhiow's nose flatly refused to identify, this far along in their evolution. "Well," Huff said finally, "I concur. It only remains to decide exactly who makes the first incursion into the past."

"Assuming that none of you are particularly eager," Urruah said, "I think it should be us."

The London team looked at him with expressions varying from Huff's thoughtful interest to Auhlae's surprise to Siffha'h's faint confusion: Fhrio put his whiskers forward, positively (and, to Rhiow's mind, oddly) amused.

"Why?" Huff said. "Though I think probably none of us are all that eager . . ."

"*I* am!" Siffha'h said.

"Hush," Auhlae said. "You're young for this kind of work yet, Siffha'h."

"I am not! I've got all my teeth—"

"No."

"Why not?"

"Not now."

"As for the 'why' . . ." Urruah said.

"We're more expendable than you are," Arhu said dryly.

"Arhu!" Rhiow said.

"I wouldn't have put it quite that way," Urruah said, putting his whiskers forward, "but in a way he's right. When it comes down to the feet and the tail of it, Huff, these are *your* gates, and you know them better than we do. If something goes wrong with a timeslide anchored to one of your gates' power sources, you have a better chance to successfully troubleshoot the situation than we would. And another matter: The Powers sent us to intervene. Implicit in that, to my mind, is the suggestion that we may be best equipped, one way or another, to deal with whatever problems we uncover while working with you."

"Or it might just be ego," Fhrio said, one ear forward and one ear back. It was a joke, Rhiow thought, *just*.

"Urruah? Ego?" Rhiow said, and then stopped herself from saying "Perish the thought," since that could have implied that it *wasn't* ego. "Well, Fhrio, if you want to relieve him of the glory, I'm sure you're welcome to change places with him, and he'll stay here and mind your gates for you."

Huff threw Rhiow a very covert and very amused look as Fhrio put his other ear forward. "Oh, no indeed," he said, "I wouldn't want to deprive him. . . ."

"All right, then," Rhiow said to Huff. "I think we'll need some hours to put together what spells we want to carry with us, and to make sure things back at home are all right before we set out. If you can keep the gate in inactive mode until we get back, that'll probably be best."

"No problem with that," Fhrio said. "I'll just disconnect it from the power source entirely until you get back—when? tomorrow?—to set up the parasitic timeslide."

"Tomorrow let it be," Rhiow said, "about this time, if that suits you all."

They all got up. "And meanwhile, thanks for the work you've done," Huff said. "We're farther along than we were, though the problem looks worse than it did: at least there's been a change in status, which *you* were begging for, Fhrio, as I remember. So you may owe Arhu one after all."

"Though, Fhrio, I must admit that he overstepped the bounds," Rhiow said. "And my apologies to you for that."

Fhrio took a not entirely ceremonial swipe at Arhu's ear. "Let him behave himself after this, then."

"I will do so," Arhu said with abrupt and brittle clarity, "insofar as *you* so do as well, when we come into the dark and you cannot find the way . . ."

Rhiow blinked. It was not anything like Arhu's usual turn of phrase; she heard foretelling in it, and her fur stood up on her. She hoped Fhrio's was doing the same, for there was no mistaking the Whisperer's Dam when She chose to speak out loud . . . as She sometimes did, using Arhu as Her throat.

The resonances trembling around his words faded themselves out on the air, leaving the London team looking at one another. "I'm sorry," Rhiow said, "but it's another recent development. Arhu is a visionary, though the talent is still training. When it comes out so forcefully, though, we've learned to listen."

Fhrio shrugged his tail. "We'll see what happens," he said, sounding skeptical, but cheerfully so. "Are we all done? Then I've got a gate to see to, and a pride to go home to. See you all tomorrow."

He stalked out, leaving them all looking after him. Auhlae looked after him with some concern and said, "He goes my way home, for a little distance: I'll go with him. Siffha'h, come with me?"

"Sure," said the youngster. Auhlae rubbed faces quickly with Huff, saluted the others with a flirt of her tail, and headed off after Fhrio. Siffha'h trotted off after Auhlae, leaving Arhu gazing after her.

Rhiow lashed her tail once or twice, then said to Huff, "Truly, I am sorry if we've caused any trouble."

"If the way he acts makes you think so," Huff said, giving her an amused look out of those big green eyes, "don't. Fhrio's always like the flea down in your ear that you can't get at. But for all that, he's good at his job. Come on."

They all made their way out, slipping behind the bar and down a corridor behind it to a heavy metal door with a small cat door installed in the bottom of it: then out into a small, untidy yard stacked high with steel beer barrels and plastic soft-drink crates. At the back of the yard, a corrugated steel gateway in a high wall had a small improvised cat door cut into the steel and hinged. "Convenient," Urruah said.

"It is, isn't it?" said Huff. "But one thing. Urruah, thank you for volunteering."

Urruah looked at him in surprise. "Well, as I said, it seems appropriate. Doesn't it, Rhi?"

"It does. Accusations of ego aside."

Huff laughed at that. "Don't take him seriously, cousins: *please* don't. He's got ego enough of his own and to spare. But I do thank you."

"You're worried about Auhlae," Arhu said suddenly.

Rhiow sighed, thinking that vision was not Arhu's only problem: he was perceptive as well, but not about how to use the perception. *He needs a tact transplant,* she thought, but she suspected that this was something not even wizardry could handle. She and Urruah were just going to have to beat it into him over time, hopefully before he got so big that the corrective administration of educational whackings was no longer a viable option.

Huff looked for a long moment at Arhu before saying, "Yes, I am. I don't think you're too young to understand the situation. We've been together awhile, and she's dear to me: the thought of her in danger upsets me. If we needed to do something dangerous in the Powers' service, of course we would . . . and doubtless will. But I don't like to think of her anywhere near trouble."

Rhiow understood completely, though at the same time it seemed to her that for partners who were wizards, and who might be in trouble at the drop of a whisker, such an attitude was likely to cause one or both of them pain sooner or later.

"I know what you mean," Arhu said, and suddenly looked very young, and painfully dignified, and profoundly troubled, all at once. *Oh, dear,* Rhiow said privately to Urruah, *he* has *been bitten badly, hasn't he.*

The claw in the ear is the claw through the heart, Urruah said, quoting the old proverb. *I just hope she doesn't rip him ragged before she's through.*

"Yes," Huff said. "I thought you might. Thank you, anyway: thank you all for volunteering." And he leaned over and rubbed cheeks with Rhiow.

She was oddly moved. "Cousin, you're more than welcome. It's our job, after all. Meanwhile, we'd better get going to prepare what we need. We'll see you down by the gate, about this time tomorrow."

They made their way out the little steel door, into the alley behind the pub, and headed for the gate, and home. And all the way home, Rhiow's fur felt strange to her where Huff's cheek had brushed it.

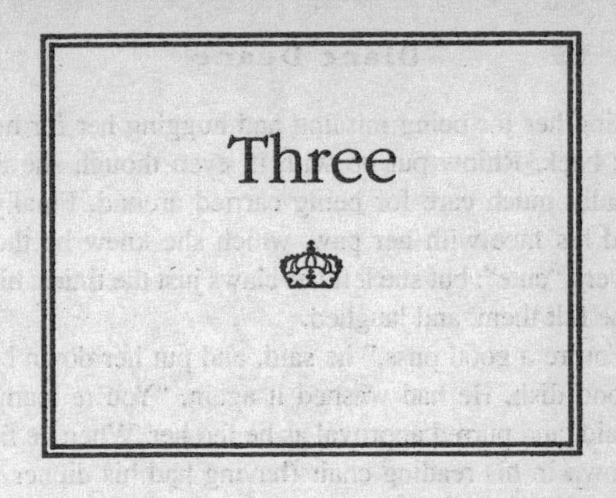

Three

They parted at Grand Central—Urruah to make his way off to his Dumpster, Arhu to the garage. Rhiow went home by one of the "high road" routes, over roofs and 'tween-building walls, rather than by the surface streets. She was already thinking about the spells she would want to bring with her the next day, the preparations she would have to make, and she was in no mood to deal with the traffic at street level. Yet at the same time Huff's touch was on her mind: nor could she stop thinking about poor Arhu's adolescent suffering over Siffha'h. *I wonder why she dislikes him,* Rhiow thought as she jumped up on a high dividing wall at the end of Seventieth Street and looked down through the maze of tiny cramped alleys that would finally lead to her own alleyway and the road up her own apartment's wall. *I hope they can sort something out. It would be nice if Arhu had another wizard more or less of his own age to be around, instead of just us old fossils.*

Iaehh hadn't seen Rhiow the night before, so when she came in the cat door now, an hour or so after he would have returned from work, Iaehh swept her up and carried her around the apartment for about ten minutes, alternately scolding her for being missing and hugging her for having come back. Rhiow put up with it, even though she didn't normally much care for being carried around. Finally she patted his face with her paw, which she knew he thought was very "cute": but she left her claws just the tiniest bit out, and he felt them, and laughed.

"You're a good puss," he said, and put her down by the cat-food dish. He had washed it again. "You're learning," she said, and purred approval as he fed her. When he finally sat down in his reading chair (having had his dinner some time ago: pizza, to judge by the smells), she jumped up into his lap and sat there washing for a good while. Iaehh picked up the remote control and turned on the living room TV, and for a good long time he sat quiet and watched the local news channel intone its litany of who had been robbed or shot in the city, what politicians were saying cutting and possibly true things about other politicians, and what the weather was going to be like the next day.

When the weather report came around for the second time, Rhiow looked up at Iaehh and saw that he was dozing. She put her whiskers forward. *Why else would he have been sitting still so long?* she thought. Even Iaehh sometimes ran out of that nervous energy that kept him running all day and made him sleep poorly at night. *At least,* sometimes *that's why he sleeps badly.* Other times, when he wept himself asleep after lying awake a long time, Rhiow knew quite well that there were other reasons. At such times she sometimes wished she could speak to his neurochemistry as she had done with Mr. Illingworth, and spare him the pain: but Rhiow knew that that would not have been within the right use of her powers. *To ease pain,* the Oath said, indeed: but when pain was what led to the growth that wizardry was also supposed to guard, one did not tamper. Her *ehhif* 's pain was difficult for her to bear, but Rhiow was not such a youngster in the exercise of the Art as to mistake the comforting of her own hurt for the salving of Iaehh's.

Now, though, he sat with his mouth slightly open, snoring very softly, while on the TV the mayor of New York complained about one of the city commissioners: and Rhiow let her eyes half-close and let the sound wash over her like running water or wind or any other noise that might have content, but not any content that she needed to pay attention to at the moment. There were more important things on her mind than city politics.

Time travel bothered her, as it bothered many wizards whose work sometimes necessitated it. For one thing, it was rarely quite so simple or straightforward as "going back in time." Even the phrase "back in time" was deceptive: the directionality of time was a variable, though the relationship of the past to the present was nominally a constant. No matter how careful you were, the possibility of careless action setting up unwelcome paradoxes was all too obvious . . . and unraveling such tangles was worse, inevitably involving more backtiming and the possibility of making things worse still.

The complications had fascinated Arhu all the way home: he had delightedly plagued Urruah with questions about a subject that until now had been off limits, about everything from what you fastened a timeslide *to,* to that ancient imponderable, the "grandfather paradox." Urruah had mentioned it, and Arhu had actually had to stop walking while he figured it out, or tried to. "It's weird," he said. "I can't see what would happen. Or, I mean, I can see two ways it would go."

"What? You mean, if you went back in time and killed your grandfather?" Urruah had said. "Well, one way, if you're still there afterwards, it means you're a by-blow. A bastard, as the *ehhif* would say. But then how *else* would you describe someone who would go back in time and kill their own grandfather? I ask you. And if you go the other way, and you succeed, then you're not there at all. And serves you right for *being* a bastard."

At that, Arhu had become so confused that he actually went quiet: and shortly thereafter they were at Grand Central, and Arhu went off to his dinner, ending the day's questioning. Rhiow had smiled somewhat wearily at that as she and Urruah parted, for the "grandfather paradox" served well enough to illuminate how difficult it could be to alter history, especially if you viewed it linearly. But in this line of work you would eventually have to deal with the question of what happened when events in some original timestream *had* actually been altered. Then you would have alternate universes to deal with. By themselves, they were bad enough. But they also brought with them the possibility that, in dealing with them, you would find yourself going back in *place* . . . which was more complex than merely backtiming, and potentially more dangerous.

Quite a few locations on Earth had a "back in place" as well as "back in time." There were other downsides than the Old Downside, less central in the hierarchy of universes, perhaps, but no less important to the creatures who loved or hated the realities to which those places were related. History, or the reality of which history is a shadow, was in full flower in these less central downsides, fully expressed there no matter how they might be repressed elsewhere—in fact, usually more vigorous in expression in direct proportion to how vigorously they had been repressed in the "real world."

And going back in *place* involved an entirely different set of dangers. You ran the risk of somehow altering the basic mythological or archetypal structure of a place, which could be immensely important in the minds of thousands or millions of sentient beings. Tampering with the mythological essence of a place—a Rubicon or a Valley Forge, in the *ehhif* metaphor, a Camelot or a Runnymede—could change not just history, but the *perception* of it as good, bad, or indifferent, a far more perilous business than changing the mere structure of time. Such shifts could create ripples and harmonics that would be capable of ripping whole worlds apart. The thought of going back in both time and place *at once* was dangerous enough to make Rhiow shudder.

But they might wind up doing just that, for London was definitely a Place, one of those hinges of *ehhif* history in this part of the world. Not that the history of place wasn't mostly an *ehhif* manifestation, anyway. Humans weighed hard on the world, and imprinted it with history and personality. But People stepped more lightly. Feline history tended to take place within individual cats, who, according to their nature, saw place as merely something they moved over or through: it was rare for one of the People to become attached to one field, one tree. Granted, your den for this season—or this week of this season—was something you would defend, for the sake of the kittens or the local hunting. But sooner or later time or loss or boredom seeped into every den like water, and you moved out, perhaps with mild regret, to escape the creeping damp and find yourself somewhere else more warm or dry. Memories of those dens you took with you as the worthwhile part of the transaction, but the dens themselves held little interest unless your kill or your kittens were in them.

What kept People in one place, if anything, was the *ehhif* they companioned: sometimes much to the Person's embarrassment—and Rhiow glanced up in affectionate amusement at Iaehh, who sat there with his head slightly to one side and his eyes closed, his mouth open, and the tiny snore emitting from it at decorous intervals. The whole business of companionment was a tangled one. Some People felt that the only way the *ehhif*-People relationship could be viewed was as slavery: others, mostly those already in such a relationship, tended to see it otherwise, in a whole spectrum of aspects from pity ("Someone has to try to teach them better") to simple affection ("Mine are well enough behaved, and they're nice to me; what's the problem?") to cheerful mercenary exploitation ("If they want to feed us, why shouldn't we enjoy eating their food? Doesn't cost anything to purr afterwards, either.").

The People who raved most about slavery and freedom found all these views despicable: starving in a gutter, they said, but starving free, was far superior to a full belly in the den of the oppressor. Rhiow, *ehhif*-companioned for a good while now, found such an attitude simplistic at best. Yet there was no denying the existence of People who had no knowledge of themselves as such: taken from their dams too early, perhaps, too soon even to drink in with the first milk and their mother's tale-purring the truth of what they were or where in the worlds their own kind came from—People who were barely self-aware, merely receptacles for food and excreters of it, dull-brained demanders of strokes and treats, "pets" in the true sense of the word: slaves to their most basic instincts, but in service to nothing any higher at all.

Rhiow shuddered a little. *But it's not that simple,* she thought. *Even among People who are self-aware, People for that matter living wild and "free," you'll find those for whom the gods and the life of the world don't matter at all, or matter far less than their last rat or a warm place to sleep. Which is worse? A cat who doesn't know she's a cat—just eats and sleeps and lives? Or one who* does *know, and doesn't care?*

A tangled issue, and not one that Rhiow would resolve. Meanwhile, there was still the problem of the upcoming intervention. She had spoken to the Whisperer on the way home and received what she was expecting: official "sanction" for time travel, if the teams decided it was necessary. She had also sorted out with Her the spells she felt most likely she would need. In the morning, before they were ready to set out, she would cross-check with Urruah to make sure they weren't carrying duplicates. And beyond that, there was nothing much she could do, except worry about what the future held for them . . . or, rather, the past. *And what good would that do?*

Rhiow closed her eyes and reduced the world to near darkness and Iaehh's tiny snore. *When I wake, I will meet my old enemy uncertainty,* she thought, *and its partners, the shadows that lie at the back of my mind and others': those darknesses that go about hunting for some action of mine to which to fasten themselves. They will lie in my road and say,* Why bother? *or* It will never work: *or they will lie out long and dark behind me, saying,* What difference have you made? It is all for nothing. *But I need pay them no mind. They are only the servants of the Lone Power, and against me and Those Whom I serve, they have no strength unless I allow them the same. My commission comes from Those Who Are, the Powers that were before time and will be after it: the Powers Who made time, and to Whom it answers. My paw, lifted to strike the shadows away from the feet of the Event enacted, holds hidden within it Their claw that strikes the Lone One to the heart, day by day. So it was done anciently; so I shall do tomorrow. And for tonight, I admit of no shadow but that of my closed eyes, and I give Their claw the resting time to sharpen itself in dream on the Tree: for at eyes' opening, together We go to battle again!*

And Iaehh's snore was the last thing she heard.

✦

When she woke up, Iaehh had already gone off to work, and apparently had carefully moved her off his lap and onto the chair without waking her when he went to bed . . . whenever that had been. The food bowls had been washed again, and were full.

Rhiow sighed with the sheer pleasure of having had a good night's sleep: it was rare enough, in her business. She got up and ate, then washed at leisure, and went out to use the box: and finally she checked the security spell on the apartment's door before heading downtown to Grand Central again.

Arhu was there early again, sitting in front of the gate. It was patent, showing the view down toward the Thames from near the main entrance to the Tower, and shedding a cool blue light around him. " 'Luck, Arhu," she said, jumping up onto the platform. "Where's Urruah?"

"He went through already," Arhu said, watching a barge full of *ehhif* tourists loading up at the dock near HMS *Belfast* for a tour down the river. "Wanted to go over early to get the timeslide set up with Fhrio: and he wanted to make sure the two Samnaun-based transfer gates were in place and working without messing everything else up."

Rhiow waved her tail slowly in acknowledgment, looking at the serene vista. It was a sunny morning over there: she had seen few of those so far. "Before we go . . ." she said.

"I'm not going to die of it," Arhu said, "so don't worry."

Rhiow blinked. "Die of what?"

"You know. Siffha'h," he said, though his voice was so mournful that Rhiow wondered if perhaps he wasn't all that sure of the outcome.

"That wasn't what I was going to ask you," she said, taking a swipe at his left ear, and missing entirely: Arhu ducked without even looking. "You *are* getting good at that," Rhiow added, unable to conceal slight admiration.

"I don't like pain," Arhu said. "It hurts."

Which is why it's such an effective teaching medium for kittens, Rhiow thought, *not least among them* you. "What I was going to ask you," she said, "was whether you had had any further insights into what was going to happen on this run."

His tail lashed. "Nothing that I can describe," Arhu said. "I keep getting flashes, but they slip away. Believe me, Rhiow, if I see anything that I can describe—then or afterwards—I'll tell you. But it doesn't always come that way. I keep getting stuff that just pops out without warning, and before I can get hold of it to see what it means, it's gone and taken all the—the meanings, the—"

"Context?"

"Yeah, the context—it all just goes. While the context's there, everything makes sense, but when I lose that . . ." He sighed. "It's really frustrating. It makes me want to hit things."

"Don't be tempted," Rhiow said, thinking of Fhrio.

Arhu laughed out loud. "I wouldn't bother. For one thing, beating him up wouldn't be any big deal, and for another, it's not exactly polite, is it?"

She blinked again. Rhiow couldn't think if she had ever before heard Arhu *use* the word *polite. If this is the kind of effect that having a crush is going to have on him,* she thought, *I'm all for it, even if it makes him ache a little.*

"So are you ready?" Arhu said.

"By all means, let's go," said Rhiow. They stepped through into the bright London day, and Arhu shut the worldgate behind them. There by the Tower entrance, the two of them sidled. They made their way among the unseeing tourists down into the Tower Hill Underground station, and down to the passages leading to the platform where the London team had confined their unruly worldgate.

The spot was busy, though not so much with wizards as with equipment. The malfunctioning gate itself was disconnected from its power source, only visible to Rhiow as the thinnest ghost oval traced in the air, like a structure woven of smoke. The "catenary," the insubstantial power conduit that was finally rooted in the Old Downside and that normally served this gate, lay coiling along the floor like some bright serpent: the end of it, which would normally have terminated in the gate, was now faired into a glowing new spell-circle that had been traced on the floor. If the last one had looked like vines twining amongst one another, this one looked more like a circular hedge. It was complex, for Rhiow could see that Urruah, rather than using specific physical objects to twist local space into the shapes he required, was using the spell structure itself. The "hedge" blazed and flowed with multicolored fire, the radiance of it stuttering here and there as one spell subroutine or another came active, did its job, and deactivated itself. Urruah was pacing around the diagram, checking his spelling, while Fhrio crouched nearby and inspected the connection of the catenary to the diagram: off to one side, Auhlae was sitting with her tail neatly tucked about her forefeet, watching him work.

"Go check your name in that," Rhiow said to Arhu. He went straight over to the spell to do it. There were few such important aspects of spelling as to make sure you were correctly named. Like all the other sciences, wizardry always works: and, as in the other sciences, if a practitioner works too casually with forces he doesn't fully understand, the results are likely to be unfortunate. A wizard whose written name specified a different nature than the usual in a given spell would come out of that spell changed, and not always in ways he or she would prefer.

Rhiow turned her attention briefly to the other gate, which was hanging at one end of the platform, shimmering in the darkness. This was one of the "transfer" gates that would be taking some of the pressure off the London complex while the malfunctioning gate structure was completely offline. A transiting wizard using one of the London gates would now find him- or herself briefly under the peak of Piz Buin, at the restored prehistoric gating facility at Samnaun in the Alps, before finishing at their intended destination. It would be a slight inconvenience, but Rhiow couldn't believe any wizard in her right mind would grudge the momentary view out of the great transverse crevasse and down the side of the mountain . . . and the skiiers above would never notice.

" 'Luck, Fhrio," Rhiow said as she walked over to him. "Everything working satisfactorily?"

"Insofar as anything can be satisfactory when it's all ripped up like this," Fhrio said, "yes." For once he sounded merely tired rather than actively quarrelsome.

"You were up all night," Rhiow said.

"Yes I was," said Fhrio, and gave her a glance as if looking to see whether she was mocking him.

All Rhiow could do, hoping he wouldn't misunderstand the gesture, was lower her head and bump his briefly. "I appreciate the effort," she said, "we all do." And she moved away before either of them would have a chance to be embarrassed.

She went over to the timeslide spell to have a look at her own name, checking the arabesques and curls of it in the graphic form of the Speech. Everything looked all right, though she checked again just to be certain. She was not about to forget one spell some years ago, worked in haste by

Urruah, that had been perfect in ninety-nine percent of its detail but in which he had changed the sign on one minor symbol. The spell would have worked all right, but Rhiow would have exited it pure white, blue-eyed, and possibly deaf. She had been teasing Urruah about *that* one for a long time, but, judging by the intent look on his face, today might not be the best time to do it.

Auhlae got up and came over to greet Rhiow as she came: they breathed breaths for a moment. "Oh, Auhlae," Rhiow said, "*more* sausages—I don't know how you cope with all this rich food. I'd be the size of a *houff* by now."

Auhlae put her whiskers forward. "I control myself mostly," she said, "but since things started to misbehave, my appetite's been raging . . . and I confess I've been humoring it. I can always eat grass for a few days, later on."

Arhu came over. "You satisfied with the way your name looks?" Rhiow said.

"It looks fine. At least it looks the way it looks in our gate at home."

"The way it did yesterday?"

"Yeah."

"Good. Always check it frequently. Lives change without warning; names change the same way."

"Yeah." He licked his nose. "Auhlae, is Siffha'h going to be here today?"

"No, Arhu, she's off with Huff making an adjustment to one of the other gates," Auhlae said. "Fhrio and I will be standing guard over this end of your timeslide while you're downtime." She craned her neck a little to look at the spell construct. "Does he do this often?" Auhlae said to Rhiow. "He's very good at it."

"He's never done it before, to the best of my knowledge," Rhiow said, glancing over that way too as Urruah sat down, apparently to take one last overview of the whole structure.

"I have a feeling he's been waiting for the chance, though." The intricacy and tightness of the spell-structure suggested to Rhiow that he had been working on this spell, or something like it, for a long time. There was no disputing its elegance: Urruah was an artist at this kind of thing. Unfortunately, there was also no disputing its dangerousness. *It's a good thing we finally have an excuse to do something like this,* Rhiow thought. *Otherwise who knows what he might have done someday.*

Then she dismissed the thought. He might sometimes be impatient and reckless, by a queen's standards anyway, but Urruah was a professional. He would not tamper with time unless and until the Powers sanctioned it. *And then when he does,* she thought, as Urruah looked up from the spell with an extremely self-satisfied expression, *he'll have the time of his life.*

"Nice work, huh?" Urruah said, getting up.

"Beautiful as always," Rhiow said. "Did you get your name right?"

He put one ear back, not *quite* having an excuse to comment. "Uh, yes, I checked."

"That being the case," she said, "hadn't we better get going? You wouldn't want to leave a spell like this just sitting around for long: it wants to work. Waste of energy, otherwise."

Urruah grinned at her, then turned to Auhlae and Fhrio, who had finished checking the catenary and had strolled over to them.

"I've structured this so that, once we pass through, it'll seal behind us," Urruah said. "If this is some kind of trap, I don't want whatever might be waiting on the other side jumping straight back down your throats. The spell will continue running on this side, though, as usual, while sealed. Afterwards, say as soon as ten minutes after opening, there are three ways it can be activated. From this side, by either of you waking up this linkage"—he patted one outside-twining branch of the "hedge" with one paw—"which will make the slide bilaterally patent. You'll be able to see through, or to pass through if you need to. You'll see I've left a couple of stems unoccupied on the 'personality' stratum for you to add names to. It can also be activated from our side by one of us pulling a 'tripwire' strand—that's in case we need an early return. Otherwise, it's programmed to reopen to bilateral patency again in two hours: that's as long as I prefer to stay, for a scouting visit."

Auhlae and Fhrio both examined the linkages that Urruah had indicated. "All right," Auhlae said, "that's straightforward enough. If you're not back in two hours?"

"Intervention at that point will have to be your decision," Urruah said. "Myself, I'd say wait an extra hour before letting anyone come after us. But you may decide against that . . . and if you do, I wouldn't blame you. The slide will remain workable for a full Sun's day, in any case. If we don't return by then . . ." He shrugged his tail. "Better check with the European supervisory wizard for advice, because my guess is you'll need to."

Auhlae and Fhrio nodded.

"Then let's do it," Urruah said to Rhiow. She flicked her tail in agreement and leaped into the circle, found the spot that Urruah had marked out for her to occupy in lines of wizardly fire: behind her, Arhu jumped too, a little more clumsily, and found his spot. *Nerves. Poor kitling,* she thought: but Rhiow's fur was not lying entirely smooth, either. She licked her nose, and tried to keep her composure in place.

Urruah jumped into the circle, dead onto his spot, as if he had been practicing for this for years. His whiskers were forward, his tail was straight up with confidence. *Disgusting,* Rhiow thought, and resisted the urge to lick her nose again.

Urruah reached out for one of the traceries of words and fire laced through the "hedge," hooked it in both his front paws, and pulled it down to the spell's activation point, standing on it.

The sensation came instantly: not of passage, as in a normal gating, but of being squeezed. *Claudication is right,* Rhiow thought, as a feeling of intolerable pressure settled in all around her, seeming to compress her from every direction at once. It was as if giant paws were trying to press her right out of existence. And perhaps they were. *This existence, anyway.*

She could not swallow, or breathe, or lick her nose, or move any part of her in the slightest. The world reduced itself to that terrible pressure—

—which suddenly was gone, and she fell down.

Into the mud.

Rhiow struggled to her feet, opened her eyes enough to register that they were in some kind of street: buildings stood up on either side. Off to one side, Arhu was pulling himself to his feet as well. Beside her, Urruah was standing up, and swearing.

"What?" Rhiow said, "what's the matter?"

"Is your nose broken?" he said. "Sweet Dam of Everything, this smells like sa'Rráhh's own litter-box. The *mud!*"

Rhiow's face was trying to contort itself right out of shape at the smell: she could only agree. The street was at least four inches deep in a thick, black mud that, to judge by the smell, was mostly horse dung: but there was rotten straw in it too, and soot, and garbage of every kind, and a smell that suggested the *ehhif*'s sewers had discovered a way to back up so thoroughly that they ran uphill. The air was not much better. It was brown, a brown such as Rhiow had not seen since she last visited Los Angeles during a smog alert: but this was far, far worse—the concentrated, inversion-confined smoke from ten thousand chimneys, most of them burning coal. You could see this air in the street with you: it billowed faintly, like smoke from a burning building in the next block. But nothing was burning—or, rather, *everything* was: wood, coal, coke, trash.

"Is the tripwire here?" Arhu asked.

"Of course it's here," Urruah said, a little crossly. "I can feel it even through this stuff. Everything's going according to plan . . . so far." He looked around at the mud. "Though I have to admit my plans did not include *this*."

"It's going to take a while for our noses to get used to this," Rhiow said, looking around her with some concern. "Meanwhile, there's no point in standing around waiting for it to happen."

"You mentioned playing in traffic," Arhu said, looking across the street as horse carriages plunged by, big drays pulled by huge horses, smaller gigs with neat-looking ponies between the shafts, or tall, slender beasts apparently bred for the hackney trade. "I'd give a lot for a nice taxi to run underneath at the moment."

"I wish you had one too," Urruah growled, glancing up the road and unwilling to put a paw in the loathsome mud. "I will never complain about New York being dirty again. *Never!*"

"Yes you will," Arhu said, more in a tone of resignation than foresight, but he knew Urruah well enough by now to be able to make the statement without resource to prophecy.

Urruah was so disgusted that he didn't even bother taking a swipe at Arhu. "For someone who lives in a Dumpster," Rhiow said, unable to resist the chance to tease him, "you're awfully fastidious."

"My Dumpster is cleaner than this," Urruah said. "A *sewage-treatment* facility is cleaner than this! If—"

"I get the message," Rhiow said. "Come on, 'Ruah, we don't have a choice. Let's do it."

They ran across the street together—

—and Arhu was completely unprepared for the motor roar that came from down the side street. In a cloud of smoke, a four-wheeled vehicle on thin-tired, spindly wheels came charging around the corner and straight at them.

There was no time to jump. Arhu's eyes rolled in terror, but it was informed terror. He threw himself flat under the vehicle's chassis: it passed over him and roared on down the street, the *ehhif* sitting in the contraption either completely unaware that they'd almost run over a cat, or completely unconcerned about it.

Urruah, who had been farther in the middle of the road, now ran over to Arhu as he picked himself up and shook himself to get the worst of the muck off. "You have to start being more careful about what you ask for," Urruah growled. "Clearly someone's listening. . . . Are you all right?"

"As long as I don't have to wash and find out what I taste like," Arhu muttered, "yes." He trotted hurriedly for the sidewalk, or what passed for it: in this neighborhood, this meant "where the mud was only an inch thick instead of three or four."

They crouched against the brick building there and looked up and down the road. It was plainly Tower Hill, running into Great Tower Street as usual, but the street names were different—George Street and Great Tower Hill—and the traffic was mostly pulled by horses. Not that that made it any slower than modern London traffic: if anything, it looked to be moving a little faster.

People walked past them, some well dressed, some seemingly poor but clean though somewhat threadbare, some practically in rags: and no one seemed to notice the mud. A few heads turned when one of the motor vehicles passed, though. Rhiow couldn't tell whether it was because they were unusual, or simply because of the noise they made. Apparently the muffler had not yet been invented.

"Now what are *those* doing here?" Urruah said. "Internal combustion engines aren't until the turn of the century."

"Neither is the word for smog," Rhiow said, looking up at the dingy, near-opaque sky, "but that doesn't seem to have stopped these people: they've got that, too."

"What time would you say this is?" Rhiow said. "The light is so peculiar."

Urruah shook his head. "Late afternoon? Not even smog could make it this dim."

"I wouldn't be too sure," Rhiow said.

"Everything here feels wrong," Arhu said. "All of it." His face had lost the disgusted expression it had worn a moment before: his eyes looked slightly unfocused.

"You're not kidding," Urruah said. "Something's happened to history . . . and I don't like the look of it. Or the smell of it."

Rhiow curled her lip at the smell from the street. "This would have been here anyway," she said, picking up one forefoot out of the mud. "The kind of sanitation we take for granted in our own time was something these *ehhif* were only beginning to see the need for. And their technology's not up to it, even if they *did* see the need. There are more people in this city than in almost any other in the world, and all they've got are brooms and dustpans . . . and four million *ehhif* and a quarter million horses inside the city limits." She smiled grimly. "Work it out for yourself. How many cubic miles of—"

"*Please,*" Urruah said, and sneezed.

They started to walk, looking for someplace clean. They found no such place, at least in the public roads. Only the moat surrounding the Tower led up to patches of green grass beneath the old stone walls. Their structure was unchanged from what Rhiow had seen in modern London, but they were stained black by who knew how many years of air pollution. Slowly the three of them made their way around toward the river, looking down it from a spot that would have been close to where Rhiow and Arhu had stood only a few hours before.

"This is all wrong," Arhu whispered. Across the river was a great palisade of buildings, all of which were taller than architecture of the *ehhif*-queen Victoria's time could possibly have been.

"This stuff shouldn't be here," Arhu said. "And look at that."

They looked at the great bridge, crowned with its pyramidal towers and boasting its high cross-walkway, which appeared on so many of the postcards and T-shirts the *ehhif* sold near Tower Hill Underground station. "That's wrong too," Arhu said.

Rhiow looked at him. "Are you sure? Even in our world, it's pretty old—"

Urruah stared off into the distance for a moment as he cocked an ear to listen to the Whisperer. "He's right, though," he said presently. "She says that in our world, this wasn't built until eighteen eighty-six. No matter what year this is in the spread we're heading for, that's still too soon."

"Interesting," Rhiow said, and shook herself to abort a beginning shiver. "Something to do with the technology, maybe?"

"They've got a whole lot too much of it, if you ask me," Urruah said.

"Of technology?" Rhiow said, and looked around her. Overhead, something very like a helicopter went by in a loud chatter of rotors. What she couldn't understand was why a helicopter needed flapping wings as well.

"Of the wrong *kind* of technology," Urruah said. "Rhi, this timeline has been contaminated . . . *seriously* contaminated."

"And you don't think it's an accident."

"Do you? Really?"

She looked around her at the vista down the river, of cranes standing up and erecting new buildings of steel and plate glass, but still somehow in a style that was essentially Victorian, complicated and, to her eye, overdecorated. She looked down the face of the river, which was full of shipping—not sail, as at least some of that shipping still should have been, but metal ships, running on internal combustion or (in just a very few cases, as in a technology that was rapidly being left behind) steam. She saw the design of many of those ships that were making their way to and from the Pool of London: lean, low, forward-thrust, angular shapes such as she had seen often enough in New York Harbor—battleships and cruisers in the modern mold, all fanged with guns and other weapons she couldn't recognize. There were a lot of those warships: they came and went as regularly, it seemed, as the tour ships that ran up and down the Thames in Rhiow's native time. For all its bustle of business and its aura of *ehhif* success and power, this London also had a grim air about it.

"No," Rhiow said. "This contamination is purposeful. The Lone One has been busy here."

"Very busy, I'd say," said Urruah. "And the contamination has to have happened a good while ago: not even *ehhif* can make changes like this overnight. We've got to find out when this alternate timeline was seeded."

Rhiow looked around her and lashed her tail in frustration. "We're going to have a good time finding that out," she said. "We can't just ask the *ehhif.*"

"We can ask People," Arhu said.

"Yes," said Rhiow, "but which ones? We could waste a lot of time talking to the wrong sources . . . and I have a feeling time isn't something we dare waste here."

They walked down to the edge of the river, looking up and down its length. The water was olive-colored and filthy, and it stank. A few desultory seabirds floated on it, or fished optimistically among the weeds and garbage for something to eat. Above it all, the dirty air billowed, unpleasantly visible.

"For all their technology, they've been oddly selective about how they use it," Urruah said. "They obviously have electricity, but why are they still burning coal in their dens? There's internal combustion being used out on the water, but why so little in the streets—why all the horses and dirt?"

"It looks like some of the *ehhif* have access to this technology, but not all that many," Rhiow said. It was a problem that their own world shared, though not quite in this way.

"You were right," Arhu said suddenly, "about it being late afternoon."

"Oh?" Rhiow said.

"Yeah. Look, the Moon's coming up."

They looked eastward down the river. Through the dirty haze, a dim round source of light had managed to rise above the buildings cluttering that end of the Thames basin. She looked at it, irrationally relieved that at least something was performing as expected around here.

But then she heard Urruah gulp. Rhiow took another look as the Moon lifted a little higher above the thickest of the murk.

"That's not our Moon," Urruah said softly.

The shape was right. The phase was gibbous. But the

face, the face was blotted with darkness, its surface scarred: not with the usual dark *maria,* but with massive craters and fissures, and great plumes and patches of dark dust.

Urruah sat down. Rhiow was too shocked to move at all.

"What in Iau's name has happened here?" she whispered.

"It's sure not the Moon we started with," Urruah said.

Rhiow couldn't take her eyes off it. "Well, even our moon at home isn't the one we started with. Things happened to it after it was born."

"But there are stories about that," Urruah said. "Not the things you mean. It was pure white, once, without a mark. Then the Lone Power in her feline form came, and saw it, and hated it. Sa'Rráhh blotted it with Her paw that was all newly stained with night, with the death She had invented. She could never bear that anything should remain the way the One made it, if She had anything to say about the matter."

"I thought the Moon was supposed to be the Old Tom's eye," Arhu said.

"Of course it is," Rhiow said. "And it's also just a big piece of rock splashed out of the Earth in its formative stages. It'd be a poor kind of world where there was just one explanation for things."

Urruah looked away from that terrible Moon to give Rhiow a wry look. "Think of it as a conditional hyperquadratic equation," he said to Arhu. "Depending on conditions and context, the same equation gives you different answers at different times. But all the answers are correct. Mythology, philosophy, and science are just three different modalities used to assess the same data, and they can coexist just fine, if you let them. In fact, they'll do it just fine whether you let them or not: they have other business than sitting around waiting to see whether *you* approve."

Arhu looked up at the smudged Moon and shivered. "I don't like it," he said.

"Believe me, you're not alone there," Rhiow said softly. Written there dark above them was a blunt, nasty restatement of the reason why there were wizards. The world, which should have been perfect, was marred: marred with and by malice long aforethought. The shadow-smudged, crater-scarred Moon of their own world was evidence enough of the Lone Power's effect in both symbolic and "real" modes. The terrible destructive force that had struck the Earth very young, in what looked like one of the earliest attempts by the Lone One to prevent the rise of life and intelligence there, had not missed. Rhiow still wondered sometimes whether It had slightly miscalculated Its aim, or whether the Powers That Be had Themselves interfered, interposing Their power just enough to help the huge mass of magma splashed out of the planet's still-molten body to draw itself together and congeal in near orbit. Even when mending the marred, They never overexerted Themselves, all too aware of the energy needed for the long battle lying ahead of them through this universe's lifetime. No attempt would have been made to fly in the face of natural law and try to get life to arise on the second world. It would have been left to cool at its own pace, its low mass mandating the loss of the sparse store of atmospheric elements that arose from it during the cooling: and all the while the fury of the frustrated Lone One would have been allowed to mark itself on the barren Moon in storm after storm of meteoric impacts, eons of merciless cratering, and the punctured crust flooding the Moon's surface with the last flows of lifeblood-lava that hardened dark into the great *maria*, the lighter elements at last all boiled away into the freezing dark of space. A dead world, now, with the mark of the Devastatrix's dark paw pressed on it, livid and chill—a clear message: *I missed, this time. But I will never rest until I finish what I began.*

The message seemed to have been much more forcefully stated in *this* universe, though. *I am much closer to finishing,* it seemed to say. Though Iau only knew what It had been up to.

"I think going home would be a good idea," Arhu said.

"Believe me, I'm with you," Urruah said, "but we have a few things to do first. We need to find out what year this is, if we can—"

"No," Rhiow said. "No, I think Arhu's idea is a good one."

"What?"

"Listen to me," Rhiow said. "Every minute we stay here makes it worse. Potentially, anyway. No, listen! Urruah, there's no question that this contamination has happened. Our being here has confirmed it . . . has made it real for us. And you know what *that* means. What's happened at *our* end of time?"

She watched Urruah start to look a lot more concerned. There was a variant of what some *ehhif* called the Heisenberg uncertainty principle that pertained to alternate universes. While you might postulate the existence of an alternate, even be faced by evidence of its existence—as Rhiow's team and the London team had been—that universe did not really "exist" for you until you visited it. Once you did, and its reality had become part of your own—not by consensus, but by direct experience—your own universe also then began to change as a result. This was one of the principles that made wizards so chary of indulging in pleasure trips outside their own universe. For one thing, there was usually plenty of pleasure to be found locally . . . and for another, once you came back from an alternate-universe jaunt, there might be no "locally" left: or not one you would recognize.

Arhu was looking from Rhiow to Urruah and back again with some confusion. "What's the matter? Is something wrong back home?"

"She's saying there might *be* no more home," Urruah said, glancing around him, "the longer we stay here. Fortunately, timelines don't wipe themselves out in a matter of seconds, the way people think, when there's a change. Causality is robust, and it tries hard to stay the way it is to begin with: the variables in the equation will slosh around for a good while before an alternate universe settles fully into place. As a rule," Urruah said. "Unless the change is so big that causality just can't resist it at all."

They all looked up at the scarred Moon again. Rhiow shuddered, then she said, "Remember when we were talking about gating offplanet? Personal small-scale gating, I mean: via a spell-circle of your own construction . . ."

Arhu looked at Rhiow.

"I think this would be a good time for you to go ahead and do it," she said to Arhu. "Mind the radiation: there's a fair amount of it, once you're out of the atmosphere's protection. All you need is a standard forcefield spell, the one we were working with last month. You can build the defense against the ionizing radiation into the forcefield at the same time you're loading in enough air to last you for the visit."

Arhu looked at her and licked his nose. "You have to wonder," Urruah said, looking away from the Moon with difficulty, "what could cause that kind of effect. I think we need to find out."

There was a long silence. "Would you come with me?" Arhu said.

Urruah glanced at Rhiow. "I'm sure he could handle it

himself," he said. "But just this once . . ." And he glanced up at the Moon again. "That is so bizarre."

They walked a little farther down the riverbank to find a place where there was less mud, just under the shadow of the Tower's walls. There was an old disused dock there, leading a little way out into the water. Gratefully enough they stepped up onto it, and Arhu headed down toward the end of it, where recent weather or wavewash had mostly scoured the rotting planks clean. Here he started to walk the circle they would need, leaving the pale tracery of graphics in the Speech behind him as he walked and muttered.

Urruah watched him with an expert's eye. "He's been practicing that one for a while," he said.

Rattled as she was, Rhiow couldn't help but smile. "The way you've been practicing that timeslide?"

"Uh, well." Urruah sat down and started to wash his face, then made a face at the taste of his paw, and stopped. "Rhi, you know I wouldn't step out of bounds. Not on this kind of stuff. It scares me."

"It's sure scaring *me,*" Rhiow said. "I can't wait to get back—it's like fleas under the skin, the fear. But it can't be helped. We need to do this first."

Arhu had finished the first layer of his circle and had tied the wizard's knot: now he was laying in the coordinates for the Moon and the pockets that would trap and hold adequate air inside the spell for the three of them. "It was a nice piece of work, regardless," Rhiow said. "That slide."

"Thanks," Urruah said. "It didn't get much approval in some quarters, though."

"Oh?"

"Fhrio."

"Just what the Snake *is* his problem?" Rhiow muttered.

"I don't know. Just generalized jealousy, I think. Or else he just really is territorial about anything to do with 'his' gates. I never thought I'd see a Person so territorial. I swear, he's like an *ehhif* that way."

"Maybe he was one in his last life," Rhiow said, putting her whiskers forward. There were numerous jokes among People about how such an accident might happen, mostly suggesting that it was a step up on the scale of things for the *ehhif*.

"Please," Urruah said. "It makes my head hurt just thinking about it."

Arhu stopped, looked up at them. "You want to come check your names?"

They walked over to the circle and jumped into it. Rhiow examined her name and found everything represented as it should be, but there was something odd about one of the symbols that was normally a constant. It was a personality factor, something to do with relationships: it was suggesting a change in the future, though whether near or far, Rhiow couldn't tell.

"Where did you get this?" she asked, prodding the symbol with one paw.

Arhu shrugged. "It came out of the Knowledge: ask the Whisperer."

Rhiow waved her tail gently at that. Sometimes such things happened to a wizard who routinely did a lot of spelling: you saw a change in the symbology before it had reflected itself in your own person, or before it seemed to have so reflected itself. Then you were faced with the question of changing it back to a more familiar form—and wondering whether you were thereby keeping yourself stuck in some situation that was meant to change gradually—or leaving it the way it was, and wondering what in the worlds it might mean. Rhiow took a long breath, looking at it, and left it alone.

Urruah straightened up, apparently having found nothing

untoward in his own name, and said, "It looks fine. Is everything else ready?"

Arhu stared at him. "You're not going to check it?"

"Why should I?" Urruah said. "You passed your Ordeal: you're a wizard. You're not going to get us killed." He sat down and started washing again, making faces again, but this time persisting.

Rhiow sat down too, there being no reason to stand. "Go on," she said to Arhu, "let's see what we see."

Arhu looked around him a little nervously, then stepped to the center of the spell and half closed his eyes, a concentrating look. Rhiow watched with some interest. Spelling styles varied widely among wizards of whatever species: there were some who simply "read" the words of a spell out of the Whispering, and others who liked to memorize large chunks; some who preferred the sound of the words of the Speech spoken aloud, and some who felt embarrassed to be talking out loud to the universe and preferred to keep their contracts with it silent. Arhu was apparently one of these, for without a word spoken—though Rhiow could feel, as if through her fur, that words in the Speech were being thought—she felt the spell starting to take: checking for her presence and Urruah's, sealing the air in around them, and then the transit—

—abrupt, quicker than she was used to, but that was very much in Arhu's style. One moment they were looking at the dirty river flowing between its sludgy banks, and the foul air snuggling down against it: then everything went black and white.

And brown. She had not been prepared for the brown: it was a strange note. They were standing on a high place, one of the Lunar Carpathians, she thought, a fairly level spot scattered with small, grainy rocks and the powdery pumice dust typical of even this area, which had suffered its share of meteoric impacts, exclusive of impacts of other types. The sphere of air held around them by the spell shed frozen oxygen and nitrogen snow around them at the interface between it and vacuum: the snow sifted out and down a little harder, sliding down the outside of the invisible sphere invoked by the spell, when any of them moved slightly and changed the way the wizardry compensated for their presence.

The brown lay streaked over the white and gray-black of the craters around them. It was ejecta from another impact, a much larger one, some miles away if Rhiow was any judge. She looked all around them for its source, but the crater was well over the short lunar horizon.

More than six miles away, anyway, she thought, glancing over at Arhu. He was licking his nose repeatedly. "Are you all right?" Rhiow asked.

"Yeah," he said, "but the spell's not. Radiation."

"The problem won't be the Van Allen belts," Rhiow said. "We're well away from them. Solar flare, possibly."

Urruah gave Rhiow a look. *You are an optimist,* he said silently.

"I don't think so," Arhu said. "I need a better look. Come on."

He started to walk upward as if on a stairway: a good trick, Rhiow thought, if he was using the air trapped with them to do it. She got up and carefully went up after him, none too concerned about the actual instrumentality at the moment—and much more concerned that the bubble of air should follow them all up, as Urruah came stepping carefully up behind her. She also took some care with how she went in the low gravity. Falling off Arhu's invisible stairway, and down and out of the spell, would be unfortunate.

The spell followed them with no problems: its diameter was at least ten meters, and Arhu had apparently designated himself as its center. They walked upward for perhaps a quarter mile before Arhu stopped, standing there in the middle of nothing and looking down on the desolate landscape. Rhiow looked down too, and drew in a long, painful breath. The crater off to the northward, the one that had produced the brown ejecta, lay plain before them. It was at least five miles in diameter, and ran all the way to the far horizon northward. Great fissures ran from it, in all directions but mostly toward the north. The bottom of the crater was glazed as if with ice, but it was not ice: it shone with a bitter, brittle gleam under the slanting light of the Sun.

"So what would you make it?" Urruah said after a moment's silence. "A megaton or so? And there are a lot more of these. Some particularly big impacts up in the northern hemisphere . . ."

Rhiow's tail lashed furiously. "The only good thing about this," she said, "is that they did this up here and not on Earth. But still—what a message."

"Yes indeed," Urruah said. "For every other pride of *ehhif* in the world to see, every time the Moon comes up. 'Look what we could do to you, if we wanted to.' The question is, which *ehhif* down there are doing it?" He glanced at the gibbous-waning Earth hanging above the horizon.

"When we come back," Rhiow said, "we're going to have to find out. The Lone One has seen to it somehow that these people have been given the most dangerous technology they could possibly get their hands on. With the assumption, I'm sure, that they'll certainly destroy themselves. What we're going to have to do is fly in the face of that certainty and stop it."

"If we can," Urruah said. He sounded rather muted: even his supreme self-confidence was having trouble dealing with this.

"Space travel as well," Arhu said. "They can come up

here and see what's here . . . and then they do *this*." He was bristling.

"If we're very lucky, we may be able to keep them from doing worse," Rhiow said. "But even here, I don't want to linger. The longer we stay in this universe, the more we endanger our own."

"Let's get back down then," Urruah said. "The timeslide won't have self-activated yet, but that doesn't matter. It functioned: that part of our test is a success. We can come back when we need to. And as for this . . ." He too was fluffed up as he looked down around him.

"Arhu," he said after a moment, "I'm sorry. You shouldn't have seen it this way, your first time out."

"No, it's all right," Arhu said. "We needed to do it: you were right. But let's go home."

He paused, standing there on nothing, and narrowed his eyes. A second later they were standing on the old dock by the Thames again, and Rhiow's ears were ringing with the *Bang!* of displaced air that accompanied their appearance. There were *ehhif* walking by the river, farther eastward, but they paid no attention to the sound at all.

"They probably think it's a car backfiring or something," Urruah muttered.

"Maybe so," Rhiow said, "and I'll be glad to get back where that kind of perception is normal for its time. Come on!"

They made their way as quickly as they dared, sidled, back to Cooper's Row, the street where the other end of the timeslide was sited. It was hard to avoid the *ehhif* sometimes, they were so crowded together, and Rhiow was bruised or kicked more than once as the team made its way toward the timeslide.

They were about to break into a run across the noise and muck of George Street again, when to Rhiow's complete astonishment, Arhu, ahead of her, suddenly darted through a thicket of walking legs and westward down George Street. "Arhu!" she cried. "What are you—"

"Just two blinks!" he said, and dodged around a corner. Rhiow and Urruah crowded against a nearby building, staring after him. Not quite two blinks later—more like two blinks and a quick scrub—he reappeared, dodging among the *ehhif.* He was unsidled, and had something large and white in his mouth: it flapped as he came. *Ehhif* pointed and laughed at him as he ran.

He ran straight past Urruah and Rhiow, and straight across George Street, weaving expertly to avoid the traffic. Rhiow and Urruah threw each other a look and went after him. All three made it to the far side together, as more horse carriages and a few more of the antique cars came splashing and rattling down through the mud at them.

Arhu was spattered but triumphant. "I saw an *ehhif* drop it," he said, and dropped it himself, going sidled again.

"How could you see him around the corner?" Urruah said, while Rhiow peered curiously at the thing. It said, THE TIMES, AUGUST 18, 1875, and everywhere else it was covered with small fine print in *ehhif* English. It would hardly have passed for a newspaper in New York; it seemed to have only three pages and no pictures.

Arhu wrinkled up his nose. "I mean, I See him," he said. "I still See him now, even though he did it already. *Au,* Rhiow, the way we talk about time doesn't work right for talking about vision. I need new words or something."

"One last check," Urruah said, and held his head up as if sniffing for something. Rhiow looked at him, bemused.

"What?" she said.

"I've been feeling around me with a detector spell ever since we got here," Urruah said. "But to no effect. You remember Mr. Illingworth? Well, there's no sign of him."

"You mean, after all this, *he's not from here?*"

"I don't know what it means," Urruah said, "and at the moment, I'm not going to hang around to find out. Come on!"

Arhu picked up the paper again, coming unsidled as he did so, and they headed down the little street together, keeping to one side, for there were some *ehhif* passing up and down it together. Urruah stopped at one point and felt around with his paw in the mud. "All right," he said, "there's the tripwire. Now if these *vhai'*d *ehhif* will just go away."

It took some minutes: there were several false starts in which the street would look like it was going to be clear, and then another *ehhif* or two or three would come along from one end or the other. This left Rhiow with nothing to do but watch her own tension increase, and try to reduce it. *Oh, please let the world still be there when we get back, our own world, please!* Meanwhile, Arhu had to keep dropping the paper and picking it up, to avoid being seen by the *ehhif.* "It's all right, isn't it?" he said suddenly. "Bringing things back?"

"Or forward in this case?" Rhiow said. "Yes. Things are all right. Anything alive, that's where the complications start."

"Quick," said Urruah. The street was empty, and he had pulled the tripwire. The circle of the timeslide spell sprang into being around them. "Ready? Brace yourselves. . . ."

Rhiow tried, but against that awful pressure there was no way you could brace, nothing you could do but endure as everything, light and breath and almost life, was squeezed out of you. *Hang on,* she thought, *it can't last much longer, hang on—*

—and suddenly things were dark again, and Auhlae and Fhrio were looking at them, bemused, from outside the circle.

"What's the matter?" Auhlae said. "Didn't it work?"

"Perfect!" Urruah said. "Right to the tenth of a second." The rest of his pleasure in the accuracy of his spelling got lost for Rhiow in a rush of astonishment and delight that the world seemed, by and large, to be the way they had left it. But the delight didn't last. She couldn't get rid of the image of that other world's Moon, and of the certainty that, unless they could work out what had gone wrong and what to do about it, their own Moon would look that way before long. Urruah was right: reality resisted being changed. But it could not resist such change indefinitely, and the rumbling dark of the Underground tunnels almost immediately looked a lot less welcome, and began to look rather like a trap.

"We should get everyone together," she said to Auhlae. "If you thought you had trouble with random temporal accesses, when we show you what we've found, you'll wish a few stray pastlings were *all* you had."

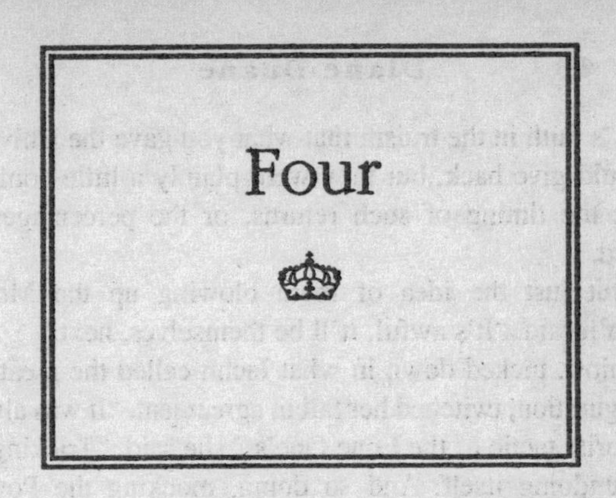

Four

"They have *nuclear weapons?"* Huff said.

"Whether they're exactly weapons the way we would define them, I don't know," Rhiow said. "We were hardly there long enough to guess anything about their delivery systems. Do they have missiles? I haven't a clue. But do they know how to produce large nuclear explosions? You'd best believe it."

Relative silence fell in the corner of the pub where the London and New York gating teams sat that evening; the only other sound was the occasional dinging and idiot music played by what the London team referred to as the "fruit machines." Rhiow much wished the machines, ranged around the back wall of this room of the pub, would emit something as innocent as fruit instead of the deafening shower and clatter of one-pound coins that came out of them every now and then when *ehhif* played with them. As evening drew on and the Mint started to fill up, the hope of a pile of those coins was starting to keep the machines busy with *ehhif* who drifted in, fed the machines money, and then shook and banged them when they didn't give it back again, with dividends. It was, in its way, a charming illustration in some *ehhif* 's faith in the truism that what you gave the Universe, it would give back, but they were plainly a little confused about the timing of such returns, or the percentages involved.

"But just the idea of them blowing up the Moon," Siffha'h said. "It's awful. It'll be themselves, next."

Rhiow, tucked down in what Iaehh called the meat loaf configuration, twitched her tail in agreement. "It was always a favorite tactic of the Lone One's," she said. "Tricking life into undoing itself. And so doing, mocking the Powers, which tend to let life take care of itself, by and large."

"They were lucky not to bring the whole thing down on top of them," Fhrio said. "Imagine if they had hit one of those deep lunar mantle faults and blown it apart. Just think of the tidal effects on the Earth . . . and then the fragment impacts later."

"I'm sure sa'Rráhh would have been delighted," Huff said. He was lying on his side, finishing one more wash after acting as courier for yet another round of snacks for the assembled group. "I wouldn't say that was her main intent in this case, as Lone Power, but it would have been entirely acceptable. As it is, it looks like the poor *ehhif* back then have been given the quickest way for an unprepared or immature species to kill itself off . . . tried and tested in other parts of this galaxy and others. And if that universe settles fully into place before we can dislodge it, we'll find ourselves living on the Earth that's a direct historical successor to that one. If 'living' is the word I'm looking for . . . because we'll be in the middle of the nuclear winter."

"Well, all we have to do now," Siffha'h said, "is figure out what to do about this."

"Oh, yes, *that's* all," Fhrio said.

Rhiow paid no more attention to this remark than the others seemed to be doing, instead glancing over toward the corner. Half hidden by the arrangement of a couple of the fruit machines, Arhu's newspaper was spread out on the floor, and he was bent over it, carefully puzzling out the words. Rhiow had always found it useful that understanding of the Speech let a wizard understand other written languages, as well as all spoken ones. Normally she didn't get too carried away by this advantage, but Arhu had been turning into a voracious reader of *ehhif* printed material of all kinds, everything from the big advertisements posted up here and there in Grand Central to scraps of newspaper and magazines that humans dropped on the platforms, or the complete papers that Urruah fished out of the garbage bins at regular intervals. Urruah had claimed, with some pride, that Arhu was taking after him in his erudition. Rhiow agreed, but was clearer about the reasons for it. Arhu was nosey, nearly as nosey as Urruah, and with a taste for gossip and scandal nearly as profound. She couldn't really complain: that insatiable curiosity was part of what made them good at being wizards. At the same time, sometimes the habit drove Rhiow nearly crazy. Urruah's endlessly relayed tales about the sexual peculiarities and mishaps of *ehhif* made her wish very much that Urruah would read more of the kind of newspapers that did not feature headlines like HEADLESS BODY IN TOPLESS BAR.

What had become immediately plain was that, in 1875 at least, *The Times* of London was not that kind of newspaper. There was hardly anything to it. A front page that was almost entirely classified ads, both commercial and private: then interior pages that reported what seemed to the publishers to be important news—most of it having to do with *ehhif* from the pride-of-prides, "Britain," or other prides closely associated with it—and then long reports about what was going on in the place where the pride-rulers sat, the "Houses of Parliament."

"This is mostly a lot of small stuff," Arhu said, glancing up at the others in the momentary quiet. "*Ehhif* buying and selling dens to live in, and renting them out: or asking other *ehhif* to come and work with them: or buying and selling little things, or asking other *ehhif* to help them find things they've lost. Some other news about shows and plays they want *ehhif* to go to: and then news about the pride-ruler and what he does all day. That's the interesting part: It's not a queen. It's a king."

Huff breathed out heavily. "Then the old queen is dead in that eighteen seventy-five," he said. "There's a major change. In our world she lived on almost into the next century."

"But the world's different, that's for sure," Arhu said. "They have all kinds of things that the Whispering says weren't there in our world's eighteen seventy-five. A lot of machines like our time's *ehhif* have: even computers, though I don't think they're as smart as the ones in our time. And they've definitely got space travel, though it's as it is in our world: only the pride-rulers use it. I think it's for weapons too, mostly."

"Orbital?" Fhrio asked.

"I don't know," Arhu said. "They don't seem eager to talk about it in here. They talk a lot about war, though. . . ." He ran one paw down the page. "See. Here's the bombing that the Illingworth *ehhif* was talking about: 'The Continental powers have once again defied the King-Emperor's edict by using mechanical flying bombs based at Calais and Dieppe to strike at civilian targets in the south of Sussex and Essex. The Royal Air Force, led by units of His Majesty's Eighth Flying Hussars, succeeded in destroying nearly all elements of the attack, but several flying bombs were knocked off course by the defending forces and impacted uncontrolled in suburban areas of Brighton and Hove, causing civilian casualties and destruction to a large area. The Ministry of War has announced that these attacks will be the cause of the most severe reprisal at a time of the Government's choosing.' "

Arhu stopped, his tail twitching slowly. Fhrio was growling under his breath. "This island has not been bombed since the second of the great *ehhif* wars in this century," Huff said. "That they should have been doing such things then. . . . Does it say what they mean by 'the Continental powers'?"

Arhu looked at the paper, reached out, and carefully turned the middle leaf of it over with his paw. "I don't see any specific pride names," he said. "Maybe they expect everybody to know what they're talking about."

Huff sighed. "There's no question that this is useful," he said, "but it's not nearly enough to base an intervention on. How I wish the Whisperer could throw some light on this."

Rhiow shook her head. "She seems unable to discuss what's happening in an alternate universe," she said. "Is it possibly outside the Whisperer's brief? Would it be speculation, even for her? Which, as we know, is something she won't indulge in. Or is this simply something we're supposed to have to find out for ourselves?"

"Whichever," Urruah said, stretching, "the result is the same. But I wouldn't take too long about it. That other universe has become real . . . and now it and ours are going to be starting to fight it out for primacy between them, though we can't feel the effects at the moment."

"We will soon enough." Fhrio growled. "The gates will be the first symptom. When something starts going wrong with them—"

"You mean besides what's going wrong already," Arhu said.

Fhrio sat up, glaring at Arhu, and lifted one paw. Urruah looked over at Fhrio.

"I wouldn't," he said. "Anybody gets to shred his ears for tactlessness, it's me. Arhu, don't you think your tone was a little snide?"

"Sorry," Arhu said, not sounding very much so. Rhiow sighed.

Arhu had gone back to reading the back page of his paper. Rhiow watched this process with amusement that she hoped was well concealed. Besides being useful, the paper had given him an excuse not to try to speak or even to look at Siffha'h for the whole early evening so far. "Hey, listen to this," he said, and began reading aloud with some difficulty, not so much because of the words themselves as because of how odd some of them seemed in context. "It's who Mr. Illingworth was talking about."

"What?" Rhiow said. Even Siffha'h sat up at that.

"I think it is, anyway. 'Maskelyne and Cook—Dark Seance. The latest novelty and most startling performance ever presented to the public . . . the seance includes the floating of Luminous Instruments, distribution of flowers with dew, appearance of materialized spirit forms, spirit hands, spirit arms, strange and apparently unearthly voices, music extraordinary, the inexplicable Coat Feat, all accomplished by Messieurs Maskelyne and Cook while bound hand and foot, the ropes secured with knots executed by the most perfect adepts in the art of rope-tying, elected by the audience.' " He paused and looked up. "That doesn't sound like such a big deal."

"It does if you're an *ehhif* and not a wizard," Urruah said. "We have *ehhif* like that at home: they do shows where they pretend to be wizards. Without the ethical element, anyway. It's 'magic' rather than wizardry; mostly they pretend to do things that would normally kill them, and make things disappear."

Fhrio muttered something under his breath. Rhiow, having occasionally shared what she suspected was Fhrio's sentiment, had to put her whiskers forward just a little. " 'In addition to the great sensation, the Dark Seance of exposés of so-called spiritualism,' " Arhu read, " 'the following leading features amuse the audience at the present program: Mr. Maskelyne's extraordinary comical illusions, extraordinary Chinese plate-spinning, lady floating in air, the animated walking-stick, the Tell Tale Hat, etc.: the original and inexplicable Corded Box Feat is performed at every representation. Every afternoon at three, every evening at eight.' " Arhu looked up again. "Spiritualism?"

Rhiow shook her head and started to tilt her head sideways to listen to what the Whisperer might have to say, but Siffha'h said suddenly, "It's where *ehhif* used to think that their dead still stayed around to speak to them after they were gone. The live *ehhif* would try to get advice from their dead ones, and ask them what was going to happen in the world . . . things like that."

"But it doesn't work that way for *ehhif,* surely," Auhlae said, sounding dubious. "When they go, they're gone, aren't they?"

A pang went through Rhiow. She stared at the floor for a moment while trying to manage it, aware of Urruah looking at her but not saying anything, just being there.

"And no matter what happens to them, I wouldn't think the advice of the dead would do the living much good in any case," Auhlae said. "Surely that must have occurred to even *ehhif.* Their priorities would be very much different."

"Nonetheless, some of them wouldn't care," Rhiow said. "Some of them miss each other very much, and they don't have the kind of knowledge we have, it would seem, about what happens to them afterwards. All they have are a lot of different stories that mostly disagree with one another." She swallowed. "It makes them feel very afraid, and very alone."

Auhlae was looking at her. "I'm sorry," she said. "My apologies, Rhiow. I hadn't realized . . ."

"It's all right," Rhiow said, though how long this statement would stay true, she wasn't sure: she tried to keep a grip on herself. "She's somewhere safe, my *ehhif,* though I haven't any idea of what she does there, how she is or what she knows, probably any more than she would normally have had of what awaited me after any given life. Maybe it's a privacy thing that the Powers preserve between species and species. Our paths cross, we live together, we part—is it really our business where *ehhif* go? Or theirs, what happens to us?"

Auhlae said nothing, merely looked at Rhiow with eyes thoughtful and a little sad. Rhiow sat still for a moment and did her best to master herself, while the back of her mind shouted *Yes it is, yes!* She held very still and concentrated on her breathing, and on not looking like an idiot in front of the others.

"Well," Huff said after a moment, "we still have a fair number of problems to deal with."

"You're not kidding," Urruah said. "I'm still trying to work out what in the worlds the 'Tell Tale Hat' might be."

"Besides that," said Huff, "Mr. Illingworth, who has been to see Maskelyne and Cook, is another problem. You said you didn't find any trace of him in that universe."

"No," Urruah said, "and I'm at a loss to know why. The most likely possibility that occurs to me is that that *wasn't* the universe we were heading for, but a close congener."

"An *alternate* alternate universe?" Siffha'h said.

"You might as well call it that," Urruah said. "When you start messing with timelines, altering them, whole sheaves of new universes are created from each branching point—some of them very likely, some of them less likely, some of them hardly there at all. The more likely they are, the more likely you are to come across them. Think of them as 'waves' in a wave tank that is chiefly populated by the two universes that are trying to achieve equilibrium. You get troughs and crests of probability and possibility as the two universes attempt to absorb one another's energy—and matter, though that's a more problematic process. The sheaves of alternates don't persist for long. As one universe or the other starts winning the argument, the other's 'alternates' vanish. Then, last of all, the universe that spawned them vanishes too; dissolves into the other one, all its energy absorbed. I think Illingworth came from the sheaf of 'possibles' surrounding the main one."

"So you're going to have to alter your timeslide's settings to find the 'core universe,' the one that engendered all these others," Fhrio said.

"Yes," Urruah said, "and as yet, I don't know *how* they're going to have to be altered, or how to construct a spell to tell it how to manage the alteration. Also, I don't understand why the settings I saved from Illingworth's gating didn't lead us straight back to his home universe. Add that to your list of problems."

"You seem to know more about timeslide theory than the rest of us," Huff said to Urruah. "Do you have any sense of how much time we might have to work in, at this end of things, before that other reality starts to supersede ours?"

"Maybe as long as a month, but I wouldn't care to bet on it," Urruah said. "My guess would be more like days—at least I think it'd be safest to play it that way."

"But, but it's just dumb!" Siffha'h burst out. "The Powers wouldn't just let an entire reality be wiped out! They'd send some kind of help!"

"They did," Rhiow said. "They sent us."

Siffha'h opened her mouth and shut it again. "But if we can't do anything about it, They'll help: They have to!"

"Do they?" Huff said. "Where does it say that in the Whispering? Listen hard."

She did, and her mouth dropped open one more time.

"You need to understand it," Rhiow said. "*We are all the help there is.* The seven of us are, apparently, the best answer the Powers That Be can offer up to this particular problem. If we fail, we fail, and our timeline fails with us. It would be nice to assume that if something goes wrong, one of the Powers will drop down out of the depths of reality to pull us up out of trouble by the tail. But such things don't normally happen: the Powers have too little power to waste. There is nothing particularly special about our timeline, except to us, because we live in it: it has no particular primacy among the millions or billions of others. For all we know, other timelines have been wiped out because of such attacks, and because their native wizards couldn't act correctly to save them. Myself, I wouldn't much care to ask the Whisperer about that at the moment: the answer might depress me. Let's just assume we must do the job ourselves, and get it right. Huff?"

He thumped his tail once or twice on the floor in disturbed agreement. "There's nothing I can add to that."

For a few moments everyone looked in every possible direction but at each other, unnerved. Then Arhu sat upright and stared toward the front room of the pub. "Oh, no, here he comes."

Rhiow looked around to see what he was talking about, but no one but their own two groups was anywhere near them. "What?" she said.

"I See him a few minutes ago," Arhu said, sounding slightly put out. "I was hoping he might change his mind, or the Seeing might turn out to be inaccurate, but no such luck. Get sidled."

They all did but Huff, who looked curiously at Arhu, then turned his head, distracted. A young *ehhif* was heading over toward the fruit machines. He was one of a type that seemed common in that part of the city, a suit-and-tie sort with a loud voice and his tie thrown over his shoulder. As he came, he was suddenly distracted by the presence on the floor of a sheet of paper. *The Times.* He bent down to pick it up.

"Oh, for Iau's sake," Arhu growled, and put one invisible paw down on the paper. Rhiow watched with interest as the *ehhif* failed to get the paper to come up off the floor: tried to pick it up again, and failed, and failed again. He got really frustrated about it, trying to get even just a fingernail under one of the newspaper's corners and peel it up, and failed at that as well, managing only to break a couple of nails. The *ehhif* straightened up again and walked off swearing softly to himself.

"Nice one," Auhlae said. "How'd you do that?"

"Made it heavy for a moment, that's all," Arhu said. "It was part of a tree once, after all. I just suggested that it was actually the *whole* tree." He put his whiskers forward. "Paper fantasizes pretty well."

"You'd better make it invisible as well," Huff said mildly. "He'll be back here with my *ehhif* in a moment. I know what that kind gets like when they're confused, or balked."

Arhu shrugged his tail. A moment later, when Huff's tall, dark-haired *ehhif* came back, there was no paper there, or seemed to be none, only Huff, lying at his ease and finishing his wash. Huff's *ehhif* took one look at the floor and saw nothing but his cat lying there and looking at him with big, innocent green eyes. Huff blinked, then threw his rear right leg over his shoulder and began to wash. His *ehhif* raised his eyebrows, and headed back to the bar.

Huff finished the second bit of washing, which had been purely for effect, and glanced over at Arhu. "Does that happen to you often?" Huff said.

"You mean Seeing? Once a day or so . . . sometimes more. I wish it was always about important things," Arhu said, looking rather annoyed, "but usually it's not. Or I can't tell if they're important, anyway, till they happen. The trouble is, they all feel important . . . until it turns out they're not."

"How very appropriate," Siffha'h murmured, and looked away.

Arhu gave her a look that had precious little lovesickness about it: it smelled more of claws in someone's ears. He opened his mouth, probably to emit something unforgivable, and Rhiow, concerned, opened her mouth to interrupt him; but at the same moment Huff said, "Arhu, have you thought of going to see the Ravens?"

"Who?"

"The Ravens over at the Tower. They have a problem rather similar to yours."

"Are they wizards?" Rhiow asked, curious.

"No," Huff said, "but they have abilities of their own that are related to wizardry, though I'd be lying if I said I understood the details. They are visionaries of a kind, though I wouldn't know if they describe the talent to themselves in precisely those terms. In any case, the few times I've talked to them, they've sounded very like Arhu. Rather confused about their tenses." He put his whiskers forward to show he didn't mean the remark to be insulting. "They might be of use to you . . . or to us, possibly, with this problem."

Arhu looked thoughtful. "Okay," he said. "It can't hurt."

"No, I would think not. Now, Urruah will be working on resetting his timeslide, recalibrating it—"

"It'll take me a day or so," Urruah said. "I want to explore as many of the possibilities as I can, as many of the universes in the sheaf, when we do our next run."

"And meanwhile there are a couple of other things we're going to need to find out," Rhiow said. "First, if there's any way to manage it at all, we must find the original contaminating event or events. If it happened using your gates, the logs may give us some hints . . . if we can ever get them to yield that data, which Urruah hasn't yet been able to do. If we can't find evidence from the gates, then we're going to have to go back to that alternate time again, much as I dislike the prospect, and search for information there. The other thing we must discover is the nature of this attack on the *ehhif*-queen, Victoria"—Rhiow went out of her way to try to get her pronunciation as close to the *ehhif* word as she could—"and also discover whether this great change in the past-world we saw would have happened anyway, or has something specific to do with her death or life."

"It very well could," Auhlae said. "She was a tremendous power in her time, though she had very little direct power—compared to some of the pride-leaders who went before her, anyway. Certainly they would have gone to war had she been assassinated, and if they were able to prove that some other pride they knew of had been involved. There was fierce rivalry between them for a long time: the shadows of it remain, though most of the *ehhif* powers in Europe are supposed to be working together now."

"Huff," Rhiow said, "how much do you know about *ehhif* history of that time? The eighteen seventies, say?"

"Very little," he said. "It's hardly my speciality: like most of us, if I need to know something I go to the Whisperer." He looked thoughtful for a moment. "But you know," he said, "there are People for whom it *is* a speciality. And they don't live far from here. In fact, there's one in particular who's famous for it. He used to live at Whitehall, but now he's out in the suburbs. You should go to see him. I'll show you the coordinates, and you can lay them into one of the other gates."

"That sounds like a good idea," Rhiow said. "Would he be available today, do you think?"

"More than likely. Probably your best bet is simply to go out there and meet with him."

"All right. What's his name?"

"Humphrey."

Rhiow blinked. "That's not a Person's name. . . ."

"It is now," Huff said, amused. "Wait till you meet him."

"Meanwhile, I think the rest of us will be minding the other gates," Fhrio said, "and watching to see if they start betraying any sign of instability. If they start acting up, we'll know we have less time to deal with our troubles than we thought."

Rhiow nodded. "And as for the rest of it," she said, "we'll meet again when it's dark, and see who's best sharpened their claws on the problem before us."

The others agreed, then got up and shook themselves preparatory to heading off in their various directions.

"Now look at this," Arhu said, crouched down again, and oblivious. " 'Princess Christiana of Schleswig-Holstein visited His Majesty and remained to lunch.' "

Urruah looked up. "Does it say what they had?" he said, coming to gaze at the paper over Arhu's shoulder.

Rhiow glanced over at Huff and wandered over to him. "You look tired," she said. "Are you all right?"

"Oh, I'm well enough," he said. "Rhiow, we're all too old for this! Except for *them*," and he indicated Arhu and, off on the other side of the room, already heading for the back door, Siffha'h. "But no matter . . . we'll cope." He sighed, looked at her, as Auhlae came wandering over and laid her tail gently over his back. "It's just hard, sometimes, discovering that after a long period of steady and not terribly dangerous work, your reward for getting it right is that you get to save the Universe." His look was dry.

"It's always dangerous to demonstrate talent," Auhlae said. "Least of all to Them. But that's our job: we accepted it when it was offered us . . . and what can we do now?"

"Do it the best we can," Rhiow said. "There's nothing else."

She rubbed cheeks with Huff when he offered, and did the same, a little more tentatively, with Auhlae. The two of them headed off toward the front of the pub; and Rhiow made her way out toward the back, and the cat door, thinking thoughts of quiet desperation but determined not to give in to them.

✦

Half an hour or so later, Rhiow was padding down a street in one of the northern suburbs of London, looking for a specific house in one small street. She had a description of the house, and a name for a Person: or rather, that peculiar *ehhif* nickname that Huff had given her. According to the Knowledge, the nickname (bizarrely) came from an *ehhif* television show, and was a reference to an astute but extremely twisty-minded politician. Rhiow was uncertain whether any Person, no matter how jovial, would really want to be called by such a name.

She found the house at last. It was actually bumped sideways into another house, in a configuration that the *ehhif* here called semidetached. There was a narrow wall of decorative concrete blocks about four feet high separating the two houses' front yards and driveways. Rhiow jumped up onto this and made her way back to where it met another wall, taller, one that divided the houses' two back gardens from one another. This was actually less a wall than a series of screens of interwoven wood, fastened end to end. Rhiow jumped up onto the nearest of them and paced along it and the subsequent screens carefully, looking down on the leftward side, as she had been instructed.

The rightward garden was less a garden than a tangle of weeds and rosebushes run amok. The left-hand one, though, had a lawn with stepping-stones in it, and carefully trimmed shrubs, and small trees making a shady place down at the far end. There was a birdbath standing in the shade, but no bird was fool enough to use it: for lying near the birdbath, upside down in the sun, was a black-and-white Person with long, fluffy fur.

Rhiow paused there for a moment looking at him as he dozed, wondering how to proceed. From a tree nearby, a small bird appeared, perched on a nearby branch, and began yelling "Cat! Cat! Cat!" at Rhiow.

She rolled her eyes. One of the great annoyances associated with becoming a wizard was, oddly, identical with one of its great joys: learning enough of the Speech to understand readily the creatures around her. It was very hard to eat, with a clean conscience, anything you could talk to and get an intelligible answer back. "In your case, though," she said to the small bird, "I'm willing to make an exception."

Except that she wasn't, really. Rhiow sighed and turned her attention away from the bird, to find that the black-and-white Person's eyes had opened, at least partially, and he was looking at her, upside down.

"Hunt's luck to you!" she said. "I'm on errantry, and I greet you."

He looked at her curiously, and rolled over so that he was right side up again. "You're a long way from home, by your accent," he said. "Come on down, make yourself comfortable."

Rhiow jumped down from the wall and walked over to

the respectable-looking Person, breathed breaths with him, and then said, "Please forgive me: I don't know quite what to call you."

"Which means you know the nickname," he said, and put his whiskers forward. "Go ahead and use it: everyone else does, at this point, and there's no real point in me trying to avoid it."

"Hhuhm'hri, then. I'm Rhiow."

"Hunt's luck to you, Rhiow, and welcome to London. What brings you all this way?"

She sat down and explained, trying to keep the explanation brief and nontechnical. But Hhuhm'hri was nodding a long time before she finished, and Rhiow realized that this was one of the more acute People she had met in a while, with a quick and deep grasp of issues for all his slightly ditzy, wide-eyed looks.

"Well, that's certainly a *different* sort of problem," Hhuhm'hri said. "At first I'd thought perhaps you were one of the People who's just been added to the standing committee on rat control."

Rhiow restrained herself from laughing. "No, the problem's a little different from that."

"Certainly a little more interesting. I must say I wouldn't want our timeline to be wiped out, either, so I'm at your disposal. Though I must admit that the temptation to alter just one piece here or there, with an eye to improving things, must be very strong."

"By and large it doesn't work," Rhiow said. "There are conservation laws for history as well as for energy. Remove one pivotal event without due consideration, and another is likely to slip in to take its place—often one that's worse than the one you were trying to prevent."

"Conservation of history . . ." Hhuhm'hri mused for a

moment. "That's the only odd thing about this, to me: if such a principle exists, why isn't it protecting you in this case?"

"Because of the nature of the Power that has intervened to cause the change," Rhiow said. "Mostly time heals itself over without a scar if the change is small, or made by a mortal. But when the Powers That Be become directly involved—and in this case, one of the oldest and greatest of Them—the fabric of time is entirely too amenable to Their will. It's unavoidable: They *built* time, after all. . . ."

Hhuhm'hri blinked. "Yes," he said. And then he added, "You'll forgive me a second's skepticism, I hope. One doesn't often expect to run into one of Them, or Their direct deeds, in the normal course of the business day."

"Of course," Rhiow said, at the same time thinking that, from the wizard's point of view, that was all anyone *ever* ran into, but this was not the moment for abstract philosophy.

"Sa'Rráhh, eh," Hhuhm'hri said after a moment. "So the bad-tempered old queen's at it again. Well, I'll help you any way I can: we'll play the Old Tom to her Great Serpent, and put a knife or two into her coils before we're done. I may not be walking the corridors of power anymore, but all my contacts are still live . . . in fact, I have rather more of them since I came out to the green leafy confines of suburbia."

Rhiow cocked her head. "I'd heard something about your retirement," she said, "from the Knowledge: but even the *ehhif* in New York noticed it. A lot of talk about you being thrown out of Downing Street—and then maybe murdered."

Hhuhm'hri put his whiskers right forward and sprawled out, blinking at Rhiow like a politician after a three-mouse lunch followed by unlimited cream: and he smiled like someone who could say a lot more on the subject than he was willing to. "It wasn't that bad," he said. "At least, as far as political scandals go." Though a lot of *ehhif* had thought it was. The new prime minister's wife, a suspected ailurophobe, had dropped a few remarks on moving into Number Ten that indicated that she thought cats were, of all things, "unsanitary." The remarks had provoked so massive an outbreak of *ehhif* public concern for "Humphrey" that an official statement from the government had been required to put matters right, making it plain that Humphrey's normal "beat" was the Cabinet Office and Number Eleven, and his position was not threatened. Shortly after that had come the photo opportunity. Rhiow had been looking over Iaehh's shoulder at the television one night and had chanced to catch some of those images: the lady in question looking conciliatory, but also rather as if she very much wished she was elsewhere, or holding something besides a cat, while "Humphrey" gazed out at the cameras, as big-eyed in the storm of strobe-flashes as a kitten seeing a ball of yarn for the first time. "Glad it wasn't me," Rhiow said. "I wouldn't have known what to do in a situation like that."

"You hold still and pray you won't walk into anything when she finally puts you down," Hhuhm'hri said, amused. "Sweet Queen above us, ten minutes straight of flash photography! I was half blind at the end of it. But other than that, I did what I had to. I shed on her." He put his whiskers forward in a good-natured way. "What *else* could I do? What kind of PR advice was she getting, to take a photo call with a black-and-white cat in a black suit? Did they expect me to stop shedding in one color? She should have worn a print, or tweed. Well, she was only new to the job. She's learned better since. While I stayed there, I steered clear of the children, by and large, which is mostly what she was worried about. No point in tormenting the poor woman. Then my kidneys began to kick up, and I thought, why should I hang about and distract these poor *ehhif*? They've got enough problems, and my replacement's trained. So I took early retirement—and there was a press scandal about that, too, unavoidable I suppose—but I was happy enough to let 'Harold' move in at Number Ten, and go off to get the kidneys sorted out and settle into domestic life. I still have more than enough to do."

"Not just the rats, in other words."

"Oh, dear me, no. As I said, now that I'm quartered out here, People who might otherwise attract notice if they came to see me in Downing Street don't feel shy about it anymore. No more cameramen hanging about all hours of the day and night . . ." He yawned. "Sorry, I was up late this morning. Tell me what kind of help you need from me, specifically."

"Advice on personalities," Rhiow said. "I need to know what People can best help us in that time, in the eighteen seventies . . . ideally, in the target year itself, where their intervention will do most good. We think it's eighteen seventy-five. The possible error, my colleague thinks, is a couple of years on either side."

"Eighteen seventy-five," Hhuhm'hri said. "Or between eighteen seventy-three and eighteen seventy-six. Not a quiet time . . ."

He mostly closed his eyes, thinking, and for a few minutes he lay there in the warm, dappled shade and said nothing. Rhiow waited, while above a growing chorus of small birds scolded at them, and her mouth began to water slightly at the thought of foreign food, whether she could talk to it or not.

"Well," Hhuhm'hri said suddenly as Rhiow was beginning to concentrate on one small bird in particular, a greenish yellow creature with banded dark wings and a bright blue cap who was hanging temptingly close on a branch of a dwarf willow. "There are certainly a fair number of resources: though the Old Cats' Network was really only getting started then. One in particular should be of best use to you, though. 'Wilberforce' told me about something that had come down to him from 'George,' or maybe it was 'Tiddles,' the one who owned Nelson . . . something concerning the British Museum's cat at that point. 'Black Jack,' the *ehhif* called him. An outstanding character—he worked at the museum for something like twenty years, and what he didn't know about the place, or about things going on in the capital in general, wasn't worth knowing. He passed everything he knew down to his replacement, 'young Jack'—and it's through that youngster that a lot of information about that time comes down to us. Either one of them would be the one you'd want to talk to, but I can give you a fair amount of the information that has come down from them, so that you'll start to get a sense of what questions you need to ask. How much background do you need?"

"All you can give me."

"Is your memory that good?" Hhuhm'hri said, looking thoughtful.

"It can be when it has to be," Rhiow said. "I can emplace everything you say to me in the Whispering as I hear it. I won't be much good for conversation while you're at it, but it'll be accessible to me and the rest of my team afterwards, and any other wizards who need the information."

"That's very convenient."

"It is," Rhiow said, though privately she thought that what would not be convenient was the headache she would have afterward. "If you'll give me a moment to set up the spell, we can get started."

✦

It was nearly five hours later that she made her way out of Hhuhm'hri's back garden: The Sun was going down, and even the dimming sunset light made Rhiow's eyes hurt. Her whole head was clanging inside as if someone were banging a cat-food can with a spoon. *And I'm ravenous, too,* she thought, heading back to the vacant lot into which she had originally gated. *Parts or no parts, if I go straight home after this, I'm eating whatever Iaehh gives me.*

It had been worth it, though. Her brains felt so crammed full of *ehhif* political and nonpolitical history of the 1870s that she could barely think: and after a sleep, she would be able to access it through the Knowledge, as if taking counsel with the Whisperer, and sort it for the specific threads and personalities they needed. It helped, too, that Hhuhm'hri's point of view was such a lucid one, carefully kept clear of uninformed opinion or personal agendas. It had apparently been an article of honor for the long line of Downing Street cats to make sure that the information they passed down the line was reliable and as free from bias as it could be, while still having an essentially feline point of view. They counted themselves as chroniclers, both of public information and of the words spoken in silence behind the closed doors of power, in Downing Street and elsewhere: and they suffered the amused way *ehhif* treated them, put up with the cute names and the often condescending attention, for the sake of making sure someone knew the truth about what was going on, and preserved it. Not that there hadn't been affection involved, as well: Hhuhm'hri had been quite close to the prime minister before the present one, and Churchill's affection for the People he lived with had been famous—Rhiow could not get rid of the image of the great *ehhif* sitting up in bed with a brandy and a cigar, dictating his memoirs and pausing occasionally to growl "Isn't that right, Cat Darling?" to the redoubtable orange-striped "Cat," veteran of the Blitz, who had worked so hard to keep his *ehhif*'s emotions stable through that terrible time.

They were an unusual group, the Downing Street cats: genuine civil servants, and talented ones. Over the many, many years they had been in residence, they had learned to understand clearly *ehhif* speech of various kinds—the first "cabinet" cats, dating back to the pride-ruler Henry VI, had been *ehhif*-bilingual in English and French—and they were assiduous about training their replacements to make sure the talent wasn't lost in this most special of the branches of the Civil Service. *Not quite wizards,* Rhiow thought, *though there may be wizardly blood in their line somewhere, or occasional infusions of it from outside.* For not all the Downing Street group were related. They were a *rrai'theh,* a working pride without blood affinities, part of the much larger pride that referred to itself as the Old Cats' Network. Rhiow wondered if, as in other nonwizardly cats, another talent to "spill over" from wizardly stock had been the one for passing through closed doors unnoticed. She suspected it had; in their line of work, such an ability would have been invaluable.

She made her way down to the Tower Hill Underground station with her head still buzzing with Hhuhm'hri's briefing. It was unnerving, the way thinking about *ehhif* affairs for four or five hours straight could make you start looking at the world the way they did. Rhiow wasn't sure she liked it. *Oh well, an occupational hazard.* But the one word that seemed to have come up most frequently in Hhuhm'hri's reminiscences was "war." Try as she might, Rhiow could not understand why *ehhif* could kill each other in such large numbers for what seemed to her completely useless purposes. Fighting for land to live on, for a territory that would provide food to eat, *that* she could understand. All People who ran in prides, from the microfelids to the great cats of this world, did the same. But they usually didn't kill each other; a fight that resulted in the other pride running away was more than sufficient. If they tried to come back, you just drove them away again.

Ehhif, though, seemed not to find this kind of fighting

sufficient. What troubled Rhiow most severely was tales of *ehhif* killing one another in large numbers for the sake of land that was nearly worthless—going to war simply because they had said that a given piece of land was theirs and some other *ehhif* had disputed the claim. Or when they went to war for the sake of prestige or injured pride: that was strangest to her of all. And it seemed to her, from what Hhuhm'hri had told her, that the pride-of-prides, which its *ehhif* called Britain, had gone to war for all these reasons, and for numerous other ones, over the past couple of centuries. Granted, they had done so genuinely to preserve their own people from being killed as well: the second of the great conflicts of this century had been one of that kind, and the British had defended themselves with courage and cleverness at least equal to their enemies'. Nevertheless, Rhiow was beginning to think she knew who most likely would have blown up atomic weapons on the Moon in 1875, if they'd had access to them.

And how did *they get them? And how can we undo it?*

It was going to take time to work that out. At least they had a little time to work with, but not much.

She made her way among the *ehhif* at the Underground ticket machines and past them, under the gates and down to the platform where the malfunctioning gate and its power source were being held. Hhuhm'hri had told Rhiow that thousands of *ehhif* had hidden in tunnels and basements near here during the bombings of London in that second great war. That had resolved, for Rhiow, the question of something she had been feeling since she came down here first—a faint buzzing in the walls, as if at the edge of hearing: the ghost-memory in the tunnels and the stones of *ehhif* sleeping nearby in the faintly electric-lit darkness. Their troubled and frightened dreams still saturated the bricks and mortar of the tunnels—and "behind" them, if you were sensitive to such things and you listened very hard, you could just catch the faintest sound of the shudder and rumble of falling bombs. That unsound, intruding at the very edge of a sensitive's consciousness, could easily get lost in or confused with the rumble of present-day trains through the stone.

At least I know what it is now, Rhiow thought, making her way to the platform and jumping up. *A relief. I thought I was going a little strange.*

Only Urruah and Arhu were there just now. "'Luck," Rhiow said, going over to breathe breaths with Urruah, who was sitting and looking at his timeslide-spell, apparently taking a break after having done an afternoon's worth of troubleshooting. The timeslide was presently lying quiescent on the platform floor, in a tangle of barely seen lines. "How's it going?"

"Slow," he said. "I wanted to have another look at the disconnected gate's logs before I started changing my own settings around."

"Find anything useful?" Rhiow asked, glancing over at Arhu. He was tucked down in meat loaf configuration with his eyes half closed, unmoving.

"No," Urruah said, following her glance and looking thoughtful. "But, Rhi, I think the logs are being tampered with."

She sat down, surprised. "By whom?"

"Or what," Urruah said. "I can't say. Normally when a gate's offline, its logs are frozen in the state they were in when the gate was taken off. I hooked the gate up again briefly to the catenary to have a look at the way the source has been feeding it power—and found that some of the logs weren't the way I remembered them. In particular, the logs pertaining to Mr. Illingworth's access were in a different state than they were when I left them. Specifically, temporal coordinates were not the same."

Rhiow looked around her and then said privately, *Fhrio?*

I don't think so. For one of us to tamper with gate's logs would normally leave marks that an expert can see, alterations in the relationships between the hyperstrings of the gate. Now, I'm an expert, and I can't find any marks. Still . . .

You're not sure. Rhiow's tail switched.

No, I'm not. If it's not Fhrio, though, I'd be tempted to look farther inward.

The Lone Power, Rhiow thought.

Urruah hissed softly. *Rhi, I* know *It's been meddling in the larger sense. The contamination of the 1875-or-thereabouts timeline is certainly Its doing. But by and large It's not going to do something like* this. *It's still one of the Powers That Be, and shares Their tendency not to waste effort Itself when It can get someone closer to the problem to do the dirty work. Myself, I'm going to keep an ear on one of us a little closer by.*

She had to agree with him there. "So what are you going to do?" she said aloud.

He shrugged his tail. "Try the altered coordinates," he said. "Or at least lay them into my timeslide and see what happens when we try to access them."

"It could very well be a trap of some kind," Rhiow said.

"Yes, but we don't have to put our foot right into it," Urruah said. "We can look before we jump. A habit of mine."

Rhiow put her whiskers forward. "All right. Anything else?"

"Well, one other possibility," Urruah said. "I think our problem in finding Mr. Illingworth's home universe, or not finding it, may have to do with the timeslide still being powered out of the malfunctioning gate's power source. We noted from what few logs were left from the microtransits earlier that the far end of the gate-timeslide was lashing around in backtime, like the end of some *ehhif*'s garden hose when they let it go with the water running at full pressure. The end whiplashes around, coming down first here, then there . . . never the same place twice. I think the fault for that could possibly lie in the power source rather than the gate."

Rhiow blinked at that. "I can't see how. The power source isn't supposed to have any coordinate information in it, or anything like that. . . ."

"I'm not sure how either," Urruah said, "but what else am I supposed to think at this point? The gate itself wasn't connected to the power source, but we still had a failure in my timeslide, although it was a small one. Big enough, though, in terms of what we were trying to do." He sighed. "I think the next time we try this, we should keep the timeslide off the gate's power source and power it ourselves."

"That's going to be hard on you," Rhiow said.

"Yeah, well, I don't see that we have the option," Urruah said.

"Excuse me," someone said pointedly from behind them.

They both looked over their shoulders. Siffha'h was sitting there behind them.

"I couldn't help overhearing," she said. "But you *do* have a power source. What about me?"

Urruah blinked. "Uh. I hadn't—"

"—thought about it? Or maybe you just don't trust me because I'm young yet." Her tone was very annoyed.

"Siffha'h," Rhiow said, "give us the benefit of the doubt, please. We're very aware that our being here at all imposes on your team somewhat. We're unwilling to impose further when there's any way that—"

"Look," Siffha'h said, "our whole reality is going to be rubbed out if we can't stop what's happening, and you're telling me you don't want to *impose?* Come on."

Rhiow glanced at Urruah, rueful but still somewhat amused. "Well," she said, "you've got a point there. 'Ruah?"

He looked at her with his tail twitching slowly. "You are unquestionably hot stuff," he said, "and anytime you want to power a timeslide of mine, you're welcome."

"You build it," Siffha'h said, "and I'll see that it takes you where you want to go. When'll you be ready?"

"Tomorrow afternoon, I think."

"Good. I'll be here."

She strolled off, tail in the air. Rhiow glanced over at Urruah. *She really does remind me of Arhu sometimes.*

Yeah, Urruah said. *In the tact department as well.*

Rhiow put her whiskers forward. *You know how it is when you're young,* she said. *Life seems short, and all the other lives a long way away. You want to be doing things.*

So do I, Urruah said. *Preferably things that'll solve this problem.* He looked rather glumly at the spell diagram for the time-slide.

"All right," Rhiow said. "Anything else that needs to be handled?"

"He said he wanted you to see what he saw," Urruah said, glancing over at Arhu, who was still crouched down in meditative mode. "I'm going to look at it later; right now this is more of a priority."

"Right."

Rhiow went softly over to Arhu: then, as he didn't react, she sat down by him and began to wash—not only because she didn't want to interrupt him in whatever he was doing, but because she felt she badly needed it. She was tired, and needed to do something to keep herself from falling asleep. Rhiow had just finished her face and was starting on one ear when she felt something thumping against her tail. It was Arhu's tail; he had come out of his study and had rolled over to his side to look up at her.

"You wash more than anybody I know," he said. "Are you nervous or something?"

She looked at him, then laughed. "Nervous? I'm terrified. If you had a flea's brain's worth of sense, you would be too."

"I'm scared enough for all of us," he said. "Especially after what I saw today."

"You went to see the Ravens," Rhiow said. "How was it?"

"Weird." He put his ears back. "I'm not sure I understood most of it, but I put it all in the Whispering, the way you showed me."

"Good," Rhiow said. "I'll have a listen, then." She crouched down, tucking her paws under her in the position Arhu had been using: comfortable enough to let go of the world around and concentrate on the inner one, not so comfortable that she would fall asleep. *Well,* she said silently to the Whisperer, *what has he got for me?*

This.

Normally the voice you heard whispering was Hers, the familiar, steady, quiet persona, ageless, deathless, and serene. But material the source of which was a mortal being would come to you strongly flavored with the taste of its originator's mind. Knowing Arhu as well as Rhiow did, this was a taste with which she was also familiar. But now, as the point of view changed to early afternoon on the riverbank, suddenly Rhiow found herself immersed in the full-strength version of it—a quick, excitable, excited turn of mind, by turns cheerful and annoyed at a moment's notice, interested in everything and with a taste for mischief . . . though also with a very serious side that would come out without warning. Rhiow actually had to gasp for a moment to catch her breath as she bounded, with Arhu, down the walkway that led to the main gateway to the Tower: past the *ehhif* who were lined up at the gate, letting the security guards there check their bags and parcels: through the gateway, looking up at the old, old stones of the arch, and through, into a cobbled street that Arhu's memory identified as Water Lane.

This little street ran parallel to the river inside the main outer wall. To the left, as Arhu went, was another wall studded down its length with several broad, circular towers: this ran on for about an eighth of a mile, to where the outer wall came to a corner and bent leftward. The stones in the left-paw wall were mostly rounded, as if they had come out of a river, but some had been cut down roughly into squarish shape, and they looked and smelled ancient. From them, as Rhiow had from the bricks and stones of the Underground, Arhu caught a faint sense of much contact with *ehhif,* but the flavor was strange, a compendium of old, faded triumph and equally old, abject fear. Arhu paused for a moment, feeling it on his fur, feeling it especially strongly from the right side when he passed a latticework gateway of metal that let out to an archway leading down to the river. *Traitor's Gate,* the Whispering said in his mind: and just briefly, as he did then, Rhiow saw, in a flicker, the way Arhu Saw with the Eye.

A flicker, there and gone. *Ehhif* standing up, *ehhif* lying down and being brought up to the gate in boats, *ehhif* dying and in fear of dying coming in, *ehhif* dead going out: queen-*ehhif* and tom-*ehhif,* proud, dejected, defiant, afraid, bitter, reluctant, confident, desperate: plots and schemes, offended innocence, furious determination, all rolled together in a moment of vision, all spread out over long years of history, circumstance, and confusion; the conflicting needs and desires, the long-planned machinations of the powerful and the requirements of the moment, terror-horror-resignation-life-death-brightness-sickness-cold-blood-release-*darkness*—

—gone. The Eye closed, and Arhu stood and shook his head, trying to clear it: and an *ehhif,* not seeing him since he was sidled, tripped over Arhu, caught himself, and went on, looking behind him to try to see the cobblestone he thought he had stumbled on.

"Ow ow ow ow," Arhu spat, and took himself over to the leftpaw wall to recover himself a little. From inside the left-paw wall came a harsh cawing, a little like *ehhif* laughter, as if someone thought it was funny.

While he stood there and panted, Rhiow shivered all over at the thought of the burden Arhu was bearing. *Better him than me,* she said, somewhat ungraciously, to the Whisperer. The vision Arhu had been trying to describe to her turned out to be more like half-vision, and all the more maddening for it. For Arhu was looking, just briefly, through the eyes of Someone Who saw everything in the world as whole and seamless: thoughts, actions, past causes and present effects, the concrete and the abstract all welded into a single staggering completion. Rhiow understood a little of Arhu's confusion and anger now, for trying to extract one piece of information from the all-surrounding vastness of the Whisperer's perception seemed impossible, like trying to fish one drop of water out of your water bowl with your claw. You would always get a little bit of something else along with it—or a *lot* of something else. Rhiow thought with embarrassment of the facile way she had been telling him to concentrate, and grab hold of one part of it.

More, she now understood much better his confusion about tenses: for in the Whisperer's mind, the world was *finished,* a made thing, a completed thing, though one that was constantly changing. It was a harrowing point of view for a Person to try to assimilate, or for any mortal being who lived in linear time and generally thought that one thing happened after another, and that the future was still indeterminate. It was not, to *Her.* The Whisperer, in Her mastery, saw it all laid out. The only place where Her uncertainties lay was in what *you* would do to change the future, in which case everything you did also became part of the ongoing completion, a law of the universe, as if it had been laid down so from the very beginning. The two visions of the future did not exclude one another, from Her point of view; they actually complemented one another, and made sense. To Rhiow, that was the most frightening concept of all.

She breathed out, wondering how she would apologize to Arhu for so completely misunderstanding what he had been dealing with, as Arhu got back his breath and his composure, and headed on down Water Lane again. Just across from Traitor's Gate was an opening into the central part of the Tower complex, through a building called the Bloody Tower. He went under this archway as well, and turned immediately left.

Built into the wall here was a house with many long peaked roofs, the Queen's House: and in front of it were arches with iron bars set in them. Behind those arches were some low, wizened trees and shrubs . . . and in the trees, and under at least one of the shrubs, sat the Ravens.

Arhu had known they would be large, but he hadn't thought they would be as large as a Person. Most of them were, though, and at least one of them, which perched on that stone wall, above the bars, was as big as Huff: as big as a small *houff.* They were all resplendently glossy black, and they looked down at him and, to Arhu's astonishment, saw him perfectly well, even though he was sidled.

"Look," one of them said. "A kitty."

"Oh, shut up, Cedric," said another of them. "You had breakfast."

Arhu licked his nose and sat down, trying to preserve some dignity in the face of so many small, black, intelligent, completely unafraid eyes staring at him. "I, uh, I'm on errantry. Hi," Arhu said.

"And we greet you, too, young wizard," said one of the

Ravens. There was a muffled noise of cawing from the far side of Tower Green: Arhu looked over his shoulder.

"How many of you are there here?" he said. "Should I go over and say hi to them, too?"

"No, they're minding their territories at the moment," said the Raven. "After all, the place is full of tourists. Later in the day, when the warders chuck them all out and lock the place up, we can all get together in the quiet and the dark and have a chat. Meanwhile, anything you say to me, they'll know. They can See it, after all."

"I'm sorry," Arhu said, "but I don't know what to call you. There are *ehhif* names on the sign over there, but—"

"No, it's all right: we use their names," said the biggest of the Ravens. "It's a courtesy to them, and from them: they've made us officers in their army, after all." She chuckled. "Even if we're only noncoms. So I'm 'Hugin,' and that's 'Hardy.' " She pointed with her beak at the Raven sitting below her. "We have other names that we tell to no one, that come down from the Old Ones, but we can't give you those. Sorry."

"Uh, it's okay. But look, is it right what the sign says over there? That the *ehhif* think this place would 'fall' without you? Fall down?"

"Cease to exist," said Hugin.

"Of course the place would fall without us," said another of the Ravens. "We've always been here. It doesn't know how to be here *without* us."

"How long is always?" Arhu said.

"How long does it have to be?" Hardy said. He was a little thinner than the others, a little smaller, which might have been deceptive, but the eye, that black, wise eye, seemed to say that this was the eldest of them. "Since there were buildings. And before that: since there were humans, what you call *ehhif*. We Saw your People come, too: We Saw them go, when the city first was burned. We stayed, and the dead . . . no others."

Arhu controlled his desire to shudder. With their great ax-like beaks, there was no mistaking these birds for anything but what they were—meat-eaters—and there was no mistaking what they would have eaten, from time to time, in this city where there had so often been large numbers of dead *ehhif. Or People, for that matter,* Arhu thought.

"It's all right," another of the Ravens said. "By the time we eat somebody, they don't mind anymore. And these days we mostly don't, anyway. The Wingless Raven gives us chicken breast." The Raven clattered its beak with pleasure. "Very nice."

"If you've been here that long," Arhu said, "you must have seen a lot."

"Even if *we* hadn't been," Hugin said, "we would still be Seeing it now. William the Conqueror: I See him walk by a puddle, right over there, and a cart goes through it and gets his hose wet, and he swears at the man driving the cart and pulls him out of his seat, throws him down into the water, too. The Romans: I See them walking their city wall, looking at the cloud of dust as Boudicca and her chariots come riding. Over there." She gestured with her beak at the remains of the wall, like a bumpy sidewalk, that stretched from past the Wardrobe Tower remains to the Lanthorn Tower, along the green that had once been the site of the Great Hall. "And poor Anne Boleyn. There she goes, over to the block. Over there." She turned and pointed with her beak in the other direction, over toward Tower Green. "Very dignified, she was. That used to be a great concern for them. And there he goes running by, one of them who didn't care about dignity so much." She pointed over to the little corner building that was presently the Tower gift shop, but once was the home of the Keeper of the Jewels. "Colonel Blood, with the Crown stomped flat and hidden under his wig, and the Rod with the Dove down one boot. He almost gets away with that, too."

"And it was you Saw that *then*?" Arhu said. "You must be pretty old." He let the skepticism show in his voice a little.

"Oh, not *us*," said Hardy. "Our ancestors. Though we See what they See: that's our job. And eventually the humans noticed that we were always here, and for once they came to the right conclusion, that the place needed us. They started trying to protect us—very self-enlightened, that. Though there have been times when the population has dropped very low." He glanced up at the sky. "During the war—the last big one here—almost all of us died except old Grip. The humans got very worried. And well they might have, with the V2s and the buzz-bombs coming down all around them. But we knew it would be all right. We Saw it then, as we See it now."

"That's why I've come," Arhu said. "It may *not* be all right, soon, in a very large-scale sort of way. We need help to find out how to stop what we think is happening from happening." He looked around him. "All this could be gone. . . ."

"No," said Hardy, "of course it won't. *This* will still be here." He squinted up at the pale stones of the Tower. "It will be *dead*, of course. No people . . . and eventually, even no Ravens. No nothing, just the dark and the cold, and the thin black cloud high up that the Sun can't come through. The wind crying out for loneliness . . . and nothing else."

"You mean it's going to happen," Arhu whispered, shocked.

"I mean it already *has* happened," said Hardy. "Now it's just a matter of Seeing how it happens otherwise. You know that: for you have the Eye too, don't you?"

"Yes. I'm not very good at it yet," Arhu said, suddenly feeling a little humble in the face of what was plainly another kind of mastery than his own.

"Oh, you will be, if you live," said another of the Ravens. "Give it time."

"I'm not so sure I'm going to have a lot of time to give it," Arhu said.

"Of course you will," Hardy said. "We're here in strength now, after all. Nothing will fall that we don't See fall first. And the more of us there are, the more certain the vision. When there was only one to See, that *was* a dangerous time."

"But there are a lot of you now."

"Oh, after this century's second war, all fortunes turned, if slowly," said Hardy. "Certainties returned. Also, we felt like breeding again. It's not like it is with your People—we don't do it unless we feel like it. And also, some of us came from other places to live here. The humans thought they brought us, of course, but we knew where we were going. We chose to come; we chose to stay."

Arhu wondered if this wasn't possibly slightly self-deluding. "But your wings are clipped," he said, rather diffidently, not knowing whether they might be insulted. "You couldn't fly away if you wanted to."

The Ravens looked at each other in silence for a fraction of a second, then burst out in loud, cawing laughter, so that some of the tourists on the other side of the Tower grounds turned to stare. "Oh, come on now," said Hugin, "surely you don't believe that, do you?"

"Uh," Arhu said. "I'm not sure I know what to believe."

"Then you're a wise young wizard," said another of the Ravens. "Why, youngster, we can go anywhere we please. We're the 'messengers of the gods,' of the Powers That Be, don't you know that? Even the humans know it. They're confused about which god, of course: they're confused about most things. But they still managed to give us use-names that are the same as the ravens they think served one of their gods, and went between heaven and Earth carrying messages. Hugin"—that Raven pointed at Hugin with its beak. "Actually she's Hugin the Second, after another one who went before her. And there's Munin the Second over there." The Raven speaking pointed at a third one.

"We go where we please," said Hugin. "You've been working with the People who manage the gate under the Tower, so you must know how we do it."

"You *worldgate?*" Arhu said.

"We transit. And we don't need spells for it, if that's what you mean," said another of the Ravens. "We don't need to use a gate that's been woven ahead of time and put in place, either. We see where to go . . . and we go. We find out what's happened, and we bring the news back. That's all."

Arhu sat down and licked his nose. "A long time now we have served Them," said Hardy. "We come and go at Their behest. That would be why *you* are here, for you're Their messenger, as we are."

"Uh," Arhu said.

Cawing came from farther up the wall: a noise of laughter. "Oh, come on, Hardy," said another raven-voice, "less of the oracular crap. Cut him some slack."

One more Raven flapped down beside Arhu, rustled his wings back into place, and paced calmly over to Arhu, looking him up and down. "No rest for the weary," it said. "But it's about time you got here. I got tired of waiting."

Arhu wasn't sure what to make of this, or of the amused way the other Ravens looked at the newcomer. "Odin," said Hardy, "have you been in the pub again?"

Odin snapped his beak. "The Guinness over there is improving," he said. "They've cleaned out the pipes since last month."

There was much muffled caw-laughter from some of the other Ravens. "Odin," said Hardy a little wearily, "is our local representative of the forces of chaos."

"You mean the Lone Power?" Arhu said, looking at Odin rather dubiously.

"No, just chaos." Hardy sighed. "Well, we all act up while we're still in our first decade, I suppose. Odin thinks it's fun to upset the Wingless Raven by getting up on the outer wall and gliding off across the road to the Queen's Head, when everybody knows perfectly well that none of us should be able to fly or glide that far at all. He walks in there and scares the landlord's dog into fits, and then the humans feed him hamburgers and try to get him drunk."

Arhu looked at Odin with new respect: any bird that could scare a *houff* was worth knowing. "Hey, listen," Odin said, "sometimes the Yeoman Ravenmaster needs to have his world shaken up a little. This way there's more to his life than just checking us over every morning and handing out chicken-breast fillets. This way, he wakes up in the middle of the night, every now and then, and thinks, 'Now how in the worlds did he *do* that?' " The raven chuckled, a rough, gravelly *arh arh arh* sound. "And it keeps him on good terms with the locals, because he has to keep coming over to the pub to get me back. After all, I can't *fly* or anything. . . ."

He roused his wings and waved them in the air, managing to make the gesture look rather pitiful and helpless. The other Ravens all laughed, though some of them sounded a little annoyed as well as amused.

"You Saw me coming here? I mean, you *See* me coming?" Arhu said.

"How would I not?" Odin said. "You've been busy. Worldgating of any kind attracts our attention: it's our business. Maybe it's why we're here. As for you, you were on the Moon recently," Odin said. "I See you there. Took you a while to manage that, too. I could get there quicker than you could, puss. And without needing spells."

"Oh yeah," Arhu said. "Well, maybe you could, *birdie*. In fact, maybe you'll show me how right now, because time's running out of things while we sit here and talk."

"He's right," said Hardy. "Well, Odin, will you make good your boast?"

"Of course I will," said Odin, sounding genuinely annoyed. "I Saw me doing it this morning, and so did you."

"*You,* though, weren't sure," said Hardy, "and you said as much at the time. You owe me a chicken breast."

Odin clattered his beak and then said, "I'm going to get a bite out of it first. . . . You See that, too, don't you?"

Hardy dropped the lower half of his beak, a gesture that looked to Arhu like a smile. He certainly hoped it was.

"The place I need to See," Arhu said, "it's an alternate universe. You do know that?"

Odin laughed. "Of course. So was the place where you went to the Moon. It's not a problem."

It's not? thought Arhu. *Iau, I hope he's right, because it would sure make things a lot easier.*

"I can tell you the coordinates for the world I'm trying to See," Arhu said. "If that's any help to you."

"You don't need to," Odin said. "I know where you're going, because I can See that we've been. All I was waiting for is you."

Time paradoxes, Arhu thought. *I thought they were kinda neat, but these guys don't seem to think any* other *way. I hope to Iau I don't get like this. I* like *keeping the past and future separate.*

"Can you ride me?" asked Odin.

"Huh? I think I might fall off," Arhu said.

"Not that way, puss. In mind."

"Since you ask, yes I can," Arhu said, somewhat annoyed. "And my *name* is Arhu."

"I knew that," Odin said. "But I couldn't know until you told me. Ready?"

The Raven huddled down under a nearby bush with his wings slightly spread out—a peculiar-looking pose. Hugin came soaring down from the stone wall, flapping her wings, and came to rest in the bush just above him. "Just a precaution," she said. "The tourists *will* come along while you're in the middle of something and tell their babies to go pet the pretty birdie." She snapped her beak suggestively. "Sometimes we have to disabuse them of the notion."

Arhu stepped through the bars and hunkered down not too far from Odin: closed his eyes, and felt around him in mind for the other's presence—

—and was caught, like a mouse, in a razory beak and claws. He struggled for a moment as something bit his neck, hard: he yowled, turned to get his claws into it—

—and everything settled into a kind of silvery darkness: no more discomfort; he was on the inside of the beak and claws now. He was soaring through what looked like cloud, faintly lit as if with twilight: the sense of day about to dawn, but in no hurry about it. The feeling was unlike skywalking, which Arhu enjoyed well enough, but this was less passive. He had wings, and the wind was in a dialogue with them.

Nicely done, something said in his head. *We could probably make a Raven of you, with about fifty years' work. Now show me the place you were in. Not the Moon, but the street.*

Arhu tried to see it again in mind as he had seen it in reality, but most of what he remembered was the smell. People's noses are wonderfully accurate and delicate. They can tell where another Person has been, or where an *ehhif* or *houff* has passed, for days afterward. But the blunting, smashing, awful weight of the smell in the London they had visited had ruined Arhu's ability to taste or smell most things for the better part of a day. Now he recalled that smell better than any other part of the experience: sickening, disgusting, like a shout inside your head, horse-bird-*houff-ehhif*-smoke-soot-garbage-shit-of-every-description. *Sorry,* Arhu gasped from inside the wings, inside the beak and claws.

Don't apologize; it's perfect, said the one who shared the inside-beak-and-claws with him. A tolerant young mind, wry, dry, somewhat disrespectful of form but respectful of talent and wisdom and wit, a fearless seeker of strange new experiences like the inside of a cat's mind, or half a pint of Guinness poured into an ashtray: that was Odin. Arhu put his whiskers forward, or tried to, and then discovered he had no whiskers: he dropped the lower half of his beak instead. As he did so, he got the faintest whiff of another name . . . and carefully turned his nose away from it. At least he still had a nose of sorts.

Now then, said the other, either missing all this or ignoring it. *The path's clear.*

They soared for a good while, circling. Every now and then Arhu would get a glimpse, through the silvery twilight, of a landscape below them: always the features were the same—the oxbowed bends of the river, the great loop of the Thames that held the Isle of Dogs, not quite an isle but a fat and noticeable peninsula. Then the cloud would close in again. Probability, Odin said. Or the lack of it . . .

And suddenly the cloud cleared, and they dropped from the heavens together like a stone. The city below them was filthy. The Moon above them was scarred.

Keep your eyes open, Odin said then. *We can't stay long. Is this it?*

Arhu looked down, trying to find the street in which they

had appeared. He found the Tower quickly enough, and the street that ran by it: and there, just visible to a feline wizard's eye, the tangle of half-seen strings that meant a sidled Person running across the mud, followed by two others. One of them fell as a motorcar rolled toward and over him—

This is it?

This is it!

All right, then. Now we start work. Let us See together.

Rhiow felt the Raven close his wings and drop like a stone: and the tense of the vision changed, just that quickly, so that Rhiow found herself wanting to shake her head in confusion. Until this moment, everything happening to Arhu had been in a clearly discernible *then.* Suddenly, though, it was *now,* all now: single threads of that seamless whole that the Whisperer saw. But changed—the Eye a bird's instead of a Person's, Seeing with a more direct and concentrated kind of vision, as if from one side of a brain rather than with the binocular vision of a predator. She was not sure she was seeing everything Arhu had, it all came so quickly. All *now,* all *here,* glimpse after glimpse tumbling one after another as the feline/raven mind fell through the cloud of probability—

—one of the London streets opening out below them, suddenly: in the middle of it, being driven along at a sedate pace, a queen-*ehhif* out for a ride in a coach pulled by horses. Men ride in front of her, and behind her, riding on other horses as guards. The queen-*ehhif* is a little stocky, plainly dressed in dark clothes. Her face is one that could have smiled but does not. The coach turns a corner in one of those broad, tree-lined avenues. People passing by pause, and bow, as the coach passes. The queen-*ehhif* waves occasionally, a very reserved gesture. The coach drives on.

An *ehhif* is standing at a corner nearby. As the coach passes he pulls out a gun, points it at the queen-*ehhif* in the coach. Shoots.

Heads turn at the sudden crack of sound. In the coach, the queen-*ehhif* looks over her shoulder, bemused, as the *ehhif* driving the coach whips up the horses. They clatter away. Others run or ride toward the *ehhif* who fired the gun. The queen-*ehhif*, unharmed, looks back, her white face sharply contrasted against the dark bonnet. This has happened to her before, but she can never quite bring herself to believe it when it does.

Now the same coach again, driving in through gates surrounding a wide green park in the countryside outside London: and then into the courtyard in front of a massive house, turreted with the same kind of great round towers as are found inside the double walls where the Ravens live. The coach drives up to the doors, and the queen-*ehhif* gets out, with a younger queen-*ehhif*, her daughter perhaps, beside her. The two of them go in together, through the great front gate, in the broad, low sunset light.

Close, Odin thought, *but not quite. Now we find the core—*

Several more flickers as the Raven and his passenger dive through patches of silvery twilight, and out again: and after a few breaths' time, the yellowy sunset light reasserts itself. But this time everything is very different. A dark carriage comes out of the gates, but its windows are shut, and draped in black. Everything about it is black: the horses, the harness, the clothes of the tom-*ehhif* who drive. The coach is a long one, long enough to take one of the boxes in which the *ehhif* put their dead before burying them. The long drive down to the roadway is lined with *ehhif*, all dressed in black, weeping. Some of them hide their faces in their hands as the coach passes them. Some of them hold *ehhif*-young up to see the coach as it goes by. Occasionally a cry breaks out from one of the grown *ehhif*, a terrible sound, as if wrested from a throat that normally would never make such a noise no matter what the circumstances. Otherwise everything is very silent, the only noises the sound of the horses' hoofs and, far away, the bell of one of the houses where *ehhif* go to entreat the Powers or the One, tolling very slow, one strike in every minute, like a failing heart.

The long black equipage winds away toward London through the brassy sunset light. The Raven flashes overhead, passing them, dodging through clouds again, coming out over the city and veering close to a shopfront in a street that is almost empty. This, in its way, shocks Rhiow more badly than anything else she has seen. She is a city Person: she is used to streets that always have someone walking or driving on them, no matter what time of day or night it is. But this place looks like it has died, or like the heart has been torn out of it. Few *ehhif* are abroad, and almost all of them are dressed in black or have black armbands, even black rags, tied about their arms. All their faces are grim: many are tearstained.

The Raven perches for a moment on a folding board that is set up outside the shopfront. The shop itself is dark and its door is shut. But outside, the piece of paper pasted to the board says, in large black letters, HER MAJESTY'S FUNERAL. It is the front page of *The Times,* and it has no other words on it except the newspaper's masthead and the date: July 14, 1874.

The Raven takes wing again before anyone should see it, vaults up into the safety of the silvery twilight again. *That is the core that you sought*, Odin says. *We have just time to see the beginning, and the end.*

The tense changed once more: *now* became *then* again, at least while Odin and Arhu were in transit. They saw more, much more, as the Raven flashed in and out through the cloud that always seemed about to break into day. Rhiow could not make sense of most of what she was sensing, and hoped Arhu would be able to do better, or that perhaps the Raven Odin could: for occasionally, like a sudden ray of light through the cloud, there would come an image so overladen with context that it was as if a thousand *ehhif* stood around her, every one of them shouting some piece of information that it was important for her to hear. A group of *ehhif*, ranged in a big room, facing each other in rows: and all shouting at one another, a terrible noise of rage and confusion, while one *ehhif* at the front of one group, in the bottom row of the benches, cried out, "Vengeance is mine, saith the Lord: I will repay!" and all the others shouted him down in a crescendo of fury, as another one leaped up and shouted, "Mr. Speaker, they say the Devil can quote Scripture to his purpose. I can do the same: and I say, 'They have sown the storm, and they shall reap the whirlwind!' " A roar of approval—and from that, abruptly, to a white-walled room where a broad, squat machine of some kind was being built by *ehhif* wearing protective suits. Then a bright, blue-skied day, and a missile or rocket leaping up on a tongue of fire from a launch pad bizarrely adorned in the curlicues of the Victorian decorative style. Then a huge aircraft passing over a city landscape, so big that it shadowed the ground, and *ehhif* looked up and pointed. Then—

—the images were gone again. The twilight returned . . . and went sinister. It was not silvery anymore: it was leaden. The sun could not come through it. Arhu and Odin spun up together on raven's wings, catching an updraft, or what passed for one in vision. This was no normal wind: the air was too thin for wind as high as they were going, as the Earth yielded up her curvature below them. Far down, away in the blue sea, Arhu could see the plume of darkness wafting up from one small point. A volcano, a mother of volcanoes, belching out great clouds of ash and dust into the upper atmosphere: a thin line that became a plume, a plume that became a pall, thin and dark and gloomy, right around the globe of the world. What was bright, and normally gleamed like polished metal where the Sun touched it, now was dull and tarnished: and clouds that should have burned white were all filmed gray. *Eighteen sixteen*, said Odin's voice, dry, noticing rather than reacting. He had Seen it before; he had Seen *all* this before. *The difference*, he said, *is that I never had to look. Looking is what makes the difference, in vision. Looking makes it so.*

They dived again, were briefly lost in the silvery twilight, the billow of possibility. When they came out, they looked down into a muddy street and saw a young, dark-complected man in casual clothing of the late twentieth century come lurching out of the middle of the air, carrying something heavy in a bag. He came staggering through the darkness, out into the street: another *ehhif* came along and frightened him. He dropped the bag, turned, and fled once more into the darkness. A few moments later, the other *ehhif* came along and picked up the bag, peeled it away from what it contained. A book, a very large book. The *ehhif* stared at the cover. Another one took the book from the one who held it: opened it, turned the pages, looking at the equations and the delicately drawn diagrams, and the dense small print.

One of them glanced up into the cloudy sky, with that thin layer of darkness streaming along above everything, as a brief, welcome ray of sun shot down through the dull day. The light fell on the book. Arhu looked at the silver *ehhif* letters on the book's cover. It said *Van Nostrand's Scientific Encyclopedia.*

Arhu looked down at the *ehhif* and heard, very softly, all about them, the laughter: the quiet amusement of Something that had given the world, just now, a brief foretaste of what was waiting for it later, in far greater intensity, when the seed it had just planted finally came to fruit. This darkness would fall again, but many times magnified: this cold would come . . . but would be permanent. By the time it passed, and the planet warmed again, all its intelligent life would be long dead.

Arhu had heard that laughter before. Once upon a time, when he was a kitten, he had found himself in a garbage bag in the East River, one that slowly filled with water, while he and his brothers and sisters clawed and scrabbled desperately on top of each other, trying to stay above the terrible cold stuff that was slowly climbing high enough around them that they would have no choice but to breathe it, and die. Only Arhu lived, saved by chance—some *ehhif* coming along and, seeing the sinking bag in the water and hearing the last faint cries of despair from inside, had fished it out, torn it open, and dumped the sodden bodies of the kittens out onto the bike path. All the while he had been in that bag, and even afterward, all the while the *ehhif* warmed him in his coat while taking the last small survivor to the local animal shelter, Arhu had sensed that laughter all around him. It was Entropy in Its personified form, the One Who invented death, sa'Rráhh as the People knew her, the disaffected and ambivalent Power that wizards called Lone: and It had laughed at the prospect of his one small death as It was now laughing at this far greater one. The fury Arhu had felt when first he recognized that laughter's source, he felt now, and it roared up in him like the voice of one of the Old Cats from the Downside, a blast of pure rage that sent Odin tumbling through the silvery twilight as if blown off course by a gust of wind.

They were not off course, though. They came out of the twilight more quickly than even Odin had expected, so that for a moment he almost lost control, dropping some hundreds of feet before he could get his wings under him again. As they tumbled, Arhu had a brief confusion of which way was up and which was down. They were high above the Earth again, but as they tumbled the lights blurred, and there seemed to be stars in the dark side of the Earth as well as in the sky.

Odin fought for stability, found it. Arhu looked down, through the Raven's Eye, and saw that there were lights on the dark side of the Earth, indeed, but they were not stars.

Europe was in shadow. London was dark. But on the Continent, from north to south, eye-hurtingly bright lights had broken out, a rash of points of fire. Paris, Berlin, Rome, Madrid, Moscow, every one was a point of light. Others blossomed as Arhu watched—Hanover, Lyons, Geneva, Lisbon, Vienna, Budapest, Warsaw, and many more: seeds of fire growing, paling, each one with its tiny pale growth above it. Arhu did not need to dive any closer to see the mushroom clouds. The seeds were planted. It would be no spring that came with their growth, but a winter that would last an age.

Arhu closed his eyes in pain. When he opened them again, he was crouched down on the ground, on the green grass near the bush in the Ravens' enclosure, and beside him, Odin was standing up and shaking his feathers into place. Hardy was sitting down on the nearby tree, now, near Hugin.

"The beginning and the end," Arhu breathed, and had to stop and try to catch his breath, for he was finding it hard just to be here and now again.

"It will pass," said Hardy. "Meanwhile, be assured; you did a good job. You See strangely, but your way might be something that we could learn in time, if you could teach us."

"Me teach *you?*" Arhu said, and gulped for air again. "Uh—I'll have to ask."

"Ask Her by all means," said Hardy. "In the meantime, I

see the nature of your problem. She was the core of that whole time, the old queen, Victoria: the events of that whole period crystallized out around her personality, and the qualities that her people projected onto her. Any universe in which she was successfully assassinated would be a threat to all the others anywhere near it in its probability sheaf. And I would suggest to you," Hardy said, bending down a little closer to Arhu, "that if the Lone One wished to make doubly sure of your universe's demise, that It would see to it that she died in *your* universe as well."

Arhu stared at him. "By making the *ehhif* here assassinate *this* Queen Victoria?"

"Indeed. It might well happen anyway, for as the two universes begin the process of exchanging energy and achieving homeostasis, that core event will be one of the first things that will try to happen in your universe." Hardy blinked and looked thoughtful. "If I were in your position, I would be sure that this world's Victoria is protected from the fate you have seen befall her counterpart. Otherwise, with two universes with dead Queens, the alternate universe will gain a great entropy advantage over the other. Should both Queens die, I doubt very much whether this world would long survive. . . ."

"Oh, great, *another* problem," Arhu said, rather bitterly. "And how can you be so calm about it?"

"Well, for one thing, it has already happened," said Hardy mildly. "For another thing, you are the ones who will cause it *not* to happen . . . if indeed you do. How should I not be calm, when I know I am giving my advice to the right person?"

Arhu blinked and turned to Odin. "Can you translate that for me?" he asked, rather helplessly.

Odin blinked too. "It made perfect sense to *me*," he said. "Which part of it specifically did you need translated?"

Arhu hissed softly. "Never mind."

"When I say it has already happened," Hardy said, "I speak of the entire chain of events from first to last: from your arrival here to work on the gates, to your final departure. Not that I know the details of *that*: you will soon know them better than we ever could. But I think that, in this timeline, this universe, Queen Victoria has not yet been assassinated. I would suspect that fact of being what has so far kept this timeline in place, and as yet largely undamaged . . . and it may also be that the difficulty you were experiencing with the oscillation of the far end of your colleague's timeslide also has to do with the unusual stability, under the circumstances, of this one. You must complete whatever consultations you have planned with speed. And at all times, the queens must be your great care. Whatever happens, protect them."

Arhu waved his tail in agreement, and stood up. He was surprisingly wobbly on his feet. "Look . . . I want to thank you. I've got to get back to the others and tell them about this: as much as I can, anyway."

"Do so. Go well, young wizard: and come back again."

"He will anyway," Odin said, and poked Arhu in a friendly way with his beak, at the back of his neck.

Arhu took a swipe at him, with the claws out, and missed on purpose. It seemed wise. He liked Odin, and anyway, that beak was awfully big. "*Dai,*" he said. "Later—"

He headed off out the gateway under the Bloody Tower with as much dignity as he could muster, while desperately wanting to fall down somewhere and go straight to sleep: and as he went out, all the stones around him were quiet . . . for the moment.

✦

Rhiow opened her eyes and looked at Arhu. He had fallen asleep. With some slight difficulty, for she was stiff, she got up and stretched, and then went over to Urruah.

"We'd better call the others in," she said. "The problem's gotten much worse."

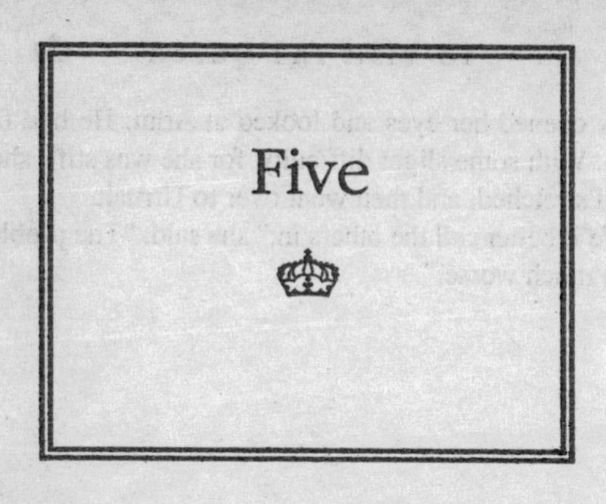

Five

The whole group met again late that night in the Mint. Urruah was the last to arrive: he had been doing work on the timeslide until the last minute, having taken a while to look at Arhu's "record" in the Whispering of his flight with Odin. All the others, one by one, took time to do the same, and also to look at Rhiow's discussion with Hhuhm'hri: and then, predictably, the argument began.

Fhrio, in particular, was skeptical about the Ravens' suggestion regarding the version of Queen Victoria in their home timeline. "It's just more work for nothing," he said. "If she's the only thing keeping this timeline in place—and the two are congruent, mostly, in terms of timeflow—then why hasn't she been assassinated already?"

Urruah's tail was lashing already. "Because someone's prevented it already," he said, politely enough. "Probably us, or someone working with us. Either the timelines have been taken out of congruence somehow—difficult—or the attempt on the queen's life has already failed. Again, probably because of us. We're going to have to consider timesliding someone back far enough to guard her—and then block any further slides to positions before our guard is in place, so that we can deal with the assassination attempt proper."

Fhrio spat. "It's a waste of time. One, I doubt the Powers will let us. There's too much temporal gating going on at the moment anyway. Too many ways to screw up past timelines. And secondly, it makes a lot more sense to concentrate on the Victoria who's in the 'nuclear' timeline. It's that universe that's the real threat, anyway."

"I don't know," Auhlae said. "I think Hardy might have had a point. If we—"

"Are you crazy?" Fhrio said. "We've got enough trouble already. Let's concentrate on one thing at a time."

"No, now you just listen to me, Fhrio. We may not be *able* to," Auhlae said. "We still have to find all the 'pastlings' and get them back into their right times: otherwise the instability of the gates is going to continue and increase all through this. We can't just drop one problem because the other seems more important all of a sudden."

"I think you're wrong," Fhrio said. "I think we have to. Even the Victoria problem will go away if we keep the first contamination, the technological one, from happening. If we could just catch that first guy with the book as he's going through the gate . . ."

"If you catch him," Huff said, "you'll probably catch what caused the slide in the first place. The Lone Power, in whatever form It's wearing this time out. Or you'll catch whatever poor stooge It's using . . . and even the stooges are likely to be trouble enough."

"Not as much trouble as the Earth dying of nuclear winter in eighteen eighty-eight or whenever!"

"If we could even just get the book, and keep it from crossing over," Huff said.

Urruah lashed his tail in agreement. "I'd say there's no question that that's the point of contamination," he said.

"I've checked in the Whispering. It's a very detailed volume, full of basic information on every possible kind of science. And possibly worst of all, it's full of *materials* science, and technical information on how to make almost everything it discusses. Manufacturing processes, temperatures, specific chemical reactions, locations of ores and chemical elements—you name it."

"That time was full of great scientific minds," Rhiow said. "They were not stupid people. Once they believed what was in that book—which they quickly would have done, once they'd tested a few of the equations in it to see what happened—they would have run wild with it. As we see they've done."

"Again, they seem to have done it somewhat selectively," Urruah said. "But the worst thing they could have started messing with, atomics, they must have started with right away, in the late teens of the century, to have got as far along as they are now. It must have seemed like magic to them, that. Until they started building the necessary centrifuges and separators for the heavy-metal ores . . . and found that the metals did what was advertised." He sighed.

"The details are going to prove fascinating enough, I'm sure," Huff said. "But now we have to find out exactly when that incursion with the young man and the book happened, and stop it."

"How?" Arhu said.

"Backtiming, stupid," said Siffha'h.

Arhu glared at her. "Look, before you start calling names," he said, "think about it. Do you really think the Lone Power's going to just let us undo what It went to so much trouble to set up? Just like that? If you do, you're even stupider than you think I am."

"That would be fairly difficult," Siffha'h retorted, "since—"

"Stop it, Siffha'h," Auhlae said sternly. "There's enough entropy loose around here at the moment without increasing it."

"Those accesses are going to be blocked," Arhu said. "Trust me."

"Is that a Seeing?" Urruah said.

"No, it's common sense," Arhu snapped, "which seems to be in short supply around here at the moment." He threw Siffha'h another annoyed look.

"Anyway," Urruah said loudly, "at the moment, there is a problem with the idea of stopping the book transfer. It is that we don't yet have a definite timing or a proper set of coordinates for that transit, even with what Odin was able to show Arhu. Until we can get a timing, we can't stop the book getting back into the Victorian era: and it will take some time and work yet for us to generate a timing that we can use . . . even an educated guess at one. So for the time being we should concentrate on what we presently *do* have a chance to stop, which is the assassination."

"How close *have* you been able to get to that timing?" Huff said.

Urruah glanced over at Auhlae. "Eighteen sixteen," Auhlae said. "That's when the Whisperer says the volcano happened. It produced something called the Year without a Summer. The usual kind of thing: the volcano spat out a lot of high-altitude ash that produced unusually rapid cooling of the atmosphere. There were places in northern Europe where it snowed in June and July that year. Harvests failed everywhere."

"If there was a perfect time to drop a book full of information on high technology into the pre-Victorian culture," Huff said, "I'd say that would have been it. The scientifically oriented *ehhif* would have tried everything in it that they then had the materials technology for, with an eye to solving their problem . . . and then, when it eventually passed, they would swiftly have started constructing everything else they could, from the 'instructions.' " He sighed. "I could wish they hadn't been half so clever."

Rhiow was in agreement with him about that. "Arhu, as regards the timing of the book's arrival, could you do anything more with the Ravens, do you think?"

Arhu lashed his tail no. "Rhiow, one of the things I gathered from Odin was that they can't spend that much time during a given period in any one timeline or alternate universe. They're messengers, all right, but they have to do their work at high speed specifically *because* they do so much out-of-timeline work. Other universes spit them out like a mouse's gallbladder if they try to stay away from 'home' too long."

She nodded. "What about vision?"

"Theirs is a little more predictable than mine," Arhu said, "but it's so different." He shrugged his tail. "I'll go and ask them tomorrow, but I wouldn't bet on them being able to help us that much more."

Rhiow waved her tail in agreement, though reluctantly. She was still bemused by the Ravens' version of vision, and wondered exactly how they were getting it. Wizards and wizardly talent among birdkind tended to vest in the predators, for some reason: possibly because they were the top of their local food chains, or possibly it was something to do with their level of intelligence. This was not something about which Rhiow had ever queried the Whisperer. She had been bemused enough, when she first became a wizard, to find that there were wizards among the *houiff*, too, and that some of them could be as sagacious as any feline. Afterward she stopped wondering why wizardry turned up in one species or another, and simply said *Dai stihó* in the Speech to another wizard when she met one, whether it had wings, or fins, or two legs or four. Now, though, she started to wonder why she had never heard of Raven-wizards. *Or is it that I just never went looking that hard for the information? There's so much to know, and so little time.*

Never mind. "All right," she said to Huff. "At least we now have a much better idea of the exact time of the assassination. We have to narrow it down further still, though."

Huff nodded. "Urruah," he said, "that's one of the other time-coordinates you're going to be trying to access when you use the timeslide next?"

"Absolutely. But there are a few other things we need to look into as well," Urruah said. "Like the small matter of the logs on the nonfunctioning gate."

Fhrio looked at Urruah sharply. "What's the matter with them?"

"They're not the way they were when we disconnected the gate from the catenary," Urruah said. "The coordinates for the Illingworth access have been changed, and I don't know how, or why. Any ideas?"

Fhrio stared at Urruah as if he were out of his mind. "They can't change. You're crazy."

Urruah glanced over at Huff: Huff looked back at him, bemused. "All right then," Urruah said, "I'm crazy." Rhiow looked with great care at his tail. It was quite still. She licked her nose, twice, very fast. "But I think you should lock that gate in a stasis, Huff, and make sure no one gets at it again. If it can manage to alter itself again while it's got a stasis on it, then obviously no cause based *here* is at fault."

Huff stared at the floor for a moment, then looked up and said, "I'll take care of it. Rhiow . . ."

She looked over at him. "Our next move?" Huff asked.

She was not used to being so obviously deferred to: it made her a little uncomfortable. After a moment's pause, she said, "Overall, I think at the moment that I have to agree with Fhrio. While I agree it's important to make sure that our home-timeline's Victoria is safe, the other one is in greater danger at the moment—or so it seems to me—and her assassination is what seems likeliest to trigger the derangement of our own timeline. I think we must therefore try to get into the 'altered eighteen seventy-four' timeline as quickly as we can: tomorrow, I think, since a lot of us are short on sleep at the moment. We'll try to find out exactly when the assassination was, and find out what we need to do to stop it. After that we can worry about the book and, last of all, about the stranded pastlings in our own time. Huff?"

He put his ears forward in agreement. "That makes sense to me. Let's do so."

"I am going to fuel Urruah's timeslide tomorrow," Siffha'h said, as if expecting an argument.

"Fine," said Huff. "Urruah had some questions about the catenary's behavior as a power source: this will resolve them. Auhlae and I will be doing general gate duty tomorrow, but we'll be on call if something else comes up. When should we all meet?"

"About this time?" Urruah said.

"Good enough."

The group broke up. Fhrio threw a very annoyed look at Urruah as he went out, and Urruah sat down and started washing, while the others, glancing at him, left.

Rhiow touched cheeks with Auhlae and Huff as they went out, then sat down by Urruah while he scrubbed his face. "Well, you seem to have managed to attract a lot of someone's annoyance today," she said softly, when the others, except for Arhu, were gone. "What was all that about?"

"Well, I spent a late night working with Auhlae a couple of nights ago," Urruah said, "and he seems to have taken issue with that."

"Fhrio? What business is that of his?"

"I'm not sure."

Rhiow sighed. "It doesn't take much to get him going in any case," she said. "Probably it means nothing. Are you all right, though?"

"Oh, I'm fine. It's just that—" He shrugged his tail, started washing his ears. *Rhi, usually there's a certain level of good humor about these joint jobs. It seems to be missing in this one.*

It's the level of stress, I'd imagine, Rhiow said. *This is not your usual joint job.*

"No," he said, "I suppose not." He stopped washing, and sighed, putting his ears forward as Huff came back in. "Huff," he said, "do you want any help with that stasis?"

"No," Huff said, "I'll manage it." He sat down and looked around him a little disconsolately.

"All right then," Urruah said. "Rhi, I'll see you in the morning. Go well, Huff." He headed out toward the cat door in the back of the pub.

Rhiow looked at Huff for a moment, then got up and went to sit by him. "Are you all right?" she asked.

"Oh—yes, I suppose so," he said, sounding a little distracted. "It's just that . . . I don't know . . . I'm not used to coping with these stress levels, and everyone around me seems to be losing their temper half the time. My team's unhappy and I don't know why, and there doesn't seem to be much I can do about it."

Rhiow put one ear back: it was a feeling she'd had occasionally. "Oh, Huff, it'll sort itself out . . . you'll see. It *is* the stress, truly: this problem isn't the kind of thing any of us would normally have to handle in the course of work. And to be suddenly thrown together with strangers, no matter how well intentioned they are, and then try to deal with something like this . . . it isn't going to be easy for anyone." She put her whiskers forward a little. "You're such an easygoing type anyway," Rhiow said, "that it must be difficult for you to deal with the frictions: they must seem kind of foolish to you."

He gave her a rueful look. "Sometimes," he said, "yes. Yes, you're right." He sighed. "Stranger or not," he said, "it's nice to have someone around who understands. But then you're not exactly a stranger anymore."

"No, of course not. When we get all this solved, Huff, you should come visit us in New York. We'll show you and your team around the gates at Grand Central, 'do the town' a little. Urruah knows some extremely good places to eat."

"I know," Huff said, sounding a little more amused. "I keep hearing about them." His whiskers were right forward now.

"I bet," Rhiow said, resigned. "Look . . . we've got a long day ahead of us tomorrow. I should get home. You try to get some rest, Huff, and we'll see you later on."

He waved his tail in agreement. "Go well," he said. They touched cheeks: and Rhiow went out the back, through the cat door, and down the alley, heading for the Tower Hill Underground station, thinking, a little absently, how nice it was that it no longer felt strange to rub cheeks with Huff at all.

✦

She got home very late, by New York time, and found Iaehh in bed and snoring. As quietly as she could, Rhiow curled up with him, too tired even to care whether he would roll over on top of her in the middle of the night, as he often did while feeling for someone else who should have been in the bed, but wasn't. She sighed at the thought of what now seemed about a hundred years ago: a time when both her *ehhif* were here and happy, and her life managing a gating team had seemed relatively simple and uncomplicated . . .

About a second later, she woke up. *Oh, unfair,* she

thought. It was typical that, on a night when you most needed the sense of being asleep for a long time, you instead got that "cheated" feeling of having been asleep almost no time at all.

It was, however, nearly six in the evening. Iaehh wasn't back from work yet, but he would be soon, and if she didn't get out fairly quickly, he would turn up and delay her. Rhiow sighed and got right up, stretching hard fore and aft: ate (finding the bowls washed and filled again), then washed and used the box, and headed out for Grand Central. Half an hour later Rhiow was in London, on the platform in the Underground station, watching Urruah reconstructing his timeslide. Auhlae was there, and Siffha'h: Arhu was sitting off to one side, ostensibly watching Urruah fine-tuning his spell, but (to Rhiow's eyes) actually staying rather pointedly out of Siffha'h's way.

"Perfect timing," Urruah said, looking up. "I'm just about set here."

"You have all those extra coordinate-sets that you wanted to test laid in as well?" Rhiow asked, strolling over to the "hedge" of burning lines that was the spell diagram. It looked taller than it had been before.

"Yes indeed," Urruah said. "We'll take them in order after we check out the main one, the 'scarred' timeline. Everybody, come and check your names. We're ready to rock and roll."

Rhiow jumped into the circle to reexamine her name. Auhlae jumped in after her, remarking, "I would have thought you were more interested in the classical line of things, Urruah."

His whiskers went forward. "Always. But I believe one's interest in music should be balanced."

"If it's *ehhif* music you're talking about," Siffha'h said as she jumped into the circle as well, "you're too balanced by half. All that screeching."

Urruah chuckled. "Wait till you're older and you have more leisure to develop your tastes."

"Older," Siffha'h said. "I'm sick of hearing about it. And I'm getting older right now waiting for you People to get your acts together!" She glared at Arhu.

Arhu, taking no apparent notice, made a small, elegant jump, which landed him precisely on the spot Urruah had laid out for him inside the circle. He bent down, checked his name, and then turned his back to Siffha'h, yawning, and sat down with his tail wrapped around his toes.

"Huh," said Siffha'h, glancing at Arhu and planting her forepaws in the power-feed area of the spell. She looked over at Urruah.

"Everybody sidled?" he said. "Good. First set of coordinates is ready," he said. "The spell's on standby. Feed it!"

"Consider it fed," Siffha'h said.

The world vanished in a blast of light and power so vehement that Rhiow was glad she had been sitting down: otherwise she would have fallen over. This was not anything like Urruah's style of power-feed, decorous and smooth like a limo starting and stopping. This was a crash of power and pressure, happening all at once from all around, like being at the center of a lightning strike. In the middle of it all she thought she heard something like a yowl of frustration, but she couldn't be sure. When the light cleared away again, Rhiow half expected to smell ozone: she had to sit there for a moment or so and shake her head, waiting for her eyes to work again. After a few moments they did, but she still saw a residual blur of green light at the edges of vision for a little while, the remnant of the image of the first flash of the spell-circle as it came up to power.

She looked around and saw that they were all once more

sitting in a muddy street: and Rhiow sighed at the thought of what getting clean again was likely to taste like. The sky above them was that of early morning, clear and blue: a surprising contrast to the last time. "All right," Urruah said, "there's the tripwire. I've closed the gate." Then Urruah looked up and around, and said suddenly, "And we've got a problem."

"What?" said Rhiow.

He was looking up at the Moon, which stood high in the southern sky at third quarter. They all looked too.

The Moon was white, with only the faintest blue shadows.

"Oh, *vhai,*" Auhlae said, *"this isn't the contaminated timeline!"* She turned to Urruah. "This is the predecessor to *our* London! Our world! For pity's sake, Urruah, how did that happen?"

Urruah was dumbfounded. "Auhlae, you saw the settings, we worked on them together—you tell *me!"*

"I'll tell you how it happened," Siffha'h said, staggering to her feet. "We were being blocked. Couldn't you feel it? Urruah?"

"I'm not sure."

"Nice excuse," Arhu muttered.

"Oh, go swallow your tail!" Siffha'h spat. "Who asked you for anything like an opinion? As if you could produce one out your front end instead of your rear for a change. *We were being blocked!* Something knocked us sideways. Something *vhai*'d well doesn't want us in the alternate timeline! Like the Lone One!"

She was bristling with fury, as much from winding up in the wrong place, Rhiow thought, as for having her competence called into question. But there was another possibility that had occurred to Rhiow: that the other timeline was becoming stronger, strong enough now to begin interfering with *any* temporal gating. *But there's no evidence of that . . . yet.*

"It could happen," Rhiow said. "For the meantime, we shouldn't stand here arguing." She glanced over at Urruah. "It's not a wasted trip, 'Ruah. We still have some things to check on, and some sources who would be helpful to talk to here. Among other things, would you say this is at least the right year?"

Urruah blinked. "Let's send Arhu to steal a newspaper."

"There's no need to steal anything," Arhu muttered. "These *ehhif* drop their newspapers all over the place, besides pasting them up on boards near the newsstands."

They walked out onto George Street, sidled, and glanced around them with a little more sense of leisure than they had felt the last time, for this was after all their home universe: there was no reason to rush away from it. Rhiow looked across the street and saw that the Tower Hill Underground station did not exist as yet. She listened, and the Whisperer told her that the worldgate complex was, at this point in its development, housed a little behind them, somewhere under the Fenchurch Street railway station.

"Maybe we should try to look up the local gating team," Siffha'h said, glancing around her.

"Much as I wouldn't mind being social with them," Rhiow said, "I think we have other things to concentrate on at the moment. Is that one of your 'newsagents' down there, Arhu?"

"Yeah. Come on."

He led them eastward as far as Trinity Square. "The mud's sure the same," Urruah said, with resignation.

"Yes, but at least there aren't any crazed car drivers here," Rhiow said. "Not that it's much of a consolation. They'll come soon enough. . . ."

In Trinity Square they paused by a little shop that had a

board outside with many newspapers pinned up to it and ready to be torn off, like pages of a calendar. "Try that with *The New York Times*," Urruah murmured.

Rhiow put her whiskers forward at the thought. The group hung back, out of the way of the *ehhif* making their way up and down the sidewalk, while Arhu went up to have a look at the newspaper.

He came trotting back with a satisfied expression. "April eighteenth, eighteen seventy-four."

"All right," Rhiow said. "A little early, but at least it's the right year. Let's go up to the British Museum and see 'Black Jack.' "

It was a long walk, nearly a mile and a half. All of them were footsore and extremely dirty by the time they got there, for no one felt it wise to expend the wizardry needed for skywalking when there might be much more important business to be handled without notice. So they went as city cats would, though sidled: down Tower Hill onto Great Tower Street and over onto Eastcheap: down Cannon Street onto the street called St. Paul's Churchyard, under the shadow of the massive dome of St. Paul's: up Ludgate Hill to Fleet Street, and then up Chancery Lane, northward to High Holborn and finally into Bloomsbury. By the time they got to Museum Street, they were all hungry, and Auhlae looked at the mud on her beautiful fur and made a despairing face.

"I can't wash like this," she said, "I just *can't*. There's no time, and . . ." She sighed, and said a few words under her breath in the Speech. The mud dried and went straight to powdery dust. She shook herself hard, and for a moment was in the center of a small chocolate-colored cloud. Then the dust settled, leaving her more or less the color she should have been.

"Now there's a thought," Rhiow said. "Auhlae, you're a genius."

A few moments later there were several chocolate-colored clouds, and somewhat cleaner People emerging from them. "Now I feel better," Auhlae said, smoothing down the fur behind her ears. "I wouldn't like to meet a Person of note looking like I just crawled out of a sewer."

They walked in through the iron gates of the museum, toward the noble main façade with its columns and Greek-style portico, all carved with what one might have taken at first for *ehhif* gods until a better look revealed them to be allegorical figures discreetly labeled DRAMA and POETRY and PROGRESS OF THE HUMAN RACE. They walked up the stairs and waited for some *ehhif* to open the doors for them, a matter of a few seconds only: then they went through into the main entrance hall, and glanced up at the huge statue of an *ehhif* that leaned there, looking out thoughtfully at the world.

"Who's that?" Arhu said. "Another fake god?"

"It's a great taleteller, dear," Auhlae said, "one who told his stories a couple of hundred sunrounds ago, from this time anyway. Hsshah'spheare, his name was."

"Whether he's that great," said someone off to one side in the great echoing hall, "when the best-known mention he makes of our People is to suggest turning one of them in a frying pan, is a question yet to be resolved. But never mind that at the moment."

They all turned to see a big, *big* black-and-white cat come pacing along the marble floor toward them. With his white bib and white feet, he gave the general impression of wearing *ehhif* formal wear. "Welcome," he said. "I'm glad to see you!"

"We're on errantry, as you've guessed, having seen us sidled," Rhiow said, "and we greet you very well: we've come some way to see you. Do I have the honor of addressing Black Jack?"

The big handsome Person put his whiskers forward. "That's how the *ehhif* know me: I suppose the name has got about by now. But you might more properly call me Ouhish, though, if you will. And I'm very glad to see you so soon: I hadn't thought you could possibly turn up with such speed."

Rhiow looked at Urruah and the others, then back at Ouhish. "I'm sorry. You say you sent for some wizards?"

"Yes," Ouhish said.

"Well," Urruah said, "we're confused, now. We thought we came on business of our own. But we'll be glad to help you in any way we can."

"You're saying you *weren't* sent?" Ouhish said.

Rhiow paused for a moment, then laughed. "Oh, no. Wizards are always sent . . . one way or another. It's just that the Powers That Be don't always tell us that They're doing it. Tell us your trouble, and we'll do our best to assist you."

"Well," Ouhish said, "let's go somewhere quiet where we can make introductions and get things sorted out. Will you follow me?" And he led them in through the pillared vestibule, and into the depths of the museum.

It was a splendid place by any calculation, *ehhif* or feline. Rhiow had to keep reminding herself that much of the wonderful statuary and carving here was regarded as stolen or looted, though an earlier period's *ehhif* had thought of what they were doing as "collection": and violent arguments were still going on, she knew, about the proper home for some of the more beautiful and ancient artwork like the Elgin Marbles. But in the meantime, the stuff was here, and Rhiow told herself that it seemed poor-spirited not to enjoy looking at it if she had the chance.

There was little enough statuary to start with, for Ouhish led them on through the inner vestibule and the Room of Inscriptions, its walls all covered with writings from the *ehhif* peoples of old Greece and Rome, and straight into the Reading Room. In Rhiow's time the British Museum's library functions had all been moved to another building, bigger and some said better suited for the huge size of the collection as the twenty-first century approached: but many lamented the loss of the noble old domed Reading Room, still preserved but no longer used for the purpose for which it had been intended. They walked through, now, into this place where for once *ehhif* walked as quietly as cats, and Ouhish led them off to one of the corners of the room, what was called the New Library, a beautiful wood-paneled area stacked high with laddered bookcases and card catalogs.

They sat down under a quiet table in one corner, touched noses and breathed breaths, and introduced themselves. "Now tell us what your trouble is, and we'll try to help you," Rhiow said. But Ouhish would have none of it, and insisted that they tell their story first.

Urruah lifted his eyebrows. "This is going to be complicated," he said, but he began to lay out their business for Ouhish as clearly as he could. There was no prohibition against telling other People, in the line of errantry, that you were time-traveling, but naturally you would work hard to keep from telling them anything inappropriate, anything that would hurt them in their own lives, or tempt them to hurt others. Urruah spoke for about ten minutes, choosing his details with care, and at the end of it, Ouhish tucked himself down and looked at them all with astonishment.

"More than a hundred years in the future," he said. "The questions I could ask you . . ."

"It might take us a while to work out which ones we could safely answer," Rhiow said. "But maybe you'd let us ask first, since then we'll have more leisure to deal with your problem. Have there been any attempts on the life of the queen of late?"

Ouhish looked surprised. "You mean the *ehhif*-queen? Nothing recent. Someone tried a couple of years ago."

"Did they try shooting her?" Arhu said.

"That's right. She was out driving—a madman came out and took a shot at her with a pistol. He missed, thank Iau. It's happened before, too, a few times: usually where there are crowds."

"Do the *ehhif* here not like her, then?" Siffha'h said, sounding intrigued.

"Oh, she's been greatly loved, in the past. But things change." Ouhish looked a little uncomfortable. "You know that her mate died some while back? They were very much attached. She was miserable, poor thing, and she withdrew almost entirely from public life after her mate's death. That's not something a queen of *ehhif* can do, you understand. She has duties she must perform. And the *ehhif* she rules saw that she wasn't doing those duties, or only doing them marginally: and those *ehhif* who've been saying for a long time that there should be no queens anymore, but just the pride-toms to lead everything, and decide everything—their way of thinking has been gaining ground." Ouhish looked embarrassed. "I wouldn't like to give offense, cousin," he said to Rhiow, "but I think I know your accent—and it's a government like your *ehhif*'s at home that some of these people want, and the queen got rid of as well. A lot of the *ehhif* seem to think that it will happen in the next ten years or so: or at least by the turn of the century. It's no matter to them that the queen has been showing signs of breaking out of her withdrawal, at last. It may be too late for her now."

Rhiow's tail twitched slowly while she thought that Ouhish's turn of phrase was unfortunate.

"Well," Rhiow said. "That's all rather sad. There are other dangers lying in wait for her as well: perhaps another assassination attempt . . . we don't know for sure. One of the things we came for was to try to find out a date on which the attempt might happen, so that we might prevent it."

Ouhish looked shocked. "Do you have any clues at all?"

"We saw them burying her on the fourteenth of July," said Arhu, "in a universe close to this one. We don't know how long might have elapsed between her funeral and whatever happened to her."

"I would doubt it would have been as far back as the first of the month, if they were burying her on the fourteenth," Ouhish said. "But it could be almost anytime between, say, the fifth and the eleventh. For surely they would let her lie in state for a little time." His tail was lashing. "Cousins, this is terrible news!"

"If you can spread it where it will do some good," Rhiow said, "you may be able to help prevent the attempt from succeeding. We may be able to help as well, but we also have other business to attend to, which, believe it or not, may be even more important. One thing I have to ask you: Have there been any strange occurrences in London lately?"

"Strange occurrences?"

He looked confused, but Rhiow was unwilling to help him and possibly lead him in a direction that wouldn't be fruitful. Ouhish thought for a moment, then said, "You know, there have been a lot of madmen about."

"Madmen?" Siffha'h said.

"*Ehhif* roaming the streets and raving," Ouhish said. "I remember one of our *ehhif* here in the museum mentioning a story in one of the newspapers. One of the story writers attributed it to the full of the Moon just being past. . . ."

"I wonder if some of those might be *ehhif* who stumbled through our gate and into this time," Urruah said softly. "That's something that's going to have to be looked into."

"One *more* problem," Arhu muttered.

"Yes," Rhiow said.

Ouhish's tail was lashing. "It's all hard to believe," he said. "But you *are* wizards. But still, what could be more important than the queen dying?"

"What might follow it," Arhu said, "in another universe. A war, fought with weapons you can't imagine . . . one that would cause a terrible winter to fall over the whole world. A winter that might never end . . ."

Ouhish's head snapped up: he stared at Arhu. "You *were* sent," he said. "You *are* the wizards I sent for!"

"We are?" Arhu said. *"Why?"*

"Come on," Ouhish said, and jumped up. "Come on, quickly. It's not me you need to be talking to: it's Hwallis."

"Hwallis?" Rhiow said, now completely bemused.

"That's right. He's an *ehhif.* Come on, I'll take you upstairs and introduce you. He won't have gone off for his midday feed yet. Not that it's ever easy to get him to go. He hates leaving this place."

Ouhish practically ran out of the New Library; they all had to trot to keep up with him. Hurriedly Ouhish led them back out the way they had come into the vestibule, then off to the right and up the main staircase to the second floor. They came out into a splendid great space roofed over with glass and with a high gallery or balcony around it, all filled with ancient bas-reliefs of winged *ehhif* with high crowns, beautifully carved lions, and big-shouldered bulls.

"Down this way," Ouhish said, and led them down a long, wide hallway to the right, skylit by more glass roofing above. Both sides of this hall were lined with statues and sarcophagi of the first *ehhif* who had really conversed easily with People, the Egyptians: artwork and carving and papyrus were everywhere, in astonishing profusion, so that even Urruah, who wasn't much of a fan of the plastic arts, stopped to stare at some of the jewelry—the gems and gold glinting, in that subdued light, like a Person's eyes in the dark.

Despite her curiosity to find out what Ouhish was carrying on about, Rhiow herself had to stop and admire what was simply a most splendid statuary group of Queen Iau and her daughters, only slightly marred by the tendency of *ehhif* of the period to put human bodies under the feline faces, as a symbol for humanlike intelligence but feline nature. Aaurh the Mighty stood there, the Destroyer by Flame, the Queen's champion, wearing the horned sun, the terrible fire with which she warred on the Queen's enemies: and Hrau'f the Silent beside her, the Whisperer, with a roll of papyrus to show that she kept the records of the universe, and passed them on to those who needed them. By them was her brother, the Queen's lover, the Old Tom, Urrau-who-Scars, Urrau Lightning-Claw: and a little separate from the others, her face turned from them but her body toward them, ambivalent as always, sa'Rráhh, mistress of the Unmastered Fire, lioness-headed lady of the stillbirth and the birth that kills the Queen in labor, but also mistress of the Tenth Life: the Lone Power in Its feline recension, deadly, but never to be scorned, for some day she would be forgiven and rejoin the Pride. Paramount among them all stood Queen Iau, a Person's head set rather incongruously on the human shoulders, but wearing a look of indomitable wisdom, power, and compassion: and Rhiow put her whiskers forward. "*Ehhif* the artist might have been," she said, "but whoever made this, he or she *knew* Them. Blessings on him or her, wherever that one might be in the worlds. . . ."

Ouhish had stopped to let them catch up: he put his whiskers forward at Rhiow. "Interesting," he said, "but Hwallis says something very like that. Come on: I want you all to meet."

He hurried down the hallway nearly to its end, then

turned left suddenly and showed them a wood-paneled side door, which was open a crack. Ouhish put his paw into it and pulled it open. "In here," he said.

He led them into what turned out to be a warren of little offices and storage spaces behind the exhibition halls. It was a strangely homely place after the grandeur and silence of the outer halls. Other statues were here, pushed carefully up against the walls, some being repaired for cracks or broken noses; near one doorway a bucket and some mops and brooms stood handy; another small room had a sink and some cleaning rags and solvents, and buckets of different kinds of grout for polishing stone. Other rooms were stacked and piled high with books: one was filled with crates that held piles of papyrus rolls and books.

And in one room they came to, there was an *ehhif* bent over a long table. The table was covered with something that might have been dust, and the *ehhif* was working, slowly and carefully, to unwrap something that lay in the midst of the dust. As they came in behind him, he sneezed.

"Hwallis," said Ouhish in Ailurin, very loudly so that the *ehhif* would be able to hear him, "there are guests here."

The *ehhif* turned. He was young: maybe no more than eighteen, Rhiow thought—a tall, dark-haired, long-faced young man, dressed in a shirt with its sleeves rolled up, and long dark pants with suspenders. He looked at the doorway, and at Ouhish, and he said, in Ailurin, "Where?"

The People glanced at each other, surprised. "It's all right," Ouhish said, "you can unsidle."

They did. The young *ehhif* looked at them with some surprise, and said to Ouhish, with very passable intonation, "Are these the People you asked to come?"

Rhiow was very impressed. She said, in the Speech rather than in Ailurin, "Young sir, since you plainly know that our kind exists, then I tell you that we're wizards on errantry, and we greet you. I'm Rhiow: here are my colleagues Urruah, Auhlae, Arhu, and Siffha'h. Ouhish says he sent for us, and though we came on other business originally, he thinks you have need of our services. So tell us what your problem is, and we'll help if we can. But speak your own language, if you like: we'll understand you well enough, and we can help Ouhish to do so too if there's need. We have complicated matters to discuss, I think, and there's no need for any of us to guess at what we mean. Even if you do have a good accent."

The young *ehhif* opened and closed his mouth, and then said, "Good heavens. Well, allow me to introduce myself. I'm Edward Wallis Budge."

The others waved their tails at him in greeting. Urruah sat down, looking around him. "What exactly do you *do* here?" he said.

Wallis smiled slightly. "I have the honor to hold the position of honorary assistant to the keeper of the mummied cats."

Urruah put his whiskers forward. "Boy," he said, "they don't make job titles like *that* anymore." He peered up at the table. "I suppose that if the museum needs a keeper for mummied cats, there must be a lot of them."

"Hundreds of thousands," Wallis said.

"Sweet Iau in a basket," Auhlae murmured, "what would anyone want *hundreds of thousands* of mummied cats for?"

"Please make yourself comfortable, and I'll explain," said Wallis, and he pulled out a creaky-looking ladderback chair and sat down in it. The People sat or sprawled as they pleased, and Wallis indicated the shelves and racks all around the room, all full of boxes with numbers and letters scrawled on the ends of them. "I expect you know something about the civilization of ancient Egypt," he said.

Rhiow put her whiskers forward. "They knew something

about *our* civilization," she said, "which is why so many of their carvings feature our gods."

"The *neter-teh*," Wallis said, and nodded, "the Powers That Be. Yes. Well, you'll understand that the Egyptians were very partial to cats, considering them at least partially divine, since they looked like the gods the cats had described to my people, the *ehhif*."

And suddenly he burst out laughing.

"I'm sorry," Rhiow said, "have we missed a joke?"

"No, no . . ." The young *ehhif* wiped his eyes, still trying to get control of his laughter. "It's just this situation. You here, and me explaining this, and . . . oh my." He wiped his eyes again. "I'm sorry. Anyway, the Egyptian *ehhif* back then loved their cats very much, even before someone got the idea that the cats' semidivine status might mean they would make good intercessors for humans. To the gods, the Great Gods, I mean: to the One, and the Powers. So when their cats would die, the Egyptians would have their bodies mummified, with amulets and words of power wrapped in among the bandages, the intent being to give the cats power in the Next World." He turned to the table and lifted from it one of the strips of bandage that he had been removing from the cat-mummy he had been working on. Faintly, on the linen, in a brownish ink, were written the pictogram-letters of the "hieratic" writing of old Egypt. "Then they would send the mummies to the great cat-burial ground at the city of the Queen-Cat, Bubastis."

"Some of this we knew," Auhlae said, "though I was always a little vague about the whys and wherefores."

"The idea was that the cats would tell the Gods how well their *ehhif* had treated them," Wallis said, leaning back and folding his arms, "and the Gods would be nice to the *ehhif* in return. Well, this went nicely for some centuries. The mummies got more elaborate—see, this is a fairly late one:

the mummy cases had become quite ornate." He turned to the table again and lifted down the case that had enclosed the mummy on which he had been working. It was in the small shape of a Person, but with its forefeet crossed together over its chest, the way a human mummy would have had its arms crossed: its hind legs were stretched out straight, and the whole business stood upright on a little pedestal, which was gilded, so that the Person's image stood upright as well, the way an *ehhif* would have. The image of the cat's face was inlaid with lapis lazuli whiskers, and around the cat's neck was a tracery of gold, a collar, jeweled with shining bits of colored glass.

"It's beautiful workmanship, isn't it?" Wallis said. "They took a lot of trouble over some of these. Equally, the spells and amulets buried with the People became very involved indeed; and the cemeteries at Bubastis got fuller and fuller. There were at least three hundred thousand cat-mummies at the cemetery at Beni-Hassan alone: probably there were many more. But then the Egyptian *ehhif*'s religion changed, or was supplanted by others, and that cat-mummies and the cemeteries were forgotten."

Wallis leaned back farther in the chair, uncrossed his legs, crossed them again. "Well. Their language became lost over time, and it has taken us a long time to start getting it back again. My old teacher was one of those who became involved with trying to recover it, and I went with him to Egypt, a couple of years ago, to start trying to translate some of the texts in the Pyramids. Some of those texts were very peculiar, and my teacher could make very little of them: but I came at the translation from a slightly different angle . . . and realized what some of those wall carvings meant."

"Spells," Urruah said. "They were wizardry."

"Yes," Wallis said. "Some of them. It was knowledge I

kept to myself. I am no wizard, not as I understand the term is usually meant. But I know a little of the language—Hauhai, the Great Speech?—some words of it were carved inside the Pyramids. And from other such carvings, and a great many of the papyruses we recovered, I know a fair amount of Ailurin, which was well known by the priestly class in the Old Kingdoms period. This has helped me with some of the mummies, since I've been able to tell genuine spells of protection from simple prayers, or lists of things to have the cat ask the Gods for when it gets to Heaven."

He smiled slightly, but after a breath or so, the smile turned grim. "The matter that has been troubling me," he said, "is that over the past couple of years, someone seems to have been going to great troubles to destroy as many cat-mummies as possible—especially at the old burial grounds at Bubastis, near the modern city of Alexandria in the northern river delta. No one has made any attempt on our collection here—we have several thousand cat-mummies—but the cemeteries at Bubastis are being systematically destroyed."

"By whom?" Rhiow said. "And why?"

"By British nitrate wholesalers," said Wallis, "for fertilizer."

"What?" Auhlae said.

Wallis looked uncomfortable. "You'll understand that, even as dry as Egypt is," he said, "sooner or later, if you simply bury things in the sand, they'll decay: and if you mummify them and bury them in the sand, they decay in a very controlled manner, so that finally very little is left but material that is very high in nitrites. Some bright lad got the idea of bringing huge cargo ships down there, digging up the mummies, or what was left of them, and shipping them home to England to be sold as fertilizer for *ehhif* gardens and farmland."

"Dear Iau," Auhlae said, "how—" She broke off, apparently unable to think of a word strong enough to describe her feelings.

"Now, as I understand feline thought from the writings of the old priests," Wallis said, "once you leave the body, there's no great concern for it: you've another life waiting, and you go to it and get on with it. So in that regard, whether one ends as fertilizer or food for some scavenger is probably moot. But what troubles me is how many of those mummies were buried with a specific kind of protection. Most of my fellow translators have rendered it as a charm against extreme heat and cold. But I'm not sure they're right in this. I read it as a spell, a piece of wizardry intended to protect against the Great Fire and the Great Cold that the spell insists will follow it. Some kind of destruction, 'like the Sun falling,' that's the usual phrase—and then 'a winter without end.' "

"Iau," Rhiow said softly.

"And now," Wallis said, "suddenly all these mummies, many of them with one version or another of this spell in place, are being taken away and destroyed. Ground up and thrown on people's gardens," Wallis said, with a grimace of distaste. "Whatever else we know about the Egyptians of that period, we know they were not foolish people. Their priests in particular. I am sure some of them were wizards—possibly wizards of great accomplishment. I don't believe that anyone would be so careful, over a space nearly fifteen hundred years, to make sure that all these cat-mummies had one version or another of this particular spell written in their bandages. And there are some disturbing hints in the carvings in the great tombs that suggest that removing these massed spells would be dangerous. There are mentions of some great destruction that would come. First fire, a terrible fire that will devastate the world. And then ice, ice forever . . ."

Urruah looked at Rhiow: the others all exchanged glances. "There were visionaries among those *ehhif*," Arhu said, "and they worked with the wizards of other species who lived then. Almost certainly with our people, too. What did they see?" He looked at Rhiow. "What *we* came to try to prevent?"

"It's not beyond probability," Rhiow said softly. "They might not have understood the science behind the idea of a nuclear winter, but they might have foreseen it, all right, and devised a defense. It wouldn't surprise me that it would involve our people, either: *ehhif* always connected us with warmth and the Sun . . . with reason. We told them often enough about Aaurh the Mighty, and how she warred the world free of the cold at the beginning of things, something for which sa'Rráhh always hated her." She looked up at the young *ehhif*. "Hwallis," Rhiow said, "how much of this spell against the Great Fire do you know?"

"Most of it," he said, "but not all. The whole thing, the master version of the spell, was only rarely written out because it was so long and complicated. Most often it was sketched on the bandages in an abbreviated form. Even in the earliest days of the mass mummy burials, few mummies contained it, or the carved version of it on an amulet, again because of the complexity. I had hoped to lead another expedition this year to go back to Bubastis and hunt specifically for the full form of the spell, which the carvings in the Pyramids suggested could reconfirm its protection of the world if it was pronounced by a 'person of Power,' in the right time and place. But now the cemeteries are almost empty: their contents are in the holds of cargo ships, ground to powder. Even if I went now, I wouldn't likely find what I'm looking for. What I fear is that protection against this Great Fire, this Great Ice, whatever they may be, is being lost . . . and that the way is being opened for something terrible to happen. So I asked Ouhish to see if he could get in touch with some wizards, people who might know what to do." He shrugged. "And here you are."

"It sounds like the Lone One has been purposely dismantling this protection," Urruah said. "Using pawns, as usual, to do Its work. *Ehhif*, and their innocent greed." He glanced up at Wallis. "Sorry. Nothing personal."

"No offense taken," Wallis said.

"So what do we do?" Siffha'h said.

"I would imagine try to find the whole spell," Rhiow said, "and reinstate the protection. It could very well help with other matters." She glanced at the others. "It might even make those other occurrences impossible."

"Might," said Auhlae.

"I take your point," Rhiow said. "Hwallis—would it help if we were able to look for your full version of the spell, the master spell of which these others are fragments, in other museums?"

"I don't know," he said. "Our collection of cat-mummies here is the biggest in the world."

"Not in a hundred years, it won't be," Urruah said.

Wallis looked perplexed. "I beg your pardon?"

"He means," Arhu said, "that we're from the future. And the collection of that British Museum is a lot bigger than *this* one."

"My God," the *ehhif* said. He fell silent for a moment, then said, "I can give you a description of what to look for, both in the written and the carved forms. Will that help?"

"Very much indeed," Rhiow said. " 'Ruah?"

"Show me what you have in mind," Urruah said. "No, I don't need a drawing: do it in your head. While we're both working in the Speech, I can see what you're thinking, a little. Don't rush, just make pictures. . . ."

They spent a few minutes about it, until Urruah was satisfied. "That'll do," he said. "I should have no trouble passing it on."

"And I think I know someone who might be able to help us," Rhiow said. "Come on—let's get on with our other business for the day. When we get back home we can start making some inquiries."

They all got up. Wallis rose as well. "This has been most extraordinary," he said. "When can I expect to see you again?"

"I really don't know," Rhiow said. "We're in the middle of a fairly complex business at the moment, but I think you may have helped us with it, for which we thank you very much. Ouhish, we don't have a lot of time to linger: will you tell Hwallis about what we were discussing with you earlier?"

"Gladly. I hope we see you again soon," Ouhish said, "for this problem has us both frightened."

"We'll be in touch as soon as we can," Auhlae said. And she waved her tail, amused. "It's been charming to speak with an *ehhif* who knows our language."

Wallis bowed. "*Dai stihó,*" he said.

"Thank you," Rhiow said. "I hope we may go well on this business of yours . . . and others."

Ouhish saw them out, down to the great flight of stairs reaching down to the Great Russell Street entrance. The walk back to the street where the timeslide spell was sited went a little more swiftly than the walk to the museum had, partly because of familiarity and partly because all of them were getting bolder in dealing with the traffic: though it hardly moved much faster than the fifteen miles an hour at which London motor traffic moved in their native time, the vehicles were a good deal less lethal. They found the street conveniently empty, and Urruah found his tripwire under the mud and activated the spell-circle. It rose up in an instantaneous, blazing hedge of fire around him, and hard behind him came Siffha'h, straight onto her power point, and the others all close behind.

"All right," Urruah said. "Next coordinates. The Illingworth incursion. The slide's in standby. . . ."

"Ready. *Now,*" Siffha'h said, reared up a little, and came down with her front paws down on the power point.

The blast of fire rose up around them, pressing in.

"Hello," said a high, clear voice, "what's this?"

All the People's heads jerked up. He could plainly see them, and had waded halfway into the circle already, waist-high in the "hedge" of fire—a young *ehhif,* in shorts and a white shirt and a short dark coat, and he was looking at them, and at the circle, in astonishment. *What's he doing in here; how* can *he be in here—get him out!* was Rhiow's first thought. But there was no time. The spell was already blazing with Siffha'h's blast of power, and they were all vanishing together, the People, the spell-circle, the *ehhif* boy. . . .

There was no way to stop it, any more than an *ehhif* would have been able to get out of a moving vehicle at high speed. The pressure built. There was a cry from the boy, lost in a roar of sound that Rhiow couldn't understand. Then everything began to shake—and that she understood too well. *Unauthorized ingress into a timeslide or worldgating,* she thought, *the whole spell comes apart and flings everyone in it into not-time or not-space. Iau, not like this, why must it end like this!*

The pressure increased unbearably: Rhiow lost all sense of herself. *So much for this life,* was her last thought.

But it was not. What seemed a long time later, Rhiow found herself lying on the concrete floor of the unused platform beneath Tower Gateway Underground station: and near her was the boundary of the timeslide spell, all the virtue drained out of it. The others lay about in the positions they had held in the spell—and, sitting down by them, his knees drawn up against his chest, trembling, was the young *ehhif,* looking at his surroundings, and the People, in terror.

Rhiow got up, slowly, feeling as if one of the big draft horses of the 1874 streets had been jumping all over her. Next to her, Urruah was pushing himself up onto his feet, where he just managed to stand, wobbling, and look at the *ehhif* boy.

The boy wet his lips and croaked, "Kitty kitty?"

Urruah looked at Arhu, who was awake as well, and getting up. "*Another* problem," Urruah said.

Rhiow was forced to agree.

The argument which life seemed lately to have been becoming broke out again with unusual vehemence in the next few minutes: and it would have gone on for much longer, Rhiow thought, had there not been a young *ehhif* gazing in astonishment at the sight of five cats all apparently staring silently at one another with their tails lashing.

Auhlae was not very pleased with Urruah. *"You didn't make the timeslide exclusive!"*

"Why should I have made it exclusive?" Urruah said, aggrieved. "No one was going to be able to see us, and the spell was told to sort for transit times that wouldn't endanger any being that came along—"

"Vhai," Rhiow said. "Urruah, the *language* was pretty vague. You know how literal spells are!"

"Rhi, what was the point, when *no one should have been able to see we were there,* or the spell." He hissed softly. "Sorry. Sorry. But Rhi"—he looked over at the young *ehhif*—"*ehhif* can't see wizardry, as a rule. What *is* he? *Is* he a wizard? If so, why does he look so panicked? Or is he someone who's about to be called to the Art but hasn't been given the Oath yet? Are we supposed to induct him somehow?"

"The Powers forfend," Rhiow muttered. "That's hardly our job. We had enough trouble that way with Arhu." But then she smiled slightly. "And a certain other party . . ."

"Was that who you were thinking of going to for help with the mummy problem?" Urruah said.

"The very same. It'll have to wait a little longer now."

"You may as well go take care of it," Urruah said, "because whatever else we might have had planned for this timeslide, *this* business has ruined it." He flirted his tail at the young *ehhif*. "The slide's half deranged: it's going to take another half day at least to put it back the way it ought to be."

"Well, all right. But meantime we can't sit here ignoring *him*. And lend Auhlae a paw, for Iau's sake: she looks terrible. And call Huff—he'd better know about this sooner rather than later."

"Right."

Rhiow walked over to the boy and sat down in front of him, tucking her tail in around her feet and trying to radiate calm instead of what she felt, which was complete confusion and terror. "Young human," she said to him in the Speech, "please don't be afraid."

"I'm not," he said. He had a narrow, intelligent face and he was holding it very still, despite what was going on inside him, and how young he was. He could hardly be more than fifteen.

"Good. There's no need to be, though you're in a strange place, and something that must seem very odd has just happened to you. What's your name?"

"Artie," he said.

"Artie. I'm Rhiow. These others lying and sitting around here are friends of mine: we'll get you introduced to them shortly. Would you tell me what you think just happened to you?"

"I saw a circle of light in the street," he said. "A circle of fire. But it didn't look like fire."

"It wasn't," Rhiow said. "It was wizardry."

"You mean magic?" the boy said, his eyes widening.

"You could call it that. But not the kind of magic that is just one of your people making it look like something has vanished. *True* magic: wizardry."

"Then it is real," he whispered. "My uncle said it might be."

"Your uncle's wise," Rhiow said, wondering meantime if there was yet another wizard about to be involved in this business and, in a way, hoping not: there were already more than enough complications to this intervention. "But, Artie, you should understand that most humans, most *ehhif,* as we call them, can't see wizardry and don't know that it exists."

"I saw it, though. . . ."

"Yes," Arhu said, coming up beside Rhiow and sitting down to look at the boy. "He's a key."

Rhiow glanced over at him. "To what?"

"I don't know. But They've sent him," Arhu said. "The Powers. I saw him, while Odin and I were flying."

"The Powers? What Powers?" Artie said.

"That's going to take some explaining," Rhiow said. "Meanwhile, Artie, we have to get you back where you belong as quickly as we can."

"I'm not going," he said. "I want to see where this is first!"

Rhiow and Arhu glanced at each other. "I don't think we're going to be able to help it," Arhu said. "And, Rhi, you can't just toss him back where he came from. Why would They send him if he wasn't going to be some use? We've got to keep him."

"Where?" Rhiow said, a little desperately. "Where will he sleep? What will he eat?" She wondered if this was how an *ehhif* felt when one of their young turned up on the doorstep with a kitten-Person in their arms.

"We'll work something out," Arhu said, with a confidence that Rhiow definitely didn't feel.

He looked over at where Urruah was trying to bump the groggy Auhlae up into something like a sitting position. As he did, Huff and Fhrio came rushing in.

"Auhlae, Auhlae," Huff cried. He ran to her and began to wash her ear. It was astonishing how fast Huff could move when he wanted to, and how tender and pitiful a sight he made despite his huge size. Rhiow turned away, and found herself looking at Fhrio, who was staring at Urruah as he backed away and let Huff take care of Auhlae. Fhrio was bristling.

Oh dear, Rhiow thought. *This is going to bring them to blows sooner or later.* "Artie," she said. "Will you be all right here for a little while? No other *ehhif* will come here: this is a secret place, for reasons I'll explain to you in a while. But right now there are some things I need to attend to."

"All right," Artie said. "What's your name, puss?"

"Rhiow."

"Reeoooowww," Artie said.

"Not too bad," she said. "It's a Scots accent, isn't it? We'll work on that. It's one of the better ones for Ailurin."

Rhiow walked off a little way, then sat down again and put her ears forward, listening. *Whisperer . . .*

She heard the purr that told her the Silent One was listening.

We need help of a specific kind. There's no time for me to visit the Old Downside just now. Will you tell the Serpent's

Child that his "father's" friends need to talk to him? And will you guide him to us?

A purr of agreement, then silence.

Rhiow got up and headed over to Urruah, who was already walking toward her. " 'Ruah," she said, "do me a favor. Let me see the spell that Hwallis showed you."

He half closed his eyes. "Here."

Rhiow half closed hers as well, and let her whiskers brush close to Urruah's. A second or so later she could see what he saw, the Egyptian characters strung out in a line, but with gaps here and there where Hwallis had inferred that material was missing. Rhiow looked at the characters in her mind with a wizard's eye, letting them rearrange themselves into a long broken pattern in the graphical version of the Speech.

"It's a spell all right," she said, opening her eyes. "What an odd one, though. A lot of missing pieces. None of the power parameters are all that large, either . . . what there are of them."

"If there were meant to be thousands of these spells in the same place, all acting together," Urruah said, "they wouldn't have to be all that strong, individually."

"No," Rhiow said. "But still, if a lot of little spells are gathered together to be used for some purpose, there still *does* have to be a master spell, one that invokes the whole aggregate of power and nominates specifically what it's supposed to be used for. Otherwise all the little packets of power just fire off any old way, or seep away uncontrolled. No, I think Hwallis is right. We'll get busy on finding this, if there's any way it can be found here and now. Meanwhile, 'Ruah, do what you can about the timeslide: we've got to get at that contaminated timeline and get a date for the assassination that we can trust. Get Fhrio to help you if you can."

"I'd sooner be helped by a—"

"*Urruah,*" Rhiow said. "He is not just a fellow wizard, but a gate technician of some skill. He might see something that you miss, under the pressure of speed. We can't afford to forgo his help . . . or alienate him by not asking for that help in an area where he's gifted. Just you *handle* it."

He glared at her, then waved his tail, reluctantly acknowledging the necessity, and walked off.

Rhiow breathed out and watched him go. This kind of thing was difficult for him, but they had no choice right now. Fhrio was a problem as well, but one that Rhiow couldn't settle. The kind of behavior he routinely exhibited toward his own team would have caused Rhiow to box one of her own team members' ears to ribbons, if they had tried it. However, Huff's management style was clearly a lot less assertive than Rhiow's, and she had no right to try to impose her own style on his team. *But oh, the inclination . . .*

She sighed and just closed her eyes for a moment, wishing there were time to lie down and have a nap. When she opened her eyes again, Huff was heading over toward her. "She's all right," he said to Rhiow, very relieved.

"Of course I'm all right," Auhlae said, sounding just slightly cross as she came up behind him. "The shock of the transit just hit me hard for a moment, that's all. I'm not made of fluff."

"No, I never said you were." He head-bumped her, and Auhlae threw him an affectionate look, though the bump bade fair to knock her over again.

"Well," Huff said, when he had straightened up again, "what's the situation?"

"Our young *ehhif* is in fairly good shape," Rhiow said, casting a glance over at where Artie still sat up against the platform wall, now with his legs stretched out in front of him, watching Urruah talking to Fhrio, and the two of them poking at various parts of the timeslide. "But we're going to have to keep him with us for a while. Arhu says he's required somehow for the solution of our problem."

Auhlae blinked at that. "Is he sure?"

"Yes. Apparently he got a glimpse of him while he and Odin were off on their jaunt."

"Now there's a new one," Huff said. "Well, we'll have to work out somewhere to keep him."

"Arhu is confident that that'll be handled," Rhiow said dryly. "So we'll refer all inquiries to him. Meanwhile, have a closer look at this."

She put one paw down on the floor and began pulling it along, so that a tracery of pale fire followed it, "writing out" the partial spell that Urruah had shown her. Huff and Auhlae bent their heads down, looking at it.

"Look at this name that keeps popping up," Huff said after a moment. "In a few places. Different forms—but it's the same personality that's meant. The Bright Serpent."

"It's not the Old Serpent, though," Auhlae said, looking curiously down the length of the spell. "That would be written differently, wouldn't it."

"Yes," said Huff. "And here, the Great Shining Lizard. And another name still. Sebek."

"The one who binds together?" Auhlae said. "Would that be it?"

"I think so." Huff sat down to look at it a little more closely. "Well, it's interesting, but as spells go it's long on nouns and short on verbs. Or more specific routines like power-expenditure instructions."

"Power," Rhiow said, "yes . . ." She glanced back over toward the timeslide. Siffha'h had stood up just long enough to drag herself out of the pattern, while Urruah was starting work on it: then she had flopped down again, and was lying on her side. "Is she all right?"

"Oh, I think so." Auhlae looked over her shoulder.

"I'll check," Huff said, and got up to head over that way.

"I just . . . Don't think I'm trying to intrude, please, but I worry about her a little," Rhiow said. "She seems to push herself very hard."

"Yes," Auhlae said, "she does." She sighed. "She came to us very young. Just after her Ordeal, it was. She never said much about the details: well, as you know, that's not information one asks about—it's offered or not, the way you would treat the question of how many lives along someone is. Finally she decided she wanted to work with us, and she settled in. But she was always—" Auhlae broke off for a moment, thinking, her tail twitching. Then she said, "There was always a sense that there was something still unfinished, Ordeal or not. Something she was still looking for, and it drove her. It drives her still . . . and all this unfocused energy of hers jumps out and 'bites' people, sometimes. Or makes her bite them herself."

Rhiow sighed. "The 'unfinished business' theme turns up often enough," she said. "It happened to me, for example."

"And did you find what you were looking for?"

"I think so," Rhiow said, "though, Auhlae, to tell you the truth, sometimes even when you *have* what you were looking for, you can get confused because it doesn't look anything like the images you got yourself used to when you were still looking." She put her whiskers forward. "Well, that's another day's problem. . . . We have enough of our own at the moment."

"You're right there, cousin," Auhlae said, and sighed once more. "Let me go see if the child needs anything. She tends to give off her power in these big bursts, and then needs a lot of time to recuperate. I keep telling her she should pace herself, but does she listen?"

"I know the problem," Rhiow said.

Auhlae went off to tend to Siffha'h, and Rhiow stood up

and had a good stretch and went to the young *ehhif;* Arhu came along behind her, and behind him, Urruah. "Are you all right, Artie?" Rhiow asked.

"I'm rather hungry," he said, very woefully. "I was on my way to get a bun for lunch when I saw you."

"Well, I'll get you something," Rhiow said.

"Where?" Arhu said. "You're going to have to steal."

"No. Well, not exactly." Rhiow sighed. "Artie, would you like a sandwich?"

"A what?"

"Never mind," Rhiow said. "Do you like cheese?"

"Yes."

"I'll get you a pizza."

"From where?" Arhu said.

"Hey, bring me one, too," Urruah said.

Rhiow gave him a look. "Get your own pizza. I have enough problems. Are you and Fhrio in agreement about the timeslide?"

"He's looking at it for the moment," Urruah said. "The idea of him catching something in the spelling that I missed seems to appeal to him."

She put her whiskers forward at him. "Now who says you're all good looks and no brain?" she said. "I'll be back in a little."

Rhiow trotted over to where Auhlae was lying by Siffha'h. "Auhlae, where's one of the gates that *is* functioning? I need to run an errand."

"Back up the stairs the way we came," Auhlae said, "down the hallway and turn left to the access for the northbound Circle Line train. It's down off the left-paw end of the platform."

"Great. Right back," said Rhiow.

Sidled, she followed Auhlae's instructions and made her way up to the Circle Line platform, past the unnoticing travelers waiting for the tube train, and down the stairs at the very end of the platform. The gate's tracery was very visible: some other wizard passing through had just used it, she saw from the status-and-log weft, for a transit to Vladivostok via Chur. She reached into the control weave, got her claws into the spatial location webbing, and wove its hyperstrings together until they matched the string-coordinate qualities of the roof of her apartment building.

Normally Rhiow preferred not to do gatings of this kind: they were wasteful of energy, when you could walk. But at the moment walking was out of the question, and everything seemed to be happening at once, and she couldn't spare the time. Rhiow pulled the control weave taut, watching as the scene within its oval boundaries snapped into place. Gray gravel, ventilators sticking up . . .

Rhiow locked the gate coordinates in place, set it for selective nonpatency except for her own return, and jumped through: came down on the gravel. Hurriedly she sidled, then trotted over to the square shape that was the outlet for the building's fire stairs. The door was locked from the inside.

She walked through it, feeding the atoms of her body past the atoms of the door, and ran down the stairs a couple of flights; then she walked through a second door, the one that led to the hallway where her apartment's front door was. Rhiow galloped down the hall and walked through one last door, her own.

There was no sign of Iaehh, which was just as well. Rhiow ran over to the refrigerator, did a very small-scale skywalk up to the handle of the freezer, and put one paw through it, pulling hard. No good. She sat up on her haunches, put both forefeet through, and pulled again. This time the freezer door came open, almost knocking her down. She ducked sideways out of the reach of the swinging door and looked inside. *Thank you, Iau,* she thought, for there were about five pizzas stacked up in there. *Hmm. Pepperoni . . . not for a first-timer. Meatball . . . no. Pieces might fall off in transit. Plain with extra cheese . . .*

Her mouth was watering as she levitated the pizza out of the freezer down onto the counter. *It's been too long since I had pizza,* Rhiow thought, but the hunger she'd seen in Artie's eyes suggested to Rhiow that it was going to be a while longer. She first did a small wizardry that would release the catch of the microwave oven and push the door back: then, while that was working, she spoke to the coefficient of friction at the end of the pizza box where the glue was, then levitated the box up on its side and shook. The pizza slid neatly out onto the rotating tray in the oven.

Rhiow ran her wizardry backwards and shut the microwave door: then jumped down to the counter and stared at the controls. *You have to be a rocket scientist to run these things,* she thought, annoyed, trying to work out which control pad to push. Finally she succeeded in programming in a five-minutes run on High and started the microwave going: then took a moment to take the empty pizza box and push it down into a briefly opened pocket in spacetime, off in a corner of the kitchen. She would empty out the pocket and get rid of the box later.

The air started to fill with a very appetizing smell indeed. Rhiow's mouth watered more earnestly. *The only bad thing about this,* she thought, *is that he's going to notice it's gone. I think.* Iaehh could be slightly vague about the contents of the freezer: he and Hhuha had had some pretty heated discussions on the subject. *Either way, I'm going to have to replace it with one of the same kind as soon as I can. One more thing to think about.*

The oven *dinged*. Rhiow ran her wizardry again, forward this time, and levitated the pizza out into the air again. It was tricky: the thing was no longer solid, but kept trying to flop over in one direction or another.

Rhiow stood there for a moment considering her options. She might be sidled, but the pizza could not be, not while she was handling it either directly or with a wizardry. She was not going to walk down the apartment's hall, invisible, with a visible pizza floating along behind her. *Logistics,* she thought.

Oh vhai. She walked through the air over to the glass doors that opened on the terrace, the pizza trailing along obediently behind her, and straight out into the air to one side of the apartment. *Let the neighbors think they saw a levitating pizza,* she thought rebelliously. *If any of them are even looking.* With the pizza in tow, Rhiow skywalked up to the roof of the building, and back through the worldgate, which she shut down behind her and left in standby configuration.

That only left the tube station to deal with. Rhiow went down the stairs, then hung an immediate left and walked straight through the wall, trying to keep the directions back to the abandoned platform straight in her head. She took a few false turns, but finally found where she wanted to be: and had the satisfaction of seeing young Artie's mouth drop open as she walked straight through a wall not far from him, the pizza floating along behind her.

She put it carefully down on the floor. "It's fairly clean here," she said. "Sorry I couldn't bring a plate. Here, just pull it apart with your hands. Watch out, it's still hot."

Artie pulled his first slice off, bit it tentatively; finished it immediately and pulled off another. "Good," Rhiow said, and went over to Urruah, who was lying nearby. "Now then. What's next?"

He looked at the pizza.

"Don't even think about it," Rhiow said. "I went to a lot

of trouble over that. How's he doing?" She glanced over toward Fhrio and the timeslide.

"How would I know? I'll wait until he tells me. He might genuinely be in the middle of something I don't want to disturb." *Or I might just not want to get my head bitten off.*

Rhiow put one ear forward and one back, a wry expression. "Is Siffha'h all right, did Auhlae say?"

"Recovering," Urruah said. "She's just exhausted after doing two big power-feeds close together—and apparently the fact that something knocked us sideways affected her, too: she tried to force us through anyway, and so she took the brunt of what hit us." His tail thumped on the concrete. "She tries real hard. It's not like she has to prove anything to anyone."

"I know," Rhiow said. "If she only—"

"What's that?" Siffha'h said suddenly from the other side of the platform, pushing herself up again. "Something's coming."

Everyone looked up in alarm. Mostly they did it just in time to see the air in the middle of the platform stretch and sheen like pulled plastic wrap, then peel apart.

A dinosaur stepped out.

A casual viewer could have been forgiven for mistaking it for a dinosaur, at any rate. It stood about six feet high at the shoulder, and its long neck arched up another couple of feet to terminate in a long, lean, toothy muzzle: a pair of well-made and delicate forelegs with six claws each were folded decorously in front of the creature's chest. It stood mostly upright on its long-clawed hind legs, and a tail about five feet long lashed out behind it, helping it keep its balance. The shadowy lighting down here did not show off to best advantage the subtly patterned hide patched in red and orange, but somehow the small golden eye found the light, and kept it.

The London team stared at this apparition in astonishment: the saurian bowed to them gracefully, bobbing forward and back. "I am on errantry," it said in a soft, hissing voice, "and I greet you."

"You're well met on the errand," Huff said, still very wide-eyed. "Rhiow, is this the help you said you were sending for?"

"Indeed so. Ith, let me make you known to the London team."

She strolled over and took him around, making the introductions. Huff and Auhlae recovered their composure quickly: Fhrio, caught in the middle of doing something technical to the timeslide, simply stood for some moments with his mouth hanging open. Siffha'h gazed at Ith too, and spoke to him politely enough when introduced, but Rhiow couldn't help noticing her expression, a peculiar look of half-recognition, as if she had seen him before sometime, but couldn't place where.

Finally she brought Ith over to Artie. "And this is our 'pet' *ehhif,*" Rhiow said, with some amusement. "Artie, this is Ith."

"Oh, *rather*," said Artie, very impressed indeed. "Are you a thunder lizard?"

Ith dropped his lower jaw and flickered his long, blunt tongue slightly in what Rhiow had come to recognize as a smile. "I have not thundered at anything very recently," he said, "but in the past I have occasionally done so."

He crouched down on his back legs next to Arhu, who leaned against him companionably. "Your summons was opportune," Ith said to Rhiow, "for I was thinking of coming to see you anyway. The master gate matrices in the Old Downside, the ones that service Grand Central and many other gating complexes, have been showing signs of strain, these last few days. Gatings have not been progressing as they normally do."

"It's not just strain," Arhu said. "Let me show you."

For a few seconds they were silent together. It was not vision, Rhiow thought, but rather something to do with their old history together; they had been in one another's minds in extremely harrowing circumstances, involving their jointly completed Ordeals, and there were times when the communication between them seemed so complete and effortless that Rhiow wondered whether some kind of permanent connection between them had been wrought by the anguish and triumph they'd shared.

Ith looked up, then, and said, "You *have* been having a busy time." He clenched his claws together, interlacing them. "And now this business of the Longest Winter. Very interesting indeed."

He looked up over at the London team. "That was what killed my people in the ancient days," he said to Huff. "The Lone One, the Old Serpent, brought that fate down on us when we made our first Choice as a species. It said if we accepted Its gift, we would rule the Earth so long as the Sun shone on it. And so we did: until the blow fell burning from the sky, and the dust and the smoke of its impact rose up and hid the sun. It killed all my ancestors except the very few who, by accident or by grace of the Powers, managed to find their way into the Old Downside and take refuge in the caves there, down where the catenaries spring up from their ultimate power source. There we lived for ages, and there the Lone One ruled us, saying that someday It would lead us up into the Sun again, and we would conquer all the puny creatures that lived there and take the Earth for our own once more." He smiled, showing most of his teeth. "Well, they conquered us instead, to our great good, and my people lost their old false Father, and gained a new one.* Mostly due to my brother, my father here." He glanced down at Arhu. Arhu looked away, and purred.

"But the thought of the Winter has not been far from my mind, or my people's," Ith said to Rhiow. "It is a charged subject for us, as charged in its way as humankind's old story that you told me about the apple and the garden: and there is a serpent in that story too, though I am afraid it is not the Bright One Who is a shape I wear these days sometimes, or Who wears me—whichever. In any case, we are eager that the Winter should not come back, from whatever cause, for if it returns to the upper world, that will eventually affect the Old Downside as well. Since we have no guarantees from the Powers that this fate would never befall us again, I thought that we might seek to put guarantees of our own in place."

"You could get caught up in that kind of thing to the exclusion of everything else," Auhlae said, "if you weren't careful."

"Oh, indeed. We know well enough that every race dies," Ith said. "That alone has become obvious enough from studying other species' history. Entropy is running." The young-old, wise eyes looked a little tired already. "We cannot stop it. But this does not mean we need instantly to enter into a suicide pact with the Universe. We may forestall the event as long as possible . . . indeed the Powers would prefer that we do."

"Getting familiar with Them, are you?" Urruah said.

"No less than you," Ith said mildly. "Your good friend, Saash of the unending itch, now herself walks the floor of Heaven about the One's business, and the depths of reality echo to the thumping when she sits down to scratch. And she

*A tale told fully in *The Book of Night with Moon*.

thought of herself as 'nothing special.' I am nothing special either, but I am also Father of my people now, and so I find myself chatting often enough with my people's Grandparents as I try to make some sense out of this terrible mass of data They've wished on me, and try to claw it into some shape that our new wizards will be able to handle."

"New wizards *already?*" said Arhu.

"They are hatching out even as we speak," Ith said. "Some seem to have been trying to be born for a long time, some say they have tried many times, but were always killed in the ongoing *hethhhiiihhh.*" Rhiow blinked at the word: the Speech said *holocaust* in her ear, but there were even more terrible implications in the word, speaking of a people who for many generations had simply been born to be killed, almost all new hatchlings being destined to feed the chosen warriors of the Lone Power's planned army.

"Now, though," Ith said, "there are more than twenty already. Our latency period is fairly short, and besides, there is the time difference between the Upworld and the Downside to consider. We are, in any case, making up for much lost time, which is a good thing, considering the importance of the gates we guard. The Downside will be alive with wizardry before very long, and all the better for it: it is not good for a world to go unmanaged. But our 'wizard's manual' is still in its early stages, and I have been kept very busy trying to codify it."

"I would have thought it would have just appeared," Urruah said. "As if it had always been there, now that your people's Choice is properly made. I mean, the information's all in the Speech after all, so your people won't have trouble understanding it."

"Yes, but first there's the question of what information a wizard of our people will routinely have access to," Ith said, "and what they'll have to ask for authorization from Higher Up to get."

"I would have thought the Powers would make that distinction themselves."

"No," Ith said. "We—upper-level field operatives—are given more autonomy than you might suspect. Surprising amounts of it." He opened his mouth to grin slightly, the amiable saurian smile that showed all those teeth. "The Powers' attitude is plainly, 'You're living in this universe: why would you be so dumb as to pull down the ceiling of the cavern on yourself? Be cautious running the place, but take what risks you think need to be taken.' And does it not say in the Estivations, 'I shall walk Your worlds as You do, as if they are mine . . . for so indeed they are'? So I find *I* must make these decisions, the Powers apparently feeling that one from inside a native 'psychology' will be best fitted to understand wizardry's best implementation for that psychology. Then there's the matter of how Seniors and Advisories will be chosen, and a very basic one: how the wizardry itself will manifest to my people. We've had all kinds of different modalities—voices heard, visions seen—but they've been haphazard, and I've been told that we should try to keep it to one or two modalities for the whole species, so that legend and tradition regarding their handling will have time to build up around them. At least we don't have to try to keep wizardry secret, the way the poor *ehhif* do. My wizardly children will lead normal lives . . . as far as any wizard's life can be considered normal."

"You're getting pretty organized," Arhu said.

"Order is a wonderful thing," Ith said, "when it flows from the roots of a matter rather than being imposed from the top down. And organization usually follows, yes, but not so much so that I can't slip out for a pastrami sandwich every now and then." He grinned at Arhu. "And we should try to meet soon in that regard: I've found a good place up on Eighty-sixth between First and Second. Meanwhile, though, I have other business in hand. They tell me you need me," he said to Rhiow. "And to my people's Stepmother I can only say, 'Tell me what you need, and it's yours.' "

Rhiow put her whiskers forward.

"Meanwhile," Ith said, turning his head sideways and giving Artie one of those peculiar looks of his, like a very large bird eyeing a very large worm, "is there any more of that pizza?"

Rhiow laughed. "No! Get your own. There's probably a fairly decent pizza place not too far from where you're getting your pastrami."

"No," Ith said, "I would say Eighty-sixth is something of a desert as regards pizza. Now if you go a little farther uptown—"

"Don't!" Rhiow said. He and Arhu looked at her, startled. "Just *don't*," she said wearily. "Later. Later I will go and look for pizza with you. If there's still a reality left on Earth that involves pizza."

"All right," Ith said. "Back to the subject. While involved in the codification, I have been eagerly searching for a spell that would prevent a second Winter's fall. Now I see and hear from your interview with Hwallis that there is, or was, such a thing. The Whisperer does not know of it, though. Or if she did, it is lost."

"How would she lose anything?" Siffha'h asked.

"I do not know. But let us see the spell again, what you have of it."

Rhiow showed it to Ith where she had it laid out on the floor. He looked at it for a few moments, and then chuckled, a deep clicking noise in his throat. "Yes," he said, "there is a piece of my name, and another piece. And the Bright Serpent's name, which I would have thought was a new thing;

but now it seems it is old, and existed from ancient times. Another piece of information temporarily lost, or submerged under formerly more aggressive archetypes. And see here." He put one claw down on one symbol of the spell, which flared briefly brighter in response. "Yes, this is the Ophidian Word in one of its new variants: my people are certainly involved—either the memory of our old tragedy, or the prophecy of our later intervention against repetitions of it. And here is the symbol for the Winter, and the indicator for the conditional branches of the target designation spell. There are definitely pieces missing: and this"—he tapped another symbol—"seems to indicate how many. Six other major parts. The master structure is hexagonal." He sat back, looking satisfied. "That makes perfect sense, for the universe has a broadly hexagonal bent: things tend to come in sixes." He flexed his claws, giving a little extra wiggle to the sixth claw on each forelimb. "Particle arrays, hyperstring structures . . ."

Arhu looked accusingly at Rhiow. "I thought you told me everything came in fives."

"Not *everything*," Rhiow said, in slight desperation. "Things to do with gates."

Ith gave her that sidewise look. "Possibly we have a paired underlying symmetry here," he said. "Dual symmetries of sixes and fives, conjoined at the functional level as elevens? The even and the odd . . ."

"Or the like and the unlike," Urruah said, interested. "But together, they make a prime."

Rhiow rolled her eyes. Since coming into his own, Ith sometimes went off into mathematical conjectures that completely lost her—a side effect, she thought, of coming of a species that was only now discovering abstract reasoning for its own sake, after having spent so many millennia in the darkness, thinking about nothing but survival and food. It was perhaps some side-gift of his wizardry: or, like Urruah's never-ending fondness for food and *oh'ra*, it might just be a hobby. Either way, it tended to make her head hurt.

"Ith, you're going to have to take it up with the Powers That Be," Rhiow said, "because I haven't the faintest idea. Right now we need someone to help us look for that spell, for the other parts of it, and to get them welded together. We may need it very badly in a very short time."

"Then I will come and do that for you," Ith said. "I will search everywhere I can think of. The museum here first, as you say: and then the museum in New York as well, and elsewhere, if I must."

Arhu glanced up, looking a little uneasy. "I don't know if I like the idea of taking the Father of his People away from them just now," he said. "This could be a dangerous time."

Ith looked at him with mild surprise. "Do fathers not go out to find food and protect their young, sometimes? The important thing is to come back afterwards. . . . Besides, events in one universe spread to others, sooner or later. By acting now, perhaps I save myself the need to act more desperately later."

"That may or may not be," Huff said, "but in any case, it's still very good of you to come and help us. I mean . . ." He sounded slightly flustered. "We are, after all, People . . . and you are, after all . . ."

"A snake?" Ith dropped his jaw amiably. "Well, People have in the past taken a certain amount of interest in the welfare of another people's universe: mine. We could have been left to die in the dark, or to live out our lives as slaves, under the Lone Power's influence. But others risked themselves for us. Perhaps there is no 'payback,' but paying forward is certainly an option open to us. So let us not speak of it anymore."

He rocked a little on his haunches, reaching back in mind

again to the interview with Wallis that Arhu had shown him, and looking down at the fragmentary spell again. " 'A person of Power,' " said Ith, "must enact the spell. Does that mean, perhaps, a Person? One of your People? Or could it be just any wizard?"

"It depends if they call themselves persons or not, I suppose," Rhiow said. "Ith, your guess is as good as mine, but I think we're going to need the rest of the spell before we can draw any conclusions about that."

"Well enough, then: I will go."

"I want to go too!" Artie said suddenly, jumping up. "I haven't seen any magic practically since I got here. I want to see some more!"

Rhiow glanced at Ith, about to object: then she stopped herself. *Cousin, if you can take charge of him for a while, it would take a worry off our minds. He's at the wrong end of time, and it's not good for an* ehhif *to know too much about its own future without preparation . . . for which we've had no time. The museum will be a controllable environment, one not too strange to him.*

Consider it done.

"Well, Ith," Rhiow said out loud, "if you take Artie with you, he can help you look for the spell, while you keep him invisible. You should have fun with that," Rhiow said to Artie. "You're going to keep walking into things, though, so be warned."

"I will bring him gladly," said Ith. "Artie, are you willing?"

"I should say so!"

"All right. Artie," Rhiow said, "who are you staying with in London?"

"My uncle and aunt," he said, suddenly looking rather concerned. "They were expecting me back for teatime."

"Well," Urruah said, "if we can get the timeslide to work

properly, there'll be no problem returning him to just a few seconds before or after we found him, or he found us." *And if we can't get the slide to work properly, then shortly it won't matter one way or the other.*

Rhiow made a face at the thought. *And what happens to us then?* she thought. *We become refugees to some other timeline that hasn't been ruined. If we can find any such. And Artie will share the same fate.*

No, she thought. *No need to give up just yet. There's a lot more work to be done.*

"Very well," Ith said, and stood up. "Artie, prepare yourself: we will go to the British Museum and walk invisible among the displays. Or perhaps"—and that little golden eye glinted—"late tonight, when none but the night watchmen are about, perhaps one of them will look into the Prehistoric Saloon and wonder if he saw one of the displays move, and wink its eye."

He winked, and Artie burst out laughing as he dusted himself off, which was about all the preparation he could make. "Ith, you wouldn't," Rhiow said, trying to sound severe. Ith seemed to have picked up some of Arhu's taste for mischief along with the taste for deli food. Unfortunately, it was difficult to scold someone who was so old and grave, and at the same time so young, and whose wickednesses were of such a small and genteel sort.

"Perhaps I would not," Ith said, bowing to Rhiow. She put her whiskers forward in ironic amusement at the phrasing. "In any case, I will take care of him," Ith said. "If nothing else, when he needs to rest, I can take him to the Old Downside, where he will see all the 'thunder lizards' his heart desires."

"How are your people doing?" Urruah asked. "Settling in nicely?"

"They love the life under the sky," Ith said. "For some of

them, it is as if the old life in the caves never happened. And truly, for some of them, it is better that way. For others . . . they remember, and they look up at the Sun and rejoice."

"Have there been any problems with our own people?" Rhiow said. The only other intelligent species populating that ancient ancestor-dimension of Earth were the Great Cats of whom *Felis domesticus* and its many cousins were the descendants: sabertooths and dire-lions, who had taken refuge in that paradisial otherworld many ages before.

"Oh, no," Ith said mildly, and flexed his claws. "None that have been serious. They were unsure whether we were predators or prey, at first. They are sure now." He grinned, showing all those very sharp teeth.

Rhiow chuckled. "Get out of here," she said. "And go well. Artie, be nice to him. He bites."

"He wouldn't bite *me,*" said Artie.

"No, I would not," Ith said. "Though perhaps in future you should wait for more data before you theorize, Artie; there are other creatures where we are going who might be less willing to give you the benefit of the doubt." Ith grinned. "Now come stand by me. Watch, and take care; when the air tears, it does so raggedly, and the boundaries between here and there are sharp."

They stepped into the air together and were gone, the tear in it healed up behind them.

Huff stared after them. "How does he *do* that?" he said. "There wasn't even any noise from the displacement of the air."

Rhiow shook her head. "In some ways, he's become a gate himself," she said. "Otherwise, I don't understand it. Ask Her. Meanwhile—what about that timeslide?"

✦

It took several more hours to get it working to both Urruah's and Fhrio's liking. Rhiow tried to catch a nap while this was going on, but her anxiety kept waking her up, so that when Urruah finally came to rouse her, she was awake anyway.

"Is the slide ready?" Rhiow asked, stretching fore and aft.

"As far as I can tell. For all Fhrio's rotten temper," he added very softly, "he's a good gating tech, and there's nothing wrong with his understanding of timeslide spells. He rearranged some subroutines I'd thought looked pretty good, and I have to admit that now they look better."

"Annoyed?" Rhiow said.

"Me? Nothing wrong with me that a pizza won't cure," Urruah said, "and the end of this job. We can jump again in fifteen or twenty minutes. Fhrio is doing the last fine-tuning: Siffha'h says she's ready to go again, and Auhlae concurs."

"Good." She glanced around. "Where are they?"

"They've gone off to relieve themselves first. Huff went off too, just for a snack of something."

"Right."

They went over together to look at the timeslide. Rhiow walked around it thoughtfully, trying to see what Fhrio had done. He was sitting, gazing at the whole structure with his eyes half-shut, a little unfocused: a technique Rhiow used herself, sometimes, to see the one bit of a spell or a routine that was out of place.

She stopped at one point and looked to see where a whole group of subroutines had been added, a thick tangle of interwoven branchings in the "hedge." There were numerous calls on spatial locations that were not far from this one, as far as Rhiow could tell, and all of which were in this time. "What are these?" Rhiow said curiously.

Fhrio glanced up. "I found myself wondering," he said, "whether we were sending a lion to kill a mouse. I mean, by looking for our pastlings one at a time by tracing specific accesses one at a time. I thought, since the *ehhif* here have support systems that are supposed to be picking up their lost and sick people from the city area, at least, why don't we let it work for us? So this set of routines visits every *ehhif*-hospital in the greater London area, and scans it for a few seconds for anyone in that facility who wasn't born within the last hundred years. If it finds anyone like that, it picks them up and brings them along with us, in stasis. Then we get back here and analyze their temporal tendencies in situ, with the gate to help, if we can get the online gate logs to co-operate."

Rhiow looked the construction over. It was elegant, compact, and looked like it ought to work, but many constructs of this kind looked like they should, and the only way you could find out was by testing them live. "Fhrio," she said, "it's handsome-looking, and beautifully made. Let's run it and see what it does." She paced around to the other side of the timeslide, checked her name in passing, then leaped into the circle and looked thoughtfully at the other sets of coordinates stacked up in the routines to be examined: mostly derived from microtransits of the malfunctioning gate. "If Siffha'h can push us through to all of these," Rhiow said, "we're going to be in great shape."

"I hoped you'd think so," Fhrio said. And he looked over at Urruah, and bared his teeth in amusement. "Pity you weren't smart enough to manage something like this, O 'expert one.' Even your own team leader admits it."

Urruah blinked and opened his mouth.

"Urruah," Rhiow said softly, "would you excuse us?"

His eyes went wide. "Uh, sure," he said.

He went away with great speed, Rhiow didn't know where; nor did she care at the moment. "All right, Fhrio," Rhiow said. "I'm tired of hearing it in the background, or unsaid. Get on with it and say what you have to say."

He stared at her, his ears back. "I don't like him around here," Fhrio said after a moment. "Or the other one. There are too many toms around here as it is. Huff and I have about worked things out. We're all right together, if not precisely in-pride. But *those* two! Him, with his big balls hanging out, leering at Auhlae. And him, with his little balls hanging out, just a furry little bundle of drool and hope and hormones, leering at Siffha'h. They both give me the pip, and the sooner they're out of here the better I'll like it."

"Well," Rhiow said, and nearly bit her tongue, she could think of so many things to say, and so few of them appropriate. "Thank you for letting me know. In Urruah's case, he's always been one for appreciating the queens, though in Auhlae's case, he knows she's mated and happy so, and you're completely mistaken about his intentions toward her. If you don't believe another wizard telling you so, then you'll have to go have it out with him—after *I* finish with you. For the second time, that is, after I extract from your hide the price of calling the competence of one of my teammates into question, and for openly suggesting that I might agree with you in your assessment. And as for Arhu, whatever business he has with Siffha'h is theirs to determine, not yours or mine: she's her own queen now, no matter what your opinions on the matter may be. What you think of that stance is your business, but if you meddle with a young wizard under my protection, I will shred your hide myself, and see if you have the nerve to do anything about it. So beware how you conduct yourself."

Fhrio stared at her as if she had suddenly appeared out of the air from another planet. "Meanwhile," Rhiow said, "I intend to do my job to the best of my ability, no matter how pointlessly annoying I find you. You seem to be doing your job . . . marginally. But if you can't manage your reactions to my team a little more completely, I'll require Huff to remove you from this intervention, which is within my rights as leader of a senior gating team sent on consultation. Then we'll bring in as a replacement someone less talented, perhaps, but a little more committed to not damaging the other wizards whom the Powers have sent to save this situation . . . and entirely incidentally, *you.* Now take yourself away until Huff comes back, and be glad I've left your ears where Iau put them, instead of so far down your throat they'll make bumps in your tail."

He stared at her without a word, and after a long moment he turned away.

Rhiow sat down and licked her nose four times in a row, feeling hot under her fur: furious with herself, furious with Fhrio, and just generally very upset. She was bristling, and her claws itched, and she was mortified. *I hate being this way,* she thought. *I hate* having *to be this way. I hate having to pull rank. Oh, Iau, did I do wrong?*

The Queen was silent on this subject, as on so many others. Rhiow breathed out and tried to get control of herself again. She was so busy concentrating on this that she didn't notice when Siffha'h came in and jumped into the circle beside her.

"I said, are you all right?" Siffha'h said.

"Oh. I will be shortly," Rhiow said. "Thanks for checking." Siffha'h had straightened up and was now staring across the platform. Rhiow glanced that way to see what was there. It was Arhu. He was staring back. For a long few moments it held: then, to Rhiow's surprise, it was Arhu who lowered his eyes first and looked away.

Rhiow jumped out of the circle and meandered over to where Arhu was, sat down by him, and started composure-washing with a vengeance. Under cover of this, she said very quietly to Arhu, a little exasperated, "What *is* it with you two?"

"She hates me," Arhu said.

Urruah reappeared, sat down beside them, and started to wash as well. "But she has no reason to," Rhiow said.

"*She* seems to think she does."

Rhiow blinked at that. "How do you know?"

"I See it."

Urruah glanced up briefly at that. "This is new," he said.

"I'm Seeing a lot of things since I went flying with Odin," Arhu said. "It's as if discovering a new way to See has made some kind of difference. It's happening more often, for one thing."

"So what did you See about her?"

"It's nothing specific. In fact, once I tried to See, on purpose, and—" He shrugged his tail. "Just nothing. Like she was blocking me somehow."

"How would she do that?" Urruah said, mystified. "I wouldn't have thought there was any way to block vision."

"I wonder if she'd discuss it," Rhiow said.

"Oh, try that by all means," Urruah said. "But bring a new pair of ears."

Rhiow sighed. It would have to wait. Auhlae jumped back up onto the platform, followed by Huff. "Are we ready?" Huff said.

"Absolutely," said Rhiow, and got up to meet him by the timeslide. "I take it our first priority is the pastlings—sweeping them up, if we can, and confining them all safe in one place."

"That's Fhrio's plan," said Huff. "Where is he?"

"Here, Huff," said Fhrio, and came up from the end of the platform to join them.

"Arhu? Urruah? Let's go," said Huff.

They paced over and leaped into the timeslide-circle, taking their positions. Siffha'h put herself down on the power point and glanced up at Fhrio.

He hooked a claw into the spell-tracery that would handle the "sweep" routine. "Half a breath," he said. And then, "It's ready. Standing by . . ."

"Now," said Siffha'h, and reared up, and put her forepaws down hard.

Rhiow blinked . . . or thought she had. Then she realized it was the spell doing it for her. There was no physical sensation to this transit any more than there usually was from crossing through a gate, but the view flickered and flickered again, showing brief vistas of fluorescent-lit rooms, shocked *ehhif* faces, and assorted machinery scattered about. Every now and then, the spell would pause a little longer as it tried to determine whether some particularly ancient *ehhif* fit the criteria for which it had been instructed to search; then it would move on, almost hurriedly, as if to make up for lost time. *Blink, blink, blink,* the vistas of people in white came and went—

—And suddenly, there was someone with them in the circle. He was a sorry-looking *ehhif* indeed, with longish black hair and a hospital gown, and he was looking at them all with dopey astonishment while he rubbed his wrists, which were suddenly no longer restrained. He opened his mouth, possibly to shout for help at the sight of seven cats in a circle of light, but Fhrio slipped one paw under one of the control lines of the spell, and the *ehhif* froze just that way, staring, with his mouth open.

"It's going to start getting crowded in here," Rhiow said, unable to resist being at least a little amused. *Blink, blink, blink, blink* went the spell, and she had to start keeping her eyes closed; the effect was rather disturbing, for it was starting to go faster and faster. *How many hospitals does this city have, anyway?* Rhiow thought.

It had quite a few, and they got to visit about eight more of them before yet another *ehhif*, a tall, handsome woman in a borrowed nightshirt, found herself standing in the circle. Rhiow could tell that the nightgown was borrowed because no one from the last century was really that likely to own a nightshirt featuring a picture of a famous gorilla climbing up the Empire State Building. The woman took one look at the cats in the circle and opened her mouth to scream.

She too froze, and outside the timeslide, the *blink, blink, blink* started again. The center of the circle began filling with *ehhif*, all still as statuary by some eccentric artist, some dressed, some not very, all looking like people who have been through a great deal in a short time.

And on and on the blinking went, until Rhiow had to squeeze her eyes shut again, and even when they were shut, she could still sense the timeslide flickering from place to place, until the mere thought of it made her queasy. Then there came a surprised shout, and suddenly Artie was standing in the circle with them, looking in astonishment at the other *ehhif* who were already there.

"No," Huff said quickly, "not *him!*"

Artie vanished again, and the flickering went on. Rhiow was slightly reassured by this proof of the spell's ability to sort for the right people. But meantime she closed her eyes again and just concentrated on standing where she was and not falling over.

After a few moments, someone poked her. She opened her eyes again, swallowing, and trying to command her stomach not to do anything rash. Auhlae patted her again with the paw and said, "Are you all right?"

"If we're done with the hospital sweep," Rhiow said, "then yes."

"Is that all of them?" Arhu said.

Huff looked at Fhrio, and Fhrio waved his tail in acknowledgment. "That's all the spell could find," Fhrio said. "It's more than we had ten minutes ago, anyway."

Rhiow gulped. "Fhrio, a beautiful job. Can we leave them here safely awhile? We still have one more thing to try to do. We've got to get at the contaminated timeline and get that assassination date."

"No problem," Fhrio said. He reached into the glowing hedge of the timeslide and hooked out another line of light; the whole timeslide slipped sideways, with the people in it, but leading the *ehhif* off by themselves at one side of the platform. "I've thrown a nonpermeable shield around them. No one will be able to see them, hear them, or get at them."

"Then let's go. One more time!"

And once more the pressure built and built, and Rhiow closed her eyes against it, sure that it was going to push them straight back in through their sockets. She waited for the release of pressure that would let them all know that the slide had been successful, but it didn't come. It just built, and built, and got worse and worse—

—*Can't,* said Siffha'h. On the other side of the circle was a terrible feeling of strain, counterbalanced with the sense of some massive force planted in their way, not to be moved.

Don't bother, said someone's voice, Huff's voice, from inside the spell. *Let it go, we'll try again later!*

I—will not—let It— Siffha'h gasped. *There may not be a chance later. We're wizards—what else are we for?*

Not for killing ourselves! Rhiow cried. *Siffha'h, let it go!*

Silence, and that unbearable strain, getting worse every moment. *It won't give,* Siffha'h said between straining breaths, almost in a grunt. *It won't give. It won't—*

Let it go! Siffha'h, let it go! That was Fhrio now. *Don't try—*

Yes—it will—

And silence for a moment . . . and then the cry.

Everything fell apart. Once again Rhiow caught that odd

and terrible sound, like a roar of some frustrated beast at the very edge of things: then it was gone.

Everything was black. Rhiow lay in the blackness, content to let it be that way. *I'm so tired . . . just let me rest a little.*

She slowly became aware that Huff was standing over her. "Rhiow, are you all right? Rhiow!"

She tried to struggle to her feet, almost made it, fell down again.

"No, lie still," Huff said, and started to wash her ear.

It was such a sweet gesture, and so completely useless at the moment, that Rhiow could have moaned out loud. But she held her peace. Just for a flash the thought went through her mind: *How lucky Auhlae is. How wonderful it would be to have a tom like this to be with . . . not just in friendship, but* that *way as well. . . .* But she put it aside. "That way" was no longer a possibility for her: and Huff was spoken for.

Rhiow was conscious of wanting to lie there and let the kindly washing continue, but at the same time it made her profoundly uncomfortable, and she could think of no way to get it to stop but to produce evidence that she was all right: so she pushed herself to her feet, no matter how wobbly she felt, and bumped Huff in the shoulder with her head in a friendly way. "Come on, cousin, it's not that bad," she said. "I'll do well enough. What about the others?"

The others were by and large in no worse shape, though Siffha'h could not get up yet no matter what she did, and had to be content to lie there on the concrete while the others sat around her. "Well," Huff said, "there's no question now that eighteen seventy-four is the right year. The Lone One is actively blocking that year, and not even bothering to hide what It's doing anymore."

"Which suggests that It's getting more certain that there's

nothing we can do to keep the two universes from achieving congruency," Auhlae said.

Siffha'h was trying to sit up again: Auhlae pushed her down, forcefully, with one paw. "We have to try again," Siffha'h said weakly.

"You will try nothing whatever," Auhlae said sternly. "You are going to your den and you are going to lie there and sleep until you've recovered yourself."

"But we can't just leave it like this," Siffha'h pleaded. "We can't *wait.* The Lone One is going to block the access even more thoroughly if we don't try again right away. We won't *ever* be able to get through. And then it will kill the Queen, and everything . . . everything will die. . . ." She had to put her head down on the concrete again: she couldn't hold it up any longer.

"We *have* to wait," Fhrio said to her. "We don't have any chance of getting through at all with you in your present state. You've got to rest. There's a chance. . . ." He looked over at Urruah, unwillingly. "If you and Urruah tried it together, tomorrow morning: powering the slide . . ."

"That's going to be our best chance," Huff said, looking over at Urruah to see if he was willing: Urruah waved his tail yes. "It's not like we need to be idle in the meantime. Some of these *ehhif* don't come from the blocked year: we can concentrate on getting as many of them back to their proper times as we can. But as for eighteen seventy-four, we'll have to try again tomorrow." He looked over at Rhiow. "Do you concur?"

"It seems the best plan," Rhiow said. "We'll head back to our home ground and make sure things are secure there . . . then be back in the morning."

And there was nothing much more they could do about it than that. Home Rhiow and her team went, not in the best of moods, despite the recovery of the *ehhif* pastlings. Rhiow was feeling emotionally and physically bruised, and still guilty and upset over what she had said to Fhrio, especially in view of how successful his strategy to pick up the time-stranded *ehhif* had proven. Urruah was silent as only a tom can be who secretly feels he's been upstaged, and is determined not to acknowledge it since the realization would be beneath him. Arhu looked abstracted and grim, his thoughts turned inward, possibly to thoughts of what he had Seen or might yet See, but Rhiow was more willing to bet that his attention was bent mostly on Siffha'h at the moment. And she seriously doubted that tomorrow would turn out any better.

When they parted company and she finally got home, Iaehh was nowhere to be found, though he had filled Rhiow's bowls for her again. It was unusual for him to be out late at night by himself. *Though perhaps he's not by himself,* Rhiow thought. And why would that be so terrible a thing? It's not like he doesn't need the company of other *ehhif. Even, perhaps, one to be close to the way he was close to Hhuha.*

Yet at the same time she shied away from the idea. They had been so *very* close. There was no question of Hhuha ever being replaced in Iaehh's affections. Rhiow thought he would always love her, even though she was gone. Though why should that mean that he should have no new mate to draw close to? *It's not as if he had been spayed or anything,* she thought: and for the first time, Rhiow actually found herself feeling slightly bitter about it. *It's not as if there was an option that he might have had, which is now forever closed to him.*

She sat in the dark kitchen and stared at the food bowl and the water bowl. *Listen to me,* Rhiow thought. *My blood sugar must be in a terrible state.* Dutifully she went over to the food bowl and tried to eat, but she had no appetite, and the food tasted like mud.

She sighed and walked into the bedroom, and jumped on the bed; curled up on the pillow and got as comfortable as she could when there was no one else in the bed to snuggle up to. Sleep came quickly, but not quickly enough for Rhiow to escape the images of Siffha'h's fear and Arhu's pain, Fhrio's anger, Urruah's discomfort: and for the first time in a long while, she had no taste for the Meditations, but simply put her head down and waited for oblivion to descend, however briefly.

✦

Come the morning, or the early afternoon, rather, she woke ravenous and lively again. Iaehh had been and gone, once more filling her bowls: though she was glad of the convenience, Rhiow wished that her schedule would stabilize enough to let her spend an evening with him. For the time being, though, work was going to have to take precedence—so that there would, hopefully, be evenings enough to spend after it all was over.

After "breakfast" at two in the afternoon, and her toilet, she made her way leisurely down to Grand Central and made the rounds of the gates. They seemed to be running normally, but Rhiow remembered Ith's remark about the main gate matrices misbehaving, and could only hope that things would remain stable for the time being—stable enough, at least, for the Penn gating team to handle any minor difficulties that might arise.

Meanwhile, she had one other piece of business to attend to, and she was fairly sure where she might find it. She went down to the train platforms and made her way over to Track 24, where the third and most frequently used of the Grand Central gates was positioned, invisible as usual to all but the wizards who used it. Sidled, Rhiow sat up on her haunches and reached into the control weave, caught the appropriate hyperstrings in her claws, and wove them together; then she let the configuration snap back into the weft. The transit oval of the gate responded immediately, showing her a view as if from the mouth of a cave: outside the cave's mouth, golden light streamed by in broad rays, through the branches of trees that could not be seen.

Rhiow braced herself, tensed, and leaped through the gate. She came down on stone on the far side, but "down" was not as far down as usual. She lifted one paw to look at it—an old habit. It was not her usual small, trim paw, but nearly five inches across. Rhiow put her whiskers forward, glad as usual that her color at least remained the same when she visited here. The old Downside was the place where a cat's body was the size of its soul, in confirmation of the ancient privilege of feline wizards, whose ancestors had once been leonine in body, and had given up that size and power for a different kind of power—one less physical but, to Rhiow's mind, much greater.

The stone shelf where she stood reared out from the side of the Mountain and gave a dazzling view across the plains of the Old Downside, tawny in the afternoon sunlight of a summer that never seemed to go away. Above her and behind her the Mountain's huge flanks were hidden by the forests of great and ancient trees, which had been there since her People first realized what this place would mean to them down the ages: and at the top of the Mountain speared farther upward yet the highest trunk and branches of the Tree whose top rose into heaven and whose roots went down to the center of things. Rhiow looked at it in awe, as she had before, wondering when she would finally have time to go up the Mountain to sit under those great branches and hear the whispers of those who sat in them, murmuring wisdom. *Not today,* she thought, a little sadly. *Maybe later . . .*

Rhiow headed for the path that led down off the stone

shelf, down toward the nearest patch of grassland, for already she had seen what she had suspected she would—creatures running on two legs rather than four, one of them quite small, and the others all six or eight feet tall. They appeared to be racing through the long grass, and one of them tumbled and got up to race again: faintly she caught the sound of *ehhif* laughter.

Rhiow put her whiskers forward and made her way down into the long grass of the plateau, actually just one of several stepped plateaus leading gradually down to where the river poured itself toward the half-seen reaches of what would someday be the Atlantic Ocean. Across the sea of grass she could see brown-golden shapes running, muscles working under shining, scaled hide: and one of them, catching sight of what might have been mistaken for a jet-black lioness, turned and loped in a leisurely way toward her.

She trotted along to meet him. "Well, Ith," Rhiow said, "I thought you might be here at this point."

"Indeed yes," Ith said, and slowed to stand beside her: together they stared out across the grass, where a small, white-shirted figure was tearing through the grass with several small saurians in friendly pursuit. "He began to weary, ten hours or so ago: so I left him here to sleep with a few of my People for guardians, and continued the work awhile."

"But you stopped," Rhiow said.

"For the time being. I have found at least some of what you sent me for," Ith said. "Some, but not all, of the master spell against the Winter. Many a mummy of your People I unwound last night." He flexed his claws. "It is delicate work, even with wizardry to help: and they all had to be put back the way I found them. Artie," he said, looking after the boy, "is good at that. He has a sharp eye for detail, and a certain morbid fascination for dead bodies."

Rhiow snorted amusement. "It's a typical trait of young *ehhif,* I believe."

"Well, it has stood him in good stead. We have found something indeed. That spell is no mere injunction against the Winter, whether meteoric or nuclear. Even by the two missing fragments we have found, I can tell it is one of those spells that invoke the Powers That Be, not indirectly through their servants the elements or mortal beings, but directly and by Their names. Not a force to be toyed with . . . and likely to be dangerous enough even when used in a good cause."

Rhiow sat down, watching Artie run. "Is it *too* dangerous to use?"

"Perhaps," Ith said, "but I would not think we dare let that stop us. There is a word in the old Egyptian: *ba-neter,* the world-soul, the 'god-soul of the world.' *That* is the power substrate that this spell indirectly invokes. One of the Powers That Be, certainly: and I think perhaps the one that anciently both created the substance of the Earth, under the One's direction, and later Itself *became* it. What the *ehhif* I think would call the 'tutelary angel' of the Earth, or of its power for life."

"Gaia," Rhiow murmured.

"Yes, that would be another of the *ehhif* names. I would be much concerned if, in working this spell, we indeed saved the Earth from the Winter . . . but if at the same time, we awakened that Power, the Earth Herself."

Rhiow's tail lashed; she licked her nose. "I see your point," she said. "What if we wake up the Earth . . . and She doesn't like what's living on Her?"

Ith bowed in agreement. The grass not too far away from them began to hiss more loudly, and after a moment Artie came bursting out of it. "Come on, Ith," he said, "it's your turn to race!"

"I'll race with you again later," Ith said, "but in the meantime, Rhiow has stopped by to find out how we did last night."

"*This* is Rhiow?" Artie looked at her in astonishment. "You're much bigger!"

"Yes," she said, "I am, here. But it won't last: I must get back to work. Are you having a good time here?"

"Oh, yes! It's wonderful . . . it's like a little lost world."

"So it is, though not so much lost as hidden. It's more like a lost one that we have to try to get into today: the Earth of eighteen seventy-four again. Not the one you come from, but the dark one."

"Ith told me about it," Artie said. "Rhiow, please let me come too! I want to see the world where the Moon's blown up!"

Rhiow shuddered. "I can't say that I recommend it," she said. "We're going to be moving very fast today . . . there won't be time for sightseeing."

"Oh, Rhiow!"

"Now don't plague her," Ith said. "She has had a hard time of it. She will take you worldgating when things are a little less busy."

"That's right," Rhiow said, putting her whiskers forward at the way Ith was acquiring the sound of a father. "Ith, I'll be in touch with you later to let you know how we're doing. Meanwhile, keep at the work with the mummies. We need that spell."

"I will see to it. Go well."

Unable to resist, Artie put out a hand, stroked Rhiow's head. She purred and bumped against him, and then headed back toward the path that would lead up to the shelf, and the worldgate back to Grand Central, and onward to London.

✦

Her own team met her on the platform on the Underground, both looking somewhat better than they had before: and the London team, too, looked much improved for a night's sleep. The exception was Fhrio, who hadn't had any sleep but didn't seem to care. He had spent the evening analyzing the *ehhif* pastlings, with freestanding wizardries and evidence from the gate logs, and had been returning them to their proper times.

"We got every one of them back where they belong," Fhrio said, and he looked positively jolly, even though he had been up since they'd seen him last. "Every single one! At least now we know that when we get the Queen's problem handled, the gates won't be misbehaving anymore."

"When," Rhiow thought. *From your mouth to Her ear*... "It's good news," Rhiow said, and sat down to have a wash: having been a "big cat" always left her feeling oddly unkempt for a few hours—something to do with the coarser texture of the fur. "Is the timeslide ready to try the eighteen-seventy-four run again?"

"Yes it is. We're just waiting for Siffha'h now: she felt she needed a nap after her last pastling transit, to make sure she was sharp for this big one."

Right on cue, Siffha'h turned up, carefully greeting everyone but Arhu, who turned his back as soon as she came in and didn't give her the chance to reject him first. Rhiow sighed at this but said nothing about it, and only glanced sympathy at Arhu. He said nothing either, simply waiting for the action to begin.

It didn't take long, for Siffha'h was eager to get started, and so was Fhrio. They leaped into their places inside the timeslide, and Huff and Auhlae followed: hard behind them came Urruah and Arhu, and Rhiow last of all.

"Ready?" Siffha'h asked, rearing up on her haunches and shaking her shoulders a little as she prepared herself.

Fhrio hooked a claw into the timeslide wizardry. "Now—"

Siffha'h came down on the power-feed point, and the world whited out. The pressure came back. Rhiow had hoped that it might possibly be a little more bearable this time: the hope was in vain. If possible, it was worse. The sense of the power that Siffha'h was pouring into the transit was staggering, but so was the resistance. It was as if she slammed them all, repeatedly, into a wall of stone. *She's stubborn, you have to give her that,* Rhiow thought, but whatever was ranged against them was immune to stubbornness.

Siffha'h kept hammering, fruitlessly. The pressure bore and bore on Rhiow until she wanted to moan out loud . . . and suddenly it simply broke, lifted all at once, a relief so great that she felt like fainting.

She was still standing, but only just. She looked around at the others, all swaying on their feet, and at Siffha'h, who was lying prostrate, panting.

"Blocked," she gasped. "Blocked . . ."

"It's no use," Fhrio said. "We're not going to be able to get it, the information we need. We were so close, but we're locked out."

"You could try using the key the Powers sent us," Arhu said, very pointedly.

Huff and Auhlae and the others looked at one another, bemused. Rhiow closed her eyes for a moment, and called up her memories of this morning, until she stood again in the grassland of the Downside, under the sun of an endless summer. *Ith!*

Arhu has already called me, the answer came back. *Artie and I will be with you shortly.*

Urruah's tail was lashing thoughtfully. "It would make sense," he said. "The Law of Isometric Origin says that nothing can prevent your return to your home time if you're attempting to reach it, and you have the proper spell, and the spell's working. There's simply no way anything can stop you: you and your home time have too great an affinity. That should mean that even the Lone Power can't stop you . . . shouldn't it?"

Huff blinked. "It'll be interesting finding out," he said.

"Even if he's only present in the spell as an 'outrider,' it should work," Arhu said. "And if you tie him into the spell, it'll work better yet."

The air pulled open in front of them, and Artie and Ith stepped out. Artie's shirt was torn by someone's claw, and he was slightly sunburned, and had begun to freckle. To Rhiow, he looked extremely happy.

"Here is the one whom the Powers have sent you," Ith said. "I will leave him with you for the time being: I must go to continue my work. Even though there are *ehhif* in the museum today, I believe I can work around them: and anyway, I feel that I must. Time seems to be getting very short."

He flirted his tail in farewell at Artie, and stepped back through his "hole in the air," into nothingness.

Artie looked around at the People and the timeslide. "Wonderful," he said, "more magic! What do I do?"

"Come over here, young *ehhif,*" said Fhrio, "and tell me about yourself."

Fhrio spent about ten minutes asking Artie the usual pointless-seeming questions about his age and his tastes and his birthday and his favorite colors: all the things that went into the most basic sketch of a wizard's name. It took no longer than that for Fhrio to add the string of symbols to the timeslide.

"Now step in here," Huff said to Artie. "We're going to try to move ourselves back into that other eighteen seventy-four. You're going to feel the spell pressing on you: it might make you faint."

"I'll sit down," Artie said, and did so.

The members of both teams arranged themselves. Siffha'h got up on her haunches. "Ready?" Fhrio said.

"Ready," said everyone.

Siffha'h came down. And so did the pressure—

It was different this time. Last time it had been as if Siffha'h were throwing them against a wall. This time it was as if something were behind them, pushing, pushing harder and harder against that wall the longer the timeslide was in operation. Instead of being squeezed from all sides, Rhiow felt as if she were being smashed flat in one direction only. *Frankly,* she thought, clenching her teeth, *there's not much to choose between the two sensations.*

It went on for quite a long time, Siffha'h stubbornness still very much something one could feel in the air all around one. But nothing happened.

The pressure relaxed again. Once more Siffha'h flopped down, panting, and all the People looked at each other in despair.

"What are we doing wrong?" Auhlae wondered.

Huff's tail lashed. "Absolutely nothing."

"There's no physical access," Fhrio said. "None at all."

A long silence fell.

"Then we're going to have to try one that's *not* physical," Arhu said.

Everyone looked at him.

"I think I could See what we need to know," he said, "if I had help. I kept thinking that this was something you had to do alone. Well, maybe it's not. Maybe I'm just sort of a walking spell. Maybe I can be fueled from outside, too. If she does what she can"—he refused to look at Siffha'h—"and Urruah, if you help, and if Artie is here too, then I think maybe I can do it. If you take most of the timeslide functions out of the circuit, all except for the coordinates . . ."

Fhrio waved his tail helplessly. "Why not?" he said. "It's worth a try."

"Try it with just Urruah first," Siffha'h said. And there was a note there in her voice that Rhiow had not heard before: she was afraid.

Of what?

"All right," Urruah said. "Let me take it." He moved over to the power-point position as Siffha'h pulled herself away, and planted his paws on it. "Ready, Fhrio?"

"Ready—"

Power, growing quickly, increasing to a blaze, a blast. Rhiow blinked, finding herself becoming lost in it. The pressure from behind, which is Artie; the pressure forward, which is Urruah; the impetus in the center, which is Arhu. All go forward a very little way . . . and then stop, blocked.

Blocked, yes (says a voice that sounds oddly like Hardy's). But only for actually *going*. Seeing cannot be blocked: vision is ubiquitous. It is one of the chief functions of Her nature: She sees everything . . . though in Her mercy, She does not always *look*. Looking makes it so.

Arhu looks. For a while all he can See is that scarred and leering Moon, the promise of destruction. It is meant to distract him. When he realizes this, he turns his attention away. *Show me what happens to her*, he says to the listening world. *Show me the ones who kill the queen.*

The darkness swirls and does not quite dissolve. . . .

There is little enough of them visible. They fear the daylight. In the room where they sit, talking in whispers, the curtains are drawn against the possibility of anyone seeing in. Sight they may defeat, but not vision.

"The time has come. Our people can suffer this unjust rule no longer. We must go forward with the plan."

"Are the conditions all correct? Are we sure?"

"As certain as we can be. The relationship with Germany could hardly be expected to worsen, excepting that they declare war . . . which they dare not do. Any more than the French. But both have been saber-rattling: and France has made several statements in the past few weeks that seem to threaten the monarchy. There is no point in waiting any further."

More whispers, hard even for a Person's ears to pick up. "The Mouse is in place."

"Well, then let the Mouse run," says another voice, and it chuckles.

The voices fade. Resistance rears itself against Arhu. Something knows he is watching and listening. Something is trying to push him away, back where he belongs.

The feeling of Arhu pressing back, pushing against the resistance, fighting it.

To no effect. It pushes back harder. It is winning.

A deep breath, and then a different tack. The Raven's way. *Don't push against it. Rise above it. Don't fight with the vision: let it bear you. The wings and the wind are a dialogue.*

Arhu lets go and soars: and the Eye opens fully. . . .

The letter came. The small *ehhif* picked it up, without any particular fanfare, from the kitchen of one of the wings of the castle: a letter from his sister in Edinburgh, he said to the cook, and carried it away whistling. Still whistling, he headed for the potting shed where most of his day's work took place these days—and then stepped into a thick bed of rhododendrons near the shed. Concealed there, he stood stock-still and silently tore the letter open.

He knew what it meant: he did not have to read it. All he had to do was make sure that the contents said what he had been told to expect. *Dearest John, I hope you are well. I write to tell you that I have received the ten shillings you sent, and thank you very much. If you—*

It was correct: it was all correct. The man folded the letter and put it back in the envelope, unaware with what fierce interest a Seer's eyes looked through his, and puzzled out the postmark. *July 9, 1874.*

"Tonight," the man whispered.

The vision whirled aside, shifted.

And the resistance came back. Pressing him away. Not to see the next part . . .

Come on, he said. *Help me.*

No answer.

Siffha'h, come on! This is what will make the difference!

No—do it yourself!

You said it, Arhu said, not angrily, but pleading. *"I'll take you anywhere you need to go."* This *is where we need to go!*

A long, long silence, while the pressure increases.

All right . . .

A shuffling of paws on the power-point, to make room for another. She rears up. Terrified, terrified, she comes down—

A blast of power runs down through the linkages, runs into Arhu. The pressure before him fails, melts away: the wind blows him past it—

Arhu whirls along with the wind, lets it bear him. Darkness now: not the darkness among the rhododendrons, but black night. In the silence, the man creeps along, under the cosseted trees of the Orangery, along the North Terrace. There are many doors into the silent castle, most locked, but few guarded: after all, the walls are guarded, and no one is inside the walls by night except trusted retainers of the household. There are no lights outside, on the inside of the wall: there is no need for such.

The man stops by a door just east of George the Fourth's

Tower, on the bottom level: the servants' quarters and the kitchens. This is a door that is rarely ever locked, a little secret: even servants like to be able to escape now and then. The man waits for a few minutes outside it to make sure no candle is burning inside, harbinger of some servant girl having a tryst in the midnight kitchen by the slacked-down coal fire of the biggest stove. But no light comes: and he needs none. He knows how many steps wide the kitchen is, how many stairs lead up from it to the first floor, and then how many steps, in the darkness, lead along the hallway to the second landing and the small winding stair that leads up into the eastern end of the State Apartments. It is a path he has walked five or six times now by night, and has memorized with the skill that used to let him ransack complex commercial premises in the city, in the dark, after just one walk-through by daylight.

He unlatches the door with one gloved hand, slips in through it, shuts it gently behind him. Stands still in the darkness, and listens. A faint hiss from the hot-water boiler behind the coal stove: no other sound.

Twelve steps across the kitchen: his outstretched hands finds the shut door. He eases its latch open, slips through this door too, pulls it gently to behind him. No need to leave it open: he will not be coming back this way. Six stairs up to the hallway. Two steps out into the middle of the carpet in the hall: turn left. Sixty steps down to the second landing. The carpet muffles his footsteps effectively, though he would go silently even without it: he is wearing crepe-soled shoes, which his employers would have judged most eccentric for a gardener. Well, they will have little chance to judge him further, in any regard. Others will be going to judgment tonight.

Fifty-nine steps, and he hears the change in the sound. Sixty. His toe bumps against the bottom step. Five stairs up to the landing: turn right: three steps. He puts his hand out, and feels the door.

Gently, gently he pulls it open. From up the winding stair comes a faint light: it seems astonishingly bright to him after the dead blackness. Softly he goes up the stairs, taking them near the outer side of the steps: the inner sides creak. One makes a tiny sound, *crack*: he freezes in place. A minute, two minutes, he stands there. No one has noticed. A great old house like this has a thousand creaks and moans, the sound of compressed wood relaxing itself overnight, and no one pays them any mind.

Up the remaining fifteen steps. They are steep, but he is careful. At the door at the top he halts and looks out of the crack in it where it has been left open. In the hallway onto which this stairway gives, next to a door with a gilded frame, a footman is sitting in a chair under a single candle-sconce with a dim electric bulb burning in it. The chair is tilted back against the wall. The footman is snoring.

Down the hallway, now, in utmost silence.

Half a minute later, the footman has stopped snoring . . . not to mention breathing.

Swiftly now, but also silently. Reach up and undo the bulb from its socket. Wait a few seconds for night vision to return. Then, silently, lift the door latch. The door swings open. This is the only part of his night's work, other than the hallway outside, that he has not been able to pace out in advance. Here sight alone must guide him, and the description he has been given of the layout of the room.

The outer room is where the lady-in-waiting has a bed. She is in it, sleeping sweetly, breathing tiny small breaths into the night.

Half a minute later, her sleep has become much deeper, and the sound of breathing has stopped. The nightwalker makes his way toward what he cannot see yet in this more total darkness, the inner door. He feels for the handle: finds it.

Turns the handle. The door swings inward.

Darkness and silence. Not *quite* silence: a faint rustle of bed linens, off to his left, and ahead.

Now, only now, the excitement strikes him, and his heart begins to pound. Ten steps, they told him. A rather wide bed. Her maids say she still favors the left side of it, leaving the right side open for someone who sleeps there no more.

Ten steps. He takes them. He listens for the sound of breathing . . .

. . . then reaches for the left side.

One muffled cry of surprise, under his hand . . . and no more. He holds her until she stops struggling, for fear an arm or leg should flail and knock something down. He wipes the wetness off on the bedclothes, unseen, and pauses by the end of the massive bed to tie the slim silken rope around one leg. Then he makes for the windows.

Quietly he slips behind the drapes: softly he pushes the window up in its sash, wider than need be—no need to give anyone the idea that he is a small man. He goes down the rope like a spider, rotating gently as he goes. Without a sound he comes down on the North Terrace again and makes straight off across the Home Park in the direction of the Datchet Road. Where the little road crosses the Broad Water, a brougham is waiting for him. He will be in it in five minutes, and in Calais by morning.

A quiet night's work, and the pay is good. He will never need to see the inside of a potting shed again—or a merchant bank or a high-class jeweler's after dark. That part is over. The new part of his life begins.

And at least she's happy now. *She's with Albert.* . . .

—and then the vision snapped back. A moment's confusion—

—and the vision was centering, bizarrely, on Siffha'h. Herself, she moaned and sank down, covering her eyes with her paws, and Rhiow could understand why: the mirroring must be disorienting in the extreme, self seeming to look at self, seeming to look at self, infinitely reflected—

Except that it was not Siffha'h moaning that Rhiow heard. It was Arhu. Crying in a small, frightened voice: crying like a kitten. "Oh, no," he moaned. "It's *you.* I didn't know. . . . I couldn't help it. . . . *How could I help it?"*

—an image of blackness. The rustling of a plastic bag as small, frightened bodies thrashed and scrabbled for purchase, for any way to stay above what inexorably rose around them. Cold water, black as death. Underneath him, all around him, the sound of water bubbling in . . . of breath bubbling out . . .

—Arhu fled from the platform, up the hallway: he was gone.

Both the teams, and even the dazed and horrified Artie, looked after him in astonishment—everyone but Siffha'h. In her eyes was nothing but implacable hatred.

"I won't have anything further to do with him," she said. "Don't ask me to. I will kill him if he touches my mind again. And why shouldn't I?" she said. "Since he killed me first."

Seven

Rhiow went out after Arhu at a run, and found him gone. He had done a private transit, not bothering to take long enough to get to one of the gates: she could smell the spell of it in the air of the hallway, and she thought she knew where Arhu had gone, within about ten feet.

Rhiow turned once, quickly, where she stood, and drew the circle with her tail, tying the wizard's knot with one last flirt of it. Then she instructed the wizardry to lay in identical coordinates to the last transit from this spot, and to execute them. *And don't forget the air!* she added hurriedly.

There was a loud clap as she displaced a considerable cubic volume of air from the tunnel, taking it with her. The sound of the clap had barely faded from her ears before she was standing on the cold, white pumice-dust of the Moon, looking around.

He was no more than ten feet away.

Arhu looked at Rhiow and opened his mouth to speak the words of another spell, ready to run again.

"Don't do it," she said.

Arhu sagged and let the breath go out of him, standing there looking cold and scared and very alone. It was an expression Rhiow had not seen on him since he first came to her and the other members of the team: and she had forgotten how much it hurt to see it.

"Tell me what's happening," Rhiow said. "Arhu, *please.*"

"I can't."

"You can," Rhiow said, "or I'll pull your ears off and wear them as collar jinglies."

Arhu stared at her in complete misery. "Who needs ears?"

"Arhu," Rhiow said, "this isn't the time for self-indulgence. If you've seen something that threatens the team, or you—"

"The team?" he said, and laughed bitterly. "It's a little more personal this time."

"It's not—you didn't see anything like your own *death,* did you?"

"Oh, no, not mine. Someone else's."

"Well, for Iau's sake, tell me! Maybe we can do something to stop it."

"You don't understand," Arhu said. "It's already happened." He laughed again, that bitter sound. "Listen to me, I'm sounding like the Ravens already."

Rhiow shook her head in frustration. "What's in Iau's name are you talking about?"

Arhu flopped down on the powdery Moondust. "Rhiow," he said very softly. "Siffha'h is my sister."

"What?"

"I Saw her," he said. "I Saw her in the bag . . . with me and the others, when the *ehhif* threw us in to drown. And she Saw it too, through me, just now. She Saw it all. . . . But dying didn't stop her, then. She came straight back. She must have been reincarnated within days of when she died. Maybe hours. And it took me this long to realize it. She was my twin, Rhiow—she had my same spots! And she was the one I climbed on top of, last, to keep breathing. . . ."

He was utterly devastated. For her own part, Rhiow could only stand there and look at him in complete astonishment. There always had been that resemblance between Siffha'h and Arhu; it really had been fairly striking. And the way Arhu had been drawn to Siffha'h. And then, Rhiow thought, with the suddenness of a blow, there was the simple matter of her name. *Why didn't I ever think to take it apart,* Rhiow thought. *But then, who thinks to take "Rhiow" apart for "dark-as-night"?* For in Ailurin, Siffha'h simply meant "Sif-again," or, by a pun in Ailurin, "one more time," the end of a feline phrase similar to the *ehhif* "If at first you don't succeed, try, try again."

"What do I do now?" Arhu asked hopelessly. "How can I go back? And . . . I thought it was an accident. Did I maybe kill her on purpose? My own twin? And more importantly, does she *think* I killed her on purpose?" He laughed again bitterly. "I couldn't figure out why she didn't like me. Now it makes perfect sense. How else would you treat the brother who climbed on top of your body, possibly even pushed you farther down into the water, to keep on breathing?"

His despair and grief were awful to hear: the sound of them made it difficult for her to think how best to help him. Rhiow was also acutely aware that, to some extent, Arhu's was the most unusual talent of the team, and the one that the Lone Power was most likely to attempt to undermine directly. In some ways, she and Urruah were simply support for Arhu, the youngest of them, and therefore the most powerful.

But Siffha'h was even younger, and her power might potentially be greater still. Was the Lone One working to impair her effectiveness as well? *And why did she reincarnate so quickly? Was it specifically for this job, to do something that had to be done for wizardry's sake . . . or was it for revenge?*

She had no answers, and she didn't think she was going to get them by sitting here. Certainly Arhu wasn't. "Well," Rhiow said, "what will you do about all this? Are you going to stay here on the Moon? You won't be making your team responsibilities any easier to fulfill."

"You're not taking this very seriously," Arhu snarled.

"On the contrary," Rhiow said, "I'm taking it more seriously than you are. There's a small matter of our home reality being chucked out of the scheme of things like litter-box cleanings if we don't do something to stop it. You are a key to the solution of this problem, just as Artie is, in his way; just as Siffha'h is in hers. We need to get back down there and handle it." She glanced up at the gibbous Earth hanging above the pristine white surface. "Otherwise, *that* is going to wind up looking like that other Moon."

He looked at Rhiow pitifully. "I can't face her."

"You already have faced her," Rhiow said. "It just didn't last long enough. Come back and have another try."

Arhu looked up at the glowing blue Earth. He breathed in, breathed out.

"Besides," Rhiow said, "now we know how the assassination takes place. We've got to lay our plans for how to stop it. We'll need you for that as well. And then we've got to execute those plans . . . and without you, that's impossible."

Arhu sighed and looked at Rhiow again. "You can be a real pain in the tail sometimes," he said. He was shivering all over, as if someone had thrown him in water.

Rhiow put her whiskers forward and walked over to the boundaries of his spell, let his spell and hers get familiar, and then walked through into his bubble of air. He looked at her fearfully.

She went gently up to him and began to wash his ear. "Come on," she said between licks. "You've had it out with the Lone One before. You thought It had done the worst to you that It could manage: It tried to kill your spirit, and It failed. Now It's having another try . . . and It's trying to steal your sister from you as well, if It can. It would love nothing better than to alienate you from one another at this time when, if you can work together, you can defeat It one more time . . . and It's depending on your pain doing Its work for It." She stopped washing for a moment and bent down and around to look Arhu in the eye. "Are you listening to me?"

He looked back at her, still full of grief, and a pang struck her again, for his pain looked much like hers must have looked when Hhuha died.

"It was so awful," he whispered.

"Of course it was awful," Rhiow whispered back. "Its wretched gift, death, that It tricked our People into accepting: how should it *not* be an awful thing? That was never what the Powers had in mind for us when they built the worlds. Now we have to deal with it as a matter of course. But at least in your case you've got a second chance. How many of us get a chance to meet a friend again in another life, let alone a relative? It happens, but not that often. Don't let It trick you into throwing that away as well!"

Arhu was silent for a little, staring at the ground. Rhiow sat beside him, waiting.

"All right," he said at last. He lifted a face to Rhiow that was full of fear. "But she said she was going to kill me."

"I think that would take some doing," Rhiow said. "But that small matter aside, no one kills one of my team without coming through me first. Power source she may be, but she's not the only one with a claw to her name. Let's go back."

✦

Ten minutes later they were back on the derelict platform under Tower Hill station. Huff stood looking forlorn as they came: Arhu looking a little defiant, Rhiow trying to keep her composure in the face of the storm of fury she expected from Siffha'h.

But Siffha'h was not there.

"She ran off," Huff said, "just after Arhu did." Huff looked profoundly disturbed, and Rhiow for one knew how he felt, and was sorry for him. It was unnerving to see so steady and stolid a personality suddenly at loose ends, embarrassed by the behavior of one of his team, upset by what he had glimpsed through Arhu's vision: and there was something else going on with him as well, Rhiow thought, though she couldn't easily tell what it was.

"She'll be back," Rhiow said, profoundly hoping that this would prove true. "Meanwhile we must start laying our plans. . . ."

Everyone gathered together and sprawled out comfortably on the platform, including Artie, who was acquiring a grimy look but becoming more cheerful all the time at all the exposure to "magic." When he understood what the two teams were discussing, he immediately cried, "I want to come with you!"

The People glanced at one another, concerned. "I don't know," Huff said. "If something happened to you, Artie, and we weren't able to return you to the time where you belong after all this—"

"Huff, if the timeslide's to be powered successfully," Rhiow said, "as it was the last time, he may *have* to come with us on the intervention run. We may very well have no choice in the matter."

"*If* it can be powered successfully," Fhrio muttered, "with Siffha'h missing. . . ."

"We'll deal with that issue a little later," Huff said. "To take care of any uncertainty about the dates, we must have someone guarding the Queen from at least a couple of nights before the date of the attack. I'm concerned that the Lone One might somehow get wind of what we're trying to do, and attempt to forestall us by striking earlier. But meanwhile, for planning purposes, let's assume that the slide goes well, and those of us not on guard duty find ourselves in the grounds of Windsor Castle on the evening of the ninth of July."

"What time was the attack?" Auhlae said. "I couldn't tell."

"I saw the Moon," said Rhiow. For her, that was the one image that haunted her most persistently about that whole year: every time she looked at the sky, she searched for the Moon to see what it looked like. "It was waning, and just rising then, which would have made the time about midnight, as *ehhif* reckon it, or at most half an hour past that. The Whispering can help us pin down the exact timing."

"Now, as for the murderer . . ."

"The Mouse," Fhrio said, and his jaw chattered. "Appropriate name, considering what's going to happen to him."

"It's *not* going to happen to him," Huff said forcefully. "Murdering a murderer will do nothing but play straight into the Lone Power's paws. The action would rebound in Iau only knows what kind of horrible way. Whatever else happens to him, his life has to be spared."

"At the same time," Rhiow said, "when he disappears—I assume that's something like what will happen to him, one way or another—that disappearance should be such that it raises as few questions as possible. An elegant intervention is one that leaves sa'Rráhh scratching her fleas and wondering what in the worlds happened."

"I'd be less concerned about elegance and more concerned about simply making sure the assassination doesn't happen," Fhrio growled.

"Yes," Rhiow said, "if necessary. No argument there. But the less wizardry is obvious about whatever goes on, the better."

"What started it all," Auhlae said, "was the Mouse getting that letter."

Arhu shook his head. "No. There was another one."

Rhiow looked at him in surprise. "What? Another letter?"

"You didn't see it?"

She shook her head. Arhu tucked himself down into thinking position and said, "There's another letter, sent the day before. I See the desk it's being written on, all shiny wood and leather: and the design on top of the paper. It's a kind of gateway, and on top of it there's a picture of what the *ehhif*-queen wears on her head."

Auhlae looked shocked. "The crowned portcullis," she said. "That's the stationery used by the *ehhif* in the House of Commons. You're telling me that the person starting this plot off is a member of Parliament?"

Arhu squinted. "The House of Commons. Is that one of the buildings in that big spiky place by the river? The one with the big clock?"

"Yes," Huff said. "The whole thing together is the Palace of Westminster."

"That's it, then. I See the river out his window as he's writing," Arhu said, still squinting slightly, and rocking back and forth a little, an odd motion, as if he were on wings. "It's getting late . . . the Sun is going down. He folds the letter up and puts it in an envelope, and he takes a pen and starts writing something up in the corner. . . . No, he stopped. He's just writing in the middle of the envelope now."

"The address," Rhiow said.

"I guess."

"What does it say?"

"His handwriting's hard to read." Arhu was silent for a moment. "Edinburgh? Where's that?"

"In the north of the country," Fhrio said.

"Then he looks around in his desk drawer for something," Arhu said, still rocking slightly. "A little piece of paper. He sticks it onto the letter, in the corner."

"Stamping it rather than franking it," Auhlae said. "That way it won't look any different from other *ehhif* 's letters, at least on the outside."

"I see. All right. Then he puts the letter in a box on a bookcase by the door, and goes out," Arhu says. "He goes down to the big room where we saw the people shouting, before." He blinked. "There are already a lot of *ehhif* there, all shouting and waving papers around. They're *loud*, down there."

"They do that," Huff said. "Don't ask me why. It's traditional."

"And these are the people who run the country?" Rhiow said. "Why do the *ehhif* here let them carry on like that?"

"Maybe they like to watch a good fight?" Urruah said.

"They're not allowed actually to fight with each other," Huff said. "The two sides are kept at sword's length and three feet apart on purpose."

"So all they do is *yell* at each other all night? All those toms?" Urruah twitched his tail in bemusement. "No singing?"

"Not in there," Huff said. "What can I tell you . . . they're *ehhif*." He put his whiskers forward. "But the letter?"

"I don't see it go out," Arhu said, "but I could hear him

thinking that that's what would happen to it. That would be the evening of the seventh, for a letter to get up north and an answer to come back on the ninth."

"If we were to steal that letter," Auhlae said, "while he was downstairs in the House shouting at the other MPs, when he came back he would think that whoever picks up the post had already come to take it away. Then he would think everything was going according to plan, and he wouldn't do anything that would stop the plan until it was already too late: *we* would have stopped it. The Mouse wouldn't run. . . ."

"And in the meantime, we can do something about *him,*" Huff said. "The *ehhif* plotting this must have planted him in the queen's household a good while before, for him to be able to get out when he wanted and sneak around like that. They would have come to trust him."

"Then let's ruin that trust," Rhiow said. "Let's transit him to somewhere in that great castle where he has absolutely no business being, and leave him trapped there. When the staff find him, they'll throw him out of the place themselves, and never let him back in again."

"It's not a bad idea," Auhlae said, waving her tail approvingly. "There are plenty of such places—" Then she stopped and put her whiskers so far forward that Rhiow thought they might take leave of her face. "Let's lock him up in the Albert Chapel," Auhlae said. "It's old, with lots of gates and bars: Henry the Seventh built it as a tomb for himself. But the queen turned the place into a memorial for her poor mate when he died, and now it's all full of gold and jewels and precious things that she had put there in his memory. Let the Mouse sit in *there* all one night, with no way to get out, and let the castle staff find him in the morning."

There was general laughter and approval at the idea, and

Artie clapped his hands. "One thing, Arhu," said Huff. "Who was it that wrote the first letter . . . the one that caused the second one to be sent?"

Arhu squinted again. "Let me watch him for a moment," he said. "There was something on his door. When he goes out again . . ."

There was a little silence while everyone let him work. Artie looked up, then, and said, "Who's going to do guard duty on the queen?"

Rhiow glanced at Huff. They both turned and looked at Arhu.

He went wide-eyed. "*Oh* no!" he said.

"It's the best bet," Huff said. "She was known to have a soft spot for little kittens."

"I'll 'little kitten' you, you big—"

"Arhu," Rhiow said, slightly exasperated. "It's useful being cute. Exploit it a little. You can take the poor *ehhif*'s mind off her troubles for a while."

"What am I supposed to do? Play with string?" Arhu looked scornful.

"If necessary, yes," Huff said. "Make sure you ingratiate yourself sufficiently with her, and she won't want to let you out of her sight . . . which, for our purposes, would be absolutely perfect."

Arhu was opening his mouth to disagree again. "You will also probably eat like royalty," Urruah said.

Arhu shut his mouth and looked thoughtful.

"I hate to mention it," Rhiow said, "but the other one who is probably going to be perfect for this job is Siffha'h. Another 'cute' one."

Arhu straightened up again. "No way!"

"We'll discuss it later," Rhiow said in a tone of voice meant to suggest that the discussion would have only one possible ending. "What about that door, Arhu? What's on it?"

He breathed out in annoyance and squinted at nothing again. "It's not coming."

"The *vhai* it's not," Urruah said, and gave him a look.

Arhu made the disgusted face again, then went slightly vague in the eyes, as if trying harder.

"McClaren," he said suddenly. "Does that make sense?"

"Is that what's on the door?" Fhrio said.

Arhu twitched his tail yes.

"Bad," Fhrio said. "The only ones who get their names on their doors are government ministers."

Auhlae and Huff looked grim. "Rhi, who was he?" Urruah said.

"From what Hhuhm'hri told me, probably the chancellor of the exchequer," she said, listening anew to the material she had read into the Whispering. "They changed these jobs around every now and then, though not as often as they do now. I would probably need to talk to Ouhish to get a more accurate date."

"I'm not sure we need it," Huff said. "We know he's involved. I would love to find some way to betray his part in the conspiracy as well, but it may not be possible. Almost certainly the letter he writes to the third party in Edinburgh isn't going to contain anything that would incriminate him: he wouldn't be so stupid, even in those less investigative days, as to commit something of that kind to House stationery. He probably used that more as a guaranteed form of identification to his contact than anything else."

They all lay and thought for a moment. "No," Huff said, "unless someone comes up with a brilliant idea about how to reveal him, we're going to have to be satisfied with stopping the attempt itself and removing the assassin permanently from the queen's ambit. Any other thoughts?"

If there were any, they were briefly derailed as the air down at the end of the platform tore softly, and a taloned shape stepped through.

"Ith!" Artie cried, jumped up and ran to him, and shook Ith's claw in a manner so suddenly and incongruously *ehhif*-adult that Rhiow burst out laughing and immediately had to pretend to have a hairball. While this was going on, Ith greeted Artie and came pacing over to the teams. He crouched down on those long back legs, the great-claw of each foot grating on the stone.

"How did you do?"

Ith hissed, a most satisfied sound. "The spell is complete," he said. "I did not stop with the museum in London. New York and Berlin, also, I visited, and Cairo, and the new Egyptian wing of the museum in Munich, apparently the biggest such collection in the world now. I am afraid a security camera might have caught me in Berlin: I was in a hurry." That toothed jaw dropped in a slight smile. "I will be interested to see how they explain what the videotape may show. But first tell me how you fare."

They told him: and Arhu, finally, looked at Ith for a long moment in which he seemed to say nothing. Ith listened, with his head on one side, and then knitted his foreclaws together in that gesture that could mean contemplation or distress—in Rhiow's experience, Ith's claws were more to be trusted as an indicator than his face or his eyes, which did not work like a Person's.

"So our old Enemy puts Its fang into your heart again, brother," Ith said, working the claws together so that they scraped softly against one another. "It is folly. The same venom will not work twice—you will begin to develop an immunity."

"I'm glad *you* think so," Arhu said bleakly.

"Gladness is far from you just now," Ith said, "but we

will see. Meanwhile, Huff, Rhiow, tell me what we must now do to save the queen."

They outlined the plan to him, and Ith listened to it all, his foreclaws working gently at each other all the while. At last, when they were done, he bowed agreement to what they had said.

"It all sounds well," said Ith. "But there is another possibility for which you must also prepare. Your plan, no matter how well laid, may nonetheless fail. If you do not get it right the first time, there is little chance that the Lone Power will let you into that timeline again. It will erect such barriers against you that half the world's wizards brought to bear against them at once would not prevail. Then the queen will die, and the consequences will begin."

The People, and Artie, all looked at one another. "That possibility must be prepared for," Ith said. "If nothing else, the Winter must be prevented. That at least. No matter if our timelines die, and all of us, and all the *ehhif* and all the People, and even all *my* people—if we can only keep the Winter from happening, then there will be survivors, and the world will eventually grow green again."

"He's right," Huff said, looking over at Auhlae. She waved her tail in agreement.

"Well, you have the complete spell," Urruah said. "So we're all right in that regard." He caught the look in Ith's eye. "Aren't we?"

"The spell is indeed complete," Ith said. "But I am less certain than I was when I started that it will function."

"What?" Rhiow said. "Why?"

"Here," Ith said, and moved a little aside to make a clear space on the floor.

He constructed the spell for them as Urruah had constructed the timeslide, as a three-dimensional diagram in the Speech. But it was far more than merely six-parted, as Ith had originally suggested. The three-dimensional figure on which it was based was a near-spherical array of hexagons, each surrounded by five pentagons: a truncated icosahedron, the Whispering called it. But this figure was four-dimensional, bearing the same relationship to the symmetry of a normal icosahedron as a tesseract did to that of a cube. Many other icosahedra flowered hyperdimensionally from the "faces" of the spell construct into a vaguely spherical cage of light that seemed both to close itself in and to try to enclose anything else within reach as well. Arhu was not the only one squinting, now: everyone was having trouble grasping the spatial relationships of the thing.

"Iau, it makes my head hurt just looking at it," Fhrio said, though with a certain amount of admiration.

"To achieve this construct," Ith said, "I unwrapped four hundred thirty-eight mummies, and extracted spell fragments from some sixty or seventy amulets. It is a great help to be able to use one's wizardry to see into the mummy first before you must unwrap it: otherwise I would be claw-deep in bandages yet." He tilted his head this way and that, bird-like, admiring his handiwork. "It is, as you see, something of a power-trap. A net of fives and sixes. That structure confines wizardly energy within it, concentrating it for use. But there is a problem." The claws began to fret gently at one another again. "The recitation parameters of the spell—you see them there, reflected at the major lower-order vertices of the construct—require the physical presence of a threshold number of mummies: a massive, strictly physical reinforcement. Originally, that would have been the main cat-mummy burial site at Bubastis. But that is now gone, as we know."

"Are you saying that this won't work?" Fhrio asked, peering at the spell.

"No. I am saying that it *may* work, but if it does, I will

not understand how. And you may be right: it may not function at all . . . in which case there is no protection against the Winter. And in that case, you *must* succeed."

Silence fell among the gathered People. Arhu kept studying the spell-construct, and his gaze went vague, but Rhiow, looking over at him, became less sure that it was the construct on which he had his eye, or Eye.

He turned to her all of a sudden. "Eight hundred thousand People you said was the threshold number for gating to start in an area," Arhu said. "How *big* an area? And do those eight hundred thousand People have to be *alive?*"

Rhiow didn't know what to make of *that* one. *But three hundred thousand cat-mummies at Beni-Hassan alone,* Hwallis had said. *And there were probably many more. . . .*

"I don't know," Rhiow said at last. "Normally, you would think so. But the Egyptians' relationship with their cats plainly didn't stop when the cats *were* dead. Indeed, they didn't think they *were* dead, not in the sense that *ehhif* use the word now: the whole idea of preserving the body itself indicates that someone thinks you might need it again."

Rhiow fell silent and thought about that for a moment. Until now she had been holding this particular *ehhif* belief as somewhat barbaric, almost funny, the result of a misunderstanding, for indeed People had told the *ehhif* of those long-past days how their own lives went: nine lives, nine deaths, and if you had done more good than evil, there followed a tenth life in a body immune to the more crass aspects of physicality, like injury, decay, and age—the fully realized Life of which the previous nine had been rough sketches. The *ehhif*, as so often happened, had gotten some of the details of this story muddled, and thought "their" cats were telling them about immortality after life in a physical body. With this understanding, the *ehhif* of Egypt, an endlessly practical people, had started working on ways to preserve the bodies of the dead—human as well as feline—with an eye to making sure those bodies would last until they were needed again. Over nearly a millennium of practice, mummification had become a science (as these *ehhif* regarded such things), elaborate, involved—and, here and there, with a touch of wizardry about it.

Now, though, this set of circumstances seemed less silly to Rhiow, and much more intriguing. The One, and Her daughters the Powers That Be, rarely did anything without a purpose. Could it be that all the magnificent sarcophagi and paintings, all the riches piled and buried in all the tombs, the folly and the glory of it, were all a blind, a distraction, meant for the one Power that was less than kindly disposed toward life? A feint, a misdirection, a behavior that externally seemed humorously typical of the stupidities of *ehhif*, but one concealing something far more important? The mummified bodies of hundreds of thousands of People, lying in the sand, forgotten: a resource, a well of potential . . .

. . . a weapon.

Rhiow did not have the kind of confusion about bodies that *ehhif* all too often had. Once you were out of it for good, a body was meat: whatever happened to it, *you* didn't care, and those around you were expected to do no more (if it was convenient) than try to drag it off somewhere a little private, where the elements of the world would dispose of it in their own fashion. Rhiow knew that the People who had once inhabited those now-mummified bodies would be far beyond caring what happened to their mortal remains. Either they would have run their nine lives' term and ended so, subsumed back into the endless purr that lay behind the merely physical Universe, as was the way of most of the People; or they would be ten lives along now, in bodies so much better suited to their needs that they would laugh at the mere thought of the old ones. If their two-thousand-year-old remains had to be used somehow as a weapon against the Lone One, not one of them would object.

But those bodies were ground up, now, and spread over half the counties of this island. Certainly they were too far scattered for the kind of intervention this spell construct would require.

Rhiow looked at the construct. *Well*, she said to the Whisperer, *will it work?*

A long, long pause.

Maybe . . .

She got up and stretched. "The only thing we haven't decided," she said to Huff, "is when we're going to do this."

"It's been rather a long day," Huff said, and glanced over at Auhlae, who was giving him a thoughtful look. "To this particular piece of work, I'd like to come well rested. Tomorrow night?"

The others all nodded.

"Shall I come with you?" Ith asked.

Rhiow looked at him with some unease. "The concern about the Father of his People risking himself comes up again," she said. "You'd better take it up with Them. But I for one would value your company."

She glanced at Huff. He twitched his tail yes. "See where your responsibilities lie, cousin," he said to Ith, "and then join us if you can. But this work alone, I think, is likely to be of great use." He glanced at the icosaract.

Ith got up. "I will go to my own, then," he said, "and consult with the Powers." He bowed to the group and laid his tail over Arhu's for a moment: then he stepped into the air again, and was gone.

"What about Siffha'h?" Arhu said.

"What about her?" said Fhrio. The growl was missing . . . just.

"Nothing," Arhu said, and sighed, and got up. "Absolutely nothing at all."

"Come on, 'Ruah," Rhiow said. "Let's get home and take a look around. Huff, Auhlae . . ." She touched cheeks with them: after doing so with Huff, she paused a second, seeing something in his eyes that she couldn't quite classify.

"It'll be all right," Rhiow said.

"Of course it will," Huff said, and his whiskers went forward ever so slightly. "Till tomorrow night, cousin. *Dai stihó.*"

✦

They made their way home together, Rhiow and Urruah and Arhu, and stepped out with some relief from the long station platforms, out into the echo and bustle of the main concourse. Sidled, they walked through it without too much concern for the *ehhif.* It was getting late on a Saturday evening, and growing quiet. Above them, the "stars" burned backward in the zodiac of a feigned Mediterranean sky, but the breezes that blew by under the great arched ceiling bore mostly the scents of the last fresh-ground coffee of the day, and a lingering aroma of pizza and cold cuts.

Urruah breathed deeply. "You know," he said, "their gating complex is very historic and all, all those old buildings and castles and whatnot . . . but I like ours better."

"You just prefer the food," Rhiow said.

"Yeah, well, I intend to have a seriously big dinner tonight," Urruah said, "and then a whole night's sleep in my Dumpster. Who knows if I'll ever see it again?"

Rhiow glanced over at him. "You're really worried, aren't you," she said.

"I think I have reason. Don't you?"

There was little evidence to suggest otherwise. There was no question that the situation was dangerous. But having granted that, Rhiow saw no advantage in dwelling on it. "If worrying would help," she said, "I'd be right in there with you. But I've no evidence that it makes any difference."

"Optimist," Urruah said.

"Pessimist," Rhiow said.

"And which side do *you* come down on?" Urruah said to Arhu, who was walking between them, silent.

"Neither," Arhu said. "I'd sooner wait to See which way to jump." He looked a little dubious. "But you know, Rhiow, 'Ruah, it's all just probabilities. I See things, but there's always that little warning hovering at the edge of them. 'It may not turn out this way.' " He sighed. "Very annoying . . ."

"I don't know," Rhiow said. "I'd think it might be worse if what you saw *always* happened and there was no escape. That would be depressing. As well as boring: nothing would ever surprise you."

"Give me no surprises," Urruah said definitely. "Give me certainty over uncertainty anytime. I'll take the boredom and be grateful."

Rhiow laughed at him, but the laughter was slightly hollow. "So let's postulate best case for a moment," she said. "Say the queen *is* assassinated. Is there any slightest chance, do you think, that the war might *not* happen, despite what Arhu Saw? As he says, it's still only probability."

Urruah flirted his tail sideways in a gesture of complete uncertainty as they walked past the shining brass central information booth. "Even in our own world," he said, "the only reason *ehhif* managed to keep the Winter from falling for so long was that there were *two* great powers that had atomic weapons . . . and everyone was sure that, no matter which one of them started the fight, *everyone's* throat would be ripped out before it was finished. And even then there were close calls. That one *ehhif* president who got lucky, for example, because spies and wizards were in the right places at the right time, to help him covertly or tell him what he needed to know to maneuver properly in that nasty little game of *hauissh* that he and his enemy were playing. Luck, yes, and the Powers' intervention—and not much else—*that* saved them. But in that alternate eighteen seventy-four, there's just *one* power that has the bomb. There is no great counterbalance against the British power in this world to keep them from using it. The only thing that could save them is if their great politicians suddenly became cautious, and what do you think the odds are on *that?*"

"With the *ehhif* Disraeli as the queen's main minister at that point?" Rhiow shook her head. "From what Hhuhm'hri told me, the chances are slim and none. If the queen dies, he'll use the excuse to sweep all the lesser 'troublemaking' nations away before him. He's been looking for an excuse to do that, I'd say, for a long time: certainly in our own world he was not exactly a cautious *ehhif*, or one to back down when provoked. At this time period, in our own world, he was busy trying to get the queen to take another title, as a kind of over-queen of another pride's-pride of *ehhif*. 'Empress,' they called it. She finally let him talk her into it, or flatter her into it, rather. Granted, that turned out to be a less destructive act of aggression, but the act was dam to a litter of results, later on, that cost many *ehhif* their lives. It's still doing so, in fact." Rhiow twitched her tail, troubled.

"In other words," Urruah said, "if given the excuse, he'll bomb the rebellious prides right back into the Stone Age."

"And his own pride as well," Arhu said. "Just what the Lone One wants."

"The warning is written on the Moon," Rhiow said, "as we saw. That's what It intends the Earth to look like after It's done."

"And the situation might get still worse," Urruah said. "It

seems that these *ehhif* lose their positions, or change them, without warning and at short notice. What if someone comes in as prime minister who's *less* tolerant than the *ehhif* holding the position now?"

"Please," Rhiow said. It was an uncomfortable enough situation as it was. "Our problem is that, whoever rules that world, the period is not one that likes to refrain from technology, once it gets its hands on it. The Victorians *like* technology, the more aggressive the better. They like mastering and dominating their world . . . and each other. They have done some great works that have lasted into our own time, it's true, but they also did a great deal of evil. They routinely acted without due consideration of the effects."

"I Saw a lot of things that looked like that," Arhu said, "with Odin. The *ehhif* took what they got from the book and mostly kept it for themselves. There are a lot of *ehhif* on this planet, in that time, but the ones with the technology weren't in a sharing mood. They wanted to keep themselves the top of the 'prides-of-prides.' Every now and then they would give a little of the information to some of the other prides, the 'countries,' as a present. A way to prove how powerful they were. But the best of it, the parts that really mattered, or were really dangerous, they kept to themselves." His ears were flat back. "It's like caching food. I don't understand how they can do that."

"It would probably be pretty foolish of us to expect them not to treat nuclear technology the way they treated all the others," Urruah said. "So . . . does that answer your question?"

Rhiow sighed. "I just hope Ith can get that spell working," she said.

And there's one other thing itching me where I can't scratch it, Urruah said silently. *You shredded Fhrio's ears for him nicely. He's been behaving himself since. So why is that gate still acting up?*

That question had been a flea in Rhiow's ear as well. She lashed her tail once or twice, and said, *I really hope we find out soon. Because if it* wasn't *him, it's probably someone else in our midst.*

Urruah lashed his tail too, but had nothing to add.

They walked to the Forty-second Street entrance and looked out through the brass doors. Forty-second was in full flower, streams of traffic flowing by in both directions, and *ehhif* walking past, running, chatting, shouting, taking their time in the soft evening air. Rhiow glanced up leftward, a little over her shoulder, to see the light-accented, graceful curves of the Chrysler Building rearing up shining into the evening sky, the city light gilding it from underneath. *Even at the best of times,* she thought, *even when life seems normal, who among us can say with certainty that we'll see this world again tomorrow? Entropy stalks the world in all its usual shapes, and some less usual than others. I'll meet them, the strange and the deadly, but I don't need to crouch in fear or bristle at them in show of defiance. I know my job. My commission comes from Those Who Are. We stand together, They and I, in protection of the world They made and I keep. We may lose: there is always that chance. But meanwhile We keep watch at the borders, and contest the Lone One's passage. We will not let it be easy. We will not fall without selling ourselves dearly. And when in the worlds' evening we fall at last, and finally come home, We will find that we have brought with us what we love, bound to us forever by blood and intention: and the Lone One will stand with Its claws empty, and howl Her anger at the night. Then we will say, That was a good fight that we won: and come the dawn, We will make another world, and play the play again. . . .*

She swallowed, and glanced around her. Urruah was looking at her thoughtfully. He leaned over, bumped noses with her, and said, "See you tomorrow evening."

Urruah walked off down Forty-second to the corner of Vanderbilt, and dodged around it and out of sight. Rhiow looked away from him, over to Arhu, and said, "And what about you?"

"I think I have an appointment," he said, and bumped noses with her too, laying his tail briefly over her back. "See you later."

He walked off toward the corner of Lexington, slipped around it, and was gone.

Rhiow stood there by the doors and watched her city go by: then, sidled, she lifted her head high, stepped up into the air, and skywalked home.

✦

Iaehh was there, and in a quiet mood, when she got in. He fed her, and afterward sat in the reading chair, and Rhiow made herself comfortable in his lap and tried to doze.

She couldn't manage it for a while. He wasn't reading for a change tonight, and he didn't even turn on the TV: he just sat in the dimness and stroked her, and Rhiow just sat and let him. It was strangely like the days when Hhuha had been here, and she would simply sit with Rhiow in her lap, not doing anything but being there.

She was actually beginning to doze a little when Iaehh spoke suddenly. "No," he said, without any preamble, "no."

Rhiow looked up at him, bemused.

"You and I are just going to stay right where we are, aren't we?" Iaehh said. "And we'll cope with the world the way it is. I can handle the rent here. And you seem to be doing all right. I miss her—I bet you miss her too—but it's easier to miss someone *with* someone than to miss them alone."

Rhiow could do nothing but breathe out slowly, once, in vast relief, and then purr.

Iaehh said nothing more, and slowly he began to fall asleep, sitting just as he was. Rhiow looked up at him and saw how tired he looked: his face was more drawn than it used to be, and he was losing weight. *Maybe* I *have less to worry about now, but what are we going to do about you?* Rhiow thought. *Hhuha would not like to see you this way. You are so unhappy.*

We've got to find you somebody.

Then she felt like laughing at herself. *The world may start to stop existing next week, or the week after that, if we fail,* Rhiow thought, *and here I am thinking about matchmaking for my* ehhif. Yet there was no question that he did need somebody, and she was going to have to do something about it.

And what about me? she thought. There would be no mates for her, and no kittens. Huff might be a good acquaintance now, might be a friend later. Yet Rhiow was feeling the need for something more. *I must go looking,* she thought, *and see what's available for a wizard who's been spending too much time in work, and not enough in having a social life.*

Assuming the Universe doesn't end later this month.

She sighed and lay back in Iaehh's lap. The end of the Universe would have to take care of itself. Right now she was home with her *ehhif*, and had had a good dinner. Just this once, she would lie still and let it all pass her by: and tomorrow evening, no matter what happened, she would be able to look the Powers in the face and say, *I have been a Person: and after that, what matters?*

✦

Much later, in the darkness, Rhiow realized that she was having a vision. It shouldn't have surprised her, in retrospect, she thought: the Ravens had already shown her that vision was transferable. It hadn't immediately occurred to her that others might learn that trick—but it seemed that at least one had.

You made me do it, he said. *So you had to see what happened. It was your act, even though I enacted it.*

In the vision he was walking down the bike path next to the East River. There had been a time when he had been unable to go anywhere near that body of water: the mere sound of it had been a horror to him. Now, though, he walked down the path and listened to the water chuckling underneath the walkway, listened to it slapping against the concrete piers, and didn't mind a bit. The voices in it were friendly now.

He was looking for someone, and waiting for something: and because this was his vision, he knew he would shortly find both.

Ith had given him the hint, as often happened these days. *The same venom will not work twice—you will begin to develop an immunity.*

At first he had rejected this idea. But Ith was wise, in his way. The more you looked at something that frightened you, or horrified you, the easier it got. This was probably how *ehhif* became conditioned to killing. In their case, it was a fatal flaw. But in *this* case, the function was different. Become used to your own death, to the point where it no longer hurts you—and your Enemy is suddenly without a weapon.

He had done it twice tonight already. He was becoming an expert at dying.

The third time would pay for all.

It was not that long until he saw the pale shape of the slender young Person walking nervously down the bike path. Indeed it shouldn't have been very long: you would be a poor kind of Seer if you couldn't tell when people were going to turn up for appointments, so you didn't have to stand around waiting. As she came, he stepped out and got in her way.

Siffha'h spat at the sight of him. "*You!* Get out of my way."

"No," he said. "If you want me to move, you're going to have to fight."

"Then I'll fight. You think I'd have trouble with that? I hate you! You killed me!"

"No, I didn't. But you know Who did."

"You're crazy. Get out of my way!"

"No," he said. "Not till you admit what you are."

"Oh?" She sneered. "And what am I?"

"A twin. Half of a pair."

"Not anymore. *You* put an end to that."

"Nothing can put an end to it," he said. "Roles may change temporarily. But this time they haven't. I'm a Seer. But you—you're something else. Or you will be."

"No!"

"Yes. The other side of Seeing, the same way our colors are sort of reversed now. Doing . . . that's what you're for."

"No!"

"Yes. You're the power source, after all. Since when are queens power sources? Mostly queens think it's too boring."

"I'm not just some queen!"

"No. You're not. And you can prove it."

"How?"

"Look."

They looked up the river, in the predawn dimness.

The bag came floating toward them, if floating was the

right word. Water was seeping into it rapidly, and it was beginning to submerge.

Siffha'h saw it and shrank back. "No!"

"What are you afraid of?" Arhu said. "It's all over."

"Yes—but—" Still she shrank back.

"But," Arhu said, "there's still a sound you haven't let yourself hear."

"I don't want to hear it!"

"Neither did I. But once I did, everything changed. I couldn't hear anything else until I heard that sound: I couldn't See until I saw what was making it."

"No!"

"You know what's happening in there," Arhu said.

"I don't want to think about it!"

She tried to run, but Arhu got in front of her.

"If you don't think about it," he said, "that's *all* you'll think about for the rest of your life. You've *already* spent all your life thinking about it. All the things you do, all the spells you power, all the time you spend inside that big blast of force you like so much—it's all about being deaf and blind. You pour so much power into what you're doing, of course, that everyone around you is deaf and blind too, for the duration, and no one else notices that you can't see or hear most of the time."

"You're crazy—what are you talking about?"

He could see her glance over his shoulder. The bag was floating nearer. "You don't dare be quiet," he said. "You don't dare be still. If you do, you'll hear what's happening in there."

She took a swipe at him, a good one. It hit him across the nose. He bled, but he wouldn't give back. "You owed me that," Arhu said. "My claws must have dug into you while I was trying to keep my head above the water—"

"Shut up!"

She launched herself at him, every claw bared. Arhu went down, and together they tumbled across the sparse, flat grass by the bike path, spitting and clawing. She got her claws into him, hard. He gave as good as he got. Fur flew.

"Why did you do it?" She panted, and bit him in the throat, and bit him again. "You were my favorite, I loved you, I slept with you, I ate with you, why—"

"I wanted to live! I wanted to breathe! So did you! You stepped on my head a lot of times, you clawed me. I loved you too, I ate with you, I slept with my head on your tummy, I washed you, you washed me, but there came a time when the washing wouldn't help, the loving wouldn't help, we both wanted to live and we couldn't!"

The bag floated closer. There was a slight movement inside it, as of some tiny struggle. The smallest sound from inside: a tiny mewling . . .

"It Saw us coming," Arhu panted. "It Saw the Seer, It Saw the Doer, It knew that together we would be a danger to It, It tried to kill us both. Still, It *couldn't* kill both of us. Help was already coming: It knew one would survive. So It killed the one It thought was more of a threat, more of a power. It knew you would come back, but It counted on you being so tangled up with anger and so confused that you wouldn't know what to do with yourself, and wouldn't put your half back with the other half to make a whole again: you'd waste the power you had on things that weren't all that important, and finally die frustrated and incomplete and useless. And you can still do that. Or you can frustrate It—"

"What are you talking about?"

"Don't do. *See.* Just this once."

And she opened her eyes, which were squeezed shut against Arhu's clawing, and looked at him: and Saw.

Saw what happened inside the bag.

Not from her point of view: from *his.*

The grief. *Tired.* The pain. *They're all dead.* The resignation. *I don't want to live anymore; they're all dead.* The anguish. *Sif, she had my same spots. She's dead. I don't want to live, let it end now.* The water bubbling in . . .

And, abruptly, astonishingly, the rage built, and built, and burst up and out of her. To her amazement, it was not rage at what had happened to *her*: it was fury at what had happened to *him.* It had never been directed at anything *outside* her before, not really: not in all her short life. But now it leaped out . . . and found its target. Now she knew what it was that she had to do, what she had come back for, what business she had to finish.

Something that hung all about them in the air, something that laughed, that had been laughing forever, suddenly stopped laughing as force such as even It had not often experienced came blasting out at It. Not some unfocused curse at a generalized cruel fate, but a specific, narrow, furious line of righteous anger, a rage like a laser, aimed, directed, and tuned. The anger lanced out and found its mark.

WHAT DID YOU DO TO HIM! YOU KILLED HIM! *I'M GOING TO*—

The air in the vision, the air outside it, shuddered with a soundless scream from Something that had not been dealt so painful a blow in some time. That influence, for just a little while, fled . . .

. . . leaving Arhu crouching and squeezing his eyes shut against what his vision showed him, a shape like a Person made out of lightning, radiating fury and purpose and the ability to do anything, anything . . . for this little while.

The lightning looked at him.

"You were right," she said. "There's no spell I couldn't power now. Nothing I couldn't do. Nowhere we can't go."

"*We,*" he said.

Very slowly, she put her whiskers forward.

"Come on," she said. "Let's go practice"—she paused a

long time—four breaths, five—then said it—"brother. We're going to have a busy night."

✦

The vision faded, and in her sleep, Rhiow put her whiskers forward, and knew that a tide had turned.

Eight

It was the morning of June 6th, 1876: sunny and hot, one more day in the middle of one of the most prolonged hot spells to manifest itself in the British Isles for nearly fifty years. Temperatures had been in the eighties every day for the past two weeks. *The Times* reported that a stationary high was in place over the Isles and showed no signs of moving in the immediate future.

A small, stout woman on horseback came riding sedately up through Windsor Home Park at an easy canter. She wore a long black riding dress, and rode sidesaddle with some grace and ease. She rode around the path that skirted the East Terrace Garden, and came up to the George IV Gateway, clattering through under the archway and into the wide, graveled space of the Upper Ward. Grooms ran forward to take her horse as she stopped near the little circular tower that marked the entrance to the State Apartments. One groom bent down to offer his back as a step to the woman dismounting: another took her by the hand and helped her down.

"He is breathing better this morning, Rackham," she said

to one of the grooms. "Perhaps he will not need the mash anymore this week."

"Yes, Your Majesty."

She swept in through the entrance to the State Apartments and up the stairs, then bustled down along the hallway that ran down the length of the first floor, making for the dayroom attached to her own apartments there. Maids curtsied low and footmen bowed as she passed: one of them rose to open the door to the dayroom for her.

The queen stepped into the dayroom, and then stopped, very surprised. Tumbling about on the carpet were two small cats, one mostly white with black patches, one more black with white patches, wrestling with each other. As the queen looked at them, they rolled over and gazed at her with big, innocent golden eyes.

"Meow," said one of them, with a deliberate air.

The queen's mouth dropped open, and she clapped her hands in delight. One of the maids appeared immediately. "Siddons," said Queen Victoria, "wherever did these darling kittens come from?"

"Please, Your Majesty, I don't know," said Siddons, a beautifully dressed young woman who immediately began to wonder if she was going to get in trouble for this. "Maybe they came in from outside, Your Majesty."

"Well, we must make inquiries and see if we can discover to whom they belong," said the queen, "but they are certainly very welcome here."

She went over to them, knelt down on one knee and stroked one of them, the kitten with more black than white. They were really a little larger than kittens but were not yet full-grown cats. The one she was stroking caught her hand in soft paws and gave it a little lick, then looked up at her with big eyes again.

"Darling thing!" said the queen, and picked the little cat

up in her arms, holding it so that it lay on its back. The small cat patted her face gently with one paw and gazed up at her adoringly.

"What was that you said? 'Meow'?" said Siffha'h, still rolling and stretching on the floor. "Look at you, squirming around like you've still got your milk teeth. How shameless can you get?"

"Well, it says here that a cat may look at a king," Arhu said. "So I'm looking."

"Well, this is a queen. And it doesn't say anything about being truly sickeningly sweet to the point where Iau Herself will come down from broad Heaven and tell you you're overdoing it. My blood sugar's going dodgy just looking at you."

"You're a wizard: adjust it. Meanwhile, at least she smells nice. Some of the *ehhif* around here could use a scrub."

"Tell me about it."

"Well, come on, don't just lie there. We've got to get ourselves well settled in. Find something to be cute with."

Siffha'h got up and headed for a thick velvet bell-pull with tassels. "All right, but I'm not sure this isn't going to stunt my growth." She started to play with the tassels.

The queen burst out laughing and put Arhu down. "Oh, my dear little kitties," said the queen, "would you like something to eat?" She turned to look over her shoulder, toward the butler standing in the doorway. "Fownes, bring some milk. And some cold chicken from the buffet."

"Yes, Your Majesty."

"Now for once Urruah was right about something," Arhu said. "Milk and cold chicken. I don't suppose they've invented pastrami yet."

Siffha'h inclined her head slightly to listen to the Whispering. "You're on the wrong side of the Atlantic. They do have it in New York. . . ."

"Dear Mr. Disraeli is coming to see me before lunch," she said to the cats. "You must be kind to him and not scratch his legs. Mr. Disraeli is not a cat person."

"*Uh* oh," Arhu said.

"I wish she hadn't said that," Siffha'h said. "I won't be able to resist, now."

"Don't do it," Arhu said. "He might nuke something."

"Please," Siffha'h said. However pleasant the surroundings, none of them had been able to stop looking up at the sky for that quiet reminder of Which Power seemed to be busiest in this Universe at the moment.

"Have you been in the bedroom yet?" Arhu said.

"No."

"Better take a look, then."

"Okay."

"Hey! Don't walk—scamper."

Siffha'h scampered, producing another trill of laughter from the queen. Arhu went after her the same way. A door opened out of the dayroom into the anteroom, and from the anteroom, to the right, into the royal bedroom. The bed was quite large, and beautifully covered all in white linen.

Siffha'h looked it over critically, walking around it. "It's a good size," she said to Arhu. "But not so big that we can't put a forcefield over it that would stop a raging elephant, not to mention an *ehhif* with a knife."

"We'll have to be careful how we trigger it, though. If she gets up for something in the middle of the night, she'll hang herself on it and get upset."

"Wouldn't want that," Siffha'h said. She walked around to look at the elaborately carved headboard. "Hey, look at the nibble marks. She's had mice in here."

"Yeah, well, we need to make sure she doesn't have another one," Arhu said. "With much bigger teeth."

"Your Majesty," said a servant who appeared at the dayroom door and bowed, "the prime minister has arrived."

"Very good. Bring his usual tea. Where is the cats' chicken?"

"Coming, Your Majesty."

"Here, kitties," the queen called, "come and have some milk!"

They glanced at each other. "I am *not* used to this kind of thing," said Siffha'h. "Ler her wait a few minutes."

"Why? You're hungry."

"If we come when she calls us, she's going to get the idea that we'll do that all the time. We're People, for Iau's sake."

"Well, she's a queen, and she's used to people coming when she calls. All kinds of people. Come on, Sif, humor her a little."

"Oh, all right." They trotted into the dayroom together. The queen was holding a bowl of milk, which she put down for them.

They drank. "Oh, Sweet Iau, where are they getting this stuff?" Arhu muttered, and practically submerged his face in the bowl.

"Real cows," said Siffha'h. "Not pasteurized. Full fat. They may know what cholesterol is here, but it doesn't bother them."

Footsteps came from down the hall. A few moments later, the man who had his finger on the Victorian nuclear trigger came in and sat down. He was tall and rangy and had the abundant beard that seemed so popular at this point in time. Arhu looked up at him from the bowl and got an immediate sense of thoughtfulness, subtlety, an almost completely artificial sense of humor, and dangerous intelligence. At the same time, behind the sleek and well-behaved façade lurked emotions that, though carefully controlled, were not at all mastered. This was the kind of man who could hold a grudge, teach it to think it was a carefully-thought-through opinion, and then turn it loose to savage his enemies.

"I wouldn't shed on him if I were you," Arhu said softly. "I think you might pull back a bloody stump."

"Mr. Disraeli," said the queen, "have you seen my two lovely young guests? I am hoping they will stay with me and enliven my sad days a little."

"Ma'am, anything that brings joy to your days is a joy to your humble servant," said Disraeli, and bowed.

Siffha'h gave him an amused look. "Pull the other three," she said, "they've got bells on."

"He can't help it," Arhu said. "He has to say things like that to her all the time now, or she wonders what's wrong with him." He put his whiskers forward.

"Sit, please," said the queen, and Disraeli did so and started chatting with her informally about the state of affairs in the empire, particularly in India. Here, as in their own universe, he was trying to convince her to accept the title of Queen-Empress, and she was presently in the stage of coyly refusing it.

"But, ma'am, the nations over which our benevolent influence is extended wish only to have you assume this title as a token of their esteem."

"If esteem is to be discussed," said the queen, reaching for a piece of chicken, "then I would sooner discuss the sort that France is expressing at the moment."

"Ah, Majesty, their inflammatory republican comments are intended for their own people and their own politicians' ears. They have no import here."

"They do when the French suggest that the British monarchy is superannuated and without merit," the queen said mildly, while this time giving Siffha'h the piece of chicken she was holding, and reaching for another one for Arhu. "No, don't grab, my darling, there is plenty for you both. —And when they threaten my cousins on the various thrones of Germany. I have no desire to seem as if we wish to expand our empire—which is broad enough at the moment—at the expense of others."

"If those others will not comport themselves wisely, those of them who live on the empire's doorstep," Disraeli said gently, "surely it is in our interest to explain to them the likely results of their destabilization of the nations of Europe. We have no desire to seem threatening, of course—"

"Indeed we do not," said the queen, looking up rather sharply from the distribution of the next piece of chicken. "And I require you to see that we do not. My diplomatic boxes have been full of disturbing material of late: complaints from neighbors who feel that our purpose is to destabilize *them.* I will not leave Europe in a worse state than I found it, Mr. Disraeli."

"Indeed, ma'am," Disraeli said, "the general opinion is that it would be left in much better state if more of it were British."

The queen sniffed. "A state of which my royal father would never have approved. We are the most powerful nation on the globe: all respect us, and those who do not respect us at least fear us, which unfortunate situation at least keeps my subjects safe. Let France provoke as it please, let Italy rattle her spears. They are too short to fly far. As for France, the English Channel is now a tie that binds us, not a protective barrier. She will do nothing but harm to her own trade by cocking a snook at us across the water."

"Ma'am," Disraeli said, "these direct attacks on the monarchy are being taken, by some, as direct threats to your royal person. There are those in Parliament who have begun calling for war."

"They do that every year around tax time," the queen said mildly. "Some distractions are worth more than others, especially in a year that presents the possibility of a general election. As for my people's opinion, they love to talk about conquering Europe, but they are not eager to do it themselves."

"They would be if you asked them to," Disraeli said softly.

The queen gave him a cool look. "I have no interest in spending their blood," she said, "for no better reason than a few vague threats. I am a mother too, and I know what the blood of sons is worth."

Disraeli bowed at that. "Yet it brings us to another matter, ma'am," he said. "You are a mother not only of princes and princesses, but of a people. And those people greatly desire to see you take up your public role with more enthusiasm. We have spoken of this before—"

"And doubtless will again," said the queen, turning away from him. "Mr. Disraeli, I know your concerns. But I cannot make a show of myself when my heart would be insincere, no matter what public opinion would make of it. You cannot possibly know the pain I suffer for the lack of my dear Albert, how I long for him, how that longing makes so many things, the splendors, the pleasures, as nothing but ashes in my mouth. I will not pretend to be what I cannot be . . . and my people, who love me, will understand."

He bowed again, slowly, reluctantly: and gradually their talk passed to other things. Arhu, meanwhile, rubbed against the queen's skirts, then headed back into the bedroom.

Siffha'h followed him in. "Well?" she said. "I didn't follow all of that."

"It gets complicated. But that was the lead-up, all right," Arhu said. "The circumstances are lining up as predicted."

"You're looking smug."

"Smug?" Arhu shook his head until his ears rattled. "No. I like a high-accuracy rating: it makes me a lot less nervous . . . especially when I hear the words 'necessary expansion' from someone who has nuclear weapons when no one else does. Nope," Arhu said, "we're in the right place at the right time. Now all we have to do is wait."

✦

The timeslide/gatings that first transported the London and New York teams to 1874 and then had dropped Siffha'h and Arhu in the queen's rooms had both run into trouble, as Ith had predicted. The resistance to them had been staggering, an order of magnitude greater than the last time it was tried. But Whoever was handling the resistance had not been prepared for a power source that for the first time simply ran into it, and through it, as if it were not there. The timeslide had first aligned itself with the time and place where Artie had stumbled upon them. The teams left him off in time for tea with his Uncle Richard and, making their farewells, they gated once more and popped directly out onto Cooper's Row in the late evening of July the eighth. There, under the scarred and tarnished Moon, the teams made themselves at home, as best they could, in the Mark Lane tube station.

Rhiow found its trains surprisingly modern: the station was clean and safe, and more handsomely decorated than its contemporary counterpart. The worldgates were not there, though. As Rhiow had suspected, they were presently up in the Fenchurch Street main-line rail station, and Rhiow and Huff both had been unwilling to tamper with them or to try to contact any London-based gating team that might be supervising the gates at this time. There were already enough complications to deal with.

They waited, and saw the city as best they could, and became very expert at ridding themselves of mud in short order. In particular, they spent a fair amount of time visiting with Ouhish and Hwallis at the British Museum. Hwallis had been delighted to hear about the recovery of the full spell for protection against the Winter, but the news about what was required to activate it had come as a blow.

The intervention, however, was Rhiow's and Huff's main care, and they made their preparations slowly, despite the impatience of some members of the team. *Look, it's been two days now,* Arhu said, late on the eighth, *and I don't know how much more petting we can stand. If it's not Herself, then it's the princes and princesses. And all the servants are trying to make friends with us, too.*

I should think you could do very well out of this, Urruah said. Like the others, he was down on the twin of their derelict platform, where the timeslide spell was "stabled" until they would need it again.

Do you mean food? Please! Don't even mention it, Siffha'h said. *I'm so stuffed I'm losing the ability to scamper.*

Huff smiled at that. *A historic moment,* he said.

Have you heard from Auhlae?

Yes. Nothing unusual as yet. So far the gates are behaving themselves.

Rhiow put her whiskers forward, glad to hear it. She had also been glad when Auhlae volunteered to mind the gates during the intervention. It had taken a weight off Huff's mind: he had been very nervous indeed of the prospect of bringing her here.

Just hold on the best you can, you two, she said. *It's only a couple of days more. Have you see the Mouse?*

Yes. A very inoffensive-looking little ehhif, Arhu said. *It's no wonder he was so good at the second-story work before McClaren hired him for this job: he's pretty small. He works in the gardens every day, putting plants in pots and taking them out again, and no one gives him a second look.*

Well, you're ready for him.

There are more protections waiting to be activated around that bed than any ehhif *needs,* Siffha'h said. *And we're there too: she insists on us sleeping with her. But he's not going to have a chance to make it* this *far, anyway. Come tomorrow afternoon, he's going to find himself locked in the Albert Tower with no way out . . . and the morning after, the police will take him away.*

They'll probably charge him with suspicion of theft when they find out what kind of work he used to do, Arhu said. *I won't mind. I see the way his little eyes look at things. It's not a mouse he reminds me of; it's a rat.*

Rhiow shivered a little. The image of a rat's mind in a man's body bothered her. *Well,* she said, *keep an eye on things. Urruah has gone to the House to see about that letter.*

Good, Arhu said. *This is a nice place . . . but I'll be glad when this lady is safe. She's got her problems, but none that deserve being killed for.*

There's also the slight problem of what would happen after *she was killed.*

Don't remind me. Well, keep us up to date, Siffha'h said. *It really will be kind of a relief to get out of here. She cries about Albert every night, like it's a ritual, and the pillows get all wet. I'm amazed she doesn't catch cold.*

Rhiow's tail twitched. *Do what you can for her,* she said. *A purr at the right time can do wonders.*

We will.

Rhiow sighed and lay back on the concrete. She was missing Iaehh already, and she was beginning to get that twitchy, uncomfortable feeling that comes of staying out of one's home time too long. In addition, she was beginning to feel peculiarly . . . exposed. *I just wish I knew to what.* But the feeling of something watching them, with bad intent, was getting very strong.

No matter. It won't take very long now. Urruah will sort that letter out . . . and then we can frame the Mouse and go home.

But something kept suggesting to Rhiow that it would not be that simple.

✦

The morning of the ninth of July came up hot and still, with crickets creaking in the crevices of stone walls and under the foundations of houses. It was hot everywhere, from Land's End to John o'Groats.

Nearer the John o'Groats end of things, just after the time when the milk arrives after dawn, the postman came up the walk of a small, neat semidetached home in Edinburgh city. Before he could knock, the latch was lifted, and a small, dapper man came out. The postman handed him several letters, which the man went through swiftly. One of these he opened: then, as the postman was on the way down the walk to the street, the small man called him and stepped back inside the door of the house for a moment. When he emerged, he handed the postman another letter. The postie took it and went his way.

✦

In the Palace of Westminster, unseen, a gray-striped tabby cat walked calmly down the Commons' Corridor, looking at the paintings that adorned the walls there: the last sleep of the Duke of Argyll, the acquittal of the Seven Bishops in the reign of James II, Jane Lane helping Charles II to escape.

Marvelous stuff, Urruah thought to himself, *but is it art?*

Most of it, he thought, was the kind of painting a partisan of a subject does to try to convince other people that it's of as much historical or cultural value as *he* thinks it is. Figures of old-time *ehhif* gestured heroically or stood in stoic silence, and all of them, to Urruah's educated eye, had "Establishment" written all over them. Urruah walked among the artwork and statuary with amusement, heading for the House of Commons and restraining his urge to sharpen his claws on the more bombastic of the murals.

He was sidled, naturally, and therefore had to sidestep to miss the occasional *ehhif* parliamentarian making for the House. They seemed to hold their meetings very late. It was nearly midnight: even bouts of *hauissh*, the feline pastime that most nearly includes politics, did not usually take place quite this late during what People consider normal waking hours. Whatever, Urruah wasn't terribly concerned about what hours they kept, except as it involved one man: McClaren.

He paused by the doors to the House, a little off to one side, and listened before going in.

". . . because the expense would be so great," an *ehhif* was saying in a great, deep, rolling voice; "whilst perhaps in the next parish there might be a clergyman who turns to the east when he celebrated the Holy Communion. If a parishioner called upon the bishop to prosecute in that case, then there would be no difficulty, it would be easy to prosecute for the posture . . . but by no means easy to prosecute for the doctrine. Is it not a monstrous proposition that when unsound doctrine is preached, one must proceed by the old, slow, cumbersome ecclesiastical law, and yet there is a rapid prosecution for gestures. . . ."

Urruah stood there trying to make head or tail of this for some minutes. It seemed that the *ehhif* was talking about communicating with the One, which was certainly a courtesy and a good idea generally: but the *ehhif*'s ideas of how the One liked to be communicated with seemed amazingly confused, and also seemed to be very hung up on obscure symbology that had to be exactly observed and duplicated, or else there would *be* no communication. *If they really believe this,* Urruah thought, *maybe it's no wonder they're so asocial. The universe must seem to them like a place run by ants. Rude,* illiterate *ants.*

". . . among the leading churchmen I have found extreme distaste and dissatisfaction with the bill. It is said that the bishop, in the ninth clause, should appear 'in a fatherly character,' but before the canons came in, he must practically have pronounced that some offense had been committed which ought to be proceeded against. Thus the power of the bishop as arbitrator can never commence until he has pronounced and sanctioned the prosecution."

Urruah reared up and peered through the glass of the doors. His view was largely blocked by frock-coated men standing between him and the floor of the House, and talking nonstop.

Well, vhai*'d if* I'm *going to stand* here *all night,* he thought. Very carefully Urruah slipped through the wood paneling of the lower half of the door, slowly, so as not to upset the grain of the wood, and, being careful not to become strictly solid again until he knew exactly where the legs of the *ehhif* on the other side were. Fortunately, none of them were too close.

Once in, Urruah stood there at the back of the House and listened for a few more minutes, finally wondering why in Iau's name anyone would come here late at night to hear this kind of thing . . . unless indeed they were all insomniacs in search of treatment. Up in the strangers' gallery, various visiting *ehhif* were either asleep or on their way to being so: on the other side, journalists were scribbling frantically in notebooks, trying to keep up with what the *ehhif* who spoke was saying. Urruah wondered why anyone would bother. The man had the most soporific style imaginable, and in this hot, still room, made hotter yet by the primitive electrical lights, the effect produced put the best sleep-spells Urruah knew to shame.

Urruah peered about him again, looking for any sign of McClaren. The *ehhif* was tall and had a big beard, but unfortunately that described about half the *ehhif* in here: this was a very hairy period for *ehhif* males in this part of the world. McClaren also had a long, hawkish nose and very blue eyes, but again Urruah's view was somewhat blocked.

He's probably not here, Urruah thought. *Still, I'll take a look around.* And the impish impulse struck him.

He unsidled.

At first no one noticed him. It was late, and he was walking softly down the carpeted floor of the gangway on the Opposition side. He knew where he was headed: toward the center of the room, the "aisle," where he could get a good view of both front benches. McClaren was a Government minister, and would normally have been sitting there on the left-paw side of the Speaker as Urruah was facing the Speaker's Chair.

He looked around him at the weary, complacent faces as he came down the gangway . . . and they began to look at him. Urruah put his whiskers forward as the laughter started. *That'll wake them up,* he thought: *this'll probably make the papers tomorrow.* He came down to the aisle, took a long leisurely look across at the Government benches . . .

. . . and saw McClaren there.

Urruah stopped short, with the laughter scaling up all around him.

What's he doing here?

For he was not supposed to be here. He should have been up in his office, writing a letter.

Sa'Rráhh in a five-gallon bucket, Urruah thought, *no—*

He bolted toward the Government benches, ignoring the surprised or shocked faces turned toward him, and jumped up on the back of the first front bench, almost getting into the beard of the surprised minister sitting nearest. Urruah jumped with great speed from there to the first of the black benches, and to the next and the next, going up them like steps in a staircase and not particularly caring whose leg, shoulder, or head he stepped on in the process. The laughter became deafening. There was a door at the back of the last of the benches, at the very top. Urruah jumped down and went straight through it, this time without the slightest concern for the grain of the wood.

He raced out through the West Division lobby, through it into the little hallway at the corner of the lobby and up the staircase two floors. He knew well enough where McClaren's office was. Through that wooden door, too, he went, sidled again this time.

There was no one in the office.

Urruah stood very still for a moment and licked his nose three times in rapid succession. Then he glanced around him and looked up into the box on the bookcase.

No letter.

He jumped up onto the desk, covered with the same leather and paper blotter Arhu had Seen. There were no writings on it, but there were faint depressions, as of writing.

Urruah looked across to the small narrow fireplace at the other side of the office. *Perfect,* he thought.

He did a very small wizardry in his mind and put his paws down on the blotter, electrostatically charging it. Then he glanced over at the fireplace, and spoke courteously in the Speech to the soot up in the chimney.

Tidily, in a thin stream, it made its way across the room to him. Urruah guided it down onto the blotter, then levitated the blotter a little way up on its edge to let the soot slide down it.

It adhered here and there on the blotter, mostly to signatures. But one recent piece of writing showed up most clearly where the soot clung.

MR. JAMES FLEMING
14 KENNISHEAD AVENUE
EDINBURGH

Dear Mr. Fleming,

Thank you for yours inst. the 6th of July regarding passes to the Speaker's gallery. Such may only be granted by the Speaker after introduction by the applicant's own member of Parliament. In your case this would—

Oh, no, Urruah thought.

It's gone. It's gone already. How can it be gone?

He ran out of the office again, through the door, his heart pounding and his mouth dry with terror.

Everybody! Everybody! Windsor, now, hurry—now!

✦

He unlatches the door with one gloved hand, slips in through it, shuts it gently behind him. Stands still in the darkness, and listens. A faint hiss from the hot-water boiler behind the coal stove, the tick of cinders shifting in the box: no other sound.

He takes his twelve steps across the kitchen, reaches out his hand, finds the shut door. He eases its latch open, slips through this door too, pulls it gently to behind him. Six stairs up to the hallway. Two steps out into the middle of the carpet in the hall: turn left. Sixty steps down to the second landing, and out onto the carpet. In the darkness he passes by the doorways he knows are there, to the Picture Gallery, the Queen's Ball Room, the Queen's Audience Chamber. Silently past the Guard Chamber: no guards are there anymore—the place is full of suits of armor, some of them those of children, and silken banners and old swords and shields, the gifts of kings. *No more kings after tonight,* he thinks, with the slightest smile in the dark. *No more queens . . .*

Fifty-nine steps, and there is the change in the sound. Sixty. His toe bumps against the bottom step. Five stairs up to the landing: turn right: three steps. He puts his hand out, and feels the door.

Gently, gently he pulls it open. From up the winding stair comes a faint light: it seems astonishingly bright to him after the dead blackness. Softly he goes up the stairs, taking them near the outer side of the steps: the inner sides creak.

Something brushes against his leg. A gasp catches in his throat: he freezes in place. A minute, two minutes, he stands there.

Nothing. A cobweb. Even a place like this, with a hundred servants, can't keep all the stairwells free of the little toilers, the spinners of webs. Softly he goes on up again, one step at a time, at the edges, with care.

The remaining fifteen steps are steep, but he is careful. At the door at the top he halts and looks out of the crack in it where it has been left open. In the hallway onto which this stairway gives, next to a door with a gilded frame, is a chair under a single candle-sconce with a dim electric bulb burning in it. There should be a footman in it, but there's no sign of him. The chair is tilted back against the wall, and down by the foot of the chair is a stoneware mug: empty. The footman has gone to relieve himself. And the door in the gilded frame is slightly open.

Perfect. Down the hallway, now, in utmost silence.

Swiftly now, but also silently. Reach up and undo the bulb from its socket. No one will think a thing of it: these newfangled things burn out without warning all the time. Wait a few seconds for night vision to return. Then, silently, push the door open and step in.

The outer room is where the lady-in-waiting has a bed. She is not in it. Now the footman's absence suddenly completely makes sense, and in the darkness, he smiles. The nightwalker makes his way toward what he cannot see yet in this more total darkness, the inner door. He feels for the handle: finds it.

Turns the handle. The door swings inward.

Darkness and silence. Not *quite* silence: a faint rustle of bed linens, off to his left, and ahead. A little rasp of noise, soft. A snore? She will sleep more quietly in a moment. . . .

Now, only now, the excitement strikes him, and his heart begins to pound. Ten steps, they told him. A rather wide bed. Her maids say she still favors the left side of it, leaving the right side open for someone who sleeps there no more.

Ten steps. He takes them. He listens for the sound of breathing . . .

. . . then reaches for the left side.

One muffled cry of surprise, as the knives pierce his hand, and other knives catch him from behind, on the neck and the back of the head, a flurry of abrupt, terrible, slicing pain. He staggers back, his arms windmilling, the knife trying to find a target in the darkness. Only the training of many years, the usual number of accidents—broken glass, banged shins—keeps him quiet now as he stumbles back to find his balance again. For just a moment his hand is free of the pain, but now the front of his neck is pierced by furious jaws that bite him in the throat, claws that seize and kick. He fumbles at his throat to grab something furry and throw it away with all his might—

—and suddenly he simply can't move: he's frozen stiff, as if he were a stick of wood or one of the carved statues downstairs. Like a statue with its pedestal pulled out from under it, he topples, unable even to catch himself, or to turn so that he falls facedown and not on his back.

Yet at the last minute he doesn't fall. Some force far stronger than he is stops him, holds him suspended in air. He can't breathe, can't move, can only lie here gripped by something he can't begin to understand, and by the terror that follows.

The pain, at least, drops away from the back of his head. But suddenly there is a pressure on his chest. His eyes, wide already in the dark, go as wide as they can with shock as a face, grinning, like the face of a demon, becomes just barely visible before him.

It is the face of a black-and-white cat. From the very end of its tail, held up behind it, comes the faintest glimmer of light, like a will-o'-the-wisp. It looks at him with a face of unutterable evil, a devil come to claim him: and, impossibly, in a whisper, it speaks.

"Boy," it says, "have *you* ever picked the wrong bedroom."

It sits there on his chest while invisible hands lift him. A brief whirl of that ever-so-faint light surrounds him, going around the back of his field of vision, coming up to the front again, tying itself in a tidy bow-knot. For a second or so that light fills everything.

Then it is gone again, and he falls again, coming down on the floor with a thump. His head cracks down hard, and he almost swears but restrains himself.

But there's no carpet on this floor. This is hard stone.

Slowly, when he discovers that he can sit up again, he feels the floor around him. Marble, and old smooth tile—hesitantly he gets to his feet, begins to feel his way around.

What he feels makes no sense. A stone figure, lying on its back, raised above the floor; much other carving reveals itself under his hands, but nothing else. He would swear out loud, except that he may still be able to get out, and someone might hear him.

It is a long while before the tarnished, waning Moon rises enough for its light to stream through the stained-glass windows surrounding him with their illustrations of biblical texts, and for him to realize whose the reclining figure is. There, entombed in marble, Prince Albert lies in the moonlight, hands folded, at rest, on his face a slight grave smile, which, in this lighting, takes on an unbearably sinister aspect.

The memory of the demon face comes back to him. He swallows, feels for his knife. It's gone. Dropped upstairs in the bedroom. There's nothing he can use on the locked, barred ornamental gate to get out. There's no way he can get rid of the silken rope. They will find it on him in the morning, when they call the police. There is a specific name for the charge of being found with tools that might be used for burglary: it's called "going forth equipped." It's good for about twenty years, these days.

He sits down on the green marble bench under the scriptural bas-reliefs with their thirty kinds of inlaid marble, and begins, very quietly, to weep.

Just outside the bars, the darkness smiles and walks away on little cat feet.

Out in the Home Park, a black brougham waits until 2 A.M. precisely: then, slowly, quietly, moves off into the night.

✦

There was a tremendous fuss the next morning when the burglar was found downstairs. There was less certainty about his status as a burglar when the lady-in-waiting found, dropped next to the queen's bed, a switchblade knife of terrible length and keenness. The police came, and the police commissioner with them: he questioned the queen with the utmost respect. No, she had seen nothing, heard nothing. Her dear little kitties had been sleeping with her all night: she woke up and went to her toilette . . . and then all these horrible discoveries began to make themselves plain. The policemen took time to stroke the cats, which lay about on the white linen coverlet with the greatest possible ease and indolence, and a fairly smug look on their faces. The cat-scratches present on the "burglar's" head and neck and hands made it fairly plain where he had been, and (probably) what he had been up to. As a result, all that morning, the cats were petted and fussed and made much of. Instead of running away, as anyone might have expected with such young creatures, they stood it with astonishing stolidity.

It was nearly ten in the morning before the queen finally saw the final visitors out of her apartment, sent her lady-in-waiting away, and shut the door to have a few moments' peace. She slipped back into her bedroom, where the two young black-and-white cats had been asleep on the bed. One of them was lying on her back with her feet in the air, utterly indolent: the other had rolled over on his side and was watching her come with an air of tremendous intelligence.

"Ah, my dears," she said, and sat down on the bed beside them. "How I wish you could speak and tell me what happened last night."

The slightly larger one, the male, gave her that unutterably wise look. The queen turned her head to look out at the bright summer morning, which she might not have lived to see. The other cat rolled off her back and blinked at the queen lazily.

"Madam," she said, "do you think this life is a rehearsal? It's *not.*"

The queen's mouth dropped open.

"She's right, Queen," Arhu said, getting up and sauntering toward her. "You're acting like you've got as many lives as we have . . . and you don't. Don't you think it's time you stopped hiding in here—time you got out there and started making some use of yourself? Honestly, I'm sorry you lost your big tom with all the fur on his face. He sounds like he was nicer than the usual run of *ehhif.* But as far as I know, he's with the One now, Who'll certainly know how to treat him right: and if what I hear is anything to go by, he wouldn't like you sitting here grieving for him while you have all this work to do."

"But . . ." the queen finally managed to say. "But, oh, my dear little puss, how can you possibly know anything of the kind of pain I suffer when I think of—"

"*I'll* tell you what I know," Arhu said. "Sif, let's show her."

They showed her: the pain they knew all too well, and shared.

The queen sank back into the chair beside the bed, a few seconds later, staggered. Tears began to roll down her face.

"Beat *that,* if you can," said Siffha'h at last.

The queen hid her face in her hands.

"So don't think you have a corner on the suffering market," said Arhu. "Or on being lonely. Or that other people 'can't know.' When the sun comes up at last, we're all stuck in our own heads by ourselves. Everyone around you feels the pain of it, sooner or later—the Lone One's claw in their heart. Some feel it a lot worse than you, even if you *are* the dam to a pride of millions. So stop acting as if you're so special."

Even through the queen's tears, her jaw dropped open at that.

"And stop shirking your work," said Siffha'h. "Bad things will happen to your pride if you don't come out and do the things you were reared to do. They've started happening already. If you act now, you can stop the process."

"Oh," Arhu added, "and by the way, lay off the nuclear weapons. I know Dizzy likes them, but *this* is what will happen if you don't."

He showed her.

The queen went ashen at the sight of the Winter.

For several long minutes she was speechless: possibly a record. At the end of it, all she could whisper was, "You are little angels of God."

"Please, madam," Arhu said, "don't get confused. We're *cats.* If you mean we're messengers of the One, well, so is everybody: it's hardly an exclusive position. But this is the word. *No nukes.* You really ought to get rid of them, lest someone later be tempted to use them who isn't as morally upright as you are."

Flatterer.

She's susceptible. A good wizard uses the tools that are available.

"And make sure you don't let them get out of control while you're having them destroyed," Siffha'h said. "Some people might be tempted to get light-fingered, try to sell a few to somebody else on the grounds that no one will notice since they're being destroyed anyway."

The queen looked suddenly determined. "I have never liked them," she said softly. "I will begin work at once, if you say so."

"It would be a project," Arhu said, "that would probably be productive of some good."

The queen looked around with some surprise, for suddenly the bedroom seemed to have a lot more cats in it, and she had no idea where they might have come from. A huge gray tabby; a small, neat, black cat with golden-green eyes; a massive gray-and-tan tabby with astonishing fluffy fur; a small, tidy marmalade cat with a slightly sardonic expression. All of them looked at her with interest.

"Our colleagues," said Arhu. "We have been here on errantry on your behalf: the errand's over. They just wanted to look at you before we all left." Arhu smiled slightly. "It's in the job description."

"But, but my dear kitties," the queen said, "you cannot go now, you must stay!" Perhaps she already read the answer in their eyes. "I command it!"

"Majesty," said the black cat, with a nod of what might have been respect, "our People have their own Queen, to whom we answer: a higher authority, I believe, than even yours. We cannot stay: we have other errands to perform for Her. But She wishes you well, by us. Do well by your people, and farewell."

And then they were all gone.

The queen wept a little, as was her habit, and then started to put herself right after the events of the morning. She did not get around to reading *The Times* until almost bedtime. When she did, it took her a while to get to the parliamentary report, which she was about to skip, since for some days it had contained an interminable report about the Public Worship Regulation Bill. But suddenly, in the middle of the dry, dry text, she began to smile.

> The right hon. Gentleman was at this moment startled by a burst of laughter from the crowded House, caused by

the appearance of a large gray tabby cat, which, after descending the Opposition gangway, proceeded leisurely to cross the floor. Being frightened by the noise, the cat made a sudden spring from the floor over the shoulder of the members sitting on the front Ministerial bench below the gangway, and, amid shouts of laughter, bounded over the heads of members on the back benches until it reached a side door, when it vanished. This sudden apparition, the cat's still more sudden disappearance, and the astonishment of the members who found it vaulting so close to their faces and beards, almost convulsed the House.

The queen folded up the newspaper, put it aside, and went to sleep, determined to start making some changes the next day.

✦

"The only thing about this that still bothers me," Urruah was saying, "is where that letter went. I can't imagine how he got it out of there so fast."

"But that's the problem," said Hwallis to the London and New York teams, earlier that afternoon. "A day for a letter to get to and from Edinburgh? A whole *day?* You must be joking."

The members of the New York team looked at each other. "It's easy for us to forget," Huff said, "that once upon a time, when this country had a rail network it could be proud of, and before there were telephones, the mail could come seven times a day—in London, in some parts, as many as *twelve* times a day. And pickups were much more frequent than they are now."

"The Houses of Parliament have a pickup for members at midnight," Ouhish said. "That letter would have been on the train to Scotland half an hour later. It would have been in Edinburgh, and delivered, with the first post, sometime after five in the morning. No later than seven, anyway. If a reply was passed directly back to the postman, that letter would also have gone on a train within an hour or so, and the reply would have been in London—Windsor, in this case—by the two-o'clock post at the latest."

Rhiow shook her head. "And we think our *ehhif* have technology," she said softly. "Sometimes retrotech has its points."

They spent the afternoon at the museum and said their farewells to Ouhish and Hwallis around four: then went for one last meeting, in Green Park. Artie was out for one last afternoon in London: the next morning he was due to catch the train back to Edinburgh, and after that, he would be heading off to a school on the Continent. He was sorrowful, but his basic good cheer would not let the affair be entirely a sad one.

"But will I never see you again," Artie said, "or Ith?"

"For our own part, it seems unlikely," Rhiow said. "Mostly wizards don't do time-work without permission from the Powers. There are too many things that can go wrong. But you will remember us for a long time."

Probably not forever, she thought but didn't say. One of the factors that protected wizardry from revelation was the tendency of humans' minds to censor themselves over time, forgetting the impossible, recasting the improbable into more acceptable forms. Childhood memories, in particular, were liable to this kind of editing, as the adult mind decided retroactively what things could have happened in the "real world" and which were dreams. Yet Artie was a little unusual. There was something about him that suggested he would not easily let go of a memory, and that no matter how impossible something was, if it was true, he would cope with it . . . and hang on.

"But Ith is another story," Urruah said. "His time isn't precisely our time: the universe where he lives is closer to the heart of things, and so a little easier to get in and out of, for him. Also, he outranks us." Urruah smiled. "He's a Senior now, and Seniors have more latitude."

"No matter what else happens," Fhrio said, "remember that you helped save the queen, and many millions of people you'll never know. You'll never be able to prove it to anybody. But without you, we would not have been guaranteed entry into this timeline . . . and we couldn't have been sure to save the others. You did that. It might have been an accident at first, but afterwards, you did it willingly. We won't forget that, or you . . . and neither will the Powers."

Artie smiled at that. "I guess it's better than nothing."

"Immeasurably," Rhiow said.

They parted as sunset drew on, and made their way back to the Mark Lane Underground, where they had lodged the timeslide. As they went underground for the last time in this period, Rhiow looked up into the dirty sky. There was no Moon there, tarnished or otherwise. Depending on whether or not they managed to track back the "seed" event of this chain, it might always wear those terrible scars. But at least now there was a good chance that the world would not.

"So what's next?" she said to Huff as they made their way down to the "derelict" platform.

"That book," he said. "Fhrio, think we'll be able to wring what we need out of the gate logs when we get back?"

"I feel certain of it," he said. "And with Siffha'h to power the gating, the way she's doing now, there shouldn't be anything that can interfere."

He sounded positively cheerful, Rhiow thought. She found herself wondering, a little ironically, whether this was because of how well the mission had gone, or whether it was because soon Urruah and Arhu would be leaving.

An unworthy thought. Never mind. It's all worked out nicely. How good it's going to be to get home to Iaehh, and let life go back to normal: our own gates to take care of, no commuting.

And Rhiow smiled at herself then. Entropy was not about to stop running. Almost certainly something would go wrong with one of their own gates as soon as they got home, something finicky and pointless that would take weeks to put right.

To her horror, the thought was delightful.

They came down to the dark and quiet of the platform, and Urruah woke up the timeslide: its wizardry blazed up into the familiar "hedge" around them as everyone took their appointed places. Rhiow looked around her as Siffha'h stepped into the power point and Fhrio hooked one claw into the wizardry. "Ready?" he said. "Anybody forget anything? Now's your last chance."

Tails were flirted no all around. "All right, Siffha'h," he said. "On standby . . ."

"Now!" she said: reared up, and came down.

The pressure came. Rhiow surrendered herself to it for a change, familiar as it was. For home was on the other side.

Nine

They came out into darkness: darkness so black that not even a Person's eyes could make anything of it.

For a few moments there was nothing but silence. Then Urruah said, "What in the Queen's name—?"

The timeslide wizardry collapsed around them, as if something had stomped it flat. All of them looked around them in shock.

"What is it?" asked Arhu. "Where's the light? What's gone wrong down here?"

"Nothing," said a soft voice from away off in the darkness. "But something is finally about to go right."

"*Uh*-oh," Arhu said, and fell very abruptly silent.

"Auhlae?" Huff said. He stepped forward carefully out of the circle: Rhiow could feel him brush past her. "Are you all right? What's happened down here?"

"Nothing that hasn't been promised for a long time," came the soft voice. Rhiow strained to hear it better. It was Auhlae . . . but it wasn't.

"What's the matter?" Huff said. "Has something gone wrong with the gates?"

Laughter came out of the dark. "That's always your first question, isn't it? No, of course not. The gates are fine."

"Oh . . . good." Huff stopped, unable to see where he was going. "Then maybe you can help us find our way out of here. It's kind of dark."

"Yes," said Auhlae . . . or something using Auhlae's voice. "A refreshing change, isn't it? This is the way it should always have been from the beginning. No garish stars, no dirty little life-infested planets, nothing but the cold and the night." And indeed it was feeling rather cold down here; much more so than it should have even in London in September. "And shortly this is what it will be like on Earth as well. Perhaps not this dark. But no Sun, no heat. Peace and quiet on this worthless little mudball at last."

A faint spark of light came up from behind them: Arhu making a light. Before them, away off in the darkness, they could see two blue eyes looking at them, gleaming green in the light Arhu made. Those eyes were farther away than it should have been possible for them to be, in a direction that should have been solid wall. And the sound of the place had gone all wrong. The close, underground feeling of it was gone: or rather, pushed back a long way . . . much farther than should have been possible, as if someone had scooped out a great cavern here to replace the tunnels.

"Auhlae," Rhiow said, feeling the fur stand up all over her at the look in those eyes. "Are you sure you're all right?"

"*You,*" said the voice. "That *you* should ask. How very glad I am that you made it back. We have business to settle."

"What are you talking about?"

There was bitter laughter in the darkness. "You think I haven't noticed you trying to steal him from me? Poor simple Huff. He never was able to tell when someone was making a play for him."

Arhu's light was still dim, though Rhiow could feel him

trying, vainly, to make it brighter. She could not see Huff clearly, or the look in his eyes. "Auhlae," Rhiow said, "you're completely mistaken. No one has ever had a better mate than Huff is to you, or a more faithful one. And as for me, what possible good would he do me even if I did want him? *I'm spayed!*"

The laughter again. "As if that matters," Auhlae snarled. "Do you think I'm such a fool as to think someone's affections can't be stolen without a uterus? How coy you were about it. Oh so sweet and noble and intelligent, and then when that starts to work, then the weak little queen act, oh-dear-I've-fallen-and-I-can't-get-up . . . and all of a sudden Huff is washing your ears and whispering sweet nothings in them. There'll be precious little left of them to whisper in when *I'm* through."

Rhiow actually took a step backward in the blast of raw jealousy: it burned like a winter wind howling down Park Avenue.

You, she thought. The Lone Power always hated love, in whatever form. It would try to destroy it whenever It could, as sa'Rráhh had rebelled against her divine Dam's love in the beginning of things. That love was still waiting: but sa'Rráhh, for the most part, was unconcerned.

"It was *you* then," Rhiow said. "You were the one who let the first few microgatings through. You saw them, and you didn't do anything to stop them."

"I *didn't* see them!" the enraged voice yowled. "What kind of obsessive would read gating logs so carefully? Do you think I'm the kind of sad case you and your team are: do you think I don't have a *life?* By the time I noticed them, there had already been three or four. And I didn't think much of it. All gates have these sporadic faults; they go away if you don't try to micromanage them. But then it started happening regularly. The problem went chronic. Even then it still wouldn't really have been a problem: I could have explained it, we could have cleared it up. But then the Ravens noticed—what business was it of theirs?—and they told the Powers, and the Powers called you in. As if it was any of your business either! And after that, how could I let Huff see the gate logs, or let him know I knew anything about what had been going on? He wouldn't have understood why I didn't do anything sooner. You have no idea the kind of fuss he would make. And I couldn't let him know that I'd seen the earlier ones."

Huff was still standing there silent and astonished at all this. "So you tampered with the logs," Urruah said. "Right down to the end. And I thought *I* was an expert." He put his whiskers forward, ironic. "My compliments."

"You think you're such a great one, you," Auhlae sneered. The voice in the darkness was getting softer, more venomous: but the eyes seemed larger, somehow. "Urruah, the conqueror of every heart. I didn't want you!"

"I didn't want *you*," he said, rather mildly.

There was a breath's pause of sheer disbelief, and then a scream. "You did! You did! How could you not want me, when Huff did!"

"Auhlae," Rhiow said softly, "Huff didn't care whether other toms wanted you or not. *He* wanted you. That was more than enough for him. Don't you see that even now?"

"As if *you* know anything about him, or me," Auhlae hissed. "*I* know why you came. One failure and that's it, isn't it? And They were glad enough to give you an excuse to move in. No forgiveness from Their high and mighty quarter, oh no! They were all too glad for you to lever me out of my place with my team and take my spot. And take Huff. Well, it's not going to happen. I found help where I least expected it."

The eyes were larger. ***He will never find out,*** the voice said now, Auhlae's voice, but not quite so much anymore. *Everything will be the way it was again. When all of you are dead, or gone, or lost in backtime . . . everything will be fine here.*

"For a while, Auhlae," said Rhiow desperately. *There may still be a chance to call her back, just a chance.* "Only for a while. All you can imagine is you and Huff, happy together . . . no matter what the price. But sa'Rráhh will brook no rivals. Her only love is destruction, like the one she's planning now. You can still oust her if you try: she cannot live in the unwilling heart, any more than wizardry can."

The laughter from away down in the darkness was deafening.

Rhiow stood up straight, though she was shaking. "Fairest and Fallen," she said, "greeting and defiance, now and always!" It was the language the protocol required: there was no need to be rude to the Lone One, no matter what might follow. "State your intentions: and then beware, for we are on the Queen's errantry, and you meddle with Her worlds at your peril!"

Suddenly Fhrio's voice came out of the darkness, sounding confused and angry. "Now wait just a moment. You can't talk to Auhlae as if she was—as if—"

"I told you it'd happen." Arhu growled. "You're in the dark, Fhrio . . . and you don't see what's happening right in front of you. You haven't seen for a long time. Now it's *your* turn to behave yourself. Shut up and let someone handle this who *can* see!"

Fhrio, uncertain, went silent. The laughter came again. *I meddle with the worlds as I please,* said the Lone Power, said sa'Rráhh, out of the middle of the darkness and Auhlae's surrendered body. *It is when* others *meddle that the peril begins. You have deprived Me of My darkness, long planned, and of the cold that would have fallen a hundred years ago. Very well: you have chosen. Instead that darkness shall fall* now.

It was not so much that the blackness around them began to break: it was more that advancing toward the gating teams, slowly and pleasurably, was something that made the darkness look horribly less dark by comparison. There was fire in it, but not the kind that gave any light: and many sorts of night that had at one time or another fallen over London, but not the kind with stars. The smoke of the Great Fire was there, and the blackness of the Plague: the fire-shot smoke of the destruction that had fallen from the sky in the Second World War, and the eye-smarting thick, gray smoke from the burning thatch of the most ancient settlement by the already oxbowed river. But most of all Rhiow was reminded of the billowing blackness in the uprising mushroom cloud of an atomic explosion . . . and it occurred to her that, even now, there were atomic weapons stationed in a few places within the ring of the M25 in London. They were supposed to be safe at defense establishments, but when the Lone Power Itself was walking, how safe could anything be?

Slowly the dark shape stalked toward them. It was feline: it was sa'Rráhh indeed, in the fullness of Her fury, the mistress of the Unmastered Fire, intent on their destruction. And they were totally unprepared. *Defiance indeed,* Rhiow thought. *What now?*

The light from behind her was at least getting a little stronger. The Lone One's influence was damping down every other wizardly power but Its own as It advanced slowly on them, but Siffha'h's newfound strength had not yet settled into channels where even sa'Rráhh could easily muzzle them. She was feeding Arhu power, and Arhu was making light, if nothing else: and in that light, Rhiow looked over at Huff, and said, *It's now or never, cousin. Do what you can—*

He looked at Rhiow, and stepped forward. "Auhlae," Huff cried, "I don't want her! Do you hear me? I never wanted her. You're all I want. This is all for nothing. Cast it out, or everything we've worked for all this time will be destroyed!"

Rhiow was desperately trying to assemble wizardry after wizardry in her mind, but it was no use: they were all being damped, every structure collapsing as she began to build it—and sa'Rráhh drew closer, the terrible feline shape towering over them in the darkness now, the size of a house, growing seemingly bigger by the second, filling the whole field of vision with that deadly dark burning. *"We've" worked for?* Laughter again. *It hasn't been worth anything anyway. When this is all over, the gates will be destroyed, and we won't have to do that kind of work anymore. We can settle down and just be wizards again.*

Huff took a long breath. "I will not be the kind of wizard that serves what you serve," he cried, "and I will not be the mate to that kind of wizard either!"

And he launched himself straight at sa'Rráhh's throat.

One great paw lifted and slapped him aside as if he were nothing. Rhiow, flinching, heard the bones crack: saw the body fly past her to come down hard on the seamed concrete, which was all that was left of the real world.

Sa'Rráhh looked down at Huff's body, put her whiskers forward, and smiled . . .

. . . and the smile twisted strangely. The lips wrinkled. From inside the burning eyes above them, just for a moment, something that might have been Auhlae once looked out: enraged, betrayed. She screamed, a yowling roar that drove Rhiow crouching down to try to escape it, a terrible squall of betrayal and loss—

—and then the light broke through.

All around the huge terrible form, like a cage, a four-dimensional figure appeared, a massive icosaract, its "extra" sides unfolding out all around it. The Lone Power looked around it in first astonishment and then growing rage, and began to throw itself against the "bars" of the cage. The cage shook, but it held.

Sa'Rráhh roared. *It will not avail you! The fire comes now, and then the Winter.*

There will be no Winter, came another great voice—one that was, bizarrely, not one voice, but a union of many. *This is the land of the Sun. We are the People of the Sun, and of our Mother Whose sigil the Sun is. By this spell worked, and this summons wrought, we ban the Winter, we ban the Unmastered Fire: we ban the One Who bears it!*

Rhiow and the others stood still and stared as the stars began to fall.

At least they looked like stars at first. There had been none in the impenetrable darkness. But all around the struggling, roaring shape of sa'Rráhh, bright fires started to fall from far above. They fell in pairs. As they came to the ground, they started to acquire shapes of their own: bodies formed around them. Hundreds of bodies, thousands of bodies, tens of thousands of them, all shining each like its own small sun.

Rhiow stared in wonder. They were the People of the ancient days: the hundreds of thousands of cats of the Egyptians, who had mummified them and laid them to rest. Their souls had been in the Tree, or about the One's business, for all these thousands of years: their bodies had lain in the sand for a long long time. Now they were in the gardens of Essex and Sussex, they were under the lawns of the Home Counties, they were in flowerpots outside old townhouses and scattered among the roots of the trees in Green Park: they were all over the city of London, and all around it, for miles and miles in every direction. It did not matter that the mummies of the cats of Egypt had been ground to powder along with the bandages and the amulets that each held its fragment of the protective spell. They had been in contact with them too long, in their long rest in Egypt, not to have become indelibly contaminated by the wizardry. The Great Cemetery of the city of Bubastis was now in England. And its inhabitants remembered the *ehhif* they loved, who had fed them fish and milk, and stroked them, and loved them in return. They would not let these *ehhif* perish simply because they were not the same ones.

The Lone Power struggled in Her cage, while around Her, for what seemed great distances, stars fell thick from the sky, and became People, all burning with glory. The fire of the Sun persisted in their eyes, which they turned on the Lone One where She roared and crashed about in the cage. Softly, a huge and concerted yowl began to go up from the hundreds and thousands assembled. It built until Rhiow had to crouch down again from the sheer weight and rage of the sound . . .

. . . and the People of the ancient world leaped in fury into the cage with sa'Rráhh, filling it until the Lone One could no longer be seen: and the cat fight to end all cat fights broke out under the streets of London. The noise soon became like the crash of ocean or of thunder, impossible to hear as anything but a vibration, something that got into the bones and shook the listener into submission. Rhiow lay flat, prostrate with anger but also with wonder. And the yowl, the roar, the noise, went on and on. . . .

She could not really tell when it stopped. What Rhiow did notice, though, was the gradual lightening of the scene. The People of the ancient days were streaming out of the icosaract, now: they pooled around it for a while, and then slowly began to fade, like a promising dawn fading into a gray and cloudy morning. The physical surroundings began to come back, and Rhiow pushed herself to her feet. The icosaract, finally, was empty. The last few sparks of divine fire in the eyes of the ancient People faded away, taking them with them. And in the middle of it all, on what was left of the platform, stood Ith, his foreclaws neatly folded together, and looking thoughtful as usual.

Rhiow staggered over toward him, but someone else was ahead of her. "What took you so long?" Arhu was saying to Ith, rather loudly: he was as deaf as Rhiow at the moment. As Ith lowered his head toward him, Arhu clouted the saurian a good one more or less over the ear, a gesture of affectionate annoyance. "I thought you were never going to get here!"

"At least you were able to See, on however short notice, what was coming," Ith said calmly. "I did not want to arrive with the spell half set. Our Enemy would have denatured it in a second if it had not arrived already running. Also, I would have found it hard to do so until the Lone One was distracted. And moving such a spell from one place to another while it is active is no small matter." He looked around at where the sea of radiant eyes had surrounded them. "But I must say the effect is most impressive."

Rhiow breathed out in immense relief. Her ears were ringing so badly that she could hardly hear: she and her team would be near-deaf for a day or so, she thought. *But we got away easy,* Rhiow thought sadly, looking down at Huff's body.

"Look at this mess!" Fhrio shouted as he came along to join her, slowly, with Urruah behind him. "What in the world are the *ehhif* going to make of this?" For a huge scoop of tunnel and brick and earth had simply been blasted out of the whole area.

"They'll probably think it's some kind of terrorist bomb or something," Rhiow said, looking around her at the destruction, the torn-up track and tangled, jutting rods of reinforcement-metal sticking out of the concrete. She sighed wearily and looked down at Huff again. "And what will we do with him?"

"I can bring him somewhere where that body may lie easy," Ith said. "Auhlae." He looked around. "There is no trace. She will have surrendered herself willingly. . . ."

"Yes," Rhiow said. "Though by the Queen's mercy, who knows where her soul may be? She and Huff might yet be together sometime, somewhere . . . and he saved us." She looked one more time, sadly, at his body as Ith picked it up.

"And that worked too," Urruah said, looking at the icosaract. "Nice job."

"The time was right. The place was right. The rest of it—" Ith shrugged. "A spell always works."

"Come on," Rhiow said. "Fhrio, let's check your gates . . . and then go home."

✦

It was some hours before that happened. The London team was going to need restructuring: Fhrio agreed readily enough, as its de facto team leader, that Rhiow and her team would come in occasionally to assist until new placements were arranged by the Powers. "I think it would have to be that way anyway," he said, glancing over at Arhu and Siffha'h. "I don't think they're going to be apart much for a while."

"No, I think they've got some exploring of roles to do," Rhiow said. "Meanwhile, we'll have your 'bad' gate up and running again within a couple of days. But before we go, there's one more thing we have to do."

Fhrio actually put his whiskers forward at Rhiow. "With pleasure," he said, and went off to bring up the timeslide again so that they could take care of it.

Urruah was standing talking to Ith. Rhiow wandered over to him, and as she came he turned to her and said, " 'Artie'—Don't *ehhif* usually have more than one name?"

"Some places," Rhiow said.

"So what was his? Did we ever find out?"

"Doyle," Arhu said. "Actually he had two last names—unusual. Arthur Conan Doyle."

"A very nice boy," Urruah said. "I wonder what he'll make of himself in the world."

"Hard to say," Rhiow said, "but he certainly likes dinosaurs."

"Rhiow?" said Fhrio. "Ready."

✦

Patel was standing in the entry to the District Line platform, looking around him with astonishment. His trainers were covered with mud, but there was no mud anywhere in sight: nothing but the platform directly in front of him, and a lightbulb high in the ceiling.

He clearly heard a voice say, from somewhere down low, "Sir? You've dropped your book."

He looked for the voice, but saw no one. Only his copy of *Van Nostrand's Scientific Encyclopedia* sat in its plastic bag on the floor nearby.

"Uh," Patel said. "Uh, thanks." He picked it up, staring again at his trainers: spent a fruitless moment or so trying to scrape the stinking mud off them, and then went on ahead to the platform.

Behind him, whiskers went forward: and Rhiow went back to fetch her team, with its new part-time member, and go home.

Epilogue

In the preceding narrative, only one liberty has been taken with "genuine" history—the history of our own present timeline, at least. There is no concrete evidence that E. A. Wallis Budge was yet working *officially* at the British Museum at the age of nineteen (which was his age in 1874): but he was often there "behind the scenes." Budge had finished university and was then permanently resident in London, where for several years previously he had been working intensively with museum officials, to whom Budge had been introduced by Disraeli because of an early demonstrated genius for translation. This early foundation-work would lead quickly to Budge's seminal translation of the Theban recension of *The Book of the Dead,* and to a long career at the museum. There he served as curator of Egyptian and Assyrian antiquities between 1894 and 1924, meanwhile collecting vast numbers of cuneiform tablets, Egyptian papyri, and Greek, Coptic, Arabic Syriac, and Ethiopic manuscripts, while always remaining at the cutting edge of any effort to decipher newly discovered ancient languages.

Otherwise, all dates, locations, and actions attributed to nonfictional persons are genuine. Arthur Conan Doyle, in particular, was in London for some time in 1874, visiting his uncle, the famous artist Richard Doyle (the man responsible for the creation of "Mr. Punch," as well as for thousands of *Punch* cartoons, and for illustrations in hundreds of children's books of the period). Doyle was a fairly lively diarist in his youth, but there are periods during this visit about which his diary falls unusually silent. However, acquaintances at the Jesuit school in Austria that he attended after this time mention that he suddenly began to read history voraciously, and also discovered (and fell in love with) the fantastic writings of Edgar Allan Poe.

Finally, the appearance of a gray tabby in Parliament on July 9, 1874, is not mentioned in *Hansard*, the official parliamentary publication, but is covered in some detail in *The Times* of London for the next day. Chris Pond at the Public Information Office of the Palace of Westminster says, "In the nineteenth century there were eleven private residences in the building, and I imagine the residents of some of these may have kept a cat, if for no reason other than to control mice numbers." However, there is no clear explanation of how a cat would have gotten all the way down from the residences into the Commons chamber, unobserved—unless it was not quite an ordinary cat.

A Very Partial Ailurin Glossary

A

aahfaui (n) the "presence" quality in hauissh

Aaurh (pr n) another of the feline pantheon: the "Michael" power, the Warrior; female

aavhy (adj) used; also a proper name when upper case

ahou'ffriw (n) the Canine Word: key, or "activating," word for spells intended for use on dogs and other canids

Auhw-t (n) "the Hearth": the Ailurin/wizardly term for what humans refer to as "Timeheart"—the most senior/central reality, of which all others are mirrors or variations

Auo (pr n) I

auuh (n) stray (pejorative)

auw (n) energy (as a generic term): appears in many compounds having to do with wizardry and cats' affinity for fire, warmth, and energy flows

auwsshui'f (n) the "lower electromagnetic spectrum," involving quantum particles, faster-than-light particles and wavicles, subatomics, fission, fusion, and "submatter" relationships such as string and hyperstring function

D

D does not appear by itself as a consonant in Ailurin, only as a diphthong, *dh*

E

efviauw (n) the electromagnetic spectrum as perceived by cats

ehhif (n) human being, (adj) human

eiuev (n) veldt: a large open space. As a proper noun, *Eiuev,* "the Veldt," means the Sheep Meadow in Central Park

eius'hss (n) the "control" quality in *hauissh*

F

ffrihh (n) refrigerator (cat slang: approximation)

fouarhweh (n) a position in *hauissh,* described as "classic" by commentators

fvais a medium-high voice among cats; equates with "tenor"

fwau (ex) heck, hell, crap

H

Hauhai (n) the Speech

hauissh (n) the Game

he'ihh (n) composure-grooming

hhau'fih (n) group relationships in general

hhouehhu (v) desire/want

Hhu'au (pr n) the Lion-"God" of Today; nickname for *ehhif* "Patience," one of the carved stone lions outside the New York Public Library main branch

hihhhh (excl) damn, bloody (stronger than *vhai*)

hiouh (n) excreta (including both urine and feces)

hlah'feihre (adj) tortoiseshell (fur)

houff (s n) dog

houiff (pl n) dogs

Hrau'f (pr n) daughter of Iau, the member of the feline pantheon most concerned wih creation and ordering it; known as "the Silent"

hruiss (n) fight, in compounds with words for "tom-fight," etc.

hu (n) day

hu-rhiw (id) "day-and-night"; idiom for a black-and-white cat

hwaa (n) drink

hwiofviauw (n) the "upper electromagnetic," meaning plasma functions, gravitic force, etc.; "upward"

I

iAh'hah (n) New York: possibly an approximation of the English name

Iau (pr n) the One; the most senior member of the feline pantheon; female

Irh (pr n) one of the feline pantheon; male (Urruah refers to his balls)

O

o'hra (n) opera (approximation)

R

ra'hio "radio"; a feline neologism

Reh-t (n abstract) the future; also, the name for the Lion-Power guarding it, the Invisible One of the Three guarding the steps to the New York Public Library main branch

rhiw (n) night. Many compounds are derived from this favorite word, including the name *Rhiow* (the actual orthography would be *rhiw'aow,* "nightdark," but the spelling has been simplified for the purposes of this narrative)

rioh (n) horse (but in the countryside, also ox, or any

other animal that works for humans by carrying or pulling things; "beast of burden"). A cat with a sense of humor might use this word as readily for a taxicab, shopping cart, or wheelbarrow

rrai'fih (n) pride relationship implying possible blood ties

ruah (adj) flat

S

sa'Rráhh (pr n) the ambivalent feline Power; analogous (roughly) to the Lone Power

Sef (pr n) the Lion-"God" of Yesterday; nickname for "Fortitude," one of the lions outside the New York Public Library main branch

sh'heih (n) "queen," unspayed female

siss (n) urine; a "baby word" similar to *ehhif* English "pee pee," and other similar formations

sshai-sau (adj) crazy

sswiass a pejorative: sonofabitch, bastard, brat, etc.

sth'heih (n) "tom," unneutered male

U

uae (n) milk

ur (n) nose

Urrua (pr n) the Great Tom, son and lover of Iau the Queen (from the older word *urra*, "scarred")

urruah (id) "flat nose" (compound: from *ur'ruah*)

V

vefessh (n) water; also (adj) the term cats use to indicate the fur color humans call "blue"

vhai (adj) damn, bloody

Diane Duane was born in Manhattan in 1952, a Year of the Dragon, and she was raised on Long Island, NY. She has been writing for her own entertainment ever since she could read and her first novel, *The Door Into Fire*, was published by Dell Books in 1979. Since then she has published twenty-seven novels, numerous short stories, and various comics and computer games here and there, garnering the occasional award.

Diane lives with her husband, (and frequent collaborator) Peter Morwood, near the Irish town of Baltinglass, along with four cats and several seriously overworked computers, in a hundred-year-old renovated cottage—an odd but congenial environment for the staging of space battles and the leisurely pursuit of total galactic domination.

DIANE DUANE was born in Manhattan in 1952, a Year of the Dragon, and spent her youth on Long Island, N.Y. She has been writing for her own entertainment ever since she could read, and her first novel, *The Door into Fire*, was published by Dell Books in 1979. Since then she has published twenty-seven novels, numerous short stories, and various comics and computer games here and there, gathering the occasional award.

Diane lives with her husband (and frequent collaborator) Peter Morwood, near the Irish town of [illegible], along with four cats and several semi-worked computers, in a hundred-year-old renovated cottage—an odd but congenial environment for the staging of space battles and the leisurely pursuit of intergalactic information.